ANNA

Our Mary Ann

CORONET BOOKS
Hodder & Stoughton

Copyright © 2003 by Anna Jacobs

First published in Great Britain in 2003 by Hodder and Stoughton
First published in paperback in 2004 by Hodder and Hodder and Stoughton
A division of Hodder Headline

The right of Anna Jacobs to be identified as the Author
of the Work has been asserted by her in accordance with the
Copyright, Designs and Patents Act 1988.

7

A CIP catalogue record for this title is
available from the British Library

ISBN 978-0-340-82134-3

Typeset in Plantin Light by Palimpsest Book Production Limited,
Polmont, Stirlingshire

Printed and bound by
Clays Ltd, St Ives plc

Hodder and Stoughton
A division of Hodder Headline
338 Euston Road
London NW1 3BH

To a fine group of novelists, my dear friends:

Lillian Stewart Carl

Denise Dietz

Pam Forrest

Annette Mahon

Corey McFadden

Garda Parker

Mary Jo Putney

Terese Ramin

Prologue

August 1890

Dinah Baillie got off the train in Overdale, so relieved to be back she could have wept. She hadn't told her grandparents she was coming home and didn't want to be recognised by any of her friends, so pulled her straw hat forward and bent her head to hide her face. Hurrying across to the ladies' waiting room – which was empty, thank goodness! – she closed the door and leaned against it for a minute, feeling shaky.

Taking up a position from which she could see out of the window but not be seen from the platform, she watched the crowd of passengers disperse. Only then did she leave the station.

As a child she'd played along all the back streets so knew exactly how to get to Stanley's house without being seen. But even so her nerves were jittery as she hurried along the alleys between the terraces of narrow dwellings, holding her skirt up to keep it away from the gutter. Luck was with her. Apart from a group of small girls playing skipping games, she met no one.

'Please let him be home,' she muttered as she lifted the sneck on the back gate of the Kershaws' home. She'd timed her arrival to coincide with Stanley's return from work at two o'clock. The house was usually empty on a Saturday because his mother always visited her cousin and his father went to the nearest football match. She and Stanley had used that to their advantage many a time. Her lips curved into a half-smile as she remembered his big, strong body and dark curly hair. The only man she'd ever loved.

But today something was wrong. She could see through the window that the kitchen was full of people, and with a muffled squeak of dismay she took two hasty steps sideways to hide behind the shed. What was happening?

As the back door banged open and someone came striding down towards the privy, she slipped inside the shed, determined not to leave Overdale until she'd seen Stanley and sorted their problems out! She didn't dare.

Through the tiny, smeary window she saw two men come out to stand on the back doorstep: his father and uncle, dressed in their Sunday best. Suddenly she heard them say something about 'the bride' and realised what was happening. A wedding. Who was getting married? And why was everyone gathering here? Stanley was an only child.

They went inside again and she saw people begin to leave the kitchen, heard the sound of their cheerful farewells fading towards the front of the house and the words 'See you at the church' repeated several times.

The back door opened and a man came out. She let out a low groan of relief. At last! As he passed by, she opened the shed door a few inches and hissed, 'Stanley!' He turned, looking puzzled, and she opened the door wide enough to show herself.

'Dinah!' He mouthed the word, staring at her in shock.

'I need to see you,' she whispered.

The back door of the house opened and someone called, 'Hurry up, our Stanley! You don't want to be late.'

'You go ahead, Mam. I'll catch up with you in a minute.' He closed his eyes for a moment, then opened them to scowl at Dinah. 'What the *hell* are you doing here? And today of all days.'

'I need to see you.'

'You said you never wanted to see me again! You said it very loudly. The whole street heard our final quarrel.'

Tears filled her eyes. She cried so easily now. 'I never meant it. You knew I didn't.'

'I knew nothing of the sort,' he said flatly. 'You went away and returned my letter unopened. What else was I to think?'

'Letter? What letter?'

He looked at her in puzzlement. 'The one I sent the Wednesday after you left.'

'I never even saw it.' Dinah clapped one hand to her mouth.

2

'Oh, no! My aunt must have sent it back. She was ill, frightened I'd leave her to cope on her own. She nearly died, so I couldn't get away till now. When I didn't hear from you, I wrote and asked my grandmother to tell you I was waiting for a letter.'

'Well, she passed me in the street many a time, could easily have done that, but she never even tried to speak to me.'

Dinah put one hand to her mouth, feeling tears begin to trickle down her face. 'Oh, Stanley, I didn't know. They must have got together about this.' Her aunt and grandmother were strict teetotallers and had never liked her going out with someone who worked in a brewery.

He sighed and looked at her less angrily. 'Any road, it's too late now. I'm getting wed today.'

The words echoed in her head and she couldn't believe she'd heard them correctly, could only stare at him in horror. 'You can't be!'

He glanced over his shoulder, then back at her. 'I'm sorry, Dinah. That's how it is.'

She grabbed his sleeve to stop him moving away. 'Who to?'

'Meggie.'

'That scrawny bitch! Stanley, *no!*'

'She's a nice lass and I love her.' A fond expression settled on his face. 'She's got such dainty manners and ways – and she doesn't throw temper tantrums like you.'

'You said you were fond of *me* not so long ago.'

'I was – once.' He sighed and pulled his watch out, flipping open the cover and shaking his head at what he saw. 'I have to go.'

'You can't!' She took a deep breath and said it baldly. 'Stanley, I'm expecting your child.'

He was so still she wasn't sure he'd heard but as she opened her mouth to repeat the words he swallowed audibly, then whispered, 'You can't be!'

'I can. It's due in February.'

'Oh, hell!'

'So you'll have to tell *her* you've changed your mind.'

He closed his eyes, then opened them again and looked at her with a pitying expression. 'I can't, Dinah. You see, *she's* expecting my child, too. Only hers is due in March.'

One mew of pain escaped her, then anger began to scald through her. 'You didn't wait long, did you? You must have been with her almost as soon as I'd left.'

'Aye. When my letter was returned I did it out of anger at first, heaven help me. But *she* did it out of love. And, Dinah – she's a damn' sight easier to get on with than you, and now . . . well, I love her. She *depends* on me and I'm not letting her down.'

Suddenly Dinah's fury overflowed in a red tide, as it did sometimes, and she began beating at his chest, trying to scratch his face. They'd loved passionately, her and Stanley, but they'd fought fiercely too.

He held her off, then as she continued to struggle, gave her a hard shake. 'Stop it!'

She fell against his chest, sobbing now, feeling helpless and afraid. 'What am I going to do?'

His voice was grim. 'Not cause trouble, I hope. Because it won't do you any good. I shan't change my mind. It's Meggie I'm marrying.'

Dinah drew back, wiping her eyes with one arm, staring at him pleadingly and laying one hand on her stomach. 'But this is your child as well.'

He nodded. 'Aye, I believe you there. You've too hot a temper to lie and cheat.' He felt in his pocket and pulled out his wallet. 'I'll give you some money. It's all I can do now.'

'*Money!*' She spat the word at him. 'What good is money? It's a husband I need.'

'Me and the lads went to the races last week and I had a bit of luck on the horses, couldn't seem to go wrong. I haven't told Meggie about it yet. Here, you can have half.' He thrust some pound notes into her hand.

She nearly threw them back at him, only she couldn't afford to do that. 'A few miserable pounds!' she whispered, looking down at them. 'That's not much of a heritage for your oldest child, is it?'

He shrugged. 'I can't marry two of you, can I?'

'I'll come to the church and stop the wedding.'

He looked at her pityingly. 'You can't stop it and you'll only show yourself up if you try.' He sighed. 'Go back to your aunt's, Dinah. Get her to help you, since she kept us apart. There's nothing more I can do for you.' He fumbled with his wallet, stuffing it anyhow into his pocket. 'I really do have to go.' He saw her open her mouth and added, 'I *want* to go! You and I have nothing more to say to one another.'

Dinah bent her head and sobbed. When he made no effort to comfort her, she looked up to see the back door closing behind him. Disgust roiled in her stomach and she ran into the privy where she was violently sick. She came out, wiping her mouth, hating the sour taste, and decided she might as well go into the house and get a drink of water. There'd be no one there now.

She tripped over something on the mat and looked down to see Stanley's wallet. It must have fallen out of his pocket in his haste. Picking it up, she opened it, staring in amazement when she found it still contained quite a bit of money. He must have had a really big win. Trust Stanley bloody Kershaw. He always had been lucky.

She put the wallet down on the table and got herself a drink of water, but as she was turning to leave, her eyes were drawn once more to it. He had given her only part of his money, the mean sod. She counted the rest of the notes out one by one, slapping them down on the table. Another twenty pounds. A fortune to someone like her!

Shoving the notes back into the wallet, she flung it back on the floor and turned to leave. But at the door she spun round and snatched it up again. Cramming it into her coat pocket, she hurried down the yard and slipped out of the back gate. Then she picked up her skirts and ran towards the station, terrified that he'd guess what she'd done and come after her, though she still retained enough sense to take the back alleys.

Just before she got there she stopped, shook out her skirt, adjusted her hat and blew her nose fiercely. She would get right out of his life, right away from Overdale too, and never come back, because she wasn't going to face the shame of having folk point at her in the street for bearing an illegitimate baby. This child would be hers, all hers. As she settled herself in the train she glanced down at her stomach with its slight curve, thinking, *Poor little thing! You'll never even know your father.*

Weary now, she sat staring out of the window as she began the first stage of the journey back to Blackpool, then leaned her head against the seat and closed her eyes. She'd have to plan this carefully. Her aunt wanted her to live with her permanently. If Dinah did that, she'd insist they move away from Lancashire and settle somewhere else – in the south perhaps. Too many people from Overdale came to Blackpool for their holidays, and anyway her aunt's neighbours knew Dinah wasn't married.

But if her aunt would sell the boarding house and move south, Dinah would be able to pretend she was a widow. And after what her aunt had done, keeping her and Stanley apart like that, just let her try to refuse!

Dinah's expression grew softer as she thought of the baby. Mary Ann, she'd call it if it was a girl. That had always been her favourite name. She prayed desperately that it would be a girl. She wanted nothing more to do with men.

PART ONE

1905–1913

July 1905 – Brighton

On her final day at school Mary Ann Baillie left home early,
feeling near to tears. She loved school, had lots of friends there
and was one of the top scholars. The only good thing about
leaving was that she wouldn't have to squash into a desk that
was too small for her because at fourteen she was taller than any
of the teachers and was already worrying about how tall she'd
end up.

When she got to school, she waved and ran across the yard
to where Sheila and the other older girls were sitting, plumping
down beside them to a chorus of hellos.

'I can't believe we'll not be coming here again,' Sheila said
with a sigh.

'We can still see one another at weekends,' Lucy said firmly.
'We've all agreed that we'll meet in the park on Saturday afternoons.'

Mary Ann bent her head to hide sudden tears, but of course
they noticed.

'What's wrong?' Sheila asked.

'When I told my mother about that, she said she's not having
me messing about in the park, getting into trouble.' She blinked
furiously as tears threatened. 'I don't get into trouble. Why does
she always say that?'

There was silence. Everyone knew how strict Mary Ann's
mother was.

'Perhaps now you're nearly grown up it'll be different?' Sheila
ventured.

Mary Ann shook her head, not saying anything because if she
did she'd cry again. She'd cried herself to sleep last night when

her mother had told her that she wouldn't be allowed out on Saturdays.

'Well, think how lovely it'll be to earn money at last,' Lucy said. 'I can't wait for my first wage packet. My mother says I can have that one all for myself – though I have to give her some from then onwards.' She turned to Mary Ann. 'Are you still going to work for your mother?'

'Yes.'

'Is she going to pay you?'

'Not proper wages, just spending money.' It wasn't fair. Their boarding house was comfortable and nearly always full. One day, when she was dusting, Mary Ann had found her mother's savings book with over three hundred pounds in it, an enormous sum of money. She hadn't said anything because Mum would only have flown into a temper, but she'd never forgotten it, especially when her mother later told her they couldn't afford the material for a new Sunday dress and Mary Ann would have to put a false hem on her old one.

The final day flew past far too quickly. Mary Ann won a prize for being the most capable senior girl, which had her blushing and beaming at her clapping friends as she went to receive it from the Headmaster. Sheila won the needlework prize and Lucy the arithmetic prize. All the prizes were the same: books. Mary Ann's was *God's Good Man* by Marie Corelli, which thrilled her. She loved to read stories, but her mother hated to see anyone being idle so she could only usually read at school.

When the final bell clanged, the girls were slow to leave the yard, parting from one another only after tearful promises to stay in touch.

At home Mary Ann found her mother starting to prepare the boarders' evening meal.

'You're late.'

'It was the last day. I was saying goodbye to everyone. Look!' She held out the book. 'I won a prize for being the most capable girl. It's by Marie Corelli.'

Her mother sniffed. 'You'd think they'd buy you something better than that rubbish.'

'It's not rubbish! Miss Corelli writes lovely stories and there are hundreds of books by her in the shops. All the girls read them and lots of their mothers do, too.'

'Well, I've better things to do with my time and you'll not be reading it till your work is done.' Dinah looked at the clock and clicked her tongue in exasperation. 'We're getting a new lodger from Henderson's, so we're going to be full up again. I knew they'd soon find another rep to replace poor Mr Brown. Powling, this one's called.'

Mary Ann automatically began to clear things off the kitchen table, piling up the dirty dishes in the scullery, ready to wash. 'Can I let my skirts down now I've left school?'

'At fourteen? Certainly not! You're still a child. Now stop asking silly questions and put that satchel away in the attic. You can take the book up to your bedroom while you're at it.'

'I wanted to show it to Miss Battley.'

'She won't be interested in that. Hurry up, now. I need you to peel the potatoes.'

While Mary Ann was upstairs there was a knock on the door and with a mutter of annoyance Dinah wiped her hands and went to open it. A man was standing there, smiling. She gasped in shock and could not for a moment move, thinking it was Stanley Kershaw. He was tall and well-built with dark wavy hair, but even though she'd quickly realised it wasn't Stanley, she still felt shocked by the man's superficial resemblance to her former lover.

He cleared his throat. 'Are you all right?'

She pulled herself together. 'Yes. Yes, of course. It's just – you look like someone I used to know and I was shocked.'

'It happens sometimes, doesn't it? I'm Jeff Powling, the new sales rep for Henderson's. They said they'd booked me a room here.'

For a moment she had the strangest premonition that this man was dangerous and felt an urge to slam the door in his face. Then she brushed the silly fancy aside and held the door open wide. 'Do come in, Mr Powling. We were expecting you.' She led the way up the stairs at a brisk pace.

He looked round the bedroom and nodded approval. 'I must say, you've got everything very nice, Mrs Baillie, much nicer than my last place.'

'Thank you. The evening meal is at seven o'clock sharp.' She smiled and left him to unpack, but the smile faded as she walked slowly down the stairs. She didn't want to be reminded of Stanley, had tried for years to forget him.

She hadn't managed to do it, though, because her daughter looked so much like her father, with the same wavy hair, grey eyes and broad smile.

Mary Ann met the new lodger when she helped serve the evening meal, but as she'd never seen a photograph of her real father she didn't notice anything special about him. Mr Powling had already made himself known to the others and was chatting to Miss Battley who had been lodging with them for several years and whose gruff exterior hid a kind heart, as the girl had found.

Mr Powling was quite good-looking, considering he was about her mother's age, though the smile didn't reach his eyes, especially when he was talking to Mary Ann. But he was all over her mother and the other female lodgers, the girl noticed.

And, for once, her mother was smiling and blushing as they chatted – something she had never done before with a lodger.

'Mum, why do you talk to him like that?' Mary Ann asked a few evenings later.

'Talk to who?'

'Mr Powling. Why do you smile at him and stand talking to him for so long? I don't even like him.'

Her mother drew herself up and frowned. 'It's part of our job to make sure our guests are happy. If they're not happy, they won't stay.'

'But you don't talk to the other men like that.'

'Just who do you think you are, young lady, commenting on your elders? What I do is my own business. Now go and make those beds.'

The next night her mother was smiling again and as soon as they'd served tea, she said, 'You'll have to clear up the rest tonight. Mr Powling has invited me to go with him to the music hall. I haven't been out for ages and there's a really good show on this week, apparently.'

Before Mary Ann could say a word, her mother had gone running upstairs to change, coming down again a few minutes later wearing her new Sunday outfit, an ankle-length gored skirt and a three-quarter jacket to match. On her head was a matching toque with a feather curling backwards across it.

There had been enough money for her mother's new clothes, Mary Ann thought resentfully. Scowling, she cleared up, set out the tea tray and biscuits for supper, then sat down by the kitchen fire, feeling too exhausted to go and fetch her new book. She'd never worked as hard in her life, because her mother had dismissed their maid of all work and now they managed with just the two of them and a scrubbing woman.

She stabbed the poker into the coal to get a better blaze. It was all very well her mother having a night out, but Mary Ann hadn't been able to meet her friends once since she'd left school. She wasn't allowed to go out in the evenings because her mother said she wasn't having her daughter hanging around on street corners after dark getting into trouble. Why did she always worry about that? What sort of trouble could anyone get into talking to their friends? Sheila was allowed to come to the house in the evening – only she hadn't done that after the first visit, because Mum hadn't left them alone and they hadn't been able to talk properly.

After the lodgers had had supper, Mary Ann cleared up again, washed the dishes and filled herself an earthenware hot water bottle, more for the comfort than because it was cold yet. Her room was in the back attic, away from the rest of the house, which she normally loved because it was quieter up there. But tonight she left the door open because she couldn't get to sleep until she knew her mother was safely back.

Only Mum and Mr Powling didn't return until nearly eleven o'clock.

In the morning her mother hummed as she got the breakfasts and Mary Ann noticed Mr Powling got the best of everything on his plate. She didn't say anything, though. Mum had a nasty temper if you crossed her and could slap you really hard if you upset her.

The things her mother said sometimes when she was angry could hurt even more than the slaps.

By the following week Mary Ann was so fed up of doing nothing but work, work, work that she decided to make a stand. 'I'm going out tomorrow afternoon to see Sheila and the others,' she declared on the Friday, chin up.

'I've told you before, I won't have you hanging round street corners,' her mother said automatically.

'We're meeting in the park. I haven't been out once since I left school and I'm fed up of staying in.' She loved going to the beach or walking past the old Royal Pavilion with its strange roof. She liked going on the Palace Pier and looking down at the water.

'You go out every day to the shops for me.'

'That's not the same. And I think I deserve more than a shilling a week spending money, too. I work hard and—'

Her mother's heavy hand cracked across her cheek.

'Ow!' Mary Ann began to sob loudly.

'Be quiet! The lodgers will hear you.'

'I don't care.' She dodged round the table, avoiding another smack. 'I'm not working here if I don't get paid and I can't ever go out.'

'Oh, aren't you? And what do you think you'll do instead?'

'Go into service. Gertie says her mistress wants another maid.' She shrieked and ran as her mother's face turned dark red and she raised her hand again. But as the girl tried to get out of the kitchen, she banged into someone and couldn't get past. 'Let me go!'

'Hold still, young woman. What's all this about?'

Mary Ann suddenly realised it was Mr Powling. He was holding her pressed right against him and though she tried to wriggle away, he was stronger than she was and wouldn't let her go.

He looked sideways at her mother. 'Having a bit of a tiff? Want me to leave?'

'Madam here is demanding to go out with her friends *and* she wants more money. I'm not having it.'

'Oh, is that all?'

At last he let her go and in her relief Mary Ann moved hurriedly back to her mother's side, only to get another crack on the cheek. She wasn't going to cry in front of *him*, but she thought it mean of her mother to treat her like that in front of a lodger and looked at her reproachfully. For a moment she thought she saw an expression of shame, then her mother tossed her head and turned back to Mr Powling.

'What can I do for you, Jeff?'

Mary Ann stilled. Her mother *never* called guests by their first names.

'I was wondering if you were going to be busy tonight, Dinah? Only there's another good show on and it's much more fun to go with someone.'

'Oh.' Her mother turned sideways to look at Mary Ann. 'You can manage the suppers, can't you?'

'If I can go out tomorrow.'

Her mother's expression grew angry again, but Mr Powling laughed. 'You're over-protective of her, Dinah. What harm can she come to on a Saturday afternoon?'

Mary Ann could have sworn there were tears in her mother's eyes and it was a minute before she spoke.

'Oh, very well. But only for a couple of hours, mind. Now, go and set the tables for breakfast and I want no more cheek from you, young lady.'

Mary Ann began to do the tables. A couple of times she had to go into the kitchen for something and the two of them were still there, sitting close together at the end of the table, talking in low voices, laughing sometimes. They fell silent each time she went in and didn't start talking again until she'd left and she couldn't help wondering what they were laughing about.

Well, at least she'd be able to see her friends again. But she hadn't liked it when Mr Powling caught hold of her. It wasn't nice to press against someone like that.

Gabriel Clough sat up on the moors looking down towards Overdale. He sighed and reached out to pat his dog, Bonnie. When she leaned against him, he continued absent-mindedly to caress her.

Below him was the familiar patchwork pattern of fields edged in dry stone walls. Around him the green curves of what locals referred to as 'the tops' stretched right to the horizon, a place belonging to no one, without roads or walls to bar the way. If you half-closed your eyes, it looked a bit like the sea – or as he imagined the sea would look. He'd never seen it except in pictures, never done anything much, really. Just gone to school when he had to, working on the farm before and after school, so that he was always too tired to pay much attention to his homework.

He'd left at fourteen and had been planning to leave Birtley, his home village, as soon as he was eighteen, wanting to see a bit of the world before he settled down. But just before his birthday, two years ago, his father had had a stroke, so now his parents couldn't manage without him. Farms like theirs didn't bring you a generous living at the best of times and when one of the two men was half-crippled, it was even harder to make ends meet.

Gabriel's whole life now seemed made up of nothing but work and then more work, but he could see no way out. It was a lonely life, too, he and his dog working with the sheep or tending the small crops they grew mostly to feed themselves and the stock.

Birtley was a mere hamlet, only a dozen houses, and there was no one his own age left there now because they'd all gone to work in the towns. If only his elder brother had lived, Gabriel would be working in a town now, too! But Paul had died aged eight and now there was just him, a late child born to elderly parents.

Our Mary Ann

Lower down the valley was Redvale, an old farmhouse bigger than the others hereabouts, built of brick not stone, and with more land. Nowadays its owner was just as short of money as everyone else, however. Maurice Greeson had inherited it a year ago from his father and everyone was watching to see what changes he'd make and whether he'd nudge the farm into profit. They weren't optimistic. Neither he nor his father had ever been noted for their energy or acumen.

The first change had been for him to get married to the woman he'd been walking out with for years, a woman slightly older than himself and cleverer, too. Well, everyone said she was clever. Jane Greeson had been a nurse until she married, but Gabriel couldn't see her bringing much comfort to sick people. She had a cruel face and he pitied the poor little skivvy who worked for them and always looked exhausted.

Devious might be a better word to describe their neighbour. Gabriel rolled the word round his tongue, enjoying it. He'd been good at reading and writing at school, and had always enjoyed finding exactly the right word to describe something. His father mocked him for using long words, but Gabriel didn't see what was wrong with that.

Suddenly he noticed that some stones had come loose in the top corner and heaved himself to his feet. The whole damned wall round this top field needed rebuilding, really, but let alone he wasn't an expert on dry stone walls, he didn't have the time to do it. Picking up the stones, he fitted them carefully into the gaps, surprised to find there weren't nearly enough of them. Had someone been up here stealing them? That had happened to a few folk lately.

He clambered across the wall and found footprints in the soft earth, following them down to the Greesons'. He even saw the stones, standing in a pile in a corner of their yard.

Anger rising in him, he banged on the back door, turning sharply when a dog growled behind him. 'Don't you dare!' he told it, and after hesitating for a moment, it slunk off.

'What do you want?' Maurice offered by way of a greeting.

17

Gabriel jerked his head towards the pile of stones. 'My property back.'

'I thought your dad was letting that top field go.'

'Well, he isn't letting the wall go, or giving the stones away. I need them to repair it.'

'Sorry. I'll return them later today.'

'Thanks.' Gabriel turned and walked away. On the face of it, the right response, just what you'd expect from a neighbour, but all done in a surly, grudging way. You had to keep your eye on the Greesons.

When Gabriel got home, his mother was looking worried and his father was slumped at the kitchen table, his face grey with exhaustion.

Jassy greeted her son with, 'Your father's been doing too much again.'

He looked at the old man. 'What was so urgent it couldn't wait for me to get back, Dad?'

'There's a dozen jobs waiting here while you're fiddling about in the top fields staring out across the moors.'

'I wasn't fiddling around. I was rebuilding the wall. That end bit had fallen down again. Then I had to go to Greesons' to get the rest of our stones back because Maurice had taken them.'

That jerked his father out of his misery. 'He's a menace, that fellow is, always taking things that don't belong to him. I don't know what the world's coming to when neighbour steals from neighbour like that.'

Gabriel took off his sheepskin jerkin. 'Any chance of summat to eat, Mum?'

'It's only three hours since you had your dinner,' his father grumbled.

'Aye, well, I'm hungry again.'

'You allus did eat us out of house and home.'

'It takes food to build muscles,' Gabriel tossed back at him. 'If we're not making enough money to feed me properly, we'd better sell the farm and I'll get a job in town that does buy me enough to eat.'

His father thumped his hand down on the table. 'I'll never sell one foot of our land. Never! Cloughs have farmed here for over a hundred years and they'll still be here when you're dead and buried. Well, they will if you ever get married. It's more than time you did.'

Gabriel noted the dull flush on his father's cheeks and bit off further arguments. Bert's temper had been very chancy since the seizure and he knew how anxiously his mother watched over her husband. Gabriel had told them several times that he didn't intend to marry for a few years yet, but they wouldn't listen and kept nagging him.

What the hell had he to offer a woman, anyway? Only a life of grinding hard work and poverty, that's what. This farm wasn't really big enough to provide a comfortable living for two families; few of them were up here on the moor's edge. Besides, his father stuck to old-fashioned crops and sheep when he could have been trying to produce other stuff. Gabriel had suggested getting in more hens because eggs always sold well, but no, his father said he hated hens and looking after them was women's work. He wasn't going to have any more of the stupid creatures around than were needed to provide eggs for the family.

Gabriel realised he was feeling sorry for himself again, which did no good to anyone, so he turned his thoughts to something more pleasant. It was his night for going to the library in Overdale. Thank God for libraries! Books were a cheap form of entertainment and his mother liked him to read to her in the evenings. Even his father listened, though he pretended not to.

'I've been thinking about what you suggested,' Maurice Greeson said abruptly over their evening meal.

His wife looked up, fork poised near her mouth. 'Oh, aye?'

'If you're sure you can get us some customers, I can find the money to fix the place up a bit.'

She smiled and put down the fork. 'I can definitely find customers, don't you worry. Dr Browning-Baker thinks well of me, was sorry when I left the hospital, said I was the best nurse he'd ever worked with. He knows a lot of people and he'll recommend us to his friends.' Her voice was heavy with scorn. 'Folk with money allus want to hide their little mistakes. Next time I go into town I'll arrange to see him and ask his advice. He loves dishing out advice, that one does.'

'I were thinking of going into town tomorrow.'

'I'll come with you, then.' She looked round, frowning. 'Eh, I'd expected a better life, with you owning a great big house like this.'

He shrugged and loaded his fork with more food. 'Blame my father. He let the place run down. We had rows all the time towards the end.'

She didn't argue, though she reckoned no Greeson had ever made money and Maurice wasn't any different. The house had been built by the first owner, a well-to-do farmer called Patterson. Maurice's grandfather had bought it from his widow and things had gone downhill steadily from then onwards.

But with her to guide him, she and Maurice would find a way to make money. In fact, she rather thought she had done so already.

2

September 1905 – January 1906

Mary Ann enjoyed her Saturday afternoon out enormously. It was like old times to see her friends and chat to them. They started off at the park but wound up at the beach, tossing pebbles into the sea. When she went back, however, she had to answer a lot of questions from her mother. Where exactly had she been? Who had she met? Had she been talking to any boys?

Knowing her mother would find out, because she always did, Mary Ann said airily, 'Only Sheila's brother and his friend.'

'I thought you told me it was just girls you went to meet?'

She shrugged. 'It is, usually.'

'I don't want you hanging around with boys.'

'You always say that, but I don't understand why. What's wrong with boys?'

'What's wrong is you – you're too young for boys. So keep away from them or you don't go out again.'

Mary Ann breathed deeply but didn't argue because that would only make her mother angrier. When *she* had children, she wouldn't get mad at them all the time. She'd cuddle them and talk to them like Sheila's mother did.

'The roast is nearly ready to carve, so if you keep an eye on the potatoes, I'll make a start on it. I could really have done with some help this afternoon. It's not easy looking after so many boarders, even if we do send our washing out to the laundry.'

After the meal Dinah went up to change for her own outing and Mary Ann was left with a kitchen full of dirty dishes. Her mother had not bothered to clear up as she went this time and the girl knew it was to punish her for going out. With a sigh, she got out the soda crystals and began to rinse and pile up the dirty dishes.

Three weeks later, her mother called Mary Ann into the small sitting room which they didn't often use. Mr Powling was there, smiling at them both. Why did his smiles never seem real? she wondered yet again.

'We have some news for you,' her mother said abruptly.

'You'll think it good news, I hope,' he said in that too-soft voice of his.

'Me and Jeff are going to get married.' Dinah gave him a glowing smile, then turned to look expectantly at her daughter.

Mary Ann was so shocked she could only gape at them.

'Well, aren't you going to congratulate us?' her mother said sharply.

'I was just – surprised.' She tried to think what else to say, but couldn't find the words because she knew instinctively that she didn't want her mother to marry this man. He might smile at folk – he did nothing but smile – but Mary Ann didn't trust him an inch. This was partly instinctive, but also because he kept saying things that put her in the wrong, always in that carefully kindly tone of voice. 'I – um – hope you'll be very happy.'

'I'm sure we shall,' he said, with a fond look at Dinah. Then he glanced across at Mary Ann and his eyes narrowed. 'Well, haven't you got a kiss for your new father?'

She drew back. 'You're not my father.'

'Mary Ann!'

'Well, he isn't, Mum, and he never will be.'

'You see what I have to put up with from her, Jeff,' Dinah said. 'Her generation has no respect for their elders.'

The lodgers were more enthusiastic about the match and started collecting for a wedding present.

'What are you going to give them?' Miss Battley asked Mary Ann a few days later.

'Give them?'

'Yes. As a wedding present. Your mother and new stepfather.'

'Nothing. How can I? I don't have any money. She only gives me a shilling a week.'

'But everyone else is giving them a present. It'll look strange if you don't.'

Mary Ann shrugged and got on with her work. It'd have to look strange, then. She wasn't spending even a penny on *him*. Her Saturday shilling was always spent the same day, on comics and sweets to share with her friends. She didn't intend to go without her one treat of the week to buy something for *him*.

The wedding took place three weeks later at the Register Office, with their lodgers Miss Battley and Mr Pearton as witnesses. It seemed strange to Mary Ann that Mr Powling didn't have any friends or relatives of his own, but she didn't say so. Well, they didn't have any relatives, either. Her grandparents had both died when she was a little girl, her mother said, and her great-aunt had died when she was four, so she had only the haziest memories of her.

Her mother had a new outfit for the occasion and even bought one for Mary Ann as well. But of course it had a short skirt and her hat was very childish, too, which looked silly on someone who was five foot eight inches tall.

'I don't know how we're ever going to find you a husband if you keep growing,' her mother had said only the week before. 'Men don't like women to be taller than them. I hope you don't get any taller.'

'I don't want to get married, so it doesn't matter.' The way her mother and Mr Powling were always pawing one another made Mary Ann shudder.

'Oh, you'll change your mind when you grow up. We all do.'

After the wedding Mr Powling provided beer for the men, port and lemonade for the ladies, and the lodgers all drank the newly-weds' health.

The next day the couple went away to Eastbourne for a few days and Mrs Grey from down the street came in to run the boarding house. She was worse than Mary Ann's mother for passing on all the work and by the time the couple came back, the girl was totally exhausted.

23

The two of them were even worse than they'd been before the wedding. In fact, it was downright embarrassing the way her mother and Mr Powling kept cuddling one another, even when they were not alone in the kitchen. Mary Ann felt a hot flush rise to her face every time she saw them pressed against one another.

He tried to cuddle her too sometimes, but she wasn't having that. She hated him even touching her.

But at least her mother was in a better mood these days and not half as sharp with her. And she was allowed out regularly now to meet her friends on Saturday afternoons, which *he* had insisted on. She loved going down to the beach and watching the sea. These were the only consolations about having a man like him around all the time, because something about him continued to make Mary Ann feel uncomfortable.

Gabriel's father died suddenly one Sunday morning as his wife was putting her hat on ready for church.

'I don't think I'll go with you today after all, love,' Bert said in a slurred voice. 'I'm feeling a bit dizzy like.'

Then he keeled over.

By the time Gabriel got to him, he was dead. He looked up to see his mother standing very still, one hand pressed to her breast. 'I'm sorry, Mum. There's nothing we can do.'

Jassy moved towards the table, feeling blindly for a chair and collapsing into it. Tears trickled down her cheeks and Gabriel moved across to put his arms round her. But they weren't a family for demonstrating their affection, so after a minute or two she pulled out of his embrace, dried her eyes and stood up.

'If you can carry him up to our bedroom, I'll see to him. After that, you go and fetch the doctor, son.'

They buried Bert two days later in the churchyard of the next village where many of his ancestors lay. Cousin Tom and his family came and Gabriel went across to thank them for that. Afterwards, he and his mother walked slowly home, arm in arm.

'I'd like to sell the farm,' he said abruptly. 'I think Tom might buy it. He's done quite well for himself.'

She looked sideways at him, her expression sad. 'Your father thought you'd say that, so he's left everything to me.'

Gabriel stopped moving until he had his anger under control. 'Will you *think* about selling it, at least?'

She shook her head. 'I promised Bert I wouldn't. What you do with it when I'm gone is up to you, but I'll not go back on my word to him.'

'What if I just up and leave?'

'You won't do that, lad. I know you.'

'I might.'

Jassy smiled at him. 'Nay, not you.' After a few more steps she said thoughtfully, 'Happen you'll think of summat to bring in a bit of extra brass, though.'

'And happen t'sheep'll sprout wings,' he said with savage mockery.

'Talk to your cousin. Tom's got a good head on his shoulders. His father were the same. Jane Greeson is going to take payin' guests, it seems.'

'Who'd pay to live up here?' he scoffed.

'The families of lasses as are in trouble and want 'em kept out of sight till afterwards. Lasses as'll need *her* help to birth their babbies.'

He stared at her in amazement. 'Who told you all that?'

'Jane did. Proper set up with hersen about it, she is. Says the lasses'll have to pull their weight an' help with the housework, *an'* it'll make a good profit.'

'I feel sorry for the poor things. They'll get no joy at Redvale. All Maurice an' Jane care about is money. They're made for each other, those two are. An' what's to happen to the babbies afterwards? They'll not stay secret if the lasses take 'em home when they leave.'

'They'll be adopted out. That doctor in charge at Overdale Hospital knows ways to see to that, apparently.'

He looked at her in astonishment. 'Why did Mrs Greeson tell *you* all this?'

'Because she knows I'll keep my mouth shut, an' because we'll be the only ones close enough to see the girls. They'll only be let out to walk round the top field for a bit of exercise and apart from that they'll be kept inside. She wants to make sure I won't say owt if I recognise any of 'em, which I won't, of course. I said I'd tell you an' promised her you'd keep quiet, too.'

They walked through the hamlet of Birtley in silence, then he said, 'Well, that doesn't help us, does it? We'll still be scratching for a living.'

'We'll help ourselves, son. Bert was a bit set in his ways, I know, but I shan't try to stop you making things more modern like. Or getting in those chickens if you still think they'll make money.'

He dug his hands deep in his trouser pockets and walked on without a word, bitterness curdling to acid in his stomach. Unfortunately, she was right. He couldn't just up and leave her because she'd worked as hard as his father to keep the farm going and been a good mother to him in her own stark way.

So he was still trapped here, as trapped as those poor lasses would be once they were put in Redvale. Eh, he felt sorry for them already, he did that.

Three months after the wedding Mary Ann heard her mother being sick in the mornings. It happened several times and she said idly one day in the kitchen, 'You're not coming down with something, are you, Mum? Only you've been sick a few times lately.'

Dinah flushed, hesitated then said, 'I'm expecting a baby. It does that to you sometimes, makes you sick in the mornings. I was the same when I was carrying you. It'll pass.'

Mary Ann stared at her in shock. 'A baby! *His* baby!'

'Mine, too. It'll be your brother or sister.'

'How does it – how do you get a baby?' The other girls all seemed to know and had laughed at something she'd said the other day.

'I'll tell you about that when you need to know, which is when you find a fellow and decide to get wed, and not before. Just make sure you don't let any boys mess around with you in the meantime.'

Our Mary Ann

'You're always saying that, but I don't know what you mean!'

Dinah flushed bright red. 'Don't let them kiss you or – or fondle you.'

Mary Ann laughed. '*Kiss me?* Ugh, I'd never. I don't know how you can stand it. *He's* always kissing you. It'd make me feel sick.'

'Right then, now you know, that's enough about that. My baby's not due till next August, so we'll have plenty of time to make some clothes for it. You're a good sewer and I hate sewing, so I'll give you time off to make things for the baby.'

Mary Ann beamed at her. 'I'd like that.'

'And I reckon it's time you went into long skirts and put your hair up. I think you've grown again.'

'Oh, Mum!' Mary Ann went and gave her a hug. For once, her mother didn't push her away.

'I wouldn't normally let you, not at fifteen, but you're so tall it looks silly to wear short skirts. Jeff was commenting on it only the other day. We'll buy some material for a couple of skirts and you can run them up yourself.' Dinah held her daughter at arm's length, looked up at the rosy young face and shook her head. Still innocent, and please God she stayed that way.

So mellow was her mother that Mary Ann risked asking a question that had been nagging at her for a long time. 'Was my father very tall like me? And why don't we have any photos of him?'

'Your father looked a bit like Jeff, actually. I was quite shocked by the resemblance the first time I saw him.'

'I wish my father hadn't died.'

Dinah pushed her away, her voice noticeably sharper. 'Well, he did and that's that. And he wasn't one for photos. Now, get on with your work and not a word about the baby to anyone, think on.'

'Can't I even tell Sheila?'

'No. Not yet.'

The first girl arrived at Redvale in January, travelling by cab

from Overdale. The driver had been offered double his usual
fare to bring certain young women out to the farm and to say
nothing about them to anyone. The blinds were down at the cab
windows.

Inside it a young woman sat and sobbed while her companion
ignored her completely.

'Father, please don't send me away!' she begged yet again.

He looked at her coldly. 'What else can we do with you now?
Unless you *want* people to know about your immorality?'

'Alfred and I could have got married . . .'

'I'm not having my daughter marrying a common working
fellow like that. When the time comes, *I* shall choose your
husband. Besides, Alfred couldn't have loved you or he wouldn't
have taken my money and left town.'

She began to sob again and was still sobbing when they arrived
at the farm. As the cab drew to a halt, she looked up in panic and
pressed herself back against the seat. 'I'm not getting out!'

Her father left her without a word, greeting Mrs Greeson as
coldly as he had spoken to his daughter. 'She's still in the carriage,
refusing to get out. I hope you're used to dealing with recalcitrant
young females.'

'Yes, sir. If you'd like to go inside, my maid will show you into
the parlour. Mr Greeson and I will see to your daughter.'

She beckoned her husband forward and they approached the
carriage.

'It'll do you no good to sit and weep, young woman,' snapped
Jane. 'Get out this instant!'

'I won't, I won't!'

Jane eyed her, thinking, close to total hysteria, then turned to
her husband. 'You'd better pull her out and carry her up to her
room. Stay with her and I'll bring something to calm her down
after I've spoken to the father.' She knew her visitor's name, but
did not intend to use it in front of the cab driver who was watching
everything with ill-concealed interest. She looked up at him. 'And
you had better remember your promise to keep quiet if you want
more of these double fares.'

He grinned and nodded.

Maurice reached into the cab and pulled the weeping girl to her feet. 'Either I carry you or you come of your own accord.'

She continued to sob and when he took hold of her again, she began to scream and try to throw herself backwards, so he dragged her out and threw her over his shoulder, ignoring her kicking and struggling.

Jane went in to offer the father a cup of tea, but he declined curtly.

'You'll look after her – feed her properly, Mrs Greeson?'

'Of course we shall.'

'Get the doctor in if there are any problems, and no beatings even if she is – troublesome. I want her returned in good health and unmarked.'

'Certainly, sir.'

'Browning-Baker will dispose of the baby, so please make sure it's looked after properly as well. He's found it a home already, I believe. A childless couple, well-to-do.'

'So I gather, sir. But he won't be telling me where they go.' Though if they went anywhere in the Overdale district, she'd probably notice.

He fumbled in his pocket and pulled out his wallet. 'Here's your fee.'

Jane counted the money while he watched disdainfully. 'That's correct, sir.'

'There'll be a bonus of ten guineas if you return her in a more obedient frame of mind. I have a husband lined up for her already. Best to get her married as quickly as possible afterwards, I think, if she's that way inclined.'

Jane stilled for a moment and stared at him as she considered this proposition, then nodded. 'I'll do my best, sir.'

'Very well, then. I'll take my leave of you, Mrs Greeson.'

She accompanied him to the door then went back to lock away the money before measuring out a dose of the soothing cordial that Dr Browning-Baker had prescribed for such cases.

Upstairs, Maurice was watching the young woman, who was

still weeping wildly, to make sure she didn't harm herself. He jumped in shock as his wife spoke from just behind him.

'You can leave her with me now.'

When he'd gone she jerked the young woman to a sitting position and slapped her across the face. 'Your father's left now and if you know what's good for you, you'll do as you're told till after the birth. If not, I'm quite prepared to make your life a total misery.' She smiled as she spoke. 'And while you're here, you'll be known as Dorothy. Kindly remember that. If I hear you using your proper name, I'll spank you good and hard on the bare backside.'

The young woman stiffened in shock.

'I mean that. I've tamed many a young woman in my time, so don't think you'll get the better of me. On the other hand, behave yourself and you'll find life here is—' she paused to let her words sink in '—not unpleasant. Now, we've had enough of your antics for today, so I'm going to give you this medicine. That baby of yours needs a rest even if you don't.' She picked up the small blue glass. 'Are you going to take it quietly, *Dorothy*, or shall I call my husband back to hold you down?'

So calmly did she speak and so confident did she sound that Dorothy swallowed the medicine.

Only when the young woman was drowsy did Jane leave her.

Gabriel saw the new arrival walking in the field under Jane Greeson's watchful eye a few days later. She looked unhappy and he felt sorry for her, would feel sorry for any young woman in that condition, but it wasn't any of his business. After several discussions with his cousin Tom, he'd made up his mind to try chicken farming. There were always customers for eggs and plucked fowl at the weekly markets. He asked his mother what she thought of the idea and she shrugged.

'It might work, but *I* shan't have time to look after them.'

'I don't expect you to. I thought we'd get a girl in from the orphanage. She could help with a few other things. Only – do you have enough money put by for her wages till the new venture is paying for itself?'

'Aye. But there's no need to get in a stranger. Fred Hodgett's niece is looking for a place. The mill didn't suit her, made her cough, so they want to find her something in the fresh air. Shall I ask her to call?'

'I suppose so. But you talk to her, see if you think she'll do. I can explain about the job, but I'm damned if I know how to tell whether someone will be a good worker or not.'

His mother nodded, pleased about this. If Gabriel didn't take to Dora Hodgett, she'd be gone after a few months. Jassy was utterly determined to get her son wed and if he didn't go out looking for young women, then she'd have to bring them to the house. This new business would provide a golden opportunity to do that without rousing his suspicions. Familiarity could sometimes lead to fondness.

She smiled as she went about her work. Things were settling down nicely. She missed Bert, but there was no denying he'd been old-fashioned. Gabriel was already managing things better. And she hoped that after a few years her son would be used to the farm and would stop talking about selling it. She didn't want to leave the district in which she'd been born.

3

February – September 1906

Dinah continued unwell, so Mary Ann had an even quieter birthday than usual. Not that her mother made much fuss about birthdays anyway. This time the girl had to make her own cake and her mother rushed out in the middle of eating it to be sick. Of the lodgers, only Miss Battley knew it was Mary Ann's birthday and gave her a pretty handkerchief with lace in the corner.

Her mother apologised for the lack of a birthday present and told her stepfather to give Mary Ann five shillings instead, which she'd rather have had anyway. He pulled the coins away when she reached for them, so she stopped reaching.

'Don't I get a kiss first?' he teased.

'No.' She hated even to touch him.

'Mary Ann, mind your manners!' her mother snapped. 'Give him a kiss, for heaven's sake. It's not much to ask you to show a little gratitude.'

The girl looked at the money then at Mr Powling and took a step backwards, shaking her head.

'You're an ungrateful wretch,' her mother said. 'Ungrateful and disobliging. I heard you refusing to make your father's bed this morning.'

The two of them had separate bedrooms now, because her mother being sick kept *him* awake.

'I only said I wouldn't do it while he was in there,' Mary Ann said. 'I'll do it later.'

'You'll do as you're told, young woman.'

She shook her head. If she went in there while he was in the house, he'd come in and press himself against her. He was doing it more often lately and she hated it. Other men didn't do that, so why did he? She'd almost told her mother, but something had held her back. After all, it was only her word against his and her mother was so besotted with him, she'd believe him, Mary Ann just knew she would.

'Go up to your room at once!' Dinah snapped. 'Birthday or not, I shan't tolerate disobedience.'

'Here, take this!'

Jeff tossed the money at her, but Mary Ann made no effort to pick it up, just elevated her chin and walked out.

He turned to his wife, his expression rueful. 'I do my best, but she won't even try to be friendly. She's jealous of me.'

But Dinah had pressed her hand to her mouth again and rushed into the scullery.

He watched her go, the rueful smile fading as soon as she was out of the room. It was rotten luck that she had fallen for a baby so quickly. He'd have to be more careful in future. Babies spoiled things. He'd found that out years ago. And he got babies rather easily. How he was to manage without getting his bed rations until after the birth, he didn't know. He wasn't the sort of chap to go without, never had been.

And why should he, with so many willing women around? Maybe he could find himself a nice widow in one of the towns he visited on his rounds. He'd have to keep his eyes open. If not, he might be forced look a little closer to home.

Mary Ann needed taking down a peg or two. She'd been spoiled. And she was getting some rather nice curves now.

Dinah's sickness didn't abate and by May she was stick-thin, except for the swell of her belly. They didn't try to get another lodger to replace Mr Baring, and Miss Battley, who had been there longer than anyone, started giving Mary Ann a hand because *he* never lifted a finger to help, insisting that was women's work.

'Things will all settle down once the baby's born,' Miss Battley said consolingly as she wiped the dishes one evening.

'*He* will still be here, though.'

'Why don't you like him?'

'Because . . .' Mary Ann hesitated. 'Oh, I just don't, that's all.'

Miss Battley looked over her shoulder and lowered her voice. 'Is it because he touches you?'

Mary Ann stared at her open-mouthed until water dripping from the dishcloth on to her apron front made her lower it into the water again. 'How did you know?'

'I've seen him do it once or twice. Some men are like that, unfortunately.'

'I hate it. And I hate him!'

'Shh! Keep your voice down.' After a pause, Miss Battley added, 'You might find a hatpin useful. I used to keep one handy when I was younger. Stab it into the fleshy part of his arm or leg if you're cornered.' She smiled conspiratorially.

Mary Ann bought a hatpin that very Saturday and kept it in her apron pocket from then on. She had been getting very worried lately about Jeff's attentions, hadn't known what to do.

The next time he trapped her in his bedroom she used the hatpin, which made him yell out in pain.

'You little bitch!' He glared at her, holding his arm. 'You'll be sorry you did that.'

'Why don't you just leave me alone?' she burst out.

He grinned. 'Why should I? You're very convenient and your mother isn't much use to me at the moment.'

She felt sick and took an involuntary step backwards just as the door opened.

'Are you all right, Jeff?' Dinah asked. 'Only I thought I heard you cry out.'

'I did. I stubbed my toe. I'll have to be more careful next time, won't I?'

The smile had returned, Mary Ann noticed in disgust. And he knew about the hat pin now, so would be on his guard. Whatever was she going to do if he kept on like this?

By June Gabriel was avoiding the farmhouse as much as possible during the day because Dora would insist on flirting with him and fussing over him, and it was driving him mad. She was docile and stupid, with cow-like eyes. They couldn't get rid of her, though, because the hens were providing a useful extra source of income, even after paying her wages. They'd never be rich, but together with a few other changes he'd made, the farm was now bringing in enough for them to be comfortable in their own modest way. He could even allow himself a few bob spending money every week.

One evening his mother said, 'That young woman they call Dorothy had her babby yesterday.'

'Poor lass. What's going to happen to her now?'

'She'll go home and someone else'll get the babby. The Greesons are on to a good thing there. They've got those two other lasses and no doubt more will be arriving because folk won't stop doing what's natural.' After buttering her toast she added, 'Jane Greeson was wearing a new silk dress in church on Sunday.'

'Oh, yes?' He didn't go to church with her, didn't see much point in it, really, but his mother seemed to enjoy it so Gabriel took it in turns with his cousin to drive their mothers and another friend to Overdale and back in the trap.

That morning he noticed a cab arriving at Redvale, the one with the grey horse again, and wondered if it was another girl. Then he saw Mrs Greeson come out of the house, carrying something wrapped in a bundle. When it moved, he realised they were indeed taking the baby away and wondered how the poor young mother felt about that.

He saw her sitting crying in the upper field the next day when he was working on the damned walls again but didn't think it his place to say anything. Let her have her weep in private.

It was a couple of weeks more before she left, walking meekly out to the cab with her father, who seemed very pleased about something. She looked like a puppet, though, lifeless except when someone pulled the strings.

One of the new lasses was so young, Gabriel would have called her a child and was shocked rigid the first time he saw her.

'How did someone of that age get into trouble?' he asked his mother one day after watching her cuddling a doll and crooning to it up in the top field. 'That's not natural. She doesn't even look like a woman.'

'Likely someone forced her.'

He stared at her aghast. He knew such things happened, of course he did, but to have the victim on his doorstep upset him. 'Men who do that should be taken out and shot like the mad dogs they are,' he said gruffly.

'I'd castrate fellows like that,' Jassy said in a matter-of-fact tone.

He was shocked to hear his mother using these words, but had to agree with her.

By June Mary Ann was feeling desperate because her stepfather was becoming more of a problem each day. She sometimes thought he enjoyed frightening her as much as he liked touching her. At nights she now wedged a chair under her door handle because he'd crept up the stairs a couple of times and tried to get into her bedroom.

The most horrible thing was that this was all done in near silence, with him whispering at her through the door and her whispering back for him to go away. She was terrified her mother would hear and blame her instead of him.

If only her mother hadn't been so ill she might have said something, asked for help, but that white face, the grim way her mother tried to go on working as usual, all stopped Mary Ann from confiding in her.

One afternoon her mother collapsed on the floor of the kitchen and when Mary Ann saw the blood soaking through her skirt, she ran out into the street and shrieked for a neighbour to help. After that they all came running and a passing deliveryman offered to take her to the hospital.

'You'd better wait here and tell your father,' Mrs Kenton from next door told Mary Ann. 'I'll go with her to the hospital.'

'No, I'm going, too.'

'Look, this isn't something for a girl of your age. It's women's business.'

'I'm nearly a woman and she's *my* mother.'

But they overruled her so Mary Ann had to stay home, and because she had to keep occupied or go mad she carried on making the tea for the lodgers.

When *he* came home she went into the hall to greet him. 'They took Mum to hospital this afternoon,' she said before he had even finished closing the front door. 'She fainted and there was blood everywhere.' She watched him turn and walk straight out without a word, and if anything was needed to convince her that he was a horrible person that was it. He hadn't even thought to offer her comfort.

She wished she could have gone with him, though, because she was desperate to know what was happening to her mother, but instead she had to serve the lodgers' tea, explaining to them that her mother was ill and she'd done her best with the food. Miss Battley was the only one who thought to help her clear the table, but their lodger had a heavy cold and soon retired to bed.

Mrs Kenton from next door came back at eight o'clock, knocking on the front door then walking right in, calling, 'Are you there, Mary Ann?'

The girl came running out of the kitchen. 'How is Mum?'

'She's lost the baby. Born dead, poor little thing. Your father's with her now.'

'He's *not* my father.'

Mrs Kenton glared at her. 'Is that important, now of all times?'

'It is to me. I hate him.'

'Well, he's a great comfort to your mother so you'd better keep your feelings to yourself, young woman.'

At ten o'clock *he* came home, looking tired.

'How's Mum?'

'Sleeping.' He stared at her, then looked round. 'Where is everyone?'

'In bed.'

'So you've been sitting here alone, worrying? Poor lass.'

He reached out as if to cuddle her and she skipped backwards. Surely he wasn't going to start that now? 'I've kept you some tea.'

'Good. I'm hungry.'

She served him, cleared away quickly after he'd eaten then edged towards the door. 'I'd better go to bed now. I'll have to be up early to get the breakfasts.'

'Just a minute.' He was up and across the room before she could get the door open. He laughed as he pulled her away from it.

She tried to thrust him away, but he was much stronger than her. 'Let go of me or I'll scream.'

'Scream away. I'll just say you're having hysterics because of your mother.'

The way he was looking at her made her shiver. It was as if she had no clothes on. 'Why won't you leave me alone? What do you want?'

He put his face right up to hers. 'I want what every man wants.'

She couldn't move for fear.

He laughed as he started fondling her breasts. She tried to fight back, but he was stronger than she'd expected. And somehow, she didn't dare scream.

She begged him to stop, because he was pinching her breasts now and it hurt, but he was breathing heavily and ignored her pleas.

When he dragged her across the room, she couldn't think what he was doing. He had shoved her to the ground before she had realised and quickly tied a scarf round her mouth.

When he rolled her over he climbed astride her and grinned down at her. She made a last effort to fight him and he slapped her face so hard her eyes watered. He had another scarf in his hands and used it to tie both her arms above her head to the table leg.

It was such a big, heavy old table that no one could move it on their own. All she could do now was kick out at him, but with another of those spine-chilling laughs, he sat on her again and unbuttoned her blouse, playing games with her. 'One little button. Two little buttons.'

When he got the blouse open he lifted her vest and she thought she'd die of embarrassment at having her bosom exposed. He tweaked her nipple and began to hurt her. Tears rolled out of her eyes and he stopped to flick one away.

'Oh, dear, am I being too rough? So sorry. Oops! I did it again.'

It all seemed like a nightmare, a dreadful pain-filled nightmare that wouldn't stop.

'I promised myself,' he said, standing up to unbutton his trousers, 'that I'd make you pay for that hatpin. And I promised myself I'd be the first with you, too. I enjoy breaking in virgins.'

She stared in horror at the thing that emerged from his trousers, feeling sick at the mere sight of it. He climbed on top of her and she couldn't breathe, couldn't think for the terror shuddering through her in great waves.

'You haven't been with a man yet, have you?'

She shook her head and looked at him pleadingly. But he just continued to smile.

From then on it got worse. She went rigid as he took down her drawers and poked his fingers into her. She was weeping but the sound was muffled by the gag. Then he pushed something into her down there, right inside her private parts. She thought it would kill her, but it didn't.

As he jerked around on top of her, grunting and groaning, she prayed to die but she didn't. She couldn't even faint.

When he'd finished, he pushed himself up off her and laughed, then went to get the dishcloth. Carefully he washed her and then pulled her drawers on again.

As he untied her hands, he warned, 'Don't scream or I'll knock you out.'

She rolled over and snatched up her blouse, thrusting her arms into it to cover herself even before she ripped off the gag.

'That,' he said, still blocking the way to the door, 'is what a man wants of a woman. You're a woman now, Mary Ann, and

I made you one.' He grabbed hold of her and plonked her down on one of the kitchen chairs. She was shaking too hard to resist. 'Look at me!'

She didn't want to, but he shook her and repeated his command until she did as he wished.

'If you say one word of this to your mother,' he said, his voice back to its usual light tone, 'I'll deny it ever happened. I'll say you must have been out with those lads again. If you try to tell the lodgers, I'll say you're hysterical because you're worried about your mother and all I did was try to cuddle you. Who do you think they'll believe? A man like me or a child like you?' He shook her. 'Eh?'

She shivered because she knew no one would believe her. Well, perhaps Miss Battley might, but their lodger wouldn't be able to prove anything.

'I see you're beginning to understand. This happens to a lot of girls. They just keep quiet and behave themselves. It doesn't even hurt if you don't fight and do as you're told. I'm your stepfather, whether you like it or not, so you *ought* to do as I say.' He gave another of those soft laughs of his. 'I hope your mother is in hospital for a long time because I intend to enjoy myself again with you. Now, go to bed. You have to be up early in the morning to get the breakfasts. And don't make a noise on the way up.'

She crept up to her bedroom, listening all the time in case he followed her. When she got there she put the chair back under the door handle, then washed herself all over before creeping into bed, shivering. She was beyond weeping now and she was sore – down there.

What he had done was wrong, she knew that.

Did her mother have to do *that* with him? How could she? How could anyone want to do such a terrible thing?

It took her a long time to fall asleep and she woke twice, thinking she heard footsteps on the attic stairs. When dawn shaded the bedroom to grey, she got up.

Her mother would kill her if she let the lodgers go without breakfast.

Her mother would kill her if she found out about what had happened.

And how was she going to stop him hurting her again tonight? She would surely die if he kept doing *that* to her!

She didn't die. But she hated it. And she hated him even more than she had before. One night she got up to bed on her own and wedged the door shut. The next night he tied her up and gagged her, thumping her in the stomach, which winded her. She panicked because she couldn't breathe and he just smiled as he watched her grunt and gasp for breath. Then he did it to her again. She didn't dare refuse him after that.

She thought of killing herself, but what prevented her was the thought that surely when her mother came home, this would stop?

It didn't. He just came up to her less often and laughed at her threats to tell.

'I think you can move back in with me again now, dear,' Dinah said to him one morning.

He looked at her. 'Sure it isn't a bit soon, darling? I don't want to upset you.'

She smiled at him. 'I'm very sure. I've missed having someone to cuddle.'

Mary Ann closed her eyes as relief washed through her. If he was sleeping with her mother, he wouldn't be able to sneak up to her. Her ordeal was nearly over.

Jane Greeson looked at the new girl and realised at once that she was facing trouble. Margaret Pensham wasn't in tears and she marched into the house ahead of her father with a defiant expression on her face, standing with folded arms by the window while he paid over the money.

When he had left Jane said, 'You'll be known as Jenny while you're here. Please remember that. Your parents wish to keep your real name secret.'

The young woman stared back at her. 'I'm not changing my

name and I won't answer to Jenny. I'm proud to be carrying this baby. The father is dead or he'd have married me, but he'll live on in my child.'

'If it survives. They don't all.'

Margaret stared at her. 'If you kill my baby, I'll kill you. I swear that. And if you try to take my child away from me afterwards, I'll find it, I promise you.'

'You're very full of what *you* intend to do. Let me tell you what *I* intend. You'll keep busy here, helping run the house. You'll not leave it under any circumstances, but will be allowed to take exercise in the field if you behave yourself.'

Margaret shrugged. 'I'm quite prepared to help and I won't give you any trouble because I need somewhere to stay that's not my parents' home, but I meant exactly what I said. I'm not pretending to be someone else and I'm not giving up my baby.'

She was nearly twenty-one and more mature than her years so Jane decided to bide her time and see how she behaved herself.

Gabriel noticed the new girl a few days later, sitting on the wall at the top of the field next to his. She had her head thrown back and was breathing deeply, as if enjoying the fresh air. When she noticed him, she jumped down on his side and strolled across.

'They'll probably prevent me from speaking to you, if they notice I'm here,' she said abruptly, 'but I need to get a letter to the family of my baby's father. He's dead and they don't know about the child. Will you help me?'

He didn't hesitate. 'Yes. Have you got it on you?'

'No. I didn't dare carry it around in case *she* found it. And will you let the Garbutts write back to you to confirm the arrangements?'

'Yes. Leave your letter under that big stone in the top corner of the field when you can and I'll pick it up. Watch out. Mrs Greeson is coming up the field after you.'

'If the Garbutts write back to say it's all right,' she said rapidly, 'pull the big rock off the corner of the wall and put it on again the next day. My room looks out this way and I'll see it.'

'All right. She's nearly here.' He raised his voice and said, 'It's sheep mainly, but we also keep hens on quite a large scale. It – oh, hello, Mrs Greeson. Your guest was just asking about the farming round here.'

Jane Greeson glared at the young woman. 'Get back to the house, you!'

With a shrug Margaret turned and climbed nimbly over the wall, for all her swollen waistline.

Jane looked at Gabriel. 'If she's trying to get you to help her escape, you'd better understand that she's under age and you'd be in big trouble.'

'She was just passing the time of day, that's all. I should think she's bored. You ought to get them some books and keep their minds occupied as well as their bodies. I feel sorry for those young women but for what it's worth, I think they probably get treated better here than they do in most places.'

'They do if they behave themselves.'

Gabriel didn't see Margaret taking exercise for several days afterwards, though he watched out for her. They must be keeping her inside to punish her. Next time he saw her, she was accompanied by the very young girl. He wondered how she would ever get a letter to him if she was watched every minute, but when the two of them got to the top of the field she went to lean on the wall, staring out across the moors, and he saw something white drop down on his side.

Since rain was brewing, he went out again as soon as the two young women had gone inside, reaching that part of the field by a roundabout way so that no one from Redvale saw him, then moving along his side of the wall, bent double. He found the envelope, which was weighted down with a pebble and had not blown away. Slipping it into his pocket, he crept back again, laughing at himself for this cloak-and-dagger stuff. But he'd believed the girl's story.

He posted the letter that evening when he went into Overdale to the library.

For the next few days he kept watch on Redvale, half-expecting the father's family to come and rescue Miss Pensham, but nothing happened. The girls continued to take exercise only in groups.

Then he received a letter from the Garbutts, saying they were grateful to him for helping Margaret and that they would do exactly as she'd asked.

He went up the next morning to move the big stone and the following day he put it back in place.

When he next saw her out walking Miss Pensham was looking a great deal happier and although they didn't try to speak to one another, their eyes met briefly and she winked at him.

A few days after Jeff moved back into her mother's bedroom, Mary Ann was sick when she got up in the morning. She shivered as she stared down at the mess she had made and didn't try to clear it up until her mother had gone out to the shops. Her mother noticed nearly everything and was back to her old self again, though she was even more sharp-tempered than before with her daughter.

Mary Ann was sick the next two mornings as well, and the third time her mother happened to be coming up for some fresh linen and heard her. She burst into the bedroom just as Mary Ann had finished vomiting.

'You didn't have your monthly and now you're being sick in the mornings. That usually only happens when someone is expecting a child.' Her voice was tight with suppressed anger.

Mary Ann could only hang her head. Surely she couldn't be? He'd said she was too young to be at risk.

'You've been with a man, haven't you? *Who is it?*'

The girl shook her head, knowing it would only make things worse if she told the truth. A slap took her by surprise, rocking her head sideways, and she yelped in shock and pain as another one followed it. Then her mother was hitting any part of her she could, one slap after another, and Mary Ann began crying, begging her to stop, ducking in a vain attempt to avoid the blows.

It was Jeff who came up and stood between them. 'Dinah, stop it! Stop it, I say! Everyone can hear you. What the hell's the matter?'

'She's been whoring around. She's expecting. After all my care, she does this to us.'

44

He stared at Mary Ann in dismay then turned back quickly to his wife. 'Surely not?'

'There's not much doubt about it. I noticed she didn't have her monthly, but that sometimes happens, and now she's being sick in the mornings, so I did some quick counting. She's missed two monthlies now.'

'Oh, no. How dreadful! You poor thing. You didn't deserve this on top of everything else.' He put his arms round his wife and they both stared accusingly at the girl.

'Who's the man?' Dinah repeated.

And suddenly Mary Ann had had enough. 'It was him!' she shouted, pointing. 'He forced me when you were in hospital. He *hurt* me.'

Her mother darted across the room and shook her hard. Even though she was not as tall as her daughter, rage gave Dinah added strength and she looked so wild Mary Ann was too terrified to defend herself.

Jeff Powling pulled his wife away and held her in his arms as she began to sob. He glared accusingly at Mary Ann. 'I don't know why you're making up this dreadful tale and it hurts me that you are, but I know your mother won't believe it. Tell us who the boy is, Mary Ann. You must have been doing it on your Saturday afternoons out. Who is he?'

'It's you! You know it is! You tied me up and forced me.'

Her mother stopped sobbing to shriek, 'You ungrateful wretch! Trying to come between us. You've been jealous from the start. Well, my Jeff would *never* do anything like that. Never!'

He pulled Dinah towards the door, giving a quick smirk over his shoulder at Mary Ann, as if to say, *I told you so*. Outside he stopped and said slowly, 'We need to think what we're going to do, love. Is there a key to this door? I think we'd better lock her in.'

'No, there isn't a key.'

'Hmm. Then perhaps I'd better fit a bolt to the outside. You stay here and keep watch that she doesn't try to get away and I'll nip down to the ironmonger's for one.'

It sickened Mary Ann to see how gratefully her mother looked

45

at him, and it hurt to see how hostile her expression was when she turned back to her daughter and leaned against the door post with her arms folded. 'You'll tell us who it is, or you'll not come out of that room.'

'I've told you. It was *him*.'

This time her mother didn't go mad at her, but looked so disgusted it was as bad.

Mary Ann considered pushing her aside and running away before *he* got back. But where could she go? They had no relatives, no real friends, either, and Sheila's mother would only bring her straight back.

What did other girls do when they were in trouble like this?

An hour later he had fitted a bolt and she was locked in. She went to sit on her bed, too upset for tears. She wasn't going to tell lies, though. It *was* him.

4

September 1906

Two weeks later Dinah sat in the small back parlour and admitted to her husband, 'I can't think what else to do. She won't tell me who it is, still keeps saying it's you.'

'As if I would fancy a child like her when I've got you,' he said fondly, taking her hand and raising it to his lips to press a lingering kiss there. 'She's resented me from the start, though I can't understand why. It's not as if she even remembers her own father, since he died before she was born.'

Dinah sighed and leaned against him. 'I don't know how I'm going to hold my head up when the neighbours find out.' He was silent for so long she looked sideways at him. 'What are you thinking?'

'I'm thinking how best to spare *you* the consequences of this.'

'Unless I throw her out – and I won't do that! – there's no way to spare me. It'll soon begin to show.'

'That daily maid you've hired is doing all right, isn't she?'

'Yes. Though she doesn't do as much work as Mary Ann used to.'

He ignored that. 'I know a place that takes girls in her condition then has the babies adopted. If we sent her there no one need know. You wouldn't be shamed in front of your neighbours.'

'And how much does that cost?' Dinah asked bitterly. 'It's only rich folk who can afford places like that.'

'It doesn't matter how much, because I'll pay.'

'Why should you do that?'

He gave her one of his loving looks, the sort that filled her with melting warmth. 'To spare you, my love.'

'Where is it?'

'In the north, in a small village near—' He hesitated, knowing Dinah had vowed never to go back to Overdale or let her daughter go near the place, though she would not say why. 'Near Burnley. It's run by a distant relative of mine, actually. She was a nurse, married late in life, so the young women are in excellent hands for the birth. The farm is on the edge of the moors and there are no neighbours to spy on the inmates. It's an ideal position for a business like that.'

'I'll have to think about it.'

He let the matter drop, knowing Dinah would do as he suggested. Since she'd lost the child, she didn't seem able to take any decision on her own. Which suited him very well. Once the girl was gone, he intended to make sure his dear wife didn't recover her old shrewdness.

The next morning when all the lodgers were out Dinah went up to the attic. She felt a pang of pity at the sight of her daughter's white, unhappy face, then remembered how Mary Ann had tried to come between her and her husband so hardened her heart.

'This is your last chance to tell me the truth, young woman. If not, you'll be sent away.'

'I've *told* you the truth, only you won't believe it.'

There was such weary dignity about the girl that Dinah stared at her in puzzlement. As the silence lengthened, she took a deep breath. 'Then you'll have to leave.'

Terror etched itself across the young face. *'You're turning me out?'*

'Not exactly. I'm sending you to a home for girls in your condition, a strict place where you'll be carefully supervised and – and looked after. They'll find a home for the baby.'

'You don't want me now you've got *him*.'

'Of course I want you. You can come back once you've had the child, as long as you promise this won't happen again.'

'He's the one who should promise that.' After a moment's frowning thought, Mary Ann asked, 'Where is this place? Will you come and see me?'

48

'It's in Lancashire, near the moors, and of course I shan't be coming to see you. Let alone I have the lodgers to look after, do you think I want to see my own daughter in that condition?' Dinah swept a scornful glance over Mary Ann's still-flat belly then left the attic, carefully locking the door. Her head was aching and she couldn't think straight, hadn't been well since she lost the baby, felt unhappy all the time.

She went to her bedroom, sitting weeping on the edge of her bed. After a while she realised how time was passing and dragged herself up to go and do the shopping. She used to enjoy that. Didn't enjoy anything much nowadays.

Mary Ann sat on the bed and tried to think things through. She knew she would have to go to this place until after the baby was born, and it didn't take much more thought to work out that she would never dare return to share a house with *him*. Once she'd had the baby, she'd have to run away. Only how did you do that without any money?

She went to stand by the window, staring out across the rooftops, listening to the swishing sound of the sea breaking on the pebbles of the nearby beach. She had fallen asleep many a night to that sound and loved the ocean in all its moods. She was going to miss it.

That night Jeff tried to cheer Dinah up and she made a huge effort to keep calm, but in the end her feelings overcame her and she burst into tears. 'I can do nothing with her. Will you take her to that place you told me about?'

He came to put his arms round her. 'Leave it to me. I'll send a telegram to let Jane know we're coming. And no weakening from you, darling. I know it's hard, but you have to think of *us* as well as her.'

Dinah looked at him through a mist of grateful tears and nodded.

Mary Ann refused categorically to go anywhere with Jeff, terrified at the mere thought of being alone with him. She made so much noise about it that she and her mother got into another shouting match that brought Miss Battley up the attic stairs to see what was wrong.

As there was no avoiding some sort of explanation, Dinah told her the problem in a few curt phrases.

Miss Battley looked at Mary Ann and said in her usual gruff way, 'I'll go with you if you like, Mary Ann. You'll be safe then.'

'Now look here—' Jeff began.

'We can't ask you to—' said Dinah.

Miss Battley held up one hand. 'You didn't. I offered. All you need do is pay my fare, Mr Powling. I'll take a week's holiday from work and make my own way back after we've left Mary Ann at the home. I've friends in Blackpool and will enjoy spending a few days with them.' She turned back to the girl. 'I think it's for the best that you leave, child.'

Mary Ann gave her mother one last pleading glance, but when it drew no response she nodded her consent.

'Next Monday will suit me.' Miss Battley started down the stairs.

'We're very grateful for your help,' Jeff said as he followed her.

She didn't even turn as she answered, 'I like the girl, always have. She's a hard worker. And honest.'

From the way she scowled at him when they reached the bottom he realised she had guessed something. She'd have to go, then. He didn't like her sour old-maid's face about the place anyway and he wasn't having anyone here spoiling his carefully laid plans.

On the train north Mary Ann asked to go to the toilet.

'I'll take her,' Miss Battley said at once.

'See you don't let her get away,' Jeff said.

'Where could she go on a moving train? Have a bit of common sense, man.'

When they got near the ladies' toilet, Miss Battley said, 'We need to talk privately and we'd better make it quick. You can't come back home after you've had the baby or he'll be after you again.'

Mary Ann stared at her, then felt her eyes filling with tears. 'You believe me?'

'Yes. But I haven't any proof, and anyway your mother is in no state to deal with this. She's not well, hasn't got over losing her baby yet.' She gave Mary Ann a wintry smile. 'I have a friend who runs a boarding house in Blackpool. If you go to her afterwards she'll either give you a job or help you find one. I must be getting foolish in my old age because it's my guess they'll search your luggage so I've written a note to my friend on a handkerchief in marking ink.' She glanced back along the corridor and produced a neatly folded handkerchief. 'In case anything happens to this, you'd better memorise my friend's name and address. You won't be able to do anything until after the baby's born, anyway. And here's some money. You'll need something if you have to run away.'

Mary Ann gave her a sudden hug then the tears flooded down her face and she disappeared into the ladies' toilet where she struggled to stop weeping.

It was a while before she came out.

Jeff ambled along the corridor and joined Miss Battley. 'You've been a long time. Anything wrong?'

'I think the poor child has an upset stomach,' Miss Battley said loudly. 'She came out then rushed back in again.'

'I'll wait with you. If she's not out in a couple of minutes I'm calling the guard to open the door. I don't trust her one inch. Or you.'

She gave him a frosty look. 'The feeling is mutual, I assure you.'

'Then I hope you'll find yourself some other lodgings after we get back.'

'I have done already. I don't enjoy sharing a house with a man who takes advantage of a child.'

He sucked in his breath but didn't reply, pretending not to understand her meaning.

She folded her arms and when Mary Ann came out, put her arm round the girl and stayed between her and her stepfather as they walked back to their compartment.

Overdale was full of bustling people, but the cab with the grey horse was waiting for them outside the station as they'd been told. On the way Mary Ann suddenly grabbed hold of Miss Battley's hand, ignoring the man opposite. 'I'm frightened. What if they're like *him?*'

'I intend to check that out for myself and won't leave you there until I'm sure.'

'Thank you.'

'I hate to spoil your little tête-à-tête but you have no power to prevent anything, you stupid old fool,' Jeff drawled.

Miss Battley gave him one of her withering glances. 'I can go to the police, though, and tell them what I suspect. I don't think your cousin would enjoy the resultant fuss, not if she's trying to keep her customers out of sight and her business secret. Nor would your wife, whether anything is proved or not.'

'You might overreach yourself one day,' he snarled.

'So might you.'

The farm was at the very end of a lane, with only one other building in sight, a much smaller house built in weathered stone. It was a grey, blustery day and the place Mary Ann was to stay didn't look at all welcoming, its red bricks darkened by rain and its windows looking like blank eye sockets.

'Wait for us here,' Jeff said to the cab driver.

'I s'll have to if you want to get back to Overdale,' he said placidly, 'nor I won't move away from here until you've paid me the agreed fare.'

Muttering, Jeff got out, grabbing Mary Ann's arm and pulling her roughly with him.

Miss Battley followed them quickly, her expression angry. 'There's no need to manhandle the child.'

He ignored her.

The door was opened by a buxom woman with a severe face.

'Jane, you're looking as well as ever.' Jeff's practised smile appeared again.

'And you're as full of flummery as ever. Did Florence die, then?'

'What?' His smile faded.

'Your first wife. Did she die?'

'Oh. Yes. Pneumonia. She always did have a weak chest. And Dinah suits me much better. Now, that's enough about me. Shall we get on with things?'

'Yes, bring the girl in.' She looked questioningly at the other woman.

As Jeff made no attempt to introduce her, Miss Battley introduced herself, then said, 'I need to talk to you in private before I agree to leave the child here, Mrs Greeson.'

Jane looked from her to Jeff. 'I don't understand.'

'She's an interfering old biddy and you shouldn't believe a word she says.'

'On the other hand, the police might want to investigate certain claims I could make,' Miss Battley said.

'Oh, do as she asks, if it'll keep her quiet,' snapped Jeff.

Jane led them into a sitting room. 'Come this way then, Miss Battley.'

Mary Ann spoke for the first time. 'I'm not staying here alone with *him!*'

'Can she stay with someone else, please?' Miss Battley asked.

'This is ridiculous!' he burst out.

Jane sucked in her breath at the ugly expression on Jeff's face, suddenly remembering the nasty little boy he had once been. 'The girl can wait in the kitchen.' She turned to Mary Ann. 'You will be known as Sarah while you're here.'

'She has a name of her own,' Miss Battley said. 'No reason why she shouldn't continue to use it. *She* has done nothing to be ashamed of.'

The two women stared at one another, each recognising a person who would stand no nonsense.

'Wait in here, Jeff.' Jane led Mary Ann into the kitchen where two girls were chopping vegetables. 'You can sit over there.'

She went back and beckoned to Miss Battley, taking her into a small office. 'You'd better be quick. I haven't any time to waste.'

'Very well. That man is the father of the baby. He'd been pestering the poor girl for months, rubbing himself against her, that sort of thing. I've seen him. When her mother was in hospital Mary Ann suddenly started looking terrified and it fits for the birth date, too. So he must have forced her then. Before I leave her here, I want your word that you won't let him near her again. When this is all over, I'll be happy to come for her myself and find her a home. She can't go back to that situation.'

Jane stared at her, then let out her breath in a big whoosh. 'That's a rather nasty accusation.'

'I don't make it lightly and I'm prepared to take it to the police if I have to, to save that child.'

'Rather a large child,' Jane said dryly.

'Wait till you get to know her, and you'll see that I'm right. She's still a child mentally. The mother's been overprotective with her, but the poor woman has just lost a baby and is too weak to do anything but cling to *him*.' Miss Battley fumbled in her handbag and held out a piece of paper. 'This will be my new address. *Please*, if you have any pity in you whatsoever, don't let him take that girl back.' She waited a moment, then continued, 'Now, I'd like to see her bedroom and then I want to meet your husband. I have to feel sure that she's not going from the frying pan into the fire.'

'I'm not promising anything about afterwards. I'll have to think about it.' Face expressionless, Jane put the piece of paper into a drawer and led the way upstairs.

Half an hour later, Jeff and Miss Battley climbed into the cab, rode back to the town in silence and parted company at the station without another word.

Eyes narrowed, he watched her walk into the ladies' waiting room. How the hell did she know what he'd done? He'd been very careful indeed.

Though she couldn't prove anything, he didn't dare risk the police being brought into this. He might have to take steps to keep the old biddy quiet. He wasn't going to let anyone stop him achieving his goal, not after all the hard work he'd put in.

Jane waited until the cab had clopped away, then went back into the kitchen. The three girls were chatting but working at the same time, and the new girl was peeling some potatoes. That augured well, anyway. Some of the girls had no idea how to do housework or cook. Jane couldn't abide idleness and took satisfaction in teaching them how to look after a house properly. And of course their working saved her the cost of a servant and tired them out nicely. People with time and energy on their hands could make mischief.

Gabriel was working outside one day when it suddenly occurred to him that there was nothing to stop him from going to see the sea the following summer, nothing at all. His father had hated to spend a farthing on anything other than the farm, but he and his mother now had a bit put away for a rainy day and it wouldn't break the bank to spend a little. For the first time in his life he would, he decided, take a holiday.

He broached the idea to his mother over the evening meal. 'Why don't you come with me? We can find someone to keep an eye on the farm for us.'

She shook her head emphatically. 'I prefer to sleep in my own bed.'

'Well, I'm going. I really want to see the sea. I don't know why, I just do. Have you ever seen it?'

'Nay, I've never gone further away than Overdale, nor I don't want to.' Jassy looked round complacently. 'Now that we've fixed things up a bit, I'm more than happy in my own kitchen.'

'I'll make arrangements to have things looked after here, then, but I really fancy a holiday.'

She looked at him thoughtfully then her mouth creased a little at the corners, which was the nearest she usually came to a smile.

'You're a hard worker and you've earned a rest. I reckon times are changing and folk are making a habit of gadding about the country. I shouldn't like my son to be scorned for never having left his home, though it's too late for me.' She stood for a moment, brow furrowed. 'How much do you reckon it'll cost? I'll give it you out of the savings.'

'I'll need ten pounds. I may as well go for two weeks.'

She sucked in her breath in dismay. 'That much?'

'I'm not skimping. I've always wanted to see a bit of the world and I've waited long enough. I was going to leave home for a year or two when I was eighteen – only Dad had the seizure and it wasn't possible. But if I don't go somewhere, see *something* different, I reckon I'll burst with the longing. And what I want to see most of all is the ocean.'

She could tell there'd be no changing his mind. He was like her and when she decided on something she nearly always got her way because she wasn't stupid enough to want the impossible.

Except for getting him married.

That shouldn't be impossible, surely? But he'd shown no interest in any of the girls she'd brought to the house under various excuses.

Well, let him go away and get this desire to view the sea out of his system. When he came back she'd find a different girl to help out with the chickens, choosing this one more carefully. Eventually one would catch his interest, surely?

Mary Ann settled in at Redvale, not complaining at the hard work which was augmented by plain sewing because Mrs Greeson took in finishing work from a local garment manufacturer and let the girls do the buttonholes and tidying up. Mary Ann often sat next to Margaret Pensham, and when Mrs Greeson wasn't in the room they chatted in low voices, growing very friendly.

One day as they were walking in the field, Margaret said abruptly, 'What are you going to do afterwards?'

'Find myself a job, I suppose. I'm not going back to live with *him!*'

'And the baby?'

Mary Ann's eyes filled with tears. 'My mother says it has to be adopted, and I didn't mind at first, but now it's started kicking, I don't want to do that. The baby seems more real now it's moving about.' She cradled her belly and looked down at it. 'Anyway, I like babies and I want to keep it.' When she couldn't sleep at night, she held imaginary conversations with it and had already grown to love it.

'You'll find it hard to work and look after a baby.'

'I know. But I'm used to hard work.' Living here had made Mary Ann realise that few people worked as hard as she had done.

Margaret hesitated then said, 'I'm going to tell you a secret because I trust you and I know you'd never tell the Greeson woman, whatever she said or did. When I'm twenty-one, John's parents are coming to take me away from here. I wrote to them, and Mr Clough on the next farm posted the letter for me. I asked them to write back to him if they were going to do as I suggested and we arranged a signal. They did write back because he gave the signal, then another day he hid behind the wall and told me they'd sent their love and were thrilled about my news.' She sniffed away a tear. 'I'm always crying. Silly, isn't it?'

Mary Ann patted her arm. 'I get like that too sometimes.'

'Anyway, the Garbutts can't do anything to help me till I'm twenty-one because my father would only get his lawyer to have me brought back. They all live in Overdale, you see, and he's terrified of anyone finding out about the baby.' She paused then added in a voice filled with anguish, 'He threatened to have me locked away in a madhouse if I didn't come here and stay until the baby was born. My own father!'

Mary Ann stared at her, wide-eyed with shock, then reached out to hold her hand.

Margaret squeezed her friend's warm hand and managed a watery smile. 'You'd think I'd be used to the thought of what he's like by now, wouldn't you? Anyway I've planned things rather carefully and I think it'll work. But why I'm telling you is – if you ever need help, come and see me. I'll definitely help you. You'd better memorise the Garbutts' address. That Greeson woman goes through our things regularly, you know, so I daren't write it down for you.'

'All right.' Mary Ann repeated it a few times, then nodded.

'She pretends to care for us, but I think she only cares for the money and I've listened to the way she talks to that poor maid of hers. She's got a mean mouth and a cruel nature.'

Mary Ann felt relief flow through her. Now she had two places to turn to afterwards.

'Just one thing more,' Margaret said as they stood at the top of the field looking out over the moors. 'Don't let people force you to do things you don't want. Make plans and take charge of your own life. I know you're quite young still, but you're not stupid. I can't bear weepy, droopy women who let what other people think rule their lives. John would never have treated me like that. He was a splendid man.' She blinked her over-bright eyes.

'Did you love him very much?'

Margaret nodded. As they walked down, she said, 'What happened to you was disgusting. I wanted to tell you that it needn't be like that when you go with a man. If you love someone, you *want* to do it with him.' As she saw the sceptical expression on her companion's face, Margaret chuckled. 'You'll find out one day. Come on, we'd better get back to our sewing.' She raised her reddened hand and sighed at the sight of it. 'She's using us as slaveys, you know. But working helps pass the time, at least. And I don't want to cause any trouble till I have to.'

Since Dinah continued to feel tired and strained she let Jeff take over the boarding-house accounts. She had never enjoyed figures, but preferred to know exactly how things stood so had learnt from her aunt how to keep them properly.

He had offered to help her earlier on in their marriage, laughing at how bad-tempered she always became when doing her weekly balances, but Dinah had refused. Now she handed them over to him because she kept failing to make the books balance. She felt confused sometimes and was often drowsy.

'I want to see them, though,' she said as she handed the books over.

'Don't you trust me?'

'It's not that, it's just – well, I like to know how I stand.'

He put the books back into her hands. 'If you don't trust me, my dear, I'd rather you continued to do them yourself.'

She sighed and passed them back. He was right. If she couldn't trust her own husband, who could she trust? And indeed, as the weeks passed and she got no better, she couldn't seem to care enough to insist on seeing the books.

Once, while he was away on business, she searched for them, because she was feeling a little brighter, but she couldn't find them and didn't like to ask him where he kept them. How could she appear mistrustful when he always brought her home little presents, cosseting her in a way she had never experienced before?

She had lost her daughter. She didn't want to lose her husband as well.

5

November 1906 – March 1907

One bright but chilly morning in November two cabs drew up at Redvale. Hearing the clop of hooves, Jane went to look out of the window and frowned at what she saw. She wasn't expecting any new girls. However, when a middle-aged couple got out of the first cab, both well-dressed and looking in comfortable circumstances, she guessed they'd come to look for somewhere to put their wayward daughter until her embarrassing problem was dealt with.

But why two cabs?

She went to answer the front door, smiling at them.

The man raised his hat to her. 'I'm Edward Garbutt. I believe Miss Pensham is staying here? We'd like to see her, please.'

Jane suddenly felt suspicious. 'We don't allow visitors, I'm afraid.' Mr Pensham had made it very plain that no one was to see his daughter while she was here, nor was she to communicate with anyone. 'I can give her a message if you like.'

'I want to see her and I'm not leaving until I do.' He beckoned to someone in the second cab.

The door opened and a man got out. Jane began to feel nervous. 'Sorry.' She slammed the door in her visitor's face before he could prevent her and as he began to hammer on it, she ran to the kitchen to lock that door as well. Trust Maurice to be in town when she needed him!

She turned to look at the astonished girls. 'Ah, Margaret, I need to speak to you straight away. I noticed something in the attics that I think is your fault.' She led the way out briskly and, with a puzzled glance at her friend, Margaret followed her up the back stairs.

When they got to the attics, Jane gestured to her companion to go in first and as soon as she had, slammed and locked the door on her.

Mary Ann stood frowning, hearing the hammering continuing on the front door. What was happening? Why was no one answering the door? She tiptoed into the hall, feeling anxious.

From upstairs came sounds of shouting and screaming for help.

Margaret!

The other two girls had followed her and were standing in the kitchen doorway, staring at her. 'Do you know what's happening?' one of them whispered.

Mary Ann shook her head and returned to the kitchen with them, but could not get on with her work for worrying. Margaret had confided in her that today was her twenty-first birthday and her father could no longer control what she did. She was quite sure the Garbutts would be coming to take her back to their home.

Only – if Mrs Greeson had locked Margaret in the attics, how would she manage to get away? The doors were all very old-fashioned and sturdy. Mary Ann couldn't imagine anyone breaking them down.

She realised suddenly that she was the only one who could help, even if it got her into trouble, and ran out of the kitchen into the hall. Glancing anxiously up the stairs, she hurried across to unbolt and fling open the front door.

Two men stood there. They stared at her in surprise.

'I think they've locked Margaret in the attics,' she whispered.

'Deprivation of liberty,' the lawyer snapped. 'Come on!'

The lady who must be Mrs Garbutt waited in the doorway, looking anxious.

Mary Ann paused for a moment to watch the two men hurry up the stairs, then hurried back to the kitchen. She had done all she could. Mrs Greeson would soon work out that someone had let them in and then she'd definitely be in trouble. But it'd be worth it to help her friend.

She only wished there were someone to help her.

Edward Garbutt was furious. He strode up a flight of stairs two at a time and nearly bumped into Mrs Greeson at the top. She gaped for a moment then barred his way.

'How dare you break into my house? Get out at once!'

The lawyer moved forward to stand beside his client. 'Before you go any further, you should think about what you're doing, Mrs Greeson.' He slapped a piece of paper into her hand. 'This is a legal requirement for you to let us see Miss Margaret Pensham, signed by a local magistrate. My client is offering her a home and since she's now twenty-one, she has the right to decide for herself whether she wants to accept that offer or not.'

'She's not twenty-one yet!'

'Oh, yes, she is. Today is her birthday.'

'I'll – um – go and ask her if she wants to see you.'

He shook his head. 'That's not good enough. I must hear the answer from her own lips. And should you deny us the chance to speak to Miss Pensham – whether we do it outside or inside your house is your own choice – I shall be obliged to call in the police.'

She stared at him, chewing her lip in frustration, then read the piece of paper carefully before scowling at the two men. 'Miss Pensham's father is going to be very angry indeed. Could you not speak to *him* about this?'

Mr Garbutt took a step forward. 'Mr Pensham kept the news of John's child from us and Margaret said he intended to have it adopted. I don't think he's amenable to reason. My wife and I have a right to know and love our grandchild, and can offer it – and its mother – a good home. Now, stop prevaricating and take us to her, if you please.'

Jane gave in, leading the way to the top floor and flinging open the door of an attic bedroom to reveal Margaret, standing with a candlestick in her hand, as if about to use it as a weapon. At the sight of them she dropped it on the floor and burst into tears.

With an exclamation of dismay Edward Garbutt hurried

forward to take her in his arms and let her weep on his shoulder. He patted her back awkwardly as he waited for her to recover.

The lawyer glared at Mrs Greeson and said very emphatically, 'If Miss Pensham cares to bring charges against you for this, I shall be very happy to represent her.'

Jane folded her arms and watched them, biding her time. How had they found out where Margaret was? It must be Gabriel Clough. He was the only one who could have got a letter out. She'd give him a piece of her mind once these three had left. Just let him ever ask a favour of her again! Turning to the lawyer, she said curtly, 'I'd be obliged if you'd leave my house as quickly as possible.'

Margaret straightened up. 'I need to pack my things.'

After that was done Jane escorted them out, slamming the front door behind them. How they had got in she didn't know because she'd definitely locked that door. But she meant to find out.

Mary Ann was working in the kitchen, preparing food for the midday meal. The other two young women were in the sewing room nearby.

Jane summoned all three into the kitchen. 'Which of you opened the front door to those people?'

The two who had been sewing looked at Mary Ann, who felt her stomach lurch nervously at the cold anger on Mrs Greeson's face. 'I did.' She tried not to let her fear show.

'Come through to the parlour, Mary Ann. You two get back to work.'

Taking a deep breath she followed the older woman.

'You can thank that,' Jane pointed to her bulging stomach, 'for me not giving you the beating you deserve. How dare you open that door? Who are you to act against my wishes in *my* house? You'll be confined to your bedroom on bread and water for a week. Sewing will be brought up to you, but you'll see no one, speak to no one, during that time. And from now on the only exercise you'll get will be in *my* company.'

The week which followed seemed very long to Mary Ann. She spent a lot of time staring out of the window at the moors and wondering what Margaret was doing. She also wondered what would happen to herself and her baby. Every morning and evening she recited the two addresses she had been given, the one in Blackpool and the Garbutts' address in Overdale. She meant to make sure she never forgot them. And saying them gave her the courage to continue. Sometimes to cheer herself up she imagined walking on the beach or promenade at Brighton, she had never stopped missing the sea and the tangy salt air.

When she was allowed to join the others and resume work in the kitchen, she found them unwilling even to speak to her unless absolutely necessary. She missed Margaret's liveliness and intelligence dreadfully, and she also missed going outside.

As the weeks passed, not only did her body grow heavier so did her spirits.

One of the girls had her baby and left. Two new girls joined them, both cowed and tearful.

Jane Greeson, who had had a very stiff letter from Mr Pensham demanding his money back, still could not forgive the Baillie girl for her defiance. When she answered his letter, enclosing a small refund for the proportion of time Margaret would not be with her, she tidied her desk and found the piece of paper with the address Miss Battley had given her. Smiling, she went into the kitchen with it.

'Mary Ann.'

'Yes, Mrs Greeson.'

'Your friend Miss Battley left me her new address and offered to come and pick you up after the child was born. I have decided, however, that the proper people to take care of you are your parents. I shall be informing them, and only them, when you're ready to leave. No doubt your stepfather will be the one to come for you.'

With great satisfaction she tore the piece of paper up and watched the colour drain from Mary Ann's cheeks. No one got the better of her without suffering for it, absolutely no one.

However, as a nurse she kept a careful eye on those within her care and could see the signs of depressed spirits in Mary

Ann. Since this could affect the outcome of the pregnancy and Dr Browning-Baker had already intimated that he had a couple ready to adopt the child, she allowed the girl outside for walks again, though only in the company of the others.

She would be glad when that one left and was annoyed with Jeff for bringing the girl here. If he got Mary Ann into trouble again, he could look elsewhere for a solution. His second wife must be a very stupid woman to have believed him innocent of this.

If she hadn't owed him a favour and always had a fondness for him, Jane would never have accepted the girl.

Well, the favour was paid back now and, fondness or not, he could clear up his own messes from now on.

The Garbutts took Margaret back to their comfortable house in Overdale, a large place called The Sycamores set in extensive gardens.

'We hope you'll make your home with us from now on,' Angela Garbutt told her as she showed her to a large, comfortable bedroom. 'We're thrilled to know John left a child behind and want to share the upbringing of our grandchild, if you'll let us.'

'Even though John and I weren't married?'

'We wish you had been, for your own sake, because people won't be kind to you. But it won't affect the way we treat you.'

Margaret burst into tears again and Angela gave her a long hug, then smoothed her hair back and smiled. 'I always wanted a daughter.'

A good night's sleep made Margaret feel so much better that she asked Edward Garbutt how they'd got inside the house. When he explained, she looked at him in consternation. 'Was it a tall girl with dark hair who opened the door?'

'Yes.'

'Oh, no! That was Mary Ann. She'll be in dreadful trouble for helping me, and Mrs Greeson isn't a kind woman. Is there nothing we can do to help her?'

'If she hadn't opened the door, we might have had a lot more trouble reaching you so I do feel grateful to her. I don't think there's anything we can do legally, but perhaps you could write to that farmer next door and ask him to keep an eye on her, help her if he can? Tell him we'll reimburse him for any expenses he incurs.'

Margaret wrote to Gabriel then settled down to await the birth of her child with as much fortitude as she could. But she couldn't help feeling hurt when a dray arrived filled with her possessions and the driver handed them a brusque note from her father's lawyer informing her that the Penshams had disowned her and wished never to hear from her again.

'That was cruel,' Angela said to her husband that night. 'And to do it now, just before the baby is due – well, that's a shameful way to treat your own daughter.'

'No wonder she turned to our John for love. She can't have found much at home, can she? I never did like Ronald Pensham. He's a cold fish and drives a hard bargain in business.'

'His wife daren't open her mouth in his company,' Angela said. 'It's a wonder Margaret turned out so well. But she'll find plenty of affection here. She and her baby. Oh, Edward, isn't it wonderful that John left a child?'

He smiled at her. 'Yes. And if it's a son, it'll be even more wonderful.'

While he worked Gabriel often turned in the direction of the farm next door and watched the girls walking round the field – they'd worn quite a path round the edges now. The tall one, Mary Ann, for no reason that he could fathom, caught his eye more than the others. Sometimes she seemed very young, a child in a woman's body, while at others she seemed old, bowed down by grief and hopelessness. She had a fresh-looking face and although she was too thin now, he'd guess she was of a sturdy, healthy build normally. He didn't find little wispy women attractive, never had.

The week after Margaret Pensham's escape Gabriel received a letter from her. She was happily settled at The Sycamores now and wished to thank him for all his help. She would also be grateful if he'd keep an eye on her friend Mary Ann, who might be in trouble for letting the Garbutts in. If he could ever help her friend, Margaret begged him to do so because she was sure no one else would. Mr Garbutt would be happy to reimburse him for any expenses involved.

Gabriel didn't see Mary Ann for three weeks, which worried him greatly, and when she did reappear she looked pale and subdued. What had that harridan been doing to her?

His mother joined him by the window. 'Eh, that lass looks proper down. Jane Greeson always was spiteful, even as a lass.'

'You know everyone,' he teased.

'I used to. There's too many folk now in Overdale for one person to know about.' She turned to leave. 'Gawping out of t'window won't get my baking finished. I mun get on with my work.'

As his mother clattered off down the narrow stairs, his eyes went back to Mary Ann, trudging round the field on her own, not looking at the scenery but pausing as she always did to pet the dogs. Eh, that poor lass! he thought. Every line of her body seemed to droop where before she had walked briskly, head up, enjoying the air, chatting to her friend.

'You keep out of it from now on, our Gabriel,' his mother advised when he asked her later if she could see any way of helping the girl.

'I'm just saying that if you see any way to help that lass, well, I'd be grateful if you'd do it. It's partly because of me that she's in trouble, you see. Because of that letter I posted.'

She watched him go back to work. He could never pass by someone who needed help, her Gabriel couldn't. He was a hard worker, too, a son to be proud of in every way.

If only he'd get married. But he hadn't even tried walking out with a girl. It was as if that side of him was still unawakened. Too much hard work and not enough pleasure. You didn't learn about women from books.

Dinah missed her daughter even more than she had expected to.

Of course she was still angry with the girl for getting herself into trouble – very angry – and furious with her for lying about who the father was. She had racked her brains to think which boy it could be, itching to question Mary Ann's friends but not daring to in case she revealed the shameful reason for it. But still, she did miss her daughter.

She missed Eleanor Battley, too, and had no idea why the old woman should have left them so abruptly, because she had been their lodger for years and had seemed part of the establishment. Exactly the sort you wanted. No trouble, kept her room immaculate and always quiet.

She still saw Eleanor in town sometimes but Miss Battley passed her with such an icy nod each time that Dinah did not dare stop to question her.

Then she heard that Miss Battley had been killed falling in front of a train one Saturday. It caused a great deal of talk in the newspapers and there were demands to have busy periods at the station managed more carefully, with due regard to passengers' safety.

The newspapers said one woman claimed to have noticed a man bump into the old woman and send her sprawling on to the line in front of the train, but no one else had seen anything so a verdict of 'Misadventure' was returned at the inquest.

For some time after that, the Saturday passengers waiting for the local trains were supervised by an extra porter and were not allowed to stand near the edge of the platform until the train had stopped.

Nothing like shutting the stable door after the horse had escaped, Dinah thought sadly. Poor Miss Battley!

When Jeff came home from his next trip, Dinah told him about Miss Battley and he was shocked. However, he changed the subject almost immediately. 'I'm more concerned about my wife, I'm afraid,' he said, pulling her into his arms. 'Miss Battley was an old hag who encouraged your daughter to defy me so I shan't pretend to mourn her, though of course I'm sorry to think of anyone being killed like that.'

Dinah sighed and let him talk her into an early night. He had been wonderful to her during this difficult time so she tried to pretend she still enjoyed his love-making. She didn't, though. She didn't enjoy anything lately and often felt quite distant and disoriented.

She ought to have been a very happy woman indeed, the way Jeff looked after her and tried to spare her, but every time she saw a pregnant woman it made her think of the child she had lost and of Mary Ann in that same condition. Life was so unfair. Her daughter was young to have a baby. What if she died in childbirth and they never saw her again? It did happen. No, it wouldn't, *couldn't*, not with a girl who was so strong and well-grown. Mary Ann would probably have the child very easily, the wretch.

The following evening Jeff brought out a bottle of port. 'I've heard it's fortifying so I'm going to insist you take a glass every night.'

Dinah pulled a face. 'You know I don't like strong drink.'

'Please, drink just one small glass to oblige me, my dear. I don't like to see you looking so pulled down.'

It tasted as horrible as it had when she'd tried it before, but she sipped it to oblige him.

Later, as they sat on the sofa together staring into the fire, he said, 'I wonder if you'd consider putting this house in my name?'

'Why should I do that?'

'For the sake of my stupid masculine pride.' He dropped a kiss on her temple. 'I can't forget I'm living in *your* house and that upsets me. I didn't mention it at first, but I must admit it's nagging at me like a sore tooth.'

She was not too muzzy-headed to express her own feelings. 'I'm afraid I couldn't do that, Jeff dear. My aunt left the house to me and – well, I like the fact that it's mine. It's always a great comfort to me.'

'It's your decision, of course.'

He looked so sad that she was tempted to give in and indeed lay in bed sleepless for some time worrying about it. But she simply couldn't bring herself to do it. This house was a symbol

69

of her making a success of her life in spite of Stanley Kershaw's refusing to marry her. She hadn't told Jeff about Stanley, and she still wished he had married her not that stupid Meg. Jeff was wonderful, of course he was, but Stanley – well, there had been something rather special about him. To her, at least.

She still had his wallet at the bottom of her box of treasures and couldn't bring herself to throw it out.

The months passed and as March drew near Dinah knew she had become rather chancy-tempered. Well, she had every right to be. At this very moment, her daughter might be making her into a grandmother with a child she would never see. But Jeff was right. There was no way they could acknowledge the child without betraying what Mary Ann had done.

Jeff wrote to his cousin Jane to reiterate his demand that after the child was adopted the girl should be kept at Birtley until he could come for her.

She wrote back to say it would cost him two guineas extra to keep the girl there any longer and after some thought he sent it. He wasn't having Mary Ann falling into her mother's arms and telling lies about him. He intended to set the rules in private before he'd allow her back.

He wished she needn't come back at all because that firm young body would be a temptation to a lusty man like him. However, this time he'd have to resist it.

He wasn't ready yet to carry out the rest of his plans, but he soon would be.

At the beginning of March Mary Ann realised that Mrs Greeson was watching her more carefully, had almost stopped snapping at her and often tried to tempt her into eating more. But it was hard to eat when you didn't feel hungry. Still, it was nice to have a rest from harsh words and occasional slaps.

When Mrs Greeson took her aside one day and explained what would happen when she gave birth, Mary Ann listened carefully and asked a few questions of her own about having babies.

Jane answered them patiently then sent her back to light work in the sewing room. She sat down behind her desk, feeling quite upset. These were the questions of an innocent child, not a wanton. None of the other girls had been that naïve.

And yet Jeff had insisted the girl had thrown herself at him.

Well, Mary Ann Baillie would soon learn to be more cynical about the world, especially about men's promises. All women did. And she was better armed with information about her own body now as well. You could never really trust men. Even Maurice hadn't lived up to expectations. Instead of settling down to a comfortable life as the wife of an affluent farmer, Jane had had to find ways to earn extra money for them. Which he'd have spent foolishly if she'd given him half a chance.

It worried her, though, the memory of the girl's naïveté. It made even her feel guilty. Which was ridiculous. *She* hadn't done anything wrong.

Oh, she'd be glad to get rid of that one, she would indeed.

When Mary Ann went into labour, a week later, she felt relieved rather than anything else. She was tired of feeling so clumsy, tired of her huge belly, tired of everything here.

To her surprise, Mrs Greeson was suddenly very kind to her, taking her into the birthing room and sitting with her, even holding her hand when the pains began to get stronger.

They were bad, but not too bad to bear. Mary Ann tried not to cry out, because she didn't want to show herself up, but couldn't help whimpering.

'You're doing very well,' Mrs Greeson encouraged her. 'That's my brave girl.'

The baby was born ten hours after the pains started, a little girl with a soft fuzz of dark hair.

When Mrs Greeson had cleaned up the new mother, she picked the child up and turned to leave the room. Mary Ann was out of bed in a flash, barring the way. 'She's mine! You're not taking her away.'

Jane's heart sank. Some of them were like this, and then it was even more difficult to do what their families asked. It had been the same at the hospital. 'They're very frail when they've just been born. You won't know how to look after her properly.'

'Then show me how.' Mary Ann snatched the child from her arms before she realised what the girl intended and cradled it to her.

Jane sighed, watching that magical transformation she had seen and envied so many times before: a woman's face suffused with love for her baby. It would have been better not to let Mary Ann hold the child because there was no way she could keep it. No way at all.

'I'll get you something to drink, then,' she said. 'Get back into bed first. I don't want you fainting on me.'

Mary Ann laughed. 'I've never felt less like fainting.'

When Mrs Greeson had left, she leaned on the pillows stacked against the bed head and studied her daughter's features, loving even the tiny star-shaped birthmark on her right upper arm. Such a pretty infant. At that moment, in spite of all the unhappiness of the past few months, Mary Ann didn't regret for one moment bearing her child. 'Elizabeth,' she said softly. 'That's what I'm going to call you. And whatever they say or do, I'm going to keep you and love you.' In fact she was overflowing with love for this tiny pink creature with its snuffly breaths and silky skin.

Mrs Greeson came back. 'Here. Drink your cocoa while it's hot. Don't spill it on the baby.'

Mary Ann did as she asked but refused to give up her child, snuggling down with Elizabeth still cradled in her arms.

When she woke up, she was alone.

6

March 1907

Mary Ann tried to sit up, but her head spun and she fell back on the pillow. Why did she feel so weak when she had felt well and happy before she fell asleep? After a moment she forced herself to sit upright and looked round for her baby. There was no sign of a cradle, no sign of anything except herself, the bed and a chest of drawers. Even the trolley with the medical equipment on it had gone.

Where was her baby?

She swung her legs over the side of the bed and staggered across to the door, dizziness twisting her steps so that she bumped into the wall. Before she could even open it, Mrs Greeson entered, carrying a tray.

'I thought you'd be stirring so I've brought you this. You must be thirsty after such a long sleep. Come on, back to bed with you. We have to change you and wash you.'

'My baby?'

'Sleeping peacefully in the nursery.'

Mary Ann moved back towards the bed, accepting the cup of cocoa and drinking it down to the last dregs. She was indeed thirsty. After allowing Mrs Greeson to minister to her, she closed her eyes for a moment.

When she woke again it was dark. Her head felt heavy. She laid one hand on her stomach, relishing the flatness of it, the feeling of having her own body back. Mrs Greeson must have changed her bleeding rags again. She felt clean and comfortable and didn't bother to move because she wanted some time to herself. Oh, but her head was aching! She couldn't think why. She didn't usually suffer from headaches.

She woke again just as dawn was icing the sky with silver on

73

a frosty March day. This time her head felt better and she lay frowning as she tried to work out why she'd been sleeping so much. It wasn't like her. And her mouth felt dry, as if it was lined with cotton wool. She'd ask for water this time. The cocoa had been rather bitter and she'd wished there was more sugar in it, but had been too thirsty to bother.

Mary Ann gasped as it suddenly occurred to her that maybe the cocoa had contained something to make her sleep.

Her heart began to thud as she realised why Mrs Greeson might have done this. Her baby. *They wanted to take her baby away from her.*

She eased herself out of the bed, not putting on slippers or dressing gown, just tiptoeing across the room and opening the door very slowly and carefully. There was enough moonlight for her to find her way round this part of the house, which was at the other side from where the girls usually slept. The cradle in the room Mrs Greeson called the nursery was unoccupied. The whole place smelled faintly of disinfectant.

She tiptoed into the only other room in this wing and found it unoccupied also.

She knew then that they'd taken her baby away from her. For a moment, she let herself sag against the wall, her anguish too deep for tears, then she turned blindly round and made her way back to her bedroom.

'What are you doing out of bed, young woman?' The sharp voice made her jump.

She turned to Mrs Greeson. 'Looking for my baby. What have you done with her?' Her voice broke on the words.

'Come back to bed and I'll tell you.'

Mary Ann hesitated then made her way back to her room in silence. The bed felt cold now. She sat down on it, shivering.

Mrs Greeson clicked her tongue in exasperation and bullied the girl into bed pulling the covers up. Mary Ann allowed her to do that because you couldn't think properly when you were shivering. And she needed to think, needed it more than ever before in her life.

'Well?' she asked as the older woman hesitated then sat down on the end of the bed.

'I've got some sad news for you, I'm afraid.'

'You've taken my baby away. I guessed that. Well, I'll find her again. I won't *let* you give her away.'

'My instructions were indeed to have her adopted but sadly—' there was a pause, then '—I'm afraid she died, dear. It happens sometimes with new-born babies. We don't know why. For all our care, they just – die.'

Mary Ann didn't recognise the sound at first then realised that the wail of pain had come from herself. 'I don't believe you!'

'Why should I lie to you?'

'To make me accept you giving her away. Only I won't.' She began sobbing. 'I want my baby back. She's mine!'

'I can't do the impossible.'

Suddenly Mary Ann hurled the pillow at her. 'You're lying to me. Lying! You're a hateful woman. You make your living from other people's misery, keep girls prisoners, treat them badly and . . .' She couldn't continue, could only weep hysterically.

Jane Greeson's voice was low and cutting. 'And what are you? Someone who did what she shouldn't, someone who's disgraced her family, that's who you are. Don't you dare speak to me like that. You've been better treated here than you would have been anywhere else.'

'Go away, you old hag. Leave me alone!'

There was a whistle of breath then Mrs Greeson took a step towards her, hands clenched into fists and half-raised. Mary Ann tensed. If that woman tried to hit her again, she'd hit back. She didn't know why she'd put up with the slaps for so long when she was taller and more sturdily built than her tormenter.

'Listen to me, girl, and listen carefully. I tried to spare you the truth, but no, you had to insult me. Very well, then, I'll tell you exactly what happened to your baby. You killed her.'

The words seemed meaningless at first, then they slowly sank in and Mary Ann cried out, 'I don't believe you!'

Mrs Greeson folded her arms. 'I don't care whether you do or not. It's the truth.'

'What did she die of?'

'Smothering.'

Mary Ann felt as if silence echoed round them and had to force the words out, words that came from a great distance. 'I don't understand.'

'They call it overlaying. What it means is, *you* killed her. You had her in bed with you and you lay on her. She couldn't breathe under your weight, couldn't struggle, so she died. I gave you something to make you sleep to protect you from what we had to do. The doctor certified the cause of death and took the baby away. *Born dead*, it said on the certificate. Only she wasn't born dead, was she? *You* killed her.'

'No.' It was the merest whisper of sound. 'I don't believe . . .' Mary Ann couldn't even finish the sentence, she was so filled with horror.

'Suit yourself. It's the truth, though.'

There was silence, then Mary Ann began to sob, harsh sounds that seemed even louder in the stillness of an icy winter's dawn. When she looked up, the door was closing behind Mrs Greeson. When she looked around, the whole world seemed devoid of life.

She'd killed her own baby!

With a high, keening sound of pain, she slid down and wept, beating the pillows with her fists, crying, 'No, no, no!' until her voice was hoarse. And then she wept silently. But there weren't enough tears in the world to wash away her anguish and guilt.

The letter was addressed to Jeff. Dinah studied the postmark and frowned at it. *Overdale!* Who could be writing to him from there? She put the letter down on the hallstand, only to pick it up the next time she walked past and study it again.

Surely he hadn't sent her daughter back to Overdale to have the baby? They'd been amused by the thought that they'd lived so close to one another when they were younger, though they'd never met. It was such a strange coincidence. But he knew how she felt about Overdale, knew she wanted to have nothing more to do with it or anyone there.

Jeff wouldn't be back until the next day and she couldn't bear to wait until then, so in the end she opened the letter, reading it anxiously then sighing in relief.

Mary Ann was all right. She'd had a little girl. This Mrs Greeson had had to trick her to get it away from her, pretending it had died, but it was now safely in the hands of its new parents. Mary Ann was recovering well physically, though still weeping over the supposed death of her child, and could Jeff please come and pick her up as soon as possible?

Dinah drew in a long, shuddering breath. Mary Ann had turned sixteen only the week before. She should not have to face these things at that tender age.

'Well, I tried to protect her,' she told her reflection in the mirror. 'I did try – but she takes after her father.' Guilt flooded through her. 'And me,' she whispered. For she had been as eager to love Stanley Kershaw as he had been to love her.

Mary Ann had clearly fallen into the same trap. Who with, though? It couldn't possibly be Jeff. *Couldn't!*

She mustn't fly into a rage about it when her daughter got back, though. Dinah's hot temper had cost her Stanley and that same temper had been the bane of her life. She had it under control now – most of the time, anyway. Well, she'd been too tired lately to flare up into anger.

When Jeff arrived home the following day, she tossed the letter on to the table in their small sitting room before he'd even had a chance to sit down. 'She's had the baby. They want you to go and pick her up. I'm coming with you this time.'

He looked at the letter then studied the envelope. 'This was addressed to me.'

She stared at him, surprised by the harshness of his tone. 'I knew it could only be about Mary Ann. I couldn't wait to find out if she was all right, Jeff, I just – couldn't.'

He turned on her furiously. 'Don't you ever dare open a letter of mine again!'

She gaped at him.

'I mean it! I have a particular hatred of people prying into my things—'

She knew that, knew he hated to have her tidy his drawers even.

'—and that includes my letters. All my letters. *Is – that – clear?*'

She found herself apologising, not wanting the closeness between them to be spoiled. But she still felt resentful that he'd not made allowances for a mother's feelings about her only child.

'And I'll tell you something else, Dinah. If you don't want to sour our marriage, you'll sign over this house to me. You'd better think very seriously about that. You're trying to wear the trousers and that won't do with a man like me.'

Her old temper flared suddenly. 'I'll *never* do that! *Never!* The house is mine and it's staying mine.'

'Don't you understand what that does to a man?' he yelled.

'I don't care! It's my house and it's staying mine!'

He stormed out.

Later that afternoon they made up their quarrel in bed, with her pretending to enjoy his love-making though it was the last thing she felt like.

Afterwards he said thoughtfully, 'I'm not taking you with me to fetch Mary Ann because it won't be good for you. You know you've been a bit off colour lately. And look how upset you became earlier over my perfectly reasonable request about the house. If you don't pick up soon I'm going to insist you see a doctor.'

'I hate doctors.'

'Well, I hate to see you looking so poorly and I'm definitely not taking you with me.'

'I'm going.' But he was right, she did feel dreadful.

'Darling, let me do this for you.'

'No. She's my daughter and I've missed her. I'm looking

forward to having her back again.' Dinah glanced at the clock. 'Now, I'd better get down to see to the evening meal or the guests won't be fed on time.'

He smiled as he listened to her go down the stairs. He was beginning to think he'd be glad to have the girl back again. Dinah was less and less interested in love-making and he needed it far more often than he was getting it, and not from a woman who lay beneath him like a limp rag, either. Where was the pleasure in that?

Only this time he'd coax the girl into his bed, treat her more kindly. And he'd be very careful. He didn't want any more babies spoiling his plans.

Then he frowned. He'd have to do something about Dinah. He didn't want her going north with him.

That night he prepared her final cup of tea himself and watched with loving concern as she drank it.

She didn't need persuading to stay at home the following day because she was up and down all night, vomiting. He smiled as he left the house. It was useful to have had a chemist for a father. You learned all sorts of little tricks.

'You'd better pack your things tonight,' Mrs Greeson said over the midday meal. 'You're leaving tomorrow.'

Mary Ann looked at her in surprise. 'Who's coming for me?'

'None of your business.'

'I won't go anywhere with *him*.'

'You'll do as you're told.'

The girl guessed then that it was Jeff who was coming and didn't make any further protests. If there was one thing she had learned during her time at Redvale, it was to hold her tongue and keep her thoughts to herself.

After they'd cleared up she went upstairs, ignoring the new girl's tears and pleas to come out walking with her on their last evening together. She looked at her clothes. There weren't many and it wouldn't take long to pack them. Suddenly she remembered something Margaret had said to her: *Don't let them force you to do things you don't want. Make plans. Take charge of your own life.*

It was time to take charge. Only how was she to manage this?

Mrs Greeson walked into the room carrying Mary Ann's battered suitcase. 'Stop mooning about and get on with your packing.'

Without a word, the girl began to empty the drawers.

Mrs Greeson stayed for a minute or two, watching, then left the room.

Only when she heard those heavy footsteps going down the stairs did Mary Ann stop what she was doing and find the handkerchief on which Miss Battley had written in indelible ink. She tucked it into her waistband. The coins her friend had given her were already sewn into the hem of her best skirt, which had been too small for her when she was expecting. She wouldn't be able to take her suitcase with her, because she'd have to climb out of the window and down the roof, but she could put on several layers of clothes.

She had so little money, though. How was she to go anywhere on a mere thirty shillings, let alone support herself till she'd found a job?

Going back to the window she looked out, seeing the moors to one side and, lower down, the little farm next door with its row of new chicken sheds beyond. Her eyes rested thoughtfully on the farm. Mr Clough had helped Margaret to escape. Would he help her as well? She knew she could go to Margaret's for help but that was the first place they'd come looking for her. Still, she was pretty sure her friend would pay Mr Clough back if he'd lend her the money to get to Blackpool where Miss Battley's friend lived. Mary Ann would enjoy living by the sea again, had missed it greatly.

When she went up to bed, she put on several layers of clothes under her nightdress and lay under the covers until Mrs Greeson had made her final rounds.

Once the house had been quiet for a while, she opened the window fully. There was a half-moon giving enough light to see by and a fitful wind was whining around the eaves, causing things to bump and clatter. Good. It would hide any noise she made.

She hitched up her skirts, pulling a fold from the back of the top one between her legs and fastening it at the front with a big safety pin. As she slid one leg over the window sill, she glanced back at the small, sparsely furnished room where she had been so unhappy, mentally wishing its next occupant luck. With some difficulty she pulled the window down again from outside, not wanting to show them how she had escaped, then turned her attention to getting down to the ground.

It was more frightening than she'd expected, climbing down the tiles. From two floors up the ground seemed a very long way below. At one point her foot slipped and she had to grab the brick base of the chimney stack to steady herself, grazing her knuckles. The wind seemed much stronger out here, tugging at her, and the moon went in behind the clouds.

She crouched there next to the chimney stack wondering whether to edge down backwards on her hands and knees, or to sit down and move on her bottom, a little bit at a time. You couldn't see anything if you went backwards, so she sat down and shuffled along on her bottom. That felt a little better. Not much. But this was the only way of escaping because Mrs Greeson kept all the outer doors locked and took away the keys, and most of the ground-floor windows were nailed shut.

Taking a deep breath, Mary Ann began moving again, edging carefully down the slope of the roof then shuffling sideways to where the lower roof of the kitchen met it at right angles. That felt a little better and she stopped for a moment to gather her strength for the final stretch.

At the far edge of the kitchen roof was an outhouse which had an even lower roof. This would bring her near enough to the ground to hang over the edge and drop. At least she hoped she'd be near enough.

It was harder than she'd expected getting over the edge of the main roof on to the kitchen. Once a tile cracked beneath her and the snapping sound seemed so loud she half-expected someone to come out to find what had happened.

But no one did.

Her heart stopped beating so fast and she continued. If she fell now, she'd probably not break her neck, only an arm or leg. But that'd be enough to keep her a prisoner.

She wouldn't fall, though. She wouldn't let herself.

From the outhouse roof she looked down at the ground six feet below her. There was a scurry of paws and the farm dogs came running up. One barked so she risked calling out to them and saw their tails start wagging as they recognised her voice. Thank goodness she'd made friends with them!

At the other side of the outhouse was a water butt and she managed to get one foot on its rim. From there she jumped down, tumbling over in the mud. The dogs came to poke their noses into her face and for a moment she hugged them indiscriminately, glad of their living warmth. Then she got to her feet, unpinned her skirts and hurried off across the field.

A light rain began to fall as she reached the dry stone wall that bordered it. She lifted her face to the clean feel of it, then clambered over the rough stones. She was tiring now, feeling weaker than she'd expected to.

Please let Mr Clough be willing to help her!

As she approached the smaller farm a dog started barking and came bounding towards her. She'd seen it out in the fields, heard him call it Bonnie so said its name when it approached her warily.

It bared its teeth and gave a sharp bark of two, as if summoning help. When she tried to move forward, it growled at her, so she stayed where she was, casting an anxious glance back towards Redvale.

The door of the farm opened and a voice called, 'What's up, Bonnie lass?'

'Mr Clough!' she called, tears running down her face. 'It's me.'

There was an exclamation and a figure left the house, coming to stare at her in the fitful light of the moon. He was taller than she was and suddenly she was terrified that he'd take her back to Mrs Greeson.

'Mary Ann? That's your name, isn't it?' His voice was gentle now.

'Yes.' Her voice broke on a sob. She wanted to throw herself against his chest and howl her eyes out. But she mustn't. She had to keep calm and persuade him to help her.

'What are you doing out here at this time of night? I was just going to bed.'

'I'm escaping. I climbed out of the attic window. Oh, Mr Clough, please don't take me back to her. *Please!*'

He raised his head to stare through the darkness at the big farm next door. 'Eh, you took a risk, lass.'

'I had to. She was sending me back to *him*.'

'I won't send you back anywhere, love. Come into the house. You're shivering.'

She hadn't even noticed how cold she was until then. Shivering, she let him put his arm round her shoulders and guide her towards the house. Since Jeff Powling she hadn't liked men to come near her, but somehow she didn't mind this one's touch, which was as gentle as his voice.

When he opened the door, the brightness and warmth inside made her sob suddenly.

'Come and warm yourself in front of the fire. I'll fetch my mother down to help you.'

'She won't—'

He seemed to read her mind. 'She won't send you back either, I promise.'

Mrs Clough appeared with an old matted shawl wrapped round her shoulders over a plain flannel nightdress. She looked so grim that Mary Ann's heart began to skitter about her chest again.

But she took the girl's hand in hers and said, 'Eh, she's frozen. Didn't you think to get the fire burning up and swing the kettle over the heat, our Gabriel?' Clucking in disapproval, she pulled off her own shawl and wrapped it round the girl's shoulders.

Mary Ann tried to stop her teeth chattering, tried to stop the tears, but couldn't for a long time. The old woman patted her shoulder occasionally, gave her a cup of hot milk laced with honey and folded her hands round it as she handed it over. It felt wonderfully warm and tasted delicious. The other two had cups of it as well.

'It's an old family treat,' Gabriel told her as she struggled for control of her emotions. 'Our own honey as well as our own milk.'

Mrs Clough took away the empty cup and said firmly, 'Now tell us everything, lass.'

So the whole story spilled out. Mary Ann saw the shock and disgust on their faces when she explained what her stepfather had done to her, but she didn't see disbelief – and the disgust didn't seem to be aimed at her, thank goodness.

'You believe me?' she asked in a voice that quavered.

'Aye, lass,' the old woman said. 'I believe you. You've not got a liar's face.'

'She definitely can't go back home, then,' Gabriel said.

'I have somewhere to go.' Mary Ann reached for the handkerchief and couldn't find it, fumbling among her clothing then whispering in horror, 'I've lost it.' She began to sob. 'Miss Battley wrote a letter in marking ink on a handkerchief. She knew my things would be searched but they never found that. It was to introduce me to her friend, and – and I put it in my waistband when I was escaping. Only it's gone. It's gone!'

'Do you know where her friend lives?' he asked.

'Oh, yes. I memorised the address.'

'Then you'll have to go there and tell her what the letter said. Miss Battley will confirm it for you.'

'Yes. Yes, of course. Only – her friend lives in Blackpool and I don't think I've enough money to get there.'

There was silence, then Mr Clough said gruffly, 'Don't worry. We'll help you.'

Jassy watched her son give the lass a quick smile. Eh, he was such a softie! She turned her head to study their visitor again.

She must be getting soft herself because after what she'd heard tonight, she was as determined as he to help this girl get away.

There was, she decided, something rather appealing about that young face. Mary Ann would never be pretty, for she had strong features and was already taller than most lasses, taller even than Jassy Clough who had always been known as a tall woman. But there was an honesty and freshness to her face that was much more important than mere prettiness. Beauty was all very well but integrity and courage were of more value, in Jassy's opinion. It must have taken a great deal of courage to clamber down the roof from the second floor in the dark.

'Our Gabriel has allus wanted to go to the seaside,' she said abruptly. 'Looks like he's going to get his wish. He can take you to Blackpool as soon as it's safe to leave. But we'll have to hide you in my bedroom for a day or two till they've stopped looking for you.'

'Do you think they will look for me?' Mary Ann asked. 'I mean, nobody *really* cares about me.'

'They'll definitely look. In fact, I shouldn't be surprised if they don't come over here and ask if we've seen you.' She smiled grimly. 'But I think I'm more than a match for Jane Greeson. You'll have to share my bed, though.'

'I'm grateful you'll let me.'

So that was that, thought Jassy. 'Come on, then. Let's get you upstairs.' As she tucked the girl in, her mind wandered over ways to feed her up. She looked worn to the bone, poor thing, still not recovered from the birth and sad about the baby dying.

7

Late March 1907

A couple of hours after Jeff had left, Dinah dragged herself out of bed and went down to the small sitting-room, frustrated that they'd had to bring in a neighbour to help out because she still felt so seedy. However, the vomiting seemed to have cleared her brain a bit. She hadn't really felt well since she'd lost the baby. Perhaps Jeff was right and she ought to see the doctor.

At four o'clock Maisie came in with her tea. 'You looked so weary I wanted to put some of your tonic in,' she said in her usual cheerful way. 'But I don't know where Mr Powling's put it.'

'Tonic?'

'Yes, the white powder. I saw him putting some into your tea one day and he told me about it.' She clapped one hand to her mouth. 'Ooh, I remember now, he said I wasn't to tell you because you don't like taking medicine. Don't tell him I let on, will you?'

Dinah was puzzled but didn't want to upset the girl. 'No. I won't say anything.'

'He really tries to look after you, doesn't he? Lovely, that is.'

'Yes.' Though sometimes his insistence on being 'the man of the house', the one who made all the decisions, was rather irritating to one who had grown used to having her own way, and indeed, had done quite well for herself without a man's help.

Dinah poured herself a cup of tea and stirred it absent-mindedly. Jeff had said nothing about a tonic and that wasn't like him. When he did something for her he liked to be thanked for it, preferably several times. She smiled. Like a little boy he was sometimes, needing praise.

She was feeling a little better so decided to clear out the drawers of the sideboard. They'd needed dealing with for a while and she could do that while sitting at the table. She knew Jeff wouldn't like her to touch the middle one, in which he kept his business papers, but she sorted out the drawers to either side, then began on the second of the three in the centre column. When she heard a rustling as she pulled the drawer out, she bent to check whether something was caught at the back and found a piece of crumpled paper.

Tugging it out, she smoothed it carefully, then stared at it in surprise as she read the first few lines. It was a new deed signing the house over to Jeff, something she had refused to do a couple of times now. In fact she'd ripped the last one up and thrown it at him. She'd worked so hard to get this house, looking after her aunt for years, biting her tongue at the old lady's sometimes unreasonable demands, that she couldn't give it away, not even to him.

Why did he think he'd get her to change her mind? She wouldn't. Definitely not.

Jane Greeson came across to see the Cloughs just after breakfast, and Mary Ann had to rush upstairs and hide.

Jassy quickly dumped the girl's crockery in the scullery before opening the front door.

'I wonder if I can have a word with you,' Jane said, smiling.

Jassy nodded and gestured to her to enter because you couldn't keep a neighbour standing on the doorstep on a chilly day like this. 'What about?'

'One of our girls has run away. We think her mind was disturbed. Sadly, this happens sometimes after giving birth. We're rather anxious to find her again so that we can look after her properly.'

'Which one is it?'

'The tall girl with dark hair. You must have noticed her walking round the field?'

'Aye, I've seen her.'

Gabriel came in and joined them.

'Seems that tall lass has run away, son,' Jassy said. 'Haven't seen owt of her, have you?'

'Been a bit busy this morning. Why did she run away?'

His mother nudged him with her elbow. They'd agreed that the less they said the better, and he was giving away his feelings by scowling at their visitor like that. 'Sorry we can't help you, Jane.'

'Well, if you do see her—'

Jassy went to open the front door. 'We'll let you know.'

'—we'd be grateful if you'd keep her here till I can come and collect her, for her own sake. Her poor father's worried sick about her.'

'We'll think on.' Jassy lingered to watch their visitor walk back down the lane to Redvale before coming back inside.

'Mary Ann's mind's not disturbed,' her son said flatly.

'I agree. I like the lass. She's been doing some mending for me, says she prefers to keep busy.' If the girl had been older, and if there wasn't this trouble with Jane Greeson, Jassy would be tempted to invite her to stay because she could see that Gabriel was interested in her. Well, she liked Mary Ann herself, baby or not. But it wouldn't do. The girl was too young for marriage.

Even now.

Eh, that fellow who'd hurt her had a lot to answer for, he did that.

At teatime the next day Dinah began to expect Jeff and Mary Ann to return, going to the front window a couple of times when she heard footsteps coming along the street. The restful day had done her good and she was feeling more alert than she had for a while now.

When there was a knock on the front door she went to answer it herself, shocked to see a lad in Post Office uniform holding out a telegram. In her experience they always brought bad news.

She felt wobbly as she took it inside, not daring to open it in full view of the street or even where the guests could see her. If anything had happened to Mary Ann, she would never forgive herself. Never.

MARY ANN RUN AWAY STOP STAYING ON A FEW DAYS TO
SEARCH STOP JEFF

She fell into the big armchair, hand flattened across her chest,
tears welling in her eyes. What had happened to make the girl
do that? She should definitely have gone with her husband to
fetch her daughter. Mary Ann didn't like him and probably never
would. Strange how she had taken an instant dislike to him when
everyone else liked him.

No, not everyone. Miss Battley hadn't liked him, either. Poor
woman! It was sad when someone died in an accident.

Should she go and join him now? Dinah wondered. She might
be able to help. Only then did she realise she didn't know the exact
address of the place. Jeff had taken the letter she'd opened and
she had not bothered to write the address down. She'd let a lot of
things just happen since her marriage. Why? It was so unlike her.

That had got to change.

The following morning she found to her surprise that she felt
more energetic and suddenly remembered that Jeff had been
giving her a tonic secretly. Perhaps it didn't agree with her.
What was in it? You had to be very careful what you took.
Her mother had nearly died once from taking some medicine
bought from a stall at the fair. Dinah had always been very
careful ever since.

Suddenly determined to find where he'd hidden it, she opened
Jeff's bedroom drawers one by one, not disturbing the clothes
but searching for this stupid tonic. She intended to throw the
stuff away and he could complain if he wanted to.

But she found nothing.

When she went downstairs she tried to search his drawer in the
sideboard, but found it locked and the key missing.

Frustrated, she went into the kitchen just as Maisie was starting
the breakfasts. 'Where did Mr Powling keep the tonic? Did
you see?'

Maisie frowned. 'I don't know exactly. I only saw him using
it once. He'd just come out of the store cupboard, though, the

one where you keep the cleaning materials. Maybe he keeps it in there?'

Dinah went to search through the cupboard herself, finding nothing on the lower shelves. Jeff was much taller than she was, so she had to get a stool to finish the job.

She found the packet at the back of the top shelf, not only out of sight but out of reach of anyone except him. It wasn't labelled, but it contained some white powder.

When they'd got the breakfasts over, she took some of the powder and went into town to do the shopping. Her first stop was the chemist's. She showed Mr Munger the stuff, pretending they'd found a packet and weren't sure what it contained.

He sniffed it, rubbed a few grains between his fingers and smiled at her. 'This is rat poison. Arsenic mainly. Good thing you didn't use it in your tea, eh?'

She tried to smile, but felt as if the world was spinning round her. You read about it in the newspapers, people poisoning their relatives. Arsenic was often named as the poison. They even had a nickname for it: inheritance powder.

'What happens if people take arsenic?' she asked.

'Not thinking of poisoning your husband, are you?' he teased. Then his expression became solemn. 'If I were you, I'd lock this away carefully. Even small amounts can make you feel disoriented.'

'Sleepy?' she questioned.

'Oh, yes. And nauseous. Why do you ask?'

'I'm wondering if it's got spilled into some food. I think I'll throw away all the things it might have touched.'

'You do that. You can't be too careful with poisons. I'll throw this away for you, shall I?'

She did the rest of the shopping in a daze, her mind shying away from drawing the obvious conclusion from her discovery. She felt as if she was bleeding happiness at every step, as if the whole world was turning into a grey, miserable, alien place.

Had Jeff been poisoning her? *Jeff!* Her husband. The man who said he loved her.

No, surely not?

But the powder said otherwise.

When she got home she showed Maisie the packet and the maid said, 'Yes, that's it.'

Dinah started on the chores automatically, not chatting, trying not to think even, just working hard and holding the horror at bay until she could be on her own.

'You seem ever such a lot better today, Mrs Powling,' Maisie said as they washed up the tea things together. 'Brighter.'

'Yes. I feel a lot better.'

And that seemed to prove something as well.

That night in bed Dinah went through everything in her own mind. Like the time Jeff had tried to slip a paper handing the house over to him in among the things she was signing. She'd caught him on that, even though she'd been feeling dizzy, because she never signed anything without checking what it was. Never. That came of living with her aunt, who had been suspicious of everyone and everything in her final years.

With a sick feeling in her stomach Dinah admitted to herself that Jeff must have been trying to poison her. It was only a short step from there to wondering if Mary Ann had been telling the truth about him all along. He liked his bed play. She'd never heard of a man with such an insatiable appetite for it. Well, she'd enjoyed it herself until she became ill.

No, it couldn't be true.

Could it?

It was past two o'clock by the chiming of the hall clock before she got to sleep. She had no proof, no real proof, but . . . something inside her told her that it was true.

The improvement in her health and alertness continued over the next two days, which only added to her suspicions.

She didn't sleep very well, though. Felt so guilty about Mary Ann.

The afternoon after Jane had called Gabriel noticed a cab drive up and a man get out. This would be Mary Ann's stepfather, he guessed. He'd like to get the fellow alone and punch the living daylights out of him, he would that.

He went to warn the girl and suggest she stay upstairs and try to get a glimpse of the newcomer to confirm who it was. Before she could do that, Jane brought the fellow along the lane towards the Cloughs' house. Gabriel, who'd been keeping watch surreptitiously ever since the fellow's arrival, slipped into the kitchen the back way.

'It's him!' Mary Ann called from the top of the stairs. 'You won't let him find me, will you?'

'How can he know you're here?' Jassy asked practically. 'Stay out of sight now. And Gabriel, you nearly gave yourself away last time. Treat him pleasantly or go back to work and leave him to me.'

'I'll stay,' he growled.

When someone knocked on the door, she shot her son a warning glance and went to open it. 'Jane. Come in.'

'This is Mr Powling, the father of the missing girl.'

'Pleased to meet you.' Jeff shook Jassy's hand and turned towards Gabriel, who was working on a piece of harness and had his hands covered in polish.

'Sorry I can't shake hands,' he said.

'No, no. You carry on. We don't like to interrupt you, but—' Jeff smiled at Jassy, the sort of smile that usually had old ladies eating out of his hand '—well, we wondered if you'd remembered anything? I'm so worried about Mary Ann.'

Upstairs the girl sat perfectly still on a chair just inside the doorway of Jassy's room, her hand pressed against her mouth. Even to hear his voice again made her shudder.

Jassy was relieved to see that her son's face was expressionless though she noticed his knuckles were white with tension. 'Well, you would be worried. But as we said before, we can't help you.'

'You heard nothing during the night?' Jeff pressed.

'The dog barked but she settled down again, so I didn't think anything of it,' Gabriel contributed.

'Well, if you do hear of anything, you will tell Mrs Greeson, won't you?' Jeff said.

Jane stood up. 'We'll let you get on with your work now.'

Jassy showed them out and stood on the doorstep until they'd gone back to Redvale. 'What do you think of him?' she asked Gabriel.

'A smooth-tongued type.'

'Can I come down now?' a voice called from above.

'Aye. The dogs will let us know if they come back.' Gabriel studied her anxious face as she joined them. 'I won't let him find you,' he promised, his tone quite different from when he'd been talking to their visitors.

'You're both so kind,' Mary Ann said, her voice wobbling.

'If we can't help one another, it's a poor look-out,' said Jassy. 'Now, go and bring that mending down and sit by the fire. I shall be glad not to have to darn those socks. Our Gabriel's hard on socks, he is that.'

The morning after her discovery Dinah used a screwdriver to open the middle drawer, the one where Jeff kept his things. The account books were there. She went through them carefully. The amounts for household expenditures had been changed, increased. She flipped her savings book open and moaned aloud as she found the account almost empty, only twenty pounds left out of nearly four hundred she'd had there. How had he managed to take her money out? He must have forged her signature.

It was time to start acting on what she had found out, more than time. But she didn't intend to call in the police, couldn't bear people to know what he had done to her. She would deal with this herself, as she had dealt with most other things in her life. And she wasn't going to waste one more tear on him.

Donning her best hat and coat, she went along to the bank. She had to wait nearly half an hour to see the manager, but when she got into his office she held out the savings book and asked him how so much money could have been taken out of it without her consent.

He stared at her in dismay, then summoned the head clerk who brought out the records and said Mr Powling had usually been the one to withdraw money on his wife's behalf.

'Surely your husband acted with your knowledge, Mrs Powling?'

'No. And it isn't a joint account.'

After some more delay they produced slips of paper supposedly signed by her. And if she hadn't been certain she hadn't signed these, she'd have been fooled too, it was so like her signature.

The manager chewed his lip, then said doubtfully, 'It's a bit of a delicate situation. When it's a husband and wife, well, we don't usually inquire too deeply if one draws out money for the other. What do you want us to do – call in the police?'

Dinah sat there, feeling sick, then looked up. 'No. Not the police. He's still my husband. But can you make sure he won't have access to my account again?'

'Oh, yes. We can certainly do that.'

'I'm throwing him out when he gets back. The house is still mine, at least.' She looked at him sharply. 'Perhaps we'd better check the deeds to make sure of that?'

So they did some more fussing around while she sat and waited, feeling chill and alone. She looked up as the manager came back.

'Yes, the house is still yours, Mrs Powling.'

She hated to hear that name. 'I shall be calling myself Baillie again from now on. Please see that all your records are changed to accommodate that.'

So they brought her some more forms to fill in.

When at last she had finished she walked slowly home, her heart heavy. She had been tricked, cheated out of her lifetime's savings. He couldn't love her. Why had he married her? For a few hundred pounds?

There was a telegram that evening saying Jeff had failed to find Mary Ann and was coming home the following day. Anger began to rise in Dinah again and with a growl of disgust she crumpled the piece of paper.

He thought he was coming home to continue poisoning her, no doubt.

Then another thought made her shiver.

How did she know that Mary Ann really had run away? Perhaps he had killed her daughter? Lurid pictures of him hiding a body on the moors rose before her.

The poison had disoriented her, but now her brain was working again with much of its old sharpness. No one was going to poison Dinah Baillie, hurt her daughter and steal her savings.

Not even her husband.

Should she change her mind and call in the police, let them handle this? No. The humiliation of everything being known would kill her. Besides – a grim smile settled on her face – she wanted her revenge. She intended to have that satisfaction at least amid the ruins of her life.

And then she'd look for her daughter.

Jeff left Brighton station and strode towards his home, tired after the long journey back from Lancashire. On reflection, he was glad the girl had run away and hoped the stupid little bitch never turned up again. Her mother was much easier to handle without her around.

When he opened the front door and called, 'I'm back!' there was no reply. Frowning, he went through into the kitchen, nearly tripping over a suitcase and trunk. He frowned at them. They looked like – they were! – his. What was going on here?

Dinah came through from the scullery and stood in the doorway watching him as she wiped her hands on her apron.

He could see at a glance that the effects of his little potion had worn off. He'd increase the dose slightly from now on, hurry things along a bit. 'I'm back, darling.' He held out his arms.

She made no attempt to run to him but stood there staring across the room. 'So I see. Well, I've packed your bags, so you can just pick them up and leave for good.'

He couldn't believe he'd heard aright. 'I beg your pardon?'

'You heard me. While you were away, I did some tidying out of cupboards and drawers. I found the so-called tonic you'd been giving me. Arsenic, the chemist said. You've been poisoning me, Jeff.'

'Don't be ridiculous. It was sold to me as a tonic. The chemist must have mixed up the wrong ingredients.'

'Always got an answer, haven't you? I found another document to transfer the ownership of this house to you. It had fallen down the back of the drawers. Were you intending to get me too fuddled to realise what I was signing, or were you going to sign it for me? And what then? You couldn't sell this place without me finding out. Or did you intend to murder me?'

As he opened his mouth to protest, she raised her voice and continued, 'I broke open your business drawer and found my bank book. You've stolen my savings, too. *Years* of hard work. All gone.'

He'd never seen her quite like this. Rage had put colour in her cheeks and her eyes were flashing.

'Don't be silly, Dinah darling,' he said soothingly, moving towards her. 'I don't know where you've got this wild idea from, but you couldn't be more wrong. I can explain –'

'I even believe Mary Ann now.' His wife glared at him. 'I must have been out of my mind to doubt her. She's never lied to me before. How could you?'

'Now, look—' He didn't finish the sentence but pounced on her. One quick knock on the head and he'd have the time to take a few more things of value before he left. She had some rather nice silver stashed away in the attics. He'd had his eye on it for a while.

Even as he grabbed her she screamed and snatched up the rolling pin from the table, belabouring him with it and yelling for help.

The scullery door opened and Maisie appeared, calling, 'Come in quick, Ron!'

Two burly young men came in, grinning, and Jeff backed away from them.

'I thought I might need protection,' Dinah said. 'So I hired these two.'

Jeff glared at them, then at her. 'You bitch!'

Maisie's brother took a step forward. 'Mind your language. There are ladies present.'

'Ladies!' Jeff threw back his head and roared with laughter. 'This one is no lady. She's been living in sin with me for over a year.'

Everyone stared at him but he was looking only at Dinah whose face had suddenly lost all trace of colour, even her lips seeming bloodless.

'What do you mean?' she demanded. 'We're not living in sin. We got married. I have the marriage certificate.'

He forced out a laugh. He wasn't letting her see how furious he was to have all his plans upset. 'That was just to appease you because I knew how much you cared about "respectability". What I omitted to inform you about was that my real wife was still alive and,' he grinned, 'that my name isn't Powling. So our marriage definitely isn't valid.'

She drew herself upright, forcing back the pain of what she had just learned. 'Don't let him leave,' she ordered and the two young men nodded. 'You've taken most of the money from my bank account, Jeff, or whatever your name is. Nearly four hundred pounds. I think it's only fair that you pay back what you can before you leave.'

'Seems fair enough to me.' Ron gave Jeff a rather nasty smile. 'Let's see what you've got in your pockets.'

He began yelling for help, so Ron punched him and knocked him flying, then dragged him to his feet by his coat and shook him like a rat. 'We don't – like – loud noises. We're likely to get violent if you shout again.'

Efficiently he and his pal turned out Jeff's pockets, emptying his wallet of money before shoving it back into his inside pocket.

Dinah counted the contents quickly. 'Just over fifty pounds. It's a start, at least.'

'What about his luggage?' Ron asked.

'I've packed it myself so I know there's nothing of mine in it. But he'll have brought back another suitcase. Maybe it's in the hall.'

She found it and brought it back, emptying its contents on the table. No sign of any more money. Then, out of the corner of her eye, she saw a smirk on Jeff's face and looked at the suitcase again. If he was smirking she must have missed something. She felt the lining and then the bottom. A quick glance sideways showed that his smirk had disappeared. 'Is it my imagination, Ron, or is there a false bottom to this suitcase? It feels lumpy, as if there's something under it.'

He obligingly took her carving knife and cut out the bottom, grinning as he did so. 'Tut! Tut! What a mess.'

She found more money there, another fifty pounds. That was enough to make her feel a little better, as was the fury on Jeff's face.

'I'll have you charged with theft,' he said angrily.

'I heard you myself, offering her the money because you felt so guilty,' Ron said at once. 'Didn't you hear him, Tam?'

'Aye, I did,' his taciturn friend replied in a strong Scottish accent.

'Besides,' Dinah said, 'you won't want the police brought into this, will you, Jeff? Or they might charge you with bigamy – and other things.' She looked at Ron. 'He likes to rape little girls.'

He swung round. 'Does he indeed? Dirty sod!'

Tam growled something under his breath and threw a punch at Jeff that knocked him flying again. 'A bugger like him hurt ma sister once,' he said, kicking Jeff in the ribs as he tried to get up again.

'Better leave it at that,' Ron told his friend after another few kicks.

'Aw, man, let me enjoy masel',' Tam begged. 'I've never caught one of 'em before.'

Dinah had been stuffing the things back into the suitcase anyhow and Ron obliged her by squeezing it shut, taking a slender boning knife from the drawer to cut off a sleeve which had got trapped outside. He slapped the piece of material against his hand and looked down at Jeff, who had been watching them but saying nothing. 'Good knife, this. Sharp enough to cut your throat if you ever return to annoy our friend here.' He bowed to Dinah.

She looked at Jeff. 'I'm going to the police tomorrow and I'll tell them that you've committed bigamy. It'd be better if you left the district.'

'Much better,' said Tam. 'Get up now, you sod.'

Jeff struggled to his feet, unable to hold back a groan. He felt black and blue and his lip was split.

Ron poked a forefinger in his chest. 'Very obliging of her to give you a chance to get away, don't you think?'

'Mmm.'

Dinah could think of nothing more to say but, 'Get out! I don't ever want to see you again.'

Jeff looked down at the pile of luggage. 'Someone will need to call a cab. I can't possibly carry this lot on my own.'

'We'll help you down to the cab rank with it. My friend here is very strong.'

Tam picked up the trunk as if it weighed nothing and Ron shoved Jeff forward, making him yelp with pain. 'Pick up your cases, there's a good chap.'

But Powling stopped at the door, one case in each hand, to look back. Although he didn't say a word, his eyes said it for him: *You'll be sorry one day, Dinah.*

Another shove in the back sent him stumbling along the hall.

Only when the front door had closed behind him did she fumble for a chair and collapse into it shaking, tears streaming down her cheeks. She began to rock to and fro and make sobbing, whimpering sounds.

Maisie made her mistress a cup of tea, which Dinah could not even pick up, she was shivering so hard. The maid helped her put it to her lips, one arm round her shoulders, forgetting that this was her mistress in her pity for the other woman.

'Thank you.' Dinah whispered after a while. 'You've been very kind. And your brother was such a help.'

Maisie shrugged. 'Mam doesn't like his rough ways but Ron's always been good to me.'

When her brother came back, he reported that Powling had taken a late train to London. 'We saw him on to it and watched it leave.' He grinned. 'He said he didn't want to go to London, but Tam changed his mind for him.'

Dinah nodded and paid him what they'd agreed. Her whole world had been turned upside down, but what hurt most was that Jeff wasn't really her husband. The precious respectability she felt she had achieved at last had been blown away.

When her maid urged her to go to bed, she nodded and agreed, saying wearily, 'Look after Ron and his friend. Get them whatever they want to eat or drink.'

As she lay in bed she wondered where Mary Ann was. She'd been so angry she'd forgotten to get the address from Jeff. How was she to find her daughter now? Tears rolled down her cheeks. She'd tried hard to be a good mother, but she'd failed, failed at everything a woman cared about.

'Did you ever see the like?' Maisie asked her brother when Dinah's door upstairs had closed.

He grinned at her. 'Good as a serial in the newspaper, isn't it? Now, Maisie love, that's given me and Tam a right old appetite. How about a bacon sandwich and a cup of cocoa? Madam said to feed us whatever we wanted, so maybe there's some cake, too. If that sod ever comes back we'll set Tam on to him. Hates fellows as bugger about with children, Tam does.'

'I think you frightened him, but I didn't like the way he looked at her before he left.'

Ron grinned at her and said in a rough, exaggerated voice, 'He'd better not try anything. Men who cross us live to regret it.'

She giggled. 'Ooh, you are a one, our Ron! You sounded just like a real gangster tonight.'

'I did, didn't I?' he said complacently. 'It comes in useful being big. They'll believe anything if you look fierce when you say it.'

'Powling's face when you cut that sleeve off!' She fell against him, laughing so hard tears of mirth rolled down her cheeks.

8

April 1907

Only when they'd seen Maurice Greeson drive Jeff Powling and his luggage off down the lane and later return without him did Gabriel and Jassy work on getting Mary Ann away. Gabriel drove over to Cousin Tom's house and explained the problem.

'Eh, I can't believe the wickedness of some folk,' Tom muttered, shocked to the core. 'And you can count on me to help in any way I can, you know you can. I'll be glad to help your mother on the farm till you return.'

'Take two weeks,' Jassy told her son when he returned. 'That way you'll be sure Mary Ann's settled and you can have that holiday you wanted.'

'You're sure?'

''Course I am.'

The next morning Tom turned up to take Gabriel and Mary Ann to the station in the next town, driving away with Gabriel sitting openly beside him and the girl hidden under some sacks in the back.

As the train pulled out of Bilsden station Mary Ann sat quietly beside Gabriel. It still felt strange to have a flat stomach and sometimes she would remember her little daughter's face and rest her hand for a minute on the flesh that had housed and protected her baby for all those months. If only she hadn't been so selfish about keeping the infant with her! If only Elizabeth had lived! She was quite sure that guilt for that would haunt her for the rest of her life. A tear escaped her and trickled down her cheek.

'You all right?' Gabriel asked gently.

'Better than I was.'

'You'll make a new life for yourself, I'm sure, and be happy once more.'

She nodded, thinking how kind he and his mother were. After a while, she confided, 'Gabriel, I've been worrying about what I'll do if this Miss Harris doesn't believe me.'

'Find another employer.'

'I don't have any references. And it won't look good my being with a man. Usually it's a girl's mother who goes with her when she's looking for a job. I've seen them come to my mother looking for work.'

He frowned. 'Then we'd better say I'm your brother.'

'No, my cousin,' she said after a moment, finding it utterly impossible to think of him as a brother.

'Whatever you consider best. We'll have to work out a story so we don't contradict one another.'

When they arrived in Blackpool he led the way out of the station, hesitated, then asked, 'Would you mind if we went to look at the sea first?'

'No, of course not.' He had already confided in her that he'd never seen the sea, which seemed amazing to her in a man of twenty-three.

'Give me your bag then.' He took it off her, sad that it felt so light. His mother had lent her some money and given her a few things, and she'd had the sense to wear more than one layer of clothing when she escaped, but still, this wasn't much on which to start a whole new life. Eh, she was so young to be on her own in the world!

As they came out on to the promenade he stopped to stare at the water for a moment, keeping control of his feelings for long enough to escort her across the road. He didn't even glance at the Tower, which had been fascinating holidaymakers for thirteen years, but put down their bags and stood staring at the water, his face full of wonderment.

Mary Ann smiled to see him so rapt and thought how young he looked suddenly. She didn't say anything, but left him to enjoy the sight he had longed for. She was delighted to be near the sea again herself and breathed in the briny air with relish. How anyone could live happily inland she didn't know. She never would be able to, she was sure.

A light wind was ruffling the surface of the water and a few hardy souls were walking along the sand, but the season hadn't started yet, so the two of them were able to enjoy the view in peace.

'I hadn't realised,' he said after a few minutes, 'how far it stretches. Or how it keeps moving and changing.'

'It goes right to the horizon,' she teased, 'and then it comes all the way back again. You should see it on a stormy day, or when the sun's shining on it in summer and it's so dazzling you can hardly bear to look at it. I used to stand on the Palace Pier in Brighton sometimes and imagine I was on a ship.'

He glanced sideways. 'You love it too.'

'Oh, yes. I've missed it dreadfully.' She raised her head and sniffed. 'Just smell that air. There's nothing like it, nothing in the world.'

He followed her example, then picked up their bags. 'Well, we'd better go and look for your Miss Harris. But first we'll fill our bellies. I never think well on an empty stomach.'

He took her to a café but she was too nervous to eat much. When she pushed her plate to one side and muttered something about not being hungry, he laid his hand over hers and said gently, 'I won't go back to Birtley till I'm sure you're all right, Mary Ann. You've got some money, so you can change jobs if you have to. And you know you can always come back to us if you're desperate.'

Her voice came out choked. 'I don't know how I'll ever repay you and your mother, but I'll send you the money when I can, I promise.'

'We don't need repaying. We both like to see people treated fairly and were glad to help you.' He pushed his chair back. 'Come on. Let's go and beard the dragon in its den.'

Miss Harris opened the door herself and led them through to a small back parlour, so like Mary Ann's mother's that it brought back memories which nearly overset her fragile emotions.

'What I can do for you, Mr Clough?'

'It's my cousin who's come to seek your help.' He nodded encouragingly to Mary Ann.

'Miss Battley gave me your address, said you were her friend and – and she hoped you might help me find a job.'

The woman's face grew suspicious. 'It must be a long time since you've seen her?'

'Yes. A few months. She gave me a note for you, but I'm afraid I lost it.'

Gabriel intervened. 'My cousin's mother died recently. Mary Ann's only just getting over that.'

'It'd be better to keep a young *cousin* near her family, surely, in those circumstances?'

'She needs a change, and any road there aren't any jobs where we live. We're out in the country.'

Miss Harris laid her hands flat on the table and stared at them across it. 'I think you're lying, young woman. And you are probably no more her cousin than I am, Mr Clough.'

They were both startled into silence.

'What's more, if you're such good friends with Miss Battley, how can you not know that she was killed a few months ago? Surely you kept in touch with her?'

Mary Ann gasped. 'Miss Battley's dead? Oh, no! How did it happen?'

'She fell under a train.' Mrs Harris pushed back her chair. 'I'm afraid I don't trust you, especially after this tale of a lost letter. And I don't need any more help.'

Touched by her white, miserable face, Gabriel put his arm round Mary Ann's shoulders as they walked down the street. 'I'm sorry about your friend.'

'I am too. I really liked Miss Battley. She was the only one who believed me about *him* and she was always so kind to me. She'd been with us for years.' At the end of the street Mary Ann stopped, squared her shoulders and said, 'Well, I'll just have to find myself a job, then, won't I?'

'The holiday season hasn't started yet. Will they be hiring help?'

'Some places will be getting ready now. And if I can't find a job in a boarding house, there must be something else I can do in a town this size. I don't intend to be a burden to you.'

As they continued walking, he said thoughtfully, 'Perhaps if we get lodgings, the landlady will be able to suggest something.'

Many of the boarding houses were not open, but one or two had *Vacancies* signs in the window. When they came to one which was only a street back from the sea front and looked very trim and well cared for, Gabriel stopped. 'Fancy trying this one?' At her nod he knocked on the door.

The lady who opened it eyed them suspiciously when they asked for rooms. 'You're together, are you?'

'We want separate rooms. I'm looking after my young cousin.' What was the matter with these people that they were so suspicious?

Her expression was not welcoming. 'I'm not sure whether . . .'

'If you're going to look at us like that, we'll go elsewhere,' Gabriel snapped. 'Come on, love. Let's find someone who doesn't treat us like lepers.'

'No, wait! I'm sorry. It's just – well, when young couples come, sometimes they're – not married and—' She flushed.

'Well, of course we're not married. Mary Ann's my cousin, not my lady friend.' Gabriel repeated the story they had agreed on.

'You'll be wanting an evening meal?' the landlady asked as they left Mary Ann on the second floor and moved up to the third floor for Gabriel.

'If that's not too much trouble. We can go and find a café, though, if you've nothing in for tonight.'

She drew herself up. 'I can *always* accommodate guests who wish me to cook for them. I used to be a cook in a gentleman's household until I married.'

'Then we would appreciate a meal and also your advice.'

'Oh?'

'Mary Ann's looking for work. Her mother used to run a boarding house in the south, so she's grown up helping out. Perhaps you could advise us on the best way to find her something? I'm not going home till she's settled somewhere.'

'I'll think about it and discuss it with you later over a cup of tea, Mr Clough. I'm Mrs Blake, by the way.'

She patted her hair as she walked down the stairs. He was a good-looking young man, the strong silent type. She'd discuss the situation with her daughter and get her opinion of the pair. Ivy was shrewd in everything but her own choice of men friends.

At the thought of that, Mrs Blake's expression darkened. Whatever was Ivy going to do now? That worry had been giving her a few sleepless nights.

They ate with the Blake family because they were the only guests. Mary Ann sat in almost complete silence so Gabriel made an effort to talk to their landlady and her daughter, who was a lively young woman and made him laugh several times. In the end, he found himself chatting mainly to her.

After the meal Ivy suggested the three of them go for a walk down to the beach. 'It's too late to go up the Tower, but the new promenade is well lit. We're quite proud of it. You can walk for miles there.'

'I'd like to see the sea at night,' Gabriel admitted. 'It was my first sight of it today.' He turned to Mary Ann but she looked exhausted, her eyes huge in a white face.

She stared from one to the other. 'If you don't mind, Miss Blake, it's been a long day and I'd like to get an early night.'

'Then it's just you and me, Mr Clough,' Ivy said cheerfully. 'I'll fill you a hot water bottle before I go out, love. Give me ten minutes to do that and help my mother clear away, Mr Clough, and I'll be ready for a nice brisk walk.'

Once she had her hot water bottle Mary Ann hesitated then wedged a chair under the door handle before snuggling down in the comfortable bed with a sigh of relief. She'd have to find some way of washing her blood rags tomorrow, but the flow was lessening now, thank goodness. She yawned and tried to stay awake long enough to make some plans for job-hunting, but within five minutes she was sound asleep.

Gabriel enjoyed his outing. Miss Blake was a good walking companion and could keep up a brisk pace. They continued to chat easily and she didn't seem to mind him stopping to stare at the water again when the moon came out from behind some clouds. He'd never met a lass as frank and lively as her.

'I never thought the sea would be so – omnipresent,' he said at one stage.

'Whatever that means.' She laughed. 'That's the third long word you've used on me, Mr Clough.'

'Oh, sorry. It's a habit of mine . . . collecting words, I mean, not tossing them out at people. At home I read a lot in the evenings.'

'I like to go dancing and visit the music hall. Do you dance, Mr Clough?'

'No. I haven't had much chance to learn.'

She linked her arm with his. 'Then I won't take you to the Tower Ballroom. Your cousin looked exhausted.'

'Aye, poor lass. She's had a hard time of it lately.'

Ivy's smile faded. 'She's not the only one. I had a fellow, but he dumped me and went off with another woman. Your cousin may be eager to work here. I'd give my eye teeth to get away.' She gave him a shamefaced look. 'I don't know why I'm telling you this. You must have a kind face.'

'It helps to talk about things.' He gestured towards the sea. 'Wouldn't you miss the water if you went away?'

'Not really. I like inland scenery best. It's gentler. I like to see trees and grass, not streets of boarding houses or miles of boring yellow sand.'

As they began walking again, she said, 'Tell me about your farm . . .'

She seemed so interested that he enjoyed telling her about life there and his new and more profitable venture of poultry-keeping.

When they got back her mother was waiting up for them. 'You're a bit late, Ivy.'

'Oh, I was quite safe with Mr Clough who's an absolute gentleman.' She smiled at Gabriel. 'I'll see you in the morning.'

He stood and watched her as she ran lightly up the stairs. He'd never enjoyed a young woman's company so much. If she lived in Birtley, he'd want to see more of her.

The following day, it seemed, was Ivy's day off and she volunteered to show them round Blackpool.

'I should be searching for a job,' Mary Ann objected. She couldn't enjoy anything else until that was settled.

'Oh, it won't hurt you to relax a bit first,' Ivy said. 'You're looking quite peaky.'

The weather decided to give them a taste of spring, offering a mild sunny day, the sort where you still needed a coat but could hold your face up to the sun and enjoy the first hint of warmth. After they'd walked along the seafront for a while, they visited the Tower and its menagerie with the row of cages.

'Poor creatures, shut up like that,' Mary Ann said softly.

'They have an easy life, well fed and cared for,' Ivy scoffed. 'What's to pity?'

'They've lost their freedom.'

'Freedom's not always what it's cracked up to be.'

After that they walked along the North Pier, watched a fisherman catch a couple of dabs whose flat bodies wriggled for a moment then lay still, and strolled northwards along the promenade.

Mary Ann watched enviously as Ivy and Gabriel chatted. She wished she knew how to talk to people so easily. Although Ivy wasn't exactly pretty, she was vivacious with a good figure and he was clearly enjoying her company.

They caught a tram back to the central area and went to eat a hearty midday meal at a café where Ivy seemed well-known. After that they wandered down to the Central Pier, which wasn't as smart-looking as the North one.

'People dance here in the season,' Ivy said wistfully. 'You should just see it on a summer afternoon.'

'Maybe I should come back then and you can teach me to dance,' Gabriel joked.

Their eyes met and the smiles they exchanged made Mary Ann feel quite left out.

Afterwards they strolled along the promenade again, because it was clear that Gabriel couldn't get enough of watching the sea and breathing the clean salty air.

'What's the best way for me to find a job here?' Mary Ann asked when they were sitting down in a shelter to rest.

'You could have my job any day,' Ivy said, her smile vanishing suddenly. 'I've had enough of washing dishes and making up beds to last me a lifetime. I'll never marry a fellow who runs a boarding house, never!'

Mary Ann breathed deeply, wishing the other woman would answer her seriously. 'Well, I can't take your job, so how do I set about finding one of my own?'

'We'll think about that tomorrow,' said Ivy firmly. 'Today you're on holiday. Let's see if we can put some roses in your cheeks.'

But it was hard to feel she was on holiday with the need to find work hanging over her, and anyway, Mary Ann was feeling tired again.

For once Gabriel didn't seem to notice and she felt jealous of the way he kept looking at Miss Ivy Blake, whose rosy cheeks and sparkling eyes were attracting glances from many of the men who walked past them.

But she seemed to have eyes only for Gabriel Clough.

It wasn't fair. He hadn't said a word to Mary Ann for ages.

'I think I'll walk back and have a rest now,' she said suddenly.

Gabriel turned to study her. 'Sorry. I wasn't thinking, dragging you all over the place. Can you find your way all right or do you want us to come with you?'

'Oh, it's easy enough to find the way,' she said, trying to sound cheerful. When she looked back over her shoulder, the other two had set off walking again, with Ivy hanging on Gabriel's arm now, still chatting away. Was the other woman never lost for words?

Ivy went to call at a friend's house the following morning after breakfast and asked Mary Ann and Gabriel to wait for her to return before they went out. She came hurrying in half an hour later. 'Guess what? I may have found you a job, Mary Ann.'

As they looked at her in astonishment, she took a step backwards and studied the girl, frowning now. 'Let me help you with your hair, though – you want to make a good impression, don't you? And that outfit is – well – a bit old-fashioned. People like their maids to look smart.' She hesitated then asked, 'Would you be offended if I offered you something to wear? I've got a skirt I don't use any more and I think it'd fit you, though you're a bit taller than me so we'd have to let the hem down.'

Mary Ann didn't like accepting charity, but on the other hand she was desperately short of clothes. 'If you're sure you can spare it?'

Gabriel spoke before she could. 'That's very kind of you, Miss Blake.'

'I keep telling you to call me Ivy. I'm not Miss Blake to my friends.' She pulled a wry face at him as she ushered Mary Ann out and whisked her upstairs.

Her bedroom was small, but so pretty Mary Ann couldn't hold back an exclamation. 'Oh, what a lovely room!'

'Do you like it? I did it myself.' Ivy went across to her wardrobe and began to flick through the garments there, pouncing on one. 'Here it is.' She tossed a grey skirt on the bed and then went through the blouses. Two were tossed on to the bed as well.

'What really happened to you?' she asked casually.

Mary Ann stiffened. 'I don't know what you mean.'

'You're not his cousin, I can tell that. You don't look at all like him. Were you his mistress? You seem a bit young for that.'

The girl didn't know what to say. 'I'd rather not – talk about it.'

Ivy came to stand in front of her. 'I'm asking because I

fancy him and if you and he are together, it'd be a waste of my time.'

'Oh. Well, we're not together in that way. He and his mother have been helping me. They're the kindest people. My step-father was . . .' A sob forced its way up Mary Ann's throat and she could only blurt out, 'My mother didn't believe me about what he was doing to me, so I had to get away.'

'Ah.' Ivy nodded, then said in a softer voice, 'You poor thing. That's why you have so few clothes, isn't it? You ran away from home?'

Mary Ann could only nod because she didn't want to weep. She'd wept enough.

'Well, I can give you a few things so that you look more respectable.' Ivy drew Mary Ann across to her bed. 'Get those clothes off and try on these.'

Mary Ann felt embarrassed to undress in front of her, especially as Ivy didn't hide the fact that she was studying her.

'You'll need some underclothes, too. I can spare a few things.'

A little later she went down to find Gabriel. 'Mary Ann's hemming her new skirt, so you'll have to make do with my company till she's ready.'

'That's a pleasure, but don't you have work to do?' He smiled, delighted that she was as kind as she was lively. He wished he knew more about women and how to attract them, wondered what she thought of him.

Ivy sat down and smoothed her skirt. 'My mother understands that I need a break from time to time. Look, I've been thinking. It'll seem better if I say we know Mary Ann's family slightly. She – er – mentioned that she's escaping her step-father.'

He was surprised. 'You must have a way with you to get her to tell you that.'

'Oh, we women have to stick together. Not that I've ever experienced anything like that – but I've seen that some men can be absolute beasts and I do feel for girls who are dragged down through no fault of their own, I really do.'

'You're wonderful,' he said softly, his eyes admiring.

That was one of the keys to getting on with him, she realised. Being kind to that silly little girl – who was clearly a child at heart, however tall she was.

When Mary Ann came down to join them, looking trim and neat in the new skirt and blouse, Ivy fussed over her.

Gabriel mouthed 'Thank you' to her and she winked at him, pleased with the progress she was making. Though she felt a pang of guilt at how naïve he was, how ignorant of women. It would be so easy, snaring him.

But he would be easy to live with as well, and that was important to her now.

Ivy led them a few streets away and rapped smartly on the door of a house very much like her mother's, a double-fronted terrace house with three storeys plus attics with dormer windows. The woman who opened the door to them was thin and about forty, her hair drawn back tightly into a bun. She nodded to Ivy then studied Mary Ann openly, finally assessing Gabriel just as shrewdly. 'Come in, please. Ivy told me to expect you. I'm Miss Thursby.'

Ivy introduced her companions, calling them 'friends of the family'.

With a nod their hostess led the way to the kitchen. 'I'm not open for guests yet, but I shall be putting my *Vacancies* sign in the window next week.'

The kitchen was neat and tidy, with a cat snoozing in front of the fire.

Miss Thursby gestured to the table. 'Please sit down. Now, Mary Ann, tell me about your experience in boarding houses.'

Haltingly at first, then gaining in confidence, the girl explained that she had worked for her mother, but now that she was dead had to find a job. 'And please, I don't have any references but I'm sure I can give satisfaction,' she finished breathlessly.

'I think the best thing would be for you to spend a day or two with me, so that I can see how you work.'

Gabriel spoke for the first time. 'You'll pay her for those days, of course?'

'If she gives satisfaction, yes. Can you bring her things across? The sooner she can start the better. I had a girl coming to work for me, but she gave back word yesterday and there's still a lot to do to get things ready.'

'You can stay now and I'll pack your things for you if that's all right, love?' Ivy said at once, seizing the opportunity to get rid of her. Outside she grinned at Gabriel and did a little dance of triumph as they walked along the street, which made him laugh.

It didn't take her long to pack up, and noticing the blood-stained cloths soaking in a bucket, she added some more rags to the bag, thinking, Poor girl, the curse on top of everything else. Then she grinned. That 'poor girl' was probably going to help her escape from this place and her own problems.

When they had left the suitcase at Miss Thursby's, Ivy linked her arm in Gabriel's. 'Mum doesn't need me so much for a few days and I'd be happy to show you round Blackpool.' Knowing how shy and inexperienced he was with women, she felt it would be up to her to make the running, which she didn't mind. 'I'd welcome some company, actually, because all my friends are working. If that's all right with you?' She knew in advance that he'd agree and he did, with another of those charming smiles.

She walked along by his side, chatting sometimes, at others falling silent. Gabriel Clough was a gift from the gods as far as she was concerned. If she couldn't make him fall in love with her and propose marriage by the end of the week, then she didn't deserve to have him.

Left alone with Miss Thursby, Mary Ann looked at her apprehensively, wondering what to say.

'Don't look so scared, child. I don't eat people.'

'It's just – I've never worked for anyone but my mother before. But I'm a good worker, even Mum admitted that.' For a moment her throat felt choked with tears, but she swallowed hard and managed not to weep.

Jean Thursby patted her new handmaiden's arm. 'Well, I don't ask my staff to work any harder than I do. Now, I've been airing the mattresses and I want to make up all the beds. I'll show you your bedroom then we'll get to work. It's always easier with two pairs of hands.'

The bedroom was in the attic, tiny but clean, with a narrow bed, a table, chair, chest of drawers and a small wardrobe which fitted neatly behind the door. It smelled of lavender.

Miss Thursby looked at her. 'I sleep in the front part of the attic during the season, by the way. No point in my taking up a bedroom that could be bringing in money.'

By lunchtime, Jean was satisfied that Mary Ann did know her job and didn't mind hard work. By teatime she knew she would offer the girl a permanent position. And by the following afternoon she had sensed that someone had hurt the girl very badly. A man, probably.

Well, there would be no men for Mary Ann Baillie to fear in this house. Jean Thursby deliberately chose to cater for women guests only because it made for an easier life. Many of her clients had been coming to her for years, and most of them came by recommendation.

A single woman running a boarding house had to be careful.

On the Thursday of that week Gabriel went for another walk along the promenade with Ivy. He found the sea air invigorating and enjoyed the stimulus of having so many people to watch and things to do.

'Shall you miss me when you go back?' Ivy asked suddenly.

He stopped walking to smile down at her. 'Yes, I shall. Very much indeed.'

Tears filled her eyes. 'I shall miss you too, Gabriel.' She tried to brush them away. 'Oh, dear, I shouldn't have—'

Suddenly she began sobbing and he guided her quickly to a seat, putting his arm round her shoulders. From her muffled confidences it seemed she had fallen in love with him. He stared down at her shiny brown hair, fastened back in a neat bun every morning, but with fine silky strands falling out of it by afternoon. He was amazed that a girl who was so lively and attractive could care about him, but knowing that, it seemed very simple.

'Ivy, stop crying and listen,' he said, putting his fingers under her chin to turn her face up and force her to look at him. 'My dear girl, I've grown to care about you, too, only I have to get back to the farm at the end of next week. So I wondered if – well, there isn't time to court you properly. Do you think you could possibly marry me?'

Her smile was radiant. 'Oh, Gabriel, yes, yes, yes!'

He kissed her soft, trembling lips and then folded her in his arms, enjoying the feel of her against him.

'It'll be easier if we get a special licence and get married before you leave,' she said as he drew away.

He blinked in shock. 'Don't you want time to – to prepare?'

She shook her head. 'No. I'm not letting any other girl get her hands on you. Unless . . . you don't think I'm being too forward?'

He chuckled. 'You can be as forward as you like with me. I'm not very good at this sort of thing, I'm afraid. I've never even flirted with anyone before.'

'I'll teach you how to flirt with me, then,' she said with one of her gurgles of laughter. 'Let's go and tell Ma at once. Afterwards we can nip down to the Register Office and arrange things. It'll cost extra to get married quickly, though.'

'I think I'll have to ask Mam to send me my birth certificate,' he said, frowning.

'Well, write at once, then.'

'We'll have to tell Mary Ann, too, and invite her to the wedding.'

For a minute, Ivy's smile faltered, then she shrugged. 'Of course we shall. Eh, I was so excited I'd forgotten about her.'

Not until he'd gone up to bed that night did Ivy have time to talk privately to her mother. 'He was a godsend, turning up like that.'

Her mother's expression was disapproving. 'Aren't you going to tell him?'

'No, I'm not. Chas was dark as well, so who's going to guess the baby isn't Gabriel's?'

'He might. It'll arrive early.'

'Ah, he's as naïve as they come. I'll be able to pull the wool over his eyes.' She sat thinking for a minute, then added quietly, in a tone almost of surprise, 'He's a nice fellow. I do like him. It's a pity he lives in such a god-forsaken place, but you never know. I might persuade him to sell that farm and come back here to live one day. He certainly likes the sea.'

Mrs Blake sighed. 'Well, on your own head be it, my girl.'

Mary Ann was shocked rigid at Gabriel's news. 'You're going to *marry* her?'

'Yes. Won't you wish me well?'

'Oh. Well, of course I do. I hope you'll be very happy.' But it worried her, this happening so quickly. How could they be certain they'd get on together for the rest of their lives after only one week? Still, they were both kind people so it should be all right. Gabriel was a quiet sort of man and perhaps needed a lively wife. She suddenly realised he had said something. 'Oh, sorry. What was that?'

'Will you come to the wedding?' he repeated.

'I'd love to. If Miss Thursby will let me have the time off, that is.'

Her new employer sniffed and said yes, of course.

'Isn't it romantic, them falling in love so quickly?' Mary Ann said.

'Not really. It's rash, if you ask me. She was all over another fellow only a few weeks ago. I saw them walking out together. You know what they say: *Marry in haste, repent at leisure.* Personally I'm glad I never married at all.' She looked round in smug satisfaction. 'I like to manage my own life and not hand it over to a fellow to mess about.'

9

April 1907

Gabriel wished he could have had time to tell his mother in person that he'd met the woman he wanted to marry, to introduce them and see them grow comfortable together. A letter seemed so inadequate to explain how he'd fallen in love with Ivy. He also wished he'd had time to make his little house look better for his new bride. But he was sure they'd all shake down together. After all, Ivy was such a kind lass, she'd fit in anywhere.

The wedding itself passed in a blur and he hardly managed to exchange two words with Mary Ann, though he did repeat his offer of help if she ever found herself in trouble again.

'I'll be fine,' she told him, determined not to return to Birtley whatever happened because Mrs Greeson would be bound to get in touch with her stepfather if she did, out of sheer spite. 'And I'll pay you back the money, I promise you.'

'Nay, there's no need for that.'

'I'll feel better if I do.'

Ivy came up to thread her arm in Gabriel's. 'I hear Miss Thursby is pleased with you,' she told Mary Ann.

The girl blushed. 'Is she? That's nice to know.'

'I'm afraid I have to take my husband away now because there are some people I'd like him to meet.'

So Mary Ann was left standing with an empty teacup in her hand and no one to talk to. Since there were a few cups lying around, she automatically began to clear them up because Mrs Blake seemed a bit absent-minded today, which was probably only natural with her daughter getting married so suddenly.

Mary Ann felt she'd be all right on her own here. Miss Thursby was a decent sort, and best of all there was a young maid next door,

Agnes, who had invited Mary Ann to go out for a stroll along the promenade when they both had time off together. Things were definitely looking up and even the nightmares were beginning to fade a little.

It still seemed strange that she could go wherever she liked during her time off and that she would have her own wages every single week. She missed Margaret though and intended to write to her once she was sure she was settled.

Mrs Blake came into the kitchen and found her washing up. 'Eh, love, that's kind of you.'

'I like to be useful.'

Already the older woman's attention was elsewhere.

'Is something wrong?'

'No. Well, I was just hoping they'd be happy together. They've known each other such a short time.'

'Oh, I'm sure they will. Gabriel is a lovely person and Ivy is so kind, they can't help but be happy.'

Mrs Blake smiled up at her earnest young face. 'Yes. Yes, of course. And in a few years, we'll no doubt see you getting married, too.'

Mary Ann shook her head firmly. 'No, I shan't ever get married.' She saw Mrs Blake smiling indulgently and didn't argue.

She hoped she never met her stepfather again and still had nightmares about him, but she did wish she could see her mother again, or at least find out if she was all right. Miss Battley had died unexpectedly. If anything happened to her mother, Mary Ann wouldn't even know. That was a terrible thought.

On the train going back to Overdale Gabriel described his home to his new wife in painstaking detail, promising he'd find time to put on a new room downstairs for his mother, so that they could be private together upstairs.

'Only it'll all take time, love,' he finished.

'Things always do,' she said obscurely. 'I'll help as much as I can, but I know nothing of poultry so you'll have to teach me.' She looked out of the window, wondering now that the rush of activity was over if she really would be able to keep her condition from him and what he'd say if he found out. It'd be all right if she didn't swell too quickly. Some women did, some didn't. She prayed she wouldn't.

But even if she did, she thought Gabriel too kind to throw her out. Besides, she intended to make herself useful to him, even if she did have to do some mucky jobs on the farm. Well, everything had its price, didn't it?

Mrs Clough came to the door as soon as she heard the cab horse clop to a halt. She stood there, arms folded, studying her new daughter-in-law as Gabriel helped her out of the cab. Not pretty but lively-looking. Smiled a lot. Probably nervous.

'I've given you two the front bedroom,' Jassy told them as she led the way inside. 'I've moved Gabriel's things in there, but you'll want to arrange things to suit yourself, Ivy.'

'I don't want to upset anything.'

'Eh, it's only furniture. What's to upset?'

Ivy kept a smile on her face, trying to hide her disappointment in the farm. It was much smaller than she'd expected and there were hardly any trees to be seen. The hamlet of Birtley had no shops and how was she to get into Overdale? Gabriel must have a vehicle of some sort. She'd have to learn to drive a horse. As for the moors which encircled the farm, she hadn't expected them to be so stark and wasn't at all sure she liked them.

Mrs Clough served them a good, hearty meal, cleared up in silence, refusing Ivy's help, then went up to bed.

Gabriel looked across the hearth at his wife, sitting on the sofa with her legs tucked up under her. She looked small and defenceless, her normal sparkle quenched and apprehension on her face. 'You all right? You look tired.'

When she smiled at him, he could see it was an effort. 'I hope you're not too disappointed, love. I know the farm's small, but the poultry and eggs are bringing us in a decent income now.'

'I'm not disappointed in anything,' she said firmly. 'It's just – different from what I expected. I shall get used to it and love it,

I'm sure. I was wondering how I'd get into Overdale to do the shopping, though.'

'We usually go in once a week on market day and grow quite a lot of the vegetables we eat ourselves. There's a walled kitchen garden on a south-facing slope behind the house which produces well. Actually, I've been thinking of taking a stall at the market and selling some of our eggs and chickens ourselves. You make more money like that than by selling to shops.'

She brightened up. 'A stall? I could run that for you. I bet I'd be good at it and I'd enjoy the chance to meet a few people.' Then she looked at him wryly. 'I've rushed you into this, haven't I?'

'We've both rushed into it,' he corrected.

'I'll pull my weight here,' she promised.

He went across to sit beside her and put his arm round her shoulders. As she nestled against him, he bent to kiss her and then said, 'Shhh!' as she opened her mouth to speak. 'This isn't a time to talk,' he said huskily, his hands lingering on her body.

Ivy wriggled against him, smiling. 'No. Definitely not a time to talk.'

'Am I the first?'

She sighed and grew still. 'No. I'm sorry.'

'I thought not. As long as I'm the last, that's all I care about. You're my first, though. I hope I don't – disappoint you.'

And to her surprise, he didn't. In fact he was so very gentle and caring that she found their first night together surprisingly satisfactory.

But there wasn't the surging ecstasy there had been with her former lover. She was going to miss that.

Two months later Ivy told Gabriel she was expecting a child and he was so alight with joy she felt guilty for days afterwards.

Jassy accepted their news calmly and when she was alone with her daughter-in-law said, 'We'll have to get Carrie Anders in to see you.'

Ivy stared at her. 'Who's she?'

'The local midwife.'

'Oh, plenty of time for that yet.' In fact, Ivy didn't intend to see the woman until much nearer the birth date.

However, Carrie Anders turned up at the stall next market day, a woman as thin and as sparing with her words as Jassy Clough. 'I hear you're expecting.'

'Yes. Oh, you must be Mrs Anders.'

'Yes. When's it due?'

'About six or seven months. It's early days yet.'

'I'll come and check you out one day next week.'

'Not yet, thank you. I'm feeling fine and don't like being fussed over.'

Which made Carrie say to Jassy after church the following Sunday, 'She's got something to hide, that one.'

Jassy stared at her. 'What do you mean?'

'Why doesn't she want me to come and check her out? Young women are usually eager to see that everything is going all right, especially the first time.'

'She's twenty-five. A year or so older than our Gabriel. Not all that young.'

'Even more reason for me to check her over.'

The two of them stood for a moment in a sunny corner of the churchyard, then Jassy shrugged. 'I'll keep an eye on her. She's a worker, at least, I have to give her that. She doesn't like dealing with the hens, but she does it. She's good at the market, too.'

A month later Carrie again made her way across to Jassy after the service. 'It were a windy day last Thursday,' she said without preamble. 'Your Ivy wears such skimpy clothes you could see the outline of her body. I don't want to cause trouble but I think she's further on than she says. Five months, I'd guess. Or even six.'

Jassy had come to the same conclusion and had already said goodbye to the idea that this was her first grandchild. 'Eh, it's a poor look-out, it is that. I've thought till my mind's addled an' I still can't decide whether to tell our Gabriel or not. I don't think he knows.'

They both shook their heads and went on their way.

But Gabriel didn't need telling. He might have little personal experience of the condition but he'd seen enough women carrying children not to realise that his wife was bigger than he'd have expected for this stage. Far bigger.

And he'd already decided he'd been mad to marry in such haste. Oh, it wasn't that he and Ivy didn't get on. She was invariably pleasant and was a hard worker. It was just that in everyday matters they were chalk and cheese, him liking a quiet life and books, her wanting to go out and be with people.

He'd lain awake at night turning things over in his mind, facing the implications and realising why she'd rushed him into marrying. He'd confront her about it all when his mother had left for church the following Sunday.

'We need to talk,' he said abruptly after his mother had left.

Ivy was icing a cake at the other end of the table. She cast one quick glance at his sombre expression and her heart began to thud in her chest. 'Talk away, then.'

'Whose baby is it?'

The knife dropped out of her hand and icing smeared across the tablecloth. She couldn't think what to say, could only stand there and look at him pleadingly. When he got up and came down to her end of the table, she flinched, thinking he was going to hit her.

He stopped dead. 'Nay, I'd never thump you, Ivy. What sort of bloke do you think I am?'

She began to cry, soft helpless tears. 'I'm sorry. I know I've cheated you, and you've been so kind, but I was desperate. I shouldn't have done it, though.' The sobs redoubled and she sank down on the nearest chair, burying her head in her hands.

He couldn't think how to comfort her when he was hurting so much himself, so went over to stand by the window, staring out.

When the sobs stopped he risked a glance over his shoulder. She wasn't looking at him but sitting there with her shoulders drooping. She looked vulnerable. He grimaced. Even now, he was using long words.

Another glance showed her wiping a tear away with a corner

of her apron, not looking in his direction but waiting for him to pass judgement.

He was reminded suddenly of another lass carrying a baby she hadn't wanted, walking up and down the field like those poor caged lions at the Tower Zoo. He'd seen Margaret Pensham a few times since then in Overdale and she always had a cheery word. Her son was lovely, plump and rosy-cheeked. You couldn't blame babies for what their parents did. He sighed. It wasn't right, the way women had to bear the shame and men got away with things.

But it hadn't been right for Ivy to marry him while carrying another man's child, either.

Eh, when had life ever been fair?

'What do you want to do about it?' he asked abruptly.

Ivy raised her head, her mouth open slightly, her eyes wide with surprise. 'What do *I* want to do? It's what *you* want to do, surely?'

'Did you care about me even a bit?' he asked.

She gave him a long, level look. 'Yes. I liked you very much.'

'*Liked*. Not loved.' He had been so set up with himself, thinking that a lively girl like Ivy had fallen in love with him. Served him right for being so vain. He was just a simple farmer, for all his long words.

'I've done enough lying to you, Gabriel. I didn't love you, but I couldn't have married you if I hadn't liked you. I thought we could make a decent life together. I've tried to work hard, pay you back for what you've done for me, be a good wife.'

'You've worked very hard,' he allowed. He let the silence wash between them for a minute or two, then repeated his question. 'What do you want to do?'

She risked saying it. 'Stay here. Have the child. Raise it together.'

'You won't go running back to him?'

She shook her head. 'He was just using me. A friend told me afterwards that he boasted about having me.' A small mew of pain escaped her then and she had to fight for self-control. 'That was why I was so desperate to get away. He's still living in Blackpool. I couldn't bear him to boast of fathering the child as well. He doesn't know and I don't want him to find out.'

Gabriel went back to looking out of the window. 'I shall have to think about it. I can't decide something like this without due consideration. It's too important.'

She was very still. 'I'm grateful you're even considering letting me stay.'

'Mmm. I think I'll go for a walk across the tops. Tell Mum I'll be out till evening.' He turned to leave and saw in the mirror how she stretched one hand out towards him, then drew it back and sagged against the chair. He felt sorry for her, but he didn't turn back to her. Couldn't.

He felt sorry for himself, as well. And there was no one to look after him.

In Blackpool Mary Ann was happier than she'd been since she left school. She didn't mind working hard when she could earn her own money and she loved having a friend of her own age. Agnes was such fun to be with. They could talk about anything and everything, help each other choose new material and sew clothes together on Miss Thursby's elderly sewing machine, or simply stroll along the promenade on their afternoons off and enjoy an ice cream. In the end Mary Ann even told her friend about the baby. It was wonderful not to have to pretend about anything.

Because she wasn't used to being extravagant Mary Ann found herself with money left over from her wages each week so opened a savings bank account, watching in delight as the shillings mounted into pounds. They mounted even more quickly when the holiday season got in full swing because some of the ladies gave her tips. When she asked Miss Thursby what she should do with them, her employer looked at her in amazement.

'They're yours, lass. You've earned them by working hard and being cheerful. Do what you want with them.'

Mary Ann went away beaming. Later, she told Agnes and her

friend said, 'Well, we shall be out of jobs come the winter, so make sure you save enough to tide you over.'

Mary Ann hadn't thought that far ahead, hadn't realised the jobs were temporary. 'Oh, no. What are you going to do in the winter?'

Agnes shrugged. 'I haven't decided yet. I could go home and live with my family, but I hate sharing a bed with my sisters. Or,' she looked speculatively at Mary Ann, 'we could try to find ourselves jobs and share lodgings.'

'Do you mean that?'

''Course I do. Wouldn't say it if I didn't.'

'What sort of jobs? I've only ever worked in a boarding house.'

'Doesn't matter what sort, does it, as long as it brings us enough to live off? Last year I worked in a sewing workshop, making clothes.' She grimaced. 'Boring, that was.'

As the season drew to a close, Miss Thursby heard them talking and worrying about their jobs and said abruptly one evening, 'If you're looking for somewhere to live for the winter, you and Agnes could live in the attics here free of charge if you'd give me a hand with the weekly cleaning. You'd have to find your own food, though, and see to your own washing. Then you could have your job back once the season started, Mary Ann, and I daresay Agnes will get hers back next door, though Mrs P likes to have the house to herself in winter.'

Mary Ann beamed at her employer. 'That sounds wonderful. I'll ask Agnes.'

Mary Ann wrote to Gabriel a month after his marriage, but didn't receive a reply. She wrote again, wondering if her letter had gone astray, but with the same result.

Hurt, she vowed not to write again, but the money she owed him preyed on her mind. She didn't even know how much he had spent on her because he had refused to tell her. But how could she pay him back when she didn't even know if she had his address right?

No, she couldn't have made a mistake. Anyone in Birtley knew where Clough Farm was and the postman came down the lane regularly.

All she could guess was that he didn't want to keep in touch with her.

She wrote to Margaret and got an immediate reply and after that the two of them wrote at least once a month. It was something to look forward to, receiving that letter and hearing Margaret's news.

Mary Ann decided she should just forget about Gabriel Clough and enjoy her new life—and she would if she could pay him back the money she owed. In the end she confided in Margaret, asking her if she'd seen Gabriel around the town and if she had the correct address for the farm so that she could send a postal order to him.

Ivy's child was born in October, on a fine autumn day with the sun shining and a light breeze whispering across the moors and rippling the grass so that it looked for a moment to Gabriel like the sea. After he'd brought Carrie Anders back to help with the birth, he was banished from the house. His mother had already persuaded her friend to say locally that the baby had arrived early, to spare them all embarrassment.

When it was over, Jassy came to the door and called out to him, 'It's a girl. Come and see her.'

Gabriel hesitated then shrugged and moved forward. He'd agreed to father the other man's baby so he couldn't draw back now. He went into the bedroom where Ivy was lying looking exhausted. She stared up at him fearfully.

He forced himself to go across and kiss her on the cheek. 'I'm glad it went well for you.'

She gulped audibly and tears welled in her eyes, so he went to stand by the cradle. He had expected to hate the child, or at least resent it, but how could you feel like that about a tiny baby?

'She's a bonny little creature,' he said quietly. 'What shall we call her?'

Ivy burst into tears and it took him a long time to calm her down. Afterwards he sat on the bed. 'How about Frances? I like that best of all the names we thought of.'

'Yes. Frances. Frances Mary, perhaps?' When he nodded, she added, 'I just wanted to say how *grateful* I am to you for . . .'

He put one fingertip across her lips. 'We won't speak of it again. Frances will be my daughter for all anyone knows.'

'Except your mother and her friend Carrie.'

He looked at her in surprise. 'They'll not say owt about it.'

'Are you sure?'

'Of course I am. Carrie's been a friend of my mother's for years.'

'Sorry.'

When he had left her, Ivy lay staring out across the moors. She should be happy as well as grateful, but somehow she couldn't be. This wasn't at all the sort of life she wanted to lead and Gabriel had gone even quieter since he'd found out. Half the time he had his head buried in a book in the evenings and she had to do the same in self-defence. If it weren't for the market stall in Overdale, which allowed her to get out and meet people, she'd go mad.

She smiled at the thought of it. Some of the folk there were real characters. And one of the neighbouring stallholders, Dan Barworth, could always cheer you up. He was her own age, though his wife was a few years older and a bit of a martinet. Sometimes Dan would pull a wry face at Ivy behind Mavis's back when she went on at him about keeping the stall tidy. They sold bed linen, tablecloths, towels, seconds and stuff Dan got cheap. He went round picking things up directly from the mills early in the week and then he and his wife sold the stuff at two or three nearby markets at the end of the week.

That'd be a much more interesting life than looking after chickens.

Sighing, Ivy told herself she was being stupid. She was very lucky indeed to have found a man like Gabriel. Only – the daily living together was all so much harder than she'd expected that sometimes she wished she'd stayed with her mother, had the baby, and to hell with what anyone else said. There were times when she felt as though she would burst from holding her feelings in, but mostly she just got on with things, doing the best she could.

The trouble was, as time went on she discovered that she didn't really like being a mother, neither the feeding which made her feel like a cow, nor the messy caring for the small, squirming body. She didn't really want any more children, either, but knew she'd have to give Gabriel at least one of his own to make up for Frances.

One Sunday in November Margaret Pensham turned up at the farm, driven there by Mr Garbutt's second coachman. She found Gabriel at home, as she'd expected on a Sunday, and allowed herself to be introduced to his wife before saying directly, 'May I speak to you alone, please, Mr Clough? It's about Mary Ann.'

Ivy looked at her sharply. 'If she needs help again, surely I should be involved?'

Margaret ignored that. 'Mr Clough?'

He nodded. 'We can go for a walk up the lane, if you like. It's fine out, if a bit chilly.'

'As long as we walk towards Birtley,' Margaret said with a grimace. 'I don't want to go near Redvale.'

When they were outside she asked bluntly, 'Why haven't you replied to Mary Ann's letters?'

Gabriel stopped to stare at her. 'What letters? I haven't received any.' Had been upset by that.

'She wrote twice, once in May and once in June. She's accepted that you don't want to keep in touch, but it's fretting her that she's not paid back the money you spent on her.'

'I don't want her money. A lass on her own needs something behind her.' He walked on in frowning silence then said, 'And I did write to her. Only she never responded.'

'It seems all the letters between you are going astray then.' Margaret didn't draw the obvious conclusion, but left that to him.

He stopped and closed his eyes. 'She couldn't have!'

'Pardon?'

'Sorry. I was just thinking aloud. Do you have Mary Ann's

address? My bit of paper went astray.' And now he could guess why.

'Yes.' Margaret fumbled in her handbag and pulled out a piece of paper.

'I'll get in touch with her, I promise you, and I can guarantee this letter won't get lost.'

He escorted her back to the carriage then went inside. 'What did you do with the letters, Ivy?'

'I don't know what you mean.'

'*Don't lie to me!* What did you do with Mary Ann's letters to me and mine to her? Why didn't you want me to keep in touch with her?'

She burst into tears.

He stood there with arms folded. He'd fallen for her tears before, but not any more. 'Well?'

'I was jealous.'

'Of a child like her?'

'She's going to be an attractive woman one day and I didn't want to risk anything.'

He looked at her in utter disgust. 'And I thought you were kind-hearted. You were only helping her to make me think well of you, weren't you? Well, it's backfired. I'm going to Blackpool to see her and explain personally.'

'Gabriel, no! Why can't you leave her be? She's all right. My mother met Miss Thursby in the street and she said Mary Ann had made friends and settled in well.'

'But that's still no reason for her to think her old friends have deserted her.'

'How can you call yourself an old friend?' Ivy asked scornfully. 'You hardly knew the girl. It was just an act of kindness on your part.'

'My mother and I both liked her. I hate to think of her believing we'd let her down like that. What's more, I'm not taking any money off her.' He paused and they stood scowling at one another across the table. 'I shall enjoy a few days' break.' He'd had more than enough of Ivy's complaints about motherhood.

'At this time of year? Can't you at least wait till the spring?'

'No. I'm going tomorrow and nothing you say or do will stop me.'

As Mary Ann came back from her part-time winter job in a shop, she saw a tall figure waiting outside the house and her heart began to thump as she recognised Gabriel Clough. What was he doing here?

She waited for him to speak first.

'I need to talk to you, Mary Ann,' he said without preamble. 'Will you let me buy you a meal or do you have to work tonight?'

She stared at him. 'I've finished for the day, but I need to change. Where are you staying?'

He looked down ruefully at his small suitcase. 'I haven't found anywhere yet. Most places seem to be closed for the winter.'

'Aren't you staying with Ivy's mother?'

His expression became grim. 'No. There are reasons, which I'll explain later.'

'Why don't you come inside and I'll see if Miss Thursby can suggest anywhere?'

The landlady looked at him, pursed her lips, then asked the same question. 'Why aren't you staying with your in-laws?'

He hesitated, then said, 'I've had a disagreement with my wife about something important and I don't want them involved.'

'Well, I suppose I'd better find you a room here. I don't usually take men guests but I'll make an exception for Mary Ann's cousin.'

'I'm not her cousin, just a friend who helped her out when she was in trouble,' he said at once, sick of lying to people.

'I'll still make an exception. You'll have to take pot luck for tea and they're forecasting a storm tomorrow, but if you choose to take a holiday at this time of year, who am I to argue with a paying customer?'

He smiled. 'I'd rather take Mary Ann out for a meal somewhere, if you don't mind. We need to talk privately.'

'The two of you can eat in the guests' dining-room and do your talking there afterwards. You'll have more privacy than in a café.'

'Thank you. You're very kind.'

'Mary Ann, you'd better help me make up a bed for Mr Clough and then you can light the fire in the dining-room.'

Jean Thursby wondered why she was being so kind to him, then shrugged. He was an honest fellow, you could see that in his face, and Mary Ann had been upset when he hadn't replied to her letters. It'd do them good to sort things out.

After they'd eaten Gabriel said abruptly, 'I want you to know that I never received either of your letters. Ivy intercepted them and threw them in the fire.'

She gaped at him. This was the last thing she'd have expected his wife to do.

'And when I wrote to you, I gave the letter to my wife to post when she went to town for the market – only she threw it away.'

Mary Ann found her voice. 'But why?'

'She was jealous.'

'She *can't* have been! Not of me!'

'Apparently so.' He offered the excuse he'd made up. 'I know women get strange fancies when they're expecting, but I'm still upset by what she did.'

'Thank you for telling me. But you needn't have come all this way.'

'I wanted to see for myself that you were all right. Mam and I've been worried about you.'

'I fell lucky with Miss Thursby.' Mary Ann fumbled in her pocket. 'While you're here, I want to pay you back what I owe you. I don't like to be in debt.'

He put out one hand to stop her. 'Keep it. I'm not short of a bob or two and you need something behind you.'

'But—'

'Please.'

'Oh, well. Thank you. If you're sure?'

'Do you think Miss Thursby will let me stay for a day or two? I need to get away from the farm – and from Ivy.' He found himself confiding in Mary Ann about the baby, which wasn't his, but which he loved. He could never have explained why he found himself able to talk to her so easily, but she seemed to have grown up a lot in the past year.

She listened in silence, then laid her hand on his which was clenched into a fist. 'That's so unfair, Gabriel.'

'Aye, Ivy took me for a right fool. It's my own fault for rushing into marriage but I've never had much to do with women and I was dazzled. I do love Frances, though. She's a dear little thing.'

'That's good.' Mary Ann tried to keep the image of her own baby at bay by changing the subject. 'Are you still reading as many books?'

He wasn't fooled. 'What made you look so sad just then?'

She swallowed back the tears. 'The thought of my own baby.'

Now it was his turn to hold her hand in his big, warm one. 'Don't let that spoil your life. You'll have others.'

She shook her head. 'No. I'm not going to get married.'

'That'd be a waste. You'd make any man a fine wife.'

It was only when Miss Thursby came in and cleared her throat that they realised how long they'd been sitting there talking.

Gabriel spent three days in Blackpool, standing on the sea front clutching his hat while waves crashed on the beach below and a strong wind made his overcoat flap around his legs. He wasn't one to feel the cold and somehow the stormy weather and wild winds seemed to clear much of the pain from his mind. After a day or two he began making plans to return, thinking out what he'd say to Ivy.

Mary Ann walked with him to the railway station.

'Unfortunately I think it's better if we don't write to one another,' he said awkwardly. 'It'd upset Ivy and I have to live with her.' Besides, he felt a tug of attraction to Mary Ann which had surprised him.

She nodded, accepting this but wishing she could still stay

friends with him because she liked him better than any man she had ever met.

When she told Agnes this, her friend said accusingly, 'You're half in love with him.'

'I am *not!*' But she knew she could easily have been. Only he was married and she had her new life to lead. She had a good friend, an employer who was fair and money mounting up in the bank. What more did she need?

She didn't let herself try to answer that.

When Gabriel got back he found that Ivy was pregnant again and knew this time the baby was his. That put an end to a vague wish he'd had of ending their sham of a marriage and giving her the money to live elsewhere.

Ivy faced this new pregnancy with grim endurance. As the months passed and her body swelled again, she couldn't bear Gabriel to touch her and he didn't insist, for which she was grateful.

Grateful again. She was sick to death of being grateful to him, sick of his eternal kindness and gentleness.

One day, feeling desperate to get away from those damned moors and smelly hens, she begged Gabriel to sell the farm and buy a boarding house by the seaside. 'I'm sure we'd both be much happier in a livelier place.'

He looked down his nose at her. 'I'd never take my mother's home away from her.'

'But she'd *have* a home with us! I wasn't thinking of leaving her on her own.'

'She likes living here, and anyway it's her farm not mine so I can't sell it. My father left it to her and I shan't get it till she dies, which I hope will be a long time away.'

No one had mentioned that before. Ivy felt quite sick with suppressed anger. She'd never have married him if she'd known they'd be dependent on his mother, though to give Jassy her due she didn't rub it in or try to boss anyone around. Ivy realised her husband was speaking again.

'Besides, we're doing all right here with the hens and eggs. We'd be fools to leave just in the hope of finding something better.'

'But you liked the sea, you know you did. You couldn't stop talking about it when you came home from seeing Mary Ann.'

'I like my life here, too, and I care deeply about my mother's happiness.'

His voice was so flatly emphatic that Ivy stopped trying to persuade him. She knew that tone. He could be as immovable as one of those ugly dry stone walls that hemmed them in when he didn't want to do something. Perhaps she could get her mother-in-law on her side about this instead.

But Jassy was just as intractable as her son and refused even to discuss the matter.

Ivy tried her usual tactic of giving herself a good talking-to and counting her blessings, but it didn't succeed. She could feel her spirits getting lower and lower. The only bright spot in her life was her time at the market. The rest of the week seemed grey and boring.

She was going to make sure she didn't have any more children after this one. There was a new lady doctor in Overdale and Ivy made an excuse to see her about the coming baby. While she was there she asked her advice about preventing other children being conceived, saying the farm was too poor to support any more. The doctor gave her a booklet which taught her a lot.

Ivy passed it on to Gabriel and he read it, too, then said, 'If we need anything I'll see to it.'

If, Ivy thought. What did he mean, *if?*

Their second child was born just before Christmas 1908. It was another girl and looked surprisingly like Ivy's first child, considering they had different fathers.

Gabriel insisted on calling this one Christina and would not allow them to shorten it. He never favoured the new baby more than Frances, which should have pleased Ivy, but instead irritated her because it was yet another reason she had to be *grateful* to him! He was a wonderful father to both children.

But he showed no interest in Ivy's body after Christina was

born, not the slightest bit, even though they still shared a bed. Perhaps she had let her irritation with him during her pregnancy show too much. He was always polite to her, but cool now and distant, which he hadn't been before.

If she had had any way of supporting herself and the children, she'd have left him. But she didn't. She knew she was quick to flare into anger these days. Well, he could just lump it. And his mother could lump it, too.

PART TWO
1913–1918

10

June – October 1913

Dinah Baillie threw the newspaper down with an angry snort. In Germany the Kaiser was celebrating the twenty-fifth anniversary of his accession to the throne. Who cared about him? She didn't even care about her own King these days. She had seen a girl in the street yesterday who reminded her of her daughter and had wept herself to sleep. It would be six years in September since she'd seen Mary Ann. *Six years!* She felt desperate sometimes wondering what had happened to her.

She also wished the police had been able to find Jeff and charge him with bigamy. She'd have felt so much safer if he was locked up in jail. A few times she'd thought she'd seen him in the distance and her heart had thumped in apprehension. She had never forgotten the way he'd looked at her the last time she'd seen him – such hatred in his eyes! Once she'd been quite certain it was him she'd seen and that night someone had thrown pebbles up at her bedroom window, waking her twice. She'd seen a man standing across the road looking up at her each time and been terrified.

She still had nightmares that he might hurt her in revenge for what she'd done to him – and other nightmares about what she'd let him do to her daughter.

Gertie, who had been her general maid for three years, ever since Maisie's marriage, and was a sensible woman of thirty, came in from the kitchen. 'All right if I go now, Mrs Baillie?'

'Is it that time already? Yes, of course. Enjoy your afternoon off, dear.'

The house seemed very quiet once Gertie had left. Too quiet. Dinah only took lady lodgers now and they were all out at work.

Even when they were at home you never heard much more than a distant murmur of voices. Miss Manning worked in a millinery store, such a smartly dressed woman but she kept herself to herself and was not inclined to linger for a chat. Miss Butler worked as a lady typist in a lawyer's office and had relatives in the town, so was often out. And the Mills sisters in the front bedroom were both teachers in a small private school for young ladies – and they had each other, so although they were pleasant they didn't chat much either. Anyway, Dinah thought them rather silly, all fluttery movements and fussy, overly genteel mannerisms.

She did wish she had a friend or two to chat to, wished it quite desperately sometimes, but she had never made friends easily.

A door banged at the rear of the house and she frowned as it was followed by silence. Gertie always called out when she came in.

Feeling suddenly uneasy, Dinah went to the door of her tiny sitting-room and looked down the long narrow hall towards the rear. The door handle of the kitchen turned slowly and she called, 'Who is it?' her voice fluttery and nervous.

As the door opened slowly she saw a man's silhouette and it was very familiar because she had seen it so many times in a darkened bedroom. Dear heavens, what was Jeff doing here?

She backed along the hall as the door opened fully, calling out, 'What do you want?'

'My revenge.' He smiled and began to walk towards her.

The front door was bolted and locked so she turned and ran upstairs, making for her bedroom which had a bolt on the inside of the door.

Footsteps pounded behind her on the stairs and she tried to move faster, but her narrow skirt prevented it. Just as she reached the landing he grabbed her skirt and yanked backwards hard. She let out another scream as she began to fall, colliding with him and feeling him push her deliberately downwards.

The breath was slammed out of her as she bumped and bounced down the stairs, and she could only choke out a cry for help as she crashed into the banisters then slid down the last few steps to land sprawling in the hall.

'You knew I'd be back one day,' he mocked from somewhere above her. 'And I haven't finished yet. You'll wish you'd broken your neck on the way down before I'm—'

Then there was the sound of the back door opening and Gertie's voice calling, 'It's only me, Mrs Baillie. I forgot my—'

From somewhere Dinah summoned up the strength to scream for help, and with a curse, Jeff came running down the stairs, kicking her as he passed. Through a haze of agony she heard the key turn in the front door, the top bolt slide, then the door slam open. The noise echoed in her brain as she plummeted down into pain-filled darkness.

She awoke to find herself lying in a hard, narrow bed. Opening her eyes, she saw she was in a hospital and tried to call out for the nurse, but her throat was so dry she only managed a faint croak. Drifting in and out of consciousness she lay there until at last a nurse came into her room. Her huge, starched hat seemed like a white bird and Dinah watched it float towards the bed and tremble slightly as the nurse bent over her.

She tried to ask for water but all that came out was another croak.

'You've had a bad fall, Mrs Baillie, and I'm afraid you've broken your leg. Let me get you something to drink.'

The nurses were all very kind, but her body was so bruised and painful Dinah couldn't help moaning as they tended her. And when they'd gone she wept over the indignities of being so helpless, of having to be cleaned like a baby.

The following morning the doctor came on his rounds, accompanied by Matron, and informed her that it was a bad break, though they'd managed more or less to straighten the leg.

Terror shuddered through her. 'Won't I be able to walk properly?'

'You'll manage to walk quite well, I think, but I'm afraid you'll always have a limp and that leg might ache a bit.'

Matron said briskly, 'No use weeping, Mrs Baillie. What's done is done. Be thankful that Doctor was able to set the leg properly for you. We'll move you out into the main ward soon and the company will cheer you up.'

When they'd gone, the Ward Sister came back and clicked her tongue in annoyance to find Dinah sobbing into her pillow. 'There's a policeman waiting to see you, Mrs Baillie. Do you feel well enough?'

'Yes.' She sniffed away the tears. If there was one thing she wanted, it was for them to catch Jeff. *Oh, please, let them catch him this time!*

An earnest young constable came to sit by her bed and ask her what she remembered.

'Your maid says she saw a man running down the hall towards the front door. She didn't recognise him. Did you?'

'Yes.' Dinah explained about Jeff and watched as the constable took laborious notes. When he'd finished, she looked at him pleadingly. 'He'll be back, you know. He means to kill me. You've got to catch him or I'll never be safe.'

He made soothing noises and muttered something about doing their best to bring the fellow to justice, but she didn't feel hopeful. Jeff had been too clever for them last time and probably would be again.

Only what could she do? Nothing except wait and try to take extra care. Jeff would have left town now and she'd never know when to expect him back. In the meantime, the doctor said it would be at least three months before she recovered, so she summoned Gertie to the hospital and arranged to hire another maid to help in the house, with Gertie in charge.

Later that afternoon she thought about her daughter, glad Jeff didn't know where Mary Ann was, because she was sure he'd want to hurt her, too. Though actually Mary Ann would be twenty-two now. Perhaps even Dinah wouldn't recognise her.

It was all her own fault, she knew. She'd let herself be tricked by a villain and both she and her daughter had paid dearly for that.

When she got out of hospital, she'd have to think how to protect herself better.

Agnes was waiting for Mary Ann on the corner. The sun was shining for their afternoon off and they were both looking forward to a good brisk walk along the promenade. They were wearing sensible dark skirts, six-gored, not the tight hobble skirts of the more fashionable visitors to the town. Mary Ann's was navy blue gabardine, worn with a pale pink blouse of cotton batiste, trimmed with tucks and narrow bands of lace. She'd spent hours sewing it during the winter and knew it looked good. Agnes also had a navy blue skirt, but her blouse was cream, with a shawl collar edged in lace and neat mother-of-pearl buttons down the front. Both of them wore straw hats with moderate brims and navy ribbons round the crown.

'Ooh, I'm glad to get out,' Agnes announced, linking her arm in her friend's. 'Mrs P's been on edge all morning, snapping my nose off every time I open my mouth. Her daughter and son-in-law are coming to see her this afternoon, so everything had to be just so.' With a sigh, she added, 'She's still not well, you know. I bet those two are going to take over the boarding house, and if they do I'm leaving. I can't stand that daughter of hers, always running her fingers over surfaces to check that I've dusted properly. As if I don't know my job or would cheat Mrs P!'

'Never mind them. Just look at that water. Doesn't it lift your heart to see it sparkling in the sun? I love to be outside.'

'What'd lift my heart would be a pair of nice young men to flirt with, someone to take us out for tea.' Her friend's face wobbled for a moment and she looked perilously close to tears.

Mary Ann gave her a quick hug. 'Oh, Agnes, you're better off without him. If he'd cheat on you before you got married, you'd have had a dreadful life with him afterwards.'

'I know, I know. But I did like being engaged and it felt nice to wear a ring on my days off.' She stared down at her hand. 'I sometimes think I'll never find another fellow.'

'Of course you will,' Mary Ann said bracingly. They'd had this conversation several times during the two months since Agnes had broken off her engagement after seeing her fiancé kissing another woman.

'It's all right for you, you don't care about getting married and having children, but I *want* to settle down. I'm twenty-three and that's almost on the shelf.'

Mary Ann sighed. 'Come on, love. Let's walk more quickly.'

But Agnes was in a contrary mood today. 'I can't keep up with you when you stride out like that. Just think! We were the same height when we met and now you're five foot ten tall.'

'It's a good thing I don't want to get married, isn't it? What fellow would fancy a maypole like me?'

'You always say that. But you'd not be bad-looking if you'd take a bit more care. You shouldn't drag your hair back into a bun like that, though. I'm going to try a new style for you, one I saw in *Peg's Paper*. If we puff your hair out over each ear and catch it in a looser bun at the back, I'm sure it'll suit you better.'

'I can't be bothered fussing with it.'

'I'm still going to try it, so you'd better get used to the idea.'

Mary Ann sighed. Agnes was always going on at her to make herself look more attractive, but as long as she was clean and tidy she didn't care. She'd been out with fellows from time to time, mostly at Agnes's urging, but none had caught her interest. One had persisted for a while, a pleasant enough fellow, but when she'd told him firmly that she never wanted to marry, he'd soon found himself someone else. Which showed, she felt, that he'd wanted a wife, but not her in particular.

And she hadn't really missed him because it hadn't been easy talking to him. The only man she'd ever found easy to talk to had been Gabriel Clough. She sighed, wondering how he was getting on. Funny how she'd never forgotten him.

'Let's go to the Central Pier,' Agnes said suddenly. 'There might be some dancing and we can have a twirl.'

'All right.' Mary Ann hid a smile. She'd guessed Agnes would want to go there. Central Pier was such a lively place and whenever the weather was fine there were usually people dancing on it in the open air, day and evening. She and Agnes were quite accomplished dancers now, but of course she always had to play the man when the two of them danced together because of being so tall. She didn't mind, though. She didn't mind anything as long as she could be out in the open air with the sun on her face.

She loved living in Blackpool.

The next evening Agnes nipped through the back gate and beckoned urgently to Mary Ann, who was drying the dishes in the scullery.

Miss Thursby popped her head in from the kitchen, which also looked out down the back yard. 'Your friend seems rather excited. You'd better go and see what she wants.'

Agnes clutched Mary Ann's arm and dragged her across to the garden bench. 'You'll never guess what!'

'No I won't, so tell me.'

'Mrs P's daughter is going to take over the boarding house.'

'You expected that.'

'Yes, but it means I shan't be staying after the end of the season. I'm definitely not working for *her*.'

'Oh, no! Oh, Agnes!' Mary Ann hated the thought of not having her friend next door. 'Where shall you go? You've been with Mrs P for ages.'

'I'm leaving Blackpool entirely and going to London!'

Mary Ann stared at her in shock. 'You'll never!'

'I shall too. I've seen adverts for chambermaids in the big hotels there. I fancy doing something a bit different.'

'Oh, dear, I shall miss you dreadfully.'

'No, you won't, because you're coming with me.' Agnes grasped her hand and said coaxingly, 'It's time we moved on, love. We've both been stuck in a rut for years. I stopped minding when I thought I was going to get married, but now I mind very much. I don't want to leave you, but if you refuse to come, well, I'll have to go on my own.'

'Work in London! I *can't!*' The thought of such a big city frightened her.

'Yes, you can. Oh, Mary Ann, surely you don't want us to be separated?'

She definitely didn't. 'I'll have to think about it.'

She did think about it, even consulted her employer, and to her surprise, Miss Thursby agreed with Agnes.

'Whatever you were running away from when you came to me, Mary Ann, is long in the past.' She raised one forefinger to forestall interruptions. 'I've never asked what it was and I'm not going to now. You're a hard worker and honest, which is what matters to me. However, I think it'd do you good to move out into the wider world.' She gave a wry smile. 'I say this even though I shall have trouble replacing you. I shall, of course, provide you with excellent references.'

After that Mary Ann kept waking in the night, panicking about the decision she needed to make. She had been here for six years now and it felt like home – well, as near a home as she could get. She sighed. Even if she stayed, though, her life would change and half the pleasure go out of it without Agnes.

In the end she decided to go, not only for her friend's sake but for her own. Miss Thursby was right. She was going to try to find the courage now to live life more fully. Only – it was hard. And frightening.

Her decision taken, she kept fear at bay by trying to make her preparations methodically. She had come to pride herself on her ability to organise things. She had only one person to write to – Margaret, whose son was now nearly seven. She had come to Blackpool two years previously and spent several days with Mary Ann. They still wrote to one another every month.

'A lot of people in Overdale won't socialise with me because of Johnny,' Margaret had confided wistfully. 'It gets a bit lonely at times, but Mr and Mrs Garbutt are always kind. I see my father sometimes in the street, but he walks past me as if I'm invisible.' She put up her chin. 'It also means he's never met his grandchild. Which is his loss.'

Margaret had pressed Mary Ann to come for a visit to The Sycamores, only she'd never dared go, not after she'd seen how beautifully her friend dressed and how confident she was. But still, it was nice to be asked. Her main reason for refusing, though, was that Margaret lived too near Birtley. She didn't want to run into Mrs Greeson and she didn't want to bump into Ivy Clough, either, though she'd have loved to see Gabriel and his mother again.

Mary Ann sighed. Margaret and Agnes were the only people who really cared about her in the whole world now. Fancy Ivy thinking a lovely fellow like Gabriel Clough would be interested in someone as ordinary as her! She'd still been a child at the time he rescued her, baby or no baby. She knew that now.

She dismissed him from her mind and bent over her letter.

Dear Margaret

I hope you and little Johnny are both well as I am.

This is to tell you that I'll be leaving Blackpool at the end of the season. Agnes's employer is handing over the business to her daughter and Agnes doesn't get on with her, so she and I have decided to look for jobs elsewhere. She favours London, but I don't really mind where we go, except not Brighton, of course. I don't want to bump into my mother or that man again.

Miss Thursby thinks it's the right thing to do and agrees that I've been stuck in a rut, but if so it's been a comfortable rut. Only I can't let Agnes go on her own, can I? Besides, I can always come back to Blackpool if it doesn't work out.

You won't need to worry about me because I have quite a bit of money saved now.

We're still not sure what sort of work we'll look for, whether as housemaids or chambermaids in a hotel, perhaps. I'll let you know where I end up.

Your friend,
Mary Ann

She hesitated, wondering whether this sounded all right and hoping she'd spelled everything properly. She really admired Margaret, who'd had the strength to fight back against what life had dished out and had not only escaped from her father but kept her baby.

She sometimes wondered what would have happened if her own baby had lived. Elizabeth would be a little girl now. Sometimes Mary Ann would watch children playing on the beach and pretend one of them was hers. Sometimes she'd see a girl with dark hair like her own and tears would come into her eyes.

She sighed. It did no good dwelling on painful things, only made you feel downhearted. Instead she licked the envelope and nipped out to post the letter after tea.

To her surprise she received a reply two days later.

Dearest Mary Ann

I'm so glad you're going to do something different. I was afraid you were going to stay in Blackpool doing the same thing for the rest of your life and that would have been such a waste, as I told you when I came to visit. I hope you don't mind my saying it again. It's only because I care about you.

You say you're not certain what to do, except that you want a change, so I mentioned your dilemma to dear Papa Garbutt and he came up with a suggestion. He has an interest in one or two hotels around the country. The one in Bournemouth has just been refurbished and is about to open again. They'll soon be taking on new staff and your training would make both of you suitable as chambermaids, especially if Papa Garbutt writes you a recommendation. I know what a hard worker you are and I'm sure any friend of yours would be the same. I really liked Agnes when we met.

Let me know quickly if you'd like to try it. You'd have your accommodation there, which would be a big help, even if you didn't stay in the job for more than a year or so.

Your friend,
Margaret

Mary Ann read the letter again, liking the suggestion so much more than the idea of going to London. She went to ask Miss

Thursby for a few minutes off and since they were only half-full that week, was able to go next door at once and show the letter to Agnes.

'Write back at once telling her yes,' Agnes said. 'Ooh, this is a godsend!' She nudged Mary Ann in the ribs. 'I've been terrified you'd back out, but you can't now your posh friend is helping us.'

And after that things moved along at such breakneck speed that it seemed no time until the grey, drizzly day in October when Mary Ann and Agnes walked along the platform through clouds of steam to board a train and head south for Bournemouth.

'Isn't it exciting?' Agnes enthused as the train rattled along. 'Clackety-*clack!* Clackety-*clack!*' she chanted in imitation of its sound

'No, terrifying.' Mary Ann had a secret fear of meeting Jeff Powling again in the south, for he travelled on business all the time, but didn't dare admit that to Agnes. Of course he couldn't do anything to her now, because she was probably as tall as him, but still, she definitely didn't want to see him again.

'Oh, you're just being silly.' Agnes looked at her earnestly and patted her hand. 'I know I'm dragging you with me, love, but I do believe it's what you need.' Her eyes crinkled into a smile as she added, 'As well as what I need.'

On the final leg of their long journey to Bournemouth, the train suddenly began to brake hard and rock wildly from side to side. People cried out in shock and Mary Anne, who was sitting at the inner end of the compartment, peered down the corridor, worried about Agnes who had gone to the toilet.

Just as her friend appeared at the other end of the carriage, looking terrified and having difficulty staying upright, there was a thump that shook the whole train and everyone was tossed around like rag dolls.

Mary Ann cried out as she was thrown clear across the compartment and then the world turned black around her.

11

October – December 1913

Gabriel looked out of the bedroom window at his daughters skipping in the back garden, ropes thwacking on the paved area and voices chanting some rhyme in unison. At six, Frances was only the same height as four-year-old Christina who promised to be very tall, like him. He always told them when Frances complained about the unfairness of this that she took after her mother and Christina after him.

He loved them both dearly, but the estrangement from his wife had progressed to the stage where he had built himself a bedroom off the kitchen and was now moving out of the room they'd shared uneasily for the past few years. The only thing he'd miss about it would be the view of the walled back garden and beyond it the moors, whose rippling grasses reminded him sometimes of his visits to the seaside. It'd be wonderful not to have to put up with Ivy's sharp remarks as they got ready for bed or her equally sharp silences, though.

If it weren't for Mary Ann, he'd never have met Ivy and sometimes he wished he hadn't, though not when he was with his daughters.

His wife had said nothing when he'd announced he was building himself a separate bedroom downstairs, just as she was saying nothing now. She sat in the kitchen, drinking a cup of tea in slow sips as she watched him bring his things down. But although the anger might not be there on her face, it showed in every line of her too-thin body.

In the end that annoyed him and he paused in the doorway of his new bedroom off the kitchen to ask, 'Why are you so angry? After all you don't really want me in your bed and you'll be able to have your room exactly as you like now. I told you we could afford to redecorate it.'

'Did I say a word? *Did I?* I'm sure you can do as you please in your mother's house. You always do anyway, so I've given up trying to argue. I'm glad to be rid of the mess, though. You've no idea how hard it is to keep everything clean while there's building going on.'

He bit back further angry words. What good did it do to argue? His mother still did most of the housework while Ivy tended the chickens, collected and washed the eggs, got things ready for market and worked in the vegetable garden, as well as keeping their account books. He knew she hated looking after the chickens, but when she'd hinted about giving it up and getting in a girl to help, he'd told her straight it was the least she could do, given the circumstances. She'd not said another word about it since. And she did the work efficiently – well, she did everything efficiently and that was part of the trouble. A woman like her needed more outlet for her cleverness than she could find in a quiet moorland hamlet. But he refused to feel guilty about that. She had chosen to marry him and must take the consequences.

When he'd finished moving his clothing, he looked round his new bedroom and heaved a sigh of both relief and pleasure. Although he was a normal man and found a celibate life frustrating, for him love-making without affection was a contradiction in terms and it froze something in him even to try. So he'd turned to the things he could enjoy instead.

He'd be able to read in bed now without anyone complaining. Next to his children, reading was his greatest pleasure in life. He'd moved his bookcase in here, bought a new incandesent reading lamp for the side of the bed, one with a special mantle that gave a particularly bright light. Ivy had grumbled about that, saying she had enough oil lamps to clean without him adding such a fancy one, but he intended to look after this beauty himself. He'd also found himself a small desk. Not that he did a lot of writing, but he'd seen the piece going cheap on a market stall, battered and faded by the sun but still sound, and had fancied owning it.

Ivy hadn't said a word about this purchase, either positive or negative, not one single word.

His mother hadn't commented on the move either when he'd asked her if she'd mind him building on another bedroom next to hers. She said he could do what he wanted with the house that would be his one day. So he'd had a load of stone delivered, hired a builder and helped him as much as possible to keep the costs down.

His mother had run her fingers over the desk when he'd brought it back and said it'd come up lovely with a bit of elbow grease. She'd spent days polishing it up for him until it gleamed like warm honey in the lamplight and had also made him a new bedspread and a huge fat cushion to put behind him so that he could read more comfortably in bed. She never spoke her love for him, but it showed in so many small ways.

When he'd finished moving his stuff, she joined him in the new room and went to smooth the bedspread, which was a rich ruby red. 'I thought this would look good in here and it does, warms up the grey of the stone walls nicely. We'll get you a red rug to keep your feet warm, too. These flagstones can be a bit chilly in winter, but you can light a fire sometimes. I'm glad you had a fireplace put in.'

He'd also had a grate put in her bedroom next to his because he'd noticed she moved more stiffly in the colder weather. 'Eh, you're a lovely mum!' He clipped her up in a big hug. 'Thank you for the bedspread.'

For once she let him hug her, not saying anything but patting his cheek and giving him a shy smile from the closeness of his arms. Then she pushed him away and bustled around with unnecessary vigour for the next few minutes.

Mary Ann knew nothing more until a woman's voice said, 'This one's coming round.'

A man said, 'Stay with her and make sure she's all right.'

She groaned as pain stabbed through her head and it was an effort to open her eyes. She found herself lying on the grass in the shade of some trees, one of a whole row of figures. Then she saw the train wreckage at the other side of the field and gasped. Of course! There must have been an accident.

Pushing herself up into a sitting position and trying to ignore the pounding behind her eyes, she noticed another group of people lying further away. Their heads and bodies were completely covered by blood-stained blankets and she realised with a sinking sensation in her belly that they were dead.

It must have been a very bad accident indeed to kill so many!

Dragging her eyes away from them, she looked at the people lying nearby, many of whom had torn and bloodstained clothing. When she looked down, she saw that hers was the same. One woman was weeping quietly, her arm over her eyes; a man nearby let out a groan and then began to curse in a low voice.

A woman's voice spoke near her head. 'There's been an accident, my dear. You were knocked out by the impact, I'm afraid. How do you feel now?'

Mary Ann looked at the speaker but could not answer because she was still trying to come to terms with the horrors around her. Her eyes kept going back to the remains of several carriages which formed a great tangle of twisted metal with one carriage jutting up at an angle into the air, its battered end resting on the others. Men were working on the wreckage, clambering across it and calling to one another, but they were too far away for her to hear what they were saying. Then one of them waved his hand in a beckoning gesture and another man picked his way across the wreckage to help him lift a woman's body through one of the smashed windows. Even from this distance she could see that the body was bloody and not moving at all.

A hand grasped her shoulder for a minute, so that she had to pay attention. 'How do you feel? Please answer me.'

The words came slowly. 'My head hurts – but apart from that

I'm all right. At least, I think I am.' Again Mary Ann looked at the unconscious figures lying nearby. 'I can't see my friend, though. I must find her.' She tried to get up, but the woman pushed her back down and she felt too weak to insist.

'You need to rest for a minute or two first. You had a nasty bump and there's a big bruise on one side of your forehead as well as grazes on your cheeks. I think the blood on your blouse is from someone else, though, because I can't find any other injuries.' She smiled reassuringly. 'I've no medical training, but we were passing in a car and saw the accident so stopped to help. I'm Daphne Bingram, by the way.'

'Mary Ann Baillie.' She sighed and looked at the other woman, really looked. Her nurse was older, about sixty perhaps, and well-dressed, though like everyone else's her clothes were dirtied. 'I'm all right, really I am. I just – I don't like the sight of blood. But I can't rest easy till I've found Agnes.'

'No, I suppose not. Let me help you up, then. Goodness, you're tall.'

Mary Ann leaned for a moment on the stranger's shoulder but she was feeling more in control of her body by the minute. 'Thank you for your help.'

'I'm happy to be of use. I presume your friend was in the same compartment as you?'

'Yes, but she had just gone to the toilet, so she was standing down the corridor by the far door when it happened. Where should I start to look?'

'I don't know, my dear, but I think I'd better come with you in case you get dizzy.'

They walked slowly up and down the rows of injured people because Mary Ann didn't see how Agnes could possibly have escaped injury.

But her friend wasn't there.

She turned and began to move towards the wreckage, thinking Agnes must still be trapped inside it, but before she had gone more than a few steps a man hurried across to bar their way. He was wearing the remnants of a guard's uniform and still had that official air, even though he had one arm in a sling, sticking plaster on his forehead and no cap.

'You can't go past here, miss. We're still getting bodies out.' He looked at her companion and bobbed his head. 'Sorry, your ladyship.'

'Oh.' Mary Ann looked at her too. Had the man really called her *your ladyship?* Then worry for her friend took over again. 'Agnes can't be *dead!*'

'We must hope not.' Daphne Bingram turned to the guard and said in an educated, upper-class voice, 'I think we need to check the bodies you've already found because the young woman we're seeking isn't among the injured.' She saw Mary Ann turn so white she put an arm round her waist again. 'Take a deep breath. And another. You're not going to faint on me, are you? That won't do any good.'

Mary Ann took several deep breaths. 'I'm – all right now. Really. Only – I've never seen a dead body before.' Not even her own baby's. She'd often wished they'd let her hold Elizabeth.

'Bodies are only people, my dear. Shall I go first and see if there's a young woman among them? What was your friend wearing?'

'A navy skirt, white blouse and navy jacket. She's got dark, frizzy hair and a thin face.' Mary Ann leaned against a tree as she watched Lady Bingram deal briskly with the man overseeing the dead bodies. The two of them moved along the row of still figures, with the man lifting the blanket from each female body for a moment. Every time she saw her ladyship shake her head, Mary Ann let out a shuddering breath of relief.

When the other woman came back, she said bracingly, 'Well, at least your friend's not there, my dear. We'd better look elsewhere.' She beckoned the guard over again and of course he came, standing with head cocked deferentially, waiting to see what she wanted. 'Are there any others?'

'Some folk have been taken to a nearby farm. They were the lucky ones from the rear carriages. Shaken up but with no serious injuries.'

'Agnes was in the same carriage as me,' Mary Ann said. She saw his face suddenly become expressionless and felt panic run through her. 'What are you hiding from me?'

'There are a few others who're pretty badly injured. They've got them over in the corner.' He gestured to an area shielded by what looked like sheets pinned to poles and trees.

Mary Ann immediately set off walking and when her companion ran after her, linking arms in a way that reminded her so much of Agnes, she could not prevent tears from welling in her eyes. 'We have to find her alive,' she whispered. 'We just have to.'

In the sheltered corner another well-dressed lady stopped them and Daphne quickly explained what they wanted. The stranger looked at them so sadly that for a moment Mary Ann couldn't seem to breathe.

'We've got a young woman answering that description who's badly hurt, I'm afraid. We've been trying to find someone who knows her. I think she might be your friend.'

Mary Ann had to force the words out. 'How badly is she hurt?'

'She's dying, I'm afraid.' The woman studied Mary Ann's face. 'If she's your friend, you can be of great comfort to her because she's still conscious. You must be very brave and think of her, not your own feelings. Can you do that?' When the young woman didn't reply, she added firmly, 'I shan't take you to her unless you promise me not to burden her with your grief.'

Daphne was beside her again. 'I'll go with Mary Ann. We've only just met but I think I can support her through this.'

'Lady Bingram, isn't it? Very well then.' The other woman turned back to Mary Ann. 'You're sure you can cope?'

She somehow found the strength to nod.

'Good girl. Come this way.' She led them behind the temporary screen to a corner shielded by yet more sheets. Behind it were three makeshift mattresses with still figures lying on them.

Agnes was at the end, almost unrecognisable, her face was so battered. As Mary Ann knelt by the bed, Agnes's eyes opened, flickered uncomprehendingly then settled on her friend's face. As recognition dawned she tried to smile and whispered, 'Glad you're all right, love. Nice black eye you've got there.'

Somehow Mary Ann found the strength to speak steadily. 'I was knocked out for a bit. When I came to I started looking for you. I'm so glad I've found you, love.'

The stranger leaned forward. 'They'll take you to hospital as soon as the ambulances arrive, my dear. Does it hurt?'

Agnes blinked, tried to focus on her, then abandoned the attempt and shook her head. 'Can't feel – a thing.'

'Shock does that to you.'

Mary Ann took hold of her friend's bloodied left hand because the right one was swathed in thick bandages. Somehow she managed another smile. 'I'll stay with you till you have to leave, shall I, love?'

'Please.' Agnes sighed and closed her eyes. 'So glad you're here. Feel better – now.'

Mary Ann blinked furiously and stayed kneeling beside her.

Once Agnes opened her eyes, saw her still there and smiled. 'We wanted an adventure, didn't we? Don't let the accident put you off, love. You can't stay in a rut all your life.'

Her voice was so faint Mary Ann had to lean close to hear what she was saying. 'No, I won't let it stop me.'

'Even with this, we were – so right – to come. Hope they – keep my job – till I'm better.'

There was silence and her breathing became even fainter, her chest hardly moving now.

Mary Ann bent forward to kiss her cheek. 'I'm sure they will.'

Daphne was behind her and as the minutes passed she laid one hand on the younger woman's shoulder, giving it a quick squeeze.

Mary Ann looked up gratefully. It was good to know she wasn't alone.

Agnes opened her eyes but didn't focus on anything. 'You're – a lovely – friend,' she whispered and sighed.

The silence that followed wasn't punctuated by any more of those shallow breaths.

The older woman stepped forward to kneel on the grass by Agnes's other side and feel for her pulse. Shaking her head, she closed the staring eyes, looked at Mary Ann and said simply, 'She's gone, dear.'

'She can't be dead! *She can't!*'

'I'm afraid so.'

Mary Ann bowed her head and wept on Daphne's shoulder, trying to muffle her sobs because of the other injured people nearby. After a while the older woman held her at arm's length and said in a quiet, level tone, 'You can't do anything more for her now, but I'm so glad we were in time. You were obviously a great comfort to her.'

'Was I?' Her eyes went back to the still figure on the mattress.

'Yes. And very brave.' After a pause she said, 'Now, I gather there isn't anyone else with you?'

'No.'

'Then you'd better come home with me. I'll give you a bed for the night, then we'll see what needs doing next.'

'We'll have to – let her family know,' Mary Ann said slowly, trying to think things through.

'If you give me their address, I'll send a telegram. Come on. Let's go and tell someone in authority where you're going, then we'll find my car.'

'My luggage.' Mary Ann looked down at her torn, stained clothing. 'I haven't any clean clothes.'

'We'll find it later, and in the meantime I'll lend you something to wear.'

For once Mary Ann was glad to let someone else take charge. She felt weary as well as desperately sad so let Daphne guide her across the field towards a motor vehicle. They sat in it for a few minutes, then a man in a stained chauffeur's uniform made his way across to them.

'Can you take us home now, Chesney? Miss Baillie needs a bath and a bed for the night. Then you can bring the car back and see if there's any other way to help.'

'Yes, m'lady.'

It didn't even register with Mary Ann until the next day that it was her first ride in a motor car, and even then it didn't feel important. All she could think of was that Agnes was dead. Her dearest friend.

It should have been her that was killed, not Agnes, because no one really cared about her, but her friend would be mourned by a large, loving family.

Mary Ann found the hot bath her hostess insisted on immensely comforting and stayed in it until the water was lukewarm, reluctant to face the world again. She wept once more but it didn't seem to ease the deep sadness weighing heavily inside her.

When she went back to her bedroom, clutching Lord Bingram's old dressing gown around her, she found that her hostess had provided her with some clean clothes and underclothing. The skirt and the blouse sleeves were too short, but what did that matter?

She went downstairs, feeling shy now in such grand surroundings, and met an elderly maid in the hall.

The woman looked at her sympathetically. 'Lady Bingram's waiting for you in the small sitting-room, miss.' She opened a door for Mary Ann.

'Oh, there you are, dear. Come and sit down. Peggy, will you bring us a tea tray now?' She turned back to her visitor. 'My husband doesn't get home until after six, so there's just you and me.'

Mary Ann went to sit with her in front of a bright fire, feeling numb and boneless. The thought of food nauseated her, but she drank several cups of tea then sighed and looked at her hostess. 'It's very kind of you to have me.'

'It's the least I could do. They're driving those who aren't injured into the next town and sending them on by train. I thought you'd prefer to stay here until your friend's family arrive.'

'Yes. You've contacted them?'

'I sent a telegram. I presume one of them will come down to – um – see to things.'

'Arrange the funeral, you mean?'

'Yes.'

Mary Ann realised her hostess wasn't quite sure how to treat her so said bluntly, 'I'd rather talk about Agnes than not, actually. Where have they taken her?'

'Into Bournemouth. They've taken all the dead there until after the inquest.' Daphne saw her guest's puzzled look and said gently, 'There always has to be an inquest when there's an accident or sudden death. They can't bury your friend until that's over.'

'I'll have to let the hotel know what's happened. We were supposed to be starting work there tomorrow.' Mary Ann's voice wobbled on the last words.

'We can telephone them if you like.'

'Thank you. I'd like to do that as soon as possible, if you don't mind. Only – I've never used a telephone before. Can you show me how, please?'

Telling the manager of the hotel about Agnes made her weep again and when her hostess took the ear and mouth pieces out of her hands and finished explaining, Mary Ann let her.

Daphne put down the phone and gestured to her guest to precede her into the sitting room. 'He says to take your time. Your job will be waiting for you as soon as you're well enough to cope. He sounds a decent sort.'

'Thank you.'

The rest of the day passed in a blur. Lord Bingram returned in the evening and was as kind as his wife, both of them urging Mary Ann to stay for a few days.

A telegram arrived from Agnes's father, saying he was on his way. Apparently the railway company had offered to put relatives up in Bournemouth.

It was several days before Mary Ann got her luggage back and she marvelled at how easy it felt to be with the Bingrams. Daphne was a busy woman, but not too busy to keep an eye on her guest, and the servants all went about their work in a way that said more clearly than words that they were happy here.

Mary Ann felt nervous at first at mealtimes, in case her manners weren't good enough, but after the first couple of times she realised she needn't have worried. Daphne and her husband seemed to keep open house with people of all sorts coming and going, joining them for a meal or for a couple of days. If she hadn't felt so sad about Agnes, she'd have enjoyed herself immensely, but the sadness kept taking her by surprise. Tears would come suddenly into her eyes as the sharpness of her loss sliced through her.

She decided not to return to Blackpool for Agnes's funeral, feeling she had said goodbye to her friend after the crash. That was much more important to her, bringing a great sense of comfort. She wrote to Miss Thursby explaining what had happened and enclosing the money for a bunch of flowers. She didn't even need to ask to know that her former employer would be happy to buy them for her and have them taken to Agnes's family.

Her trunk arrived at last. It had been in the guard's van and hadn't suffered too badly, but her suitcase was very battered.

'I think,' she said when she saw it, 'I'll buy a new one. That one has a bloodstain on it.' She shuddered.

'We've got an old suitcase you can have,' Daphne said at once.

'I can't keep taking things from you. You won't even let me help in the house to pay you back.'

Daphne grinned at her. 'I should think not. Guests get waited on – whether they want it or not. Besides, think how virtuous it makes me feel to help you.'

That even drew a half-smile from Mary Ann, though she felt guilty about it afterwards. How could she be smiling so soon after Agnes's death?

She lay awake for a long time that night, thinking things through as was her wont, and came to the conclusion that her friend would have been the first one to tell her to get on with life. So that was what she intended to do. She was never going to stay in a rut again. She owed that to Agnes – and to herself.

But she wouldn't forget her friend. Never, ever.

A week later Daphne escorted Mary Ann into Bournemouth to

start work at the hotel. She asked her chauffeur to take them for a quick drive round the town centre first. Mary Ann loved the tall pine trees that grew here and there, and listened with interest as Daphne explained about the various chines or ravines which broke the line of cliffs. The town centre was built around the large chine along which the Bourne Brook ran and seemed very elegant.

There were no rows of boarding houses along the sea front as in Blackpool, just a long promenade at the foot of the cliffs, with pretty gardens to walk in. But there was a pier. She did love a pier!

They drove up East Overcliffe Drive to the Charrington, which seemed very large to Mary Ann, for it was several storeys high and built in an E-shape. But to her surprise Daphne said it was only medium-sized compared to the big London hotels. It stood at the top of East Cliff, looking out across the sea, and had neat, sheltered gardens to one side, leading down to a small sheltered chine where a few guests were strolling around.

The manager, Mr Farran, fussed over Lady Bingram, escorting her to the front door himself when she left. She looked over her shoulder at Mary Ann, winked and said loudly, 'I shall be coming to see you next Sunday, don't forget, and remember that if you ever need anywhere to stay, you can always come back to us.'

He stood watching the chauffeur drive her away and came back to Mary Ann, rubbing his hands because it was a cold day. 'You fell lucky there, young woman.'

'Yes, sir. Her ladyship has been very kind to me.' She didn't call Daphne by her first name when others were around, only when they were alone together.

'Well, I'd better introduce you to the housekeeper.'

Mrs Upton was brisk and efficient. 'You may as well start work straight away. You *are* all right now, aren't you? That must have been a nasty blow to leave a bruise still.'

'I'm fine and I'd prefer to get to work. I don't like to be idle.' She'd had too many hours to sit and think at the Bingrams', but couldn't have started work until she received her luggage and her own clothes.

Bob Hall, the head porter, helped carry Mary Ann's trunk up to the room she would be sharing with a young Irishwoman called Colleen and lingered behind after his assistant had left.

'We were all sorry to hear about your loss,' he said quietly. 'If there's anything I can do to help, you have only to ask.'

She managed to say, 'Thank you,' but found it easier if people didn't display sympathy because it made her want to weep.

At first everyone spoke to her gently and treated her as if she might burst into tears at any moment, but to her relief that soon wore off in the busy life of the hotel. The work proved easy enough for Mary Ann, who'd been a bit worried about fitting in, and there was no time to be idle, thank goodness.

On her days off she went for long walks, enjoying the views from the cliffs, for you could see in the distance the Needles, a chain of rocks which formed the western end of the Isle of Wight, Bob told her. She also liked to see liners sailing towards Southampton or coming from that port. It was all so much busier than the sea off Blackpool.

From the cliff tops little paths zig-zagged down to the promenade below. It made a lovely walk into the town centre. At first she went on her own, then occasionally with her room-mate Colleen. She missed Agnes's lively conversation greatly because Colleen seemed to talk of little but her family in Ireland to whom she was sending half her wages. Or if not her family, she went on about her religion, which seemed to demand a great deal of her time and to control most of her actions.

It was all very different from Blackpool, but the sea was still the same and Mary Ann loved to catch glimpses of it as she worked in the guests' bedrooms.

Christmas passed in a blur. She didn't feel like celebrating this year, though Margaret wrote and sent a present.

Daphne Bingram also sent a card and turned up just as Mary Ann was going off duty on Christmas Eve to sweep her into town for a special tea with cream cakes.

Mary Ann couldn't understand why such a rich woman would bother with an ordinary person like her and in the end had to ask.

'Because I admired the way you coped with your friend's death. Because – oh, sometimes I grow a little tired of pretending we're better than other people just because my husband has a title. I come from the north originally like your mother. We're more down to earth up there, I think.'

As Mary Ann gaped at her frankness, Daphne added, 'Am I driving you mad? Shall I stop pestering you? I do enjoy your company, you know. I like to speak to young people and to those who work for their living, not just drones who've inherited money someone else laboured for.'

'I was worried you'd be bored and were just being kind,' Mary Ann confessed.

'Not at all. You make some very sensible comments on life and that does me good.'

As she left she reached into the car and pushed a big box into Mary Ann's hands, smiling as she said firmly, 'Not to be opened until tomorrow.'

Which made two presents Mary Ann had received, when she'd expected to get none. She had tears in her eyes as she opened them the following day, to find a book from Margaret and a very pretty dressing gown in a deep rose colour from Daphne. In losing one friend she had made another, it seemed. She bought some fine lawn and embroidered a pair of handkerchiefs for Daphne and Margaret, using a delicate white satin stitch and adding a narrow band of lace round the edge. If she said so herself, you could buy no finer in the shops.

As New Year approached and people talked about their hopes for the coming year, Mary Ann could not help contemplating her own future. For the time being she was quite content to work at the Charrington. Everyone told her you needed time to recover from the loss of a dear one, and they were right.

But she wasn't staying there for ever. She intended to do something with her life that would have made Agnes proud of her. She didn't know what yet, but something.

It seemed only right.

12

January 1914

One market day Ivy noticed that Dan Barworth's stall wasn't set up and asked the neighbouring stallkeeper where he was.

'Eh, didn't you hear?'

'Hear what? The wind over the moor is about all we hear out at our farm.'

'Mavis Barworth died on Monday. Pneumonia, it were. Came on her sudden and she was gone just like that.' He snapped his fingers.

'Goodness!'

'Only forty. She was a few year older than him, of course. You don't expect 'em to go at forty, do you? Poor Dan'll be lost without her. Such a pity they never had children. They'd be a right comfort to him now.'

Ivy didn't agree that Dan would be lost. She found him very shrewd and he'd offered her various pieces of advice in the early days of running the stall which had helped improve sales. She always looked forward to his cheerful conversation but was surprised by how much she missed him that day. Far more than she'd expected to.

'Mavis Barworth died last week,' she said over tea that night. 'Did you know?'

Gabriel nodded. 'Aye. I heard summat when I went down to the library on Tuesday.'

'You might have told me. I felt a right fool not knowing.'

He shrugged. 'You've never mentioned her. Didn't think she was one of your market friends.'

'I've been running a stall near theirs for years, for heaven's sake. Of *course* I know – knew them. Dan's been a really good friend to me. He always helps me with the heavy things.'

'Aye, well, I didn't think. Does it really matter enough to make a fuss about?'

Ivy filtered air in through her nose, itching to say more but knowing Gabriel hated disagreements and would never argue about anything. Sometimes she wondered if he hated her for what she had done to him, though he had never been anything except polite to her. *Polite!* That was not how a husband and wife should be. It was a godsend as well as a surprise that he seemed genuinely to love Frances, while the child adored him.

The following week Dan was back behind his stall, wearing a black armband and looking tired.

'I was sorry to hear about your wife,' Ivy said during a quiet period.

He glanced round as if to check that they weren't being overheard. 'I was sorry Mavis died so young, for her sake, but I'm glad to be free of her.' He gave Ivy a wry look. 'Now I suppose you'll think ill of me? Only I couldn't lie to *you* about it, lass. Me and Mavis haven't got on for years. She was a miserable creature, always mithering on about summat.'

Ivy thought it best not to comment on that.

He shot her a quick glance, hesitated, then added in a low voice, 'From things you've let drop, I've a notion you're in the same boat as I used to be – not exactly happy in your marriage?'

If he could be frank, so could she. In fact, it'd be a relief to talk to someone. 'No, not particularly.'

'I thought not.'

She didn't want him to blame Gabriel, so added, 'It's mostly my fault. I tricked him into marriage. Frances isn't his. I was desperate, but I should've known he'd guess.' She gave a shaky laugh. 'Eh, I've never told anyone about that before. You won't let on, will you?'

'Of course I won't, love. Don't you know me better than that?'

A customer came up just then and Dan turned to greet the woman and receive the inevitable condolences, his expression solemn once more.

When she'd moved on, he said in a growling undertone, 'I'm sick to death of pretending to be the grieving widower.'

'Well, don't let on how you feel to anyone except me or they'll throw a fit.'

'Aye, I know.'

As they were clearing up their stalls that afternoon he said suddenly, 'Why don't you come for a cup of tea with me in the Penny Cafe?'

'I can't do that!'

'Why not?'

'I'm a married woman.'

'You're a stallholder as well. Lots of folk nip over there for a quick cuppa after they've packed up. Any road, you don't seem married when you come to market. You're different here, more cheerful, more yourself. I've seen you shopping with your husband in Overdale and you look a bit grim sometimes, as if you're irritated with him.'

She stared at Dan in shock. 'Is it so obvious?'

'Not to most folk. It takes one to know one.' When she didn't speak for a minute or two, he repeated softly, 'Come on. Just one cup of tea. Where's the harm in that?'

'What'll I say to folk?'

'You don't need to say owt to most of 'em. You can tell your husband I needed to ask your advice about getting help in the house – which I do – unless you don't *want* to come with me?'

She did want to, wanted it very much, because his gaze was warm and he was looking at her the way a man looks at a woman he fancies. Something inside her stirred, something warm and girlish and happy. She'd missed that feeling. Gabriel wouldn't care if she dressed in old sacks, never really looked at her these days, and she avoided him as much as you could in a small house. Even when they were in the same room, there were the children and his mother, so they never really talked as she could to Dan. Had they ever done? She hesitated and was lost. 'All right. But just for half an hour. I'll have to pack up first, think on.'

'I'll help you.' They packed everything quickly and she borrowed one of the market trolleys to take what wasn't sold to her trap, which she always left at the Shepherd's Rest. There wasn't much to take home. She was good now at judging how much she could sell. And as usual Jassy would use the spare eggs to make lemon cheese, which Ivy would sell at the next market.

In the café she and Dan said nothing that could not have been overheard and certainly they didn't touch one another, but the feeling was there between them nonetheless, a ribbon of warmth flowing from one to the other as they chatted.

'I've right enjoyed your company,' Dan said quietly as he walked her back to the inn.

Ivy didn't dare tell him how much she'd enjoyed his. Far too much for her own peace of mind.

As she drove the placid mare home more slowly than usual she was lost in thought, feeling by turns guilty and excited. How was she to wait another whole week to see him, talk to him?

And how much longer could she stand this tedious life?

She'd thought she could do anything for her children, but she grew less sure of that with each year that passed. Anyway, the girls both preferred Gabriel, were all over him in the evening, letting him read stories to them, playing Snap or just curling up on his lap and staring into the fire.

When she reached the farm Gabriel came out to help with the horse. 'You're late today. I was getting a bit worried.'

'I had a cup of tea with Dan Barworth in the Penny Café after we closed up. He wanted to ask me about getting help with the housework.' She managed a cheerful smile. Well, she hoped she looked cheerful. 'Eh, you men are that ignorant about it! He hadn't a clue what sort of help he'd need.'

'Nice of you to take the trouble. But I doubt he'll be grieving for long. He's well set up and some woman or other will snare him.'

She breathed deeply but didn't say, As I snared you. He often used that phrase: women *snaring* men. It made her want to yell at him, though she rarely allowed herself that luxury.

Gabriel gazed into the distance for a moment or two, then shook his head and turned back to her. 'Look, I'll unload tonight. You go inside and get warm.'

'Thanks.' At the back door, though, she had to stop and take a couple of deep breaths before she could face Jassy Clough's shrewd gaze.

The girls were already eating their tea, so Ivy joined them at the table, making an effort to ask about their day as she counted out the takings.

It seemed ages till she could escape to her bed. She lay wakeful long after the parlour clock had chimed midnight, going over and over her time with Dan.

He fancied her, no doubt about that, and she fancied him. Gabriel might be better looking, but Dan was fun to be with.

The question was: did she want to encourage him?

The answer wasn't hard: yes, she did.

But there was another question too: where could it possibly lead if she did? She didn't intend to jump from the frying pan into the fire. Definitely not!

Quite a few of the guests left newspapers in their rooms, so Mary Ann asked Mrs Upton if she could take one to read.

'Fond of newspapers, are you?'

Mary Ann shrugged. 'I want to learn a bit more about the world, that's all. It makes you think, being in an accident like that.' And what she'd decided was that she was too ignorant about the world in which she lived.

Mrs Upton's voice grew gentler. 'Yes, I suppose it would.'

But many of the newspaper articles were too hard for Mary Ann, full of long words and talking about things that made no sense to her. One mild late January afternoon she found herself a sheltered seat just below the path that led along the top of East Cliff and sat puzzling over an article on women's suffrage, utterly amazed that women, many of them *ladies*, could act so violently.

Someone cleared their throat next to her and she looked up to see Bob Hall, the head porter, standing there cap in hand.

Anna Jacobs

'I wondered if you'd like a little company?' He added hastily, 'I don't want to intrude, though, and shan't be at all offended if you prefer to be on your own. We all need some peace and quiet at times.'

She found him pleasant enough, an earnest, hard-working man about ten years older than herself, so gestured to the seat. 'There's plenty of room.'

'I've seen you bringing newspapers out here to read,' he said. 'I do the same on fine days.'

'I'm trying to improve my mind. Only I can't understand half of this.' She tapped the newspaper sharply, her forefinger pointing to the article. 'Why are these women doing it?'

'Well, they think they should have the vote, same as men.'

'I know that and I agree with them, but I wouldn't chain myself to railings or break people's windows to get it. Why do they do such terrible things? How can that help their cause?'

'Heaven alone knows.' He glanced at her sideways. 'Would you really like the vote?'

'Yes, I would. I work as hard as any man and I've got a brain, even if it's not very well educated.'

'Don't tell Mrs Upton about your feelings. She hates suffragettes with a passion.'

'Oh, she's all right.'

He grinned. Of course Mrs Upton was all right with Mary Ann. They all knew she was the hardest worker of the bunch. Some of the other chambermaids were flibbertigibbets who skimped on the work if they thought they could get away with it. 'I don't understand a lot of the stuff in the newspapers either,' he offered. 'The *Illustrated London News* is my favourite. I like a good picture with an article. It can make you understand better what they're on about. I've got a few copies I can lend you, if you like?'

She shot him a suspicious glance but he had such a plain, kind face she couldn't imagine him having a hidden motive. All the girls liked him, which was more than you could say for Mr Preston, the new assistant manager. 'Thanks. I'd like that. I used to read *Peg's Paper*, but since the accident it seems so – well, childish. I

170

got a copy of *Home Chat* last week, but that's not much better. It didn't tell me about this sort of thing and I've no one to ask.' She frowned at the newspaper again and the silence continued for a few minutes, a comfortable silence that she didn't feel any urge to fill with meaningless words.

'You must miss your friend,' he said eventually.

She found she could talk about Agnes to him, which surprised her. She couldn't talk about her to anyone else except Daphne, though she'd written a couple of letters about her feelings to Margaret. 'I do miss her. Dreadfully. We'd been best friends since I was sixteen. It was she who insisted we move away from Blackpool and see something of the world. It's funny, but now she's gone, I feel I have to go on trying new things and improving myself – or else what was the purpose of her death?'

'Do you think there was any purpose?' he wondered aloud. 'Death just happens. Blind chance, I reckon. I was engaged once and she died. It seemed unfair. Mary wasn't pretty, but she was kind and loving. I know we'd have been happy together. Why should she die and not me?'

'That's just what I thought after the accident.'

They sat on together, their conversation turning to the hotel and this week's guests, then he pulled out his watch and flicked open the case. 'I'd better be getting back now.'

'Me too.'

When they stood up, she realised he was a bit shorter than she was, though a strong man. His hair was greying at the temples, but he had a good complexion and his face always looked newly scrubbed. She liked the way he was neat and tidy, not only in his dress but in the way he did things.

He smiled at her as they began to walk back. 'I've enjoyed our little chat.'

'So have I.'

Funny to sit and chat to a man. But she didn't feel threatened by Bob. You simply couldn't imagine him being unkind or violent to anyone, for all he was a strong man.

*   *   *

On her next afternoon off Mary Ann found Bob waiting for her at the back entrance. He flushed as he stepped forward. 'I've got the afternoon off, too, and – well, I wondered if you'd like some company? I'd thought of walking into town, having a cup of tea, perhaps. It looks like staying fine.'

She guessed it was not pure chance that he was off at this time too. Should she accept his offer? Did she want the rest of the staff talking about them? But she thought how lonely it was on her own and guessed that he was lonely too. An offer of friendship wasn't something to be refused lightly. 'I – well – all right, then.'

They made their way slowly down the cliff path and into town, with a brisk wind buffeting them as they walked. Only a few hardy souls were strolling along the beach.

'I couldn't have sat reading a paper today,' Mary Ann said, holding on to her hat and laughing in exhilaration. 'I love it when it's windy.'

'I like it best on a fine winter's day when it's not crowded with holidaymakers.'

'Me, too.'

They walked on in silence. A little later, he said, 'It's good to be with someone who can stride out.'

'It comes of being so tall.'

He smiled at her. 'It suits you to be tall. You're a strong woman. I don't think you've come into your own yet, you know.'

She stopped walking to stare at him in surprise. 'What makes you say that?'

He shrugged. 'I don't know. I just think it. I've been watching you. You're very capable. I don't think you even realise how capable.'

Which made her blink in surprise and then feel a sense of pleasure at being appreciated.

In town he insisted on buying them tea and some scones, though the scones weren't nearly as good as those offered at the hotel. She felt a little uneasy with this. Friendship was one thing. Anything else was – not acceptable.

'Can we do this again?' he asked as they walked back up the hill.

'Do what?'

'Spend our afternoon off together?'

She felt flustered. 'Won't it look – a bit particular?'

'It might. But it's only as particular as *you* let it be. We'll just stay friends, if that's all you want.'

His eyes said he wanted more, though. She swallowed hard and tried to find the words to refuse his offer without hurting or offending him, but they'd got to the hotel by then. He smiled at her, tipped his cap and hurried away – and she could only watch him go, the words still unspoken. He'd be waiting for her next week, she knew, unless she said something to stop him in the meantime.

She lay awake for a long time that night. She'd refused to let other men court her and genuinely didn't want to get married, so it wouldn't be fair to let Bob think their friendship could mean anything more.

But he'd said *only as particular as you let it be*. So perhaps he could be just a friend. She really missed having a friend whom she could see regularly. Daphne Bingram might come to see her, but Mary Ann could never feel it right to go and visit a titled lady without being invited.

As she was drifting towards sleep she realised suddenly that she didn't have to decide anything now. After another outing or two, then she'd know better how things stood.

And being with Bob might protect her from the assistant manager's attentions, which were beginning to worry her.

Two weeks later Mary Ann and Bob spent another afternoon together. As they were leaving the café to walk back to the hotel, a noise erupted further down the street in the direction of the Square, women's voices yelling.

Bob paused. 'Sounds like someone's in trouble.' As the shouting continued, he said, 'I don't like to think of anyone hurting a woman. Let's go and see what's up.'

They both began to walk towards the commotion and then stopped dead as the reason for the noise came into view.

'By heck, it's them suffragettes!' he exclaimed. 'In Bournemouth, too. The nerve of them!'

Fascinated, Mary Ann watched the small group of women come into view, marching along the centre of the road with heads held up proudly, though some of their clothes were spattered with mud and rotten fruit, or worse. They were all wearing green, white and violet sashes, and the two who looked the youngest seemed more nervous than the others.

A man next to Bob picked up a stone to throw, but he knocked it out of the fellow's hand with an angry, 'I don't agree with what they're doing either, but there's no need for that.'

The woman walking nearest to them smiled at Mary Ann and thrust a leaflet into her hand. An elderly gentleman lifted his cane and slashed it down, knocking the piece of paper away with enough force to make her cry out and stare down in shock at her hand as pain continued to shoot through it. The skin was broken and her left forefinger was bent at an odd angle. She felt suddenly queasy and didn't know what to do. She hated having to deal with injuries.

With a growl of anger, Bob snatched the man's cane and broke it by stamping on it. 'Look what you've done to her, you bully! She's only an innocent bystander, not one of *them!*'

The man flushed and stared at Mary Ann. 'I'm sorry, miss. I get angry when I see those unnatural harridans parading in front of decent people.'

'Well, behaviour like yours makes *me* want to go and join them!' she snapped, holding her left hand with her right because it hurt to move it. 'That man was going to throw a stone at them. You're hitting out blindly. This is England, not a heathen country. We're supposed to have a democracy here, with everyone having a right to free speech.' She'd been reading about that in one of the magazines left by a guest. She glanced down at her injured hand and was horrified to see that it was swelling fast. 'How do you think I'm going to do my work now?' she demanded.

A middle-aged lady who'd been standing nearby stepped forward. 'I'm a doctor. Let me see your hand, dear.'

'Women doctors, what next?' the angry man muttered.

Although the lady examined it gently, Mary Ann couldn't hold back a whimper of pain.

'I think you've broken her finger, you brute!' the woman snapped, putting her arm round Mary Ann's shoulders. 'You won't be able to use this for a while, I'm afraid, my dear.'

'But I must! I'm a chambermaid at the Charrington, not a lady of leisure.'

'Hey!'

The gentleman had been edging away, but turned round at the doctor's call.

'Excuse me, sir, but this young woman is going to need at least a week off work, probably two. And since you've caused this, I think it only fair you should pay her wages for that time.'

He fumbled in his pocket, red-faced. 'Yes. Yes, of course. How much?'

'Fifteen shillings a week,' Mary Ann muttered, embarrassed.

He thrust two sovereigns at her, looked down at the wreckage of his cane and left it lying there. Tipping his hat, he moved off, looking rather sheepish now.

'Let me come back with you to the hotel and explain,' the lady said. 'I know James Farran and he'll pay attention to me.'

Hot with embarrassment, Mary Ann muttered, 'I'm sure I can manage most jobs if I'm careful.'

'You shouldn't even try,' Bob said.

The doctor nodded. 'Your friend is right. Besides, that man's given you the money. Use it to look after yourself properly. Not everyone has that luxury.'

Mary Ann looked down at the coins, hating to keep them because it smacked of charity.

As more noise erupted from round the corner, the doctor bent down and picked up the leaflet. 'Don't you want to see what it was all about?'

'She doesn't need that thing,' said Bob, reaching out for it.

Mary Ann took it quickly with her good hand, stuffing it into her pocket. 'Yes, I do want to see it and try to understand.'

The doctor nodded approval. 'Come on, then. Let's go and see James, then I have evening surgery. I have my car nearby.'

Mr Farran greeted their new acquaintance with, 'Constance! What are you doing here?'

'Bringing your injured chambermaid home to explain to you what happened.'

He shot a puzzled glance at Mary Ann and Bob.

'A suffragette handed her a WSPU leaflet and some fool lashed out with his cane to knock it out of her hand. He acted rather too vigorously and broke her finger.'

'I didn't know you were a suffragette, Mary Ann,' the manager said disapprovingly.

'I'm not! We were just watching them march down the street.'

Bob stepped forward. 'That's right, sir.'

Just then the gentleman who had injured her entered the hotel, saw the group standing there and avoided their eyes as he made his way hurriedly towards the lift.

'It was that gentleman who did it, actually,' Constance said.

'That's Major Leffington, one of our valued guests.'

'He's a fool.' The doctor watched disapprovingly as the iron lift cage rose and clanked out of sight, then turned back to the manager. 'She's not to use that hand for a while, James. I got two weeks' wages out of him for her. Can you get someone else in temporarily?'

Mary Ann interrupted. 'I can't sit around doing nothing! I'll go mad.'

'How about office duties?' he queried, looking at Constance.

'*Light* office duties – but I'll take her home and set that finger properly first.'

He spread his hands in a gesture of resignation and smiled as if he was fond of her. 'Do what you think best, my dear. You would anyway.'

'Thank you, James. Come along, Mary Ann. We want that finger to heal straight.'

So it was that she found herself being driven to Dr Constance Peele's commodious villa where her finger was set and bandaged, a painful process which proved to her that she really wouldn't be able to use it for a while.

'You were very brave,' Constance said quietly afterwards. 'I know how that must have hurt. Do you fancy a cup of tea now?'

'Didn't you say you had surgery?'

'Not for another two hours. Do you still have that leaflet? If so, I'd like to look at it, too. The last one I saw was dreadful. It had three spelling mistakes in it. That's no way to gain people's respect.'

Mary Ann fumbled in the pocket of her coat, pulling out the piece of paper.

It was very simple, headed 'Votes For Women' and insisting that if women were fit to rear the next generation or be Queen of the land, like Victoria had been, they were equally fit to vote.

'Amazing what fury these arguments generate,' Constance said thoughtfully, handing it back. 'What are your views on the question of votes for women?'

Mary Ann looked at her cautiously.

Constance burst into laughter. 'It's all right, you can be honest with me.'

'It seems only fair. I've met some very stupid men who have the vote, so why shouldn't I have one, too?'

'Bravo! I agree with you absolutely.'

This encouraged Mary Ann to ask the question that had been puzzling her. 'What I can't understand is why the suffragettes commit such violent acts. It puts everyone against them.'

'Because they've been trying to get the vote for some time now and nothing has changed.'

'I still couldn't make a spectacle of myself or damage other people's property.'

'Me neither. I did my bit to further the women's cause by qualifying as a doctor and now I help other women as best I can. Not to mention innocent bystanders who get in the way of old fools with canes.' She grinned, an urchin's grin for all that she was about forty.

'How much do I owe you, Dr Peele?'

'Heavens, nothing at all! And my name's Constance. Now how about some tea and fruit cake? I wouldn't mind a bit of company. My husband's been away all week and I've had no one to talk to.' She smiled again as she confessed, 'I dearly love a natter.'

Bemused, Mary Ann found herself talking to another woman whose friendliness recognised no bounds of class, and promising to come back again.

'I mean it,' Constance said as she showed her guest to the door. 'I like you.'

'But – haven't you got plenty of friends already, friends of your own station?'

'Depends what you mean by friends. I occasionally go out to dinner with ladies of my own class whose heads are empty of anything as dangerous as a thought. I see poorer women in my surgery whose lives are so hard they can't think beyond where the next meal is coming from. And then I meet women like you from time to time to whom I take an instant liking so I seize the intiative. Let's face it, you wouldn't dare offer to be my friend, would you?'

'Well, no.'

'And I do have an ulterior motive, the need to understand women of all sorts. One day the suffragettes will have their demands granted and we'll get our votes, then I mean to stand for Parliament. So in a sense I'm using you. But I do like you. And you'll like my other friends, I'm sure. There are several of us who meet here from time to time to discuss women's needs. Fancy joining us one evening?'

'I'd love to.'

'Good. Now, I'll get my chauffeur to drive you home. And I mean what I say. No using that hand until it stops hurting, and even then, please go easy with it for a week or two. And keep that splint on for at least a week.'

This time Mary Ann was fully conscious of the pleasure of

riding in a motor car and throughly enjoyed the trip back to the hotel.

She intended to accept Constance Peele's invitation. Maybe through the kind doctor she could make a few women friends as well as Bob. Suddenly everything in her life seemed brighter. She smiled as she went back into the hotel, even though her hand was throbbing now.

She still intended to make Agnes proud of her.

13

February 1914

Mary Ann found working as a temporary assistant to the house-keeper and manager fascinating. It didn't matter that Mrs Upton and Mr Farran used her as a general dogsbody, sending her here and there with messages or setting her to do a variety of physically easy tasks, like making lists and checking cleaning supplies. The broken finger was painful at first, but luckily it was on her left hand and she managed to find ways to do all she was asked.

Gradually Mrs Upton relaxed a little and even began to chat to her when things were quiet, explaining how very much there was to do in a big hotel that even the staff never realised. Sarah, the senior chambermaid, looked at Mary Ann with naked jealousy and suspicion, however, and she overheard the maid telling someone, 'That one is *worming her way in*, if you ask me.' Well, if doing your job to the best of your ability was worming your way in, then she supposed she was. But she could never bear to do less than her best.

One day Mr Farran even set her to watch the reception desk when Mr Preston was suffering from a severe head cold and he had to deal with some important guests who expected personal attention from the manager in their suite.

At first she felt shy as she greeted the guests and took or handed out keys, for even at this season the hotel was half-full. Some of them stared in surprise to see a woman behind the long mahogany counter; others ignored her beyond a haughty nod of the head.

Bob bustled to and fro, dealing with luggage or sending the page boy out for a cab. Sometimes he would wink at Mary Ann as he passed and that always lifted her spirits.

When the Major came in he scowled at her, hesitated, then harrumphed and asked brusquely, 'Finger all right now?'

'Getting better, sir, thank you. And I haven't lost my wages, so I can give you your money back.'

He looked amazed then muttered, 'No need, no need!' and hurried across to the lift.

So she kept the money, which made a nice little addition to her savings bank account.

There was nothing difficult about the work she was doing and inevitably she began to wonder why a woman couldn't do such a job as well as a man. Which led her on to consider yet again during a quiet period why women shouldn't have the vote as a matter of right, for she had not been able to stop thinking about the suffragettes marching bravely along to boos and hisses. Why were people so very hostile to them?

The only problem in her new life was the assistant manager, with whom she spent as little time as possible and never alone if she could help it because he was always brushing against her. All the girls said he was a nuisance like that and joked about his octopus hands, but Mary Ann remembered another man who had rubbed against her and shuddered.

'Will you please stop touching me, Mr Preston!' she exclaimed one day.

He stood barring her way, a big man with a red face and thick lips, smiling now. 'I haven't the slightest idea what you mean.'

As she moved to pass him, he stepped sideways to bar her way. When she moved again, so did he.

'Stop this!' she exclaimed.

His grin told her he was enjoying himself and she was so angry she gave him a hard shove, taking him by surprise. She walked away before he could recover his balance, muttering, 'The cheek of it!' loudly enough for him to hear.

'Talking to yourself now?'

She turned to see Bob but couldn't return his smile. 'I've just had to push my way past Mr Preston. I'm sick of him touching me, absolutely sick of it!'

Bob's smile faded. 'He's a nuisance, that one. I'll try to keep my eye on you when he's around.'

'Thank you.' She went on her way, not feeling optimistic because Bob was mainly in the reception area and she had to go all over the hotel. She wondered why some men behaved like Preston and her stepfather.

The incidents brought the nightmares back, the ones where she tried in vain to fight off Jeff Powling. Then came the other dreams about her baby, which always made her wake up in tears.

The following evening, feeling extremely nervous, Mary Ann walked into town to Dr Peele's house for her first fortnightly gathering. She found herself in such congenial company that she soon wondered what she had been afraid of. The women discussed anything and everything, including their desire for the vote and the situation in Europe where things were apparently politically unstable.

Mary Ann drank in all the new information and even felt comfortable enough to ask questions which betrayed her utter ignorance of European or even English politics. It wasn't something she had even thought about before and she was shocked rigid when Dr Peele said it might come to war between Britain and Germany.

'Surely not?' she exclaimed, horrified. 'Not in Europe!'

'We must hope the worst doesn't happen,' Dr Peele said. 'Keep reading the newspapers and you'll find out more. And do come again next time.'

It was clear that the doctor had set herself up as a mentor to this group of women, who included a shop assistant, a faded spinster caring for elderly parents, two women who worked in an office but earned little more than half of what the male clerks did, and two nurses from a small local lying-in hospital which Dr Peele visited. All were lively-minded and ready to offer friendship to the newcomer.

Mr Peele arrived home just as the evening was winding up and was not at all what Mary Ann had expected. He seemed quiet and colourless next to his wife with her strong personality, and said very little except that he was glad to see them all enjoying themselves once again.

Mary Ann walked back to the hotel, accompanied partway by Norah, one of the clerks. At the top of the cliff she stopped for a moment to stare out across the moonlit sea. Life seemed full of promise and not for the first time it occurred to her that she didn't actually want to return to chambermaid duties, which were far less interesting than working in the office.

Margaret Pensham sat watching her son play with his toy soldiers. He was lining them up for battle on a card table and earnestly discussing military tactics with his grandfather. She looked down at her embroidery and sighed. She was, she admitted to herself, more than a little bored with her peaceful life here in Overdale – which was ungrateful when the Garbutts were so kind to her. But she needed more than to live quietly, spurned by most people of her own class, reading book after book to feed her active mind and going for long walks to try to use up the energy with which her equally active body was filled.

Only, what else could she do? She still had her son to look after and no money except for what the Garbutts gave her.

When the final tea tray of the day was brought in, Angela looked at her as they sipped. 'You're growing restless, aren't you, dear?'

Margaret blushed. 'I am a little. I'm sorry, it's not that I'm unhappy. You've been wonderful to me and Johnny. I think I've too much energy for my own good. I'm a little worried about how Mary Ann is getting on as well. I haven't had a letter from her for a while.'

The hint worked.

'I think everyone needs a change from time to time,' Edward Garbutt said in his comfortable way. 'We can look after the lad, so why don't you go and stay in Bournemouth for a few days? See that lass and make sure she's all right. You can bring her back here if she's not happy. We can always use another maid.'

'She must be missing her friend dreadfully,' Angela said. 'Such a terrible accident.'

Margaret got up and went to give them both a hug. 'You're too kind to me. And I will go to Bournemouth, if you don't mind.'

'Well, you've given us both something to live for,' Edward said gruffly. 'How can we not be grateful for that?'

His wife looked at him and nodded, as if to encourage him to say something else.

He cleared his throat noisily. 'We thought you should know, Margaret, that we've made new wills leaving most of our money to young Johnny here. But I've also settled an annuity on you, so that you won't have to worry about money. You won't be rich, but you'll be comfortable enough. And it's to be paid to you from now on, so that you'll not feel quite so dependent on us.'

Margaret felt tears well in her eyes and rushed across to hug them both again. 'I can't think what to say except thank you. I'm so lucky to have you.'

Mary Ann received a letter from her friend two days later.

I've decided that I need a change so I'm coming to see you. Can you book me a room at the hotel, a good one, mind? And I'm hoping you'll be able to manage a day or two off so that we can spend some time together. It seems a long time since Birtley, doesn't it? Remember how we used to chat until past midnight sometimes? And it was just the same when I visited you in Blackpool.

Which made Mary Ann think of Gabriel Clough, because Birtley and Blackpool were always linked in her mind with him. She sighed, wondering how he was and if he and his wife had made up their differences.

As she was booking the room for her friend she explained that Margaret was a relative of one of the owners and Mr Farran, who had been frowning at her request for a day or two off, immediately became very obliging.

'She's a dark horse, Baillie is,' he told Mrs Upton later that evening. 'She's got some very useful friends, not only Lady Bingram and Dr Peele but this relative of Edward Garbutt's as well.'

'How do you find her?'

'Very efficient. She picks things up quickly.'

'Yes. I was wondering about letting her stay on as a sort of general assistant rather than sending her back to clean bedrooms. I've come to rely on her.'

'We'll have to think about that. But if we do offer her the job permanently, she'll have to get some smarter clothes. Something dark and tailored.'

'I can help her with that.'

He chewed the corner of his lip. 'Offer her the job, then. Pound a week, all found.'

'Preston won't like it,' she warned, wondering whether she dared go further and mention the way the fellow was annoying the maids. No, better not. Preston had even better connections than Mary Ann because he was a nephew of the main shareholder.

'Well, he'll just have to lump it. For a young fellow, he's a real stick-in-the-mud.'

When Cousin Tom dropped a few hints to Gabriel that his wife was spending time with Dan Barworth every market day, he laughed and assured him that he knew all about it. But when he was on his own, the memory of their conversation brought a frown to his face.

He knew Ivy was not being unfaithful to him because there simply wasn't any time when she could have been. But he also knew how much she looked forward to market day and how much brighter she was when she came home. Was she attracted to Dan Barworth?

Characteristically he asked her straight out when she got home the following week, detaining her near the stable so that his mother wouldn't overhear.

'Is there something going on between you and Barworth?'

She gaped at him. 'What did you say?'

'You heard me.'

'No, there jolly well isn't. We have a cup of tea together after the market closes, that's all. You know about that because I told you. He's lonely, needs someone to talk to, asks my advice about his house.'

Gabriel looked at her hard. 'Well, make sure that's all that happens. I'm not putting up with goings on.'

She tossed her head. 'I could say the same thing to you. You're always out in the evening – down at the library, you say, but how do I know that's where you go?'

'Because of the sort of fellow I am.'

'Oh, and I'm the sort to have an affair, am I? Well, thank you very much! It's my only outing of the week, going to the café, and I'm not giving it up. You never take me with you when you go to see your precious cousin, or anywhere else for that matter, so you can't complain.'

With that Ivy flounced off towards the house, furious with him. In bed that night she grew even angrier, because although she was attracted to Dan – and he to her, no denying that – she'd decided that nothing could come of it. She was well and truly married, with two children to think about.

Trapped.

Nothing to look forward to but a lifetime of being *grateful!*

Margaret felt a sense of liberation as the train left Overdale. She coped easily with changing trains in London, smiling to think that Papa Garbutt had wanted to send one of his clerks with her in case she got lost or confused. She prided herself on being a modern woman and yet she knew she'd let the Garbutts cosset her too much during the past few years. They tried so hard to make up for her loss of respectability as the mother of their son's illegitimate child – and for the rejection by her own father.

But nothing could make up for the circumscribed life she was forced by convention to lead. She sometimes thought she should emigrate to the colonies and pretend to be a widow. She might just do that if anything happened to the Garbutts. No, she couldn't even then if Johnny was going to inherit the family business. Chains forged by love were no less chains, she found.

Surely there must be something useful she could do with her life?

Her spirits lifted still further as she reached Bournemouth and sat in a cab driving up the hill towards the Charrington. She was looking forward to seeing Mary Ann and really talking to her.

As she walked into the hotel she saw her friend behind the reception counter. Suddenly Mary Ann jumped and turned to glare at a youngish man who had just moved away from her with a smirk on his face. He was wearing a dark suit and a stiff white collar. Margaret frowned as he pushed rudely past Mary Ann to greet her.

'May I help you,' he glanced down at her hand before adding, 'miss?'

'*Mrs* Pensham,' she countered, because it was easier among strangers to pretend she was a widow. 'And no, you may not help me. I prefer to deal with my friend Miss Baillie.'

For a moment his expression turned ugly, then he inclined his head and stepped back but still did not move away.

There was something threatening about the way he loomed over her, so Margaret walked past him and held out her arms. Mary Ann rushed forward and the two young women hugged one another.

After watching them for a moment, Preston slipped into the manager's office. 'Have you a moment, sir? I really don't think it suitable for that female to stage gushing reunions with her friends somewhere as public as *our* foyer when she's supposed to be on duty at the counter.'

Mr Farran looked up and sighed. 'It's probably Mrs Pensham, who is a relative of Mr Garbutt, one of our major shareholders. She's a friend of Mary Ann's and has come here specially to visit her.'

Preston snapped his mouth shut and breathed deeply.

'If I may venture a word of advice,' Mr Farran went on, 'I would suggest you stop treating Miss Baillie with such suspicion and get on with your own work.'

'That's all very well, but I cannot think the front desk a suitable place for a woman.'

'Women are doing many things nowadays. Times are changing and we must change with them.'

'We don't have to let things change at the Charrington. We can still maintain decent standards here.'

'Mary Ann is capable and trustworthy, and it's my business not yours to decide who does what here.' Mr Farran saw the younger man take another deep breath, as if preparing to argue, and said sternly, 'I think *you* had better turn your attention to the accounts for cleaning supplies. They seem rather excessive to me this month. Check that we really did receive everything listed.'

He watched Preston leave then went out into the foyer. After greeting their newest guest, he suggested that Mary Ann show her friend up to her room while he arranged for some tea to be sent up for them both. 'I shan't expect you down for an hour or so, my dear.'

'Oh, thank you, sir!' Mary Ann beamed at him. 'You're very kind.'

'Papa Garbutt thinks highly of him,' Margaret said as they got into the lift cage and it clanked its way up to the second floor. 'But who's that horrible young man and what did he do to upset you just now?'

Mary Ann hesitated then confided, 'Mr Preston is the assistant manager. He keeps rubbing against me and – well, his hands are everywhere.'

'Slap his face for him the next time he behaves improperly.'

'But he's the assistant manager! I can't.'

'He still has no right to take liberties. And of course you can defend yourself.'

'I might lose my job.'

'Then you can come to us and Papa Garbutt will help you find another one. They can always use an extra maid.'

Mary Ann didn't try to argue. Ladies with money simply didn't understand how much at the mercy of such men women like her were, out of the simple need to earn their living. And anyway, she didn't want to be a maid any more. She seemed to have spent her whole life doing housework, right from when she was a tiny child. Her present work was much more interesting.

The following evening, after Mary Ann had finished for the day, the two young women sat and talked until late, finding again the same ease with one another that they had experienced at Redvale. Margaret confessed to being bored with her life and added, 'I really envy you.'

'Envy *me?*'

'Yes. You've plenty to keep you busy, people to talk to, new things happening all the time. My Johnny's a dear little boy, but he's at school now most of the time and I sit around in attendance on Mama Garbutt. She's a dear too, but . . . well, life would be easier if I weren't a *fallen woman.*' She pulled a wry face. 'Many people in Overdale seem unable to forgive me for that – especially with my father there to stoke their anger. He walks right past me in the street, you know.' She had to stop to control her feelings because thinking of that always hurt her. She didn't see her mother even in the street because she was a semi-invalid these days.

Mary Ann's hand was gentle on her friend's. 'That can't be easy for you.'

'No. To top it all, Papa Garbutt thinks England will have trouble with the Kaiser before too long. He says it could even come to war. And he's not a stupid man.'

Mary Ann looked at her in dismay. 'Dr Peele says the same thing.' She had just about persuaded herself that the good doctor was exaggerating, that it could not possibly come to war, not for Britain.

'I'm afraid they're right.' Margaret's face took on her old determined expression. 'Anyway, now that I've got some money of my own, I've decided to buy myself a motor car and learn to drive it.'

'That might be fun, though I doubt an ordinary woman like me will ever get the chance to do that.'

'There's nothing ordinary about you, Mary Ann. You'll make something of yourself, I'm sure.'

Which made the second time someone had said that to her. She was glad to have people's good opinion, of course she was, but there was nothing special about her.

The next night Mary Ann took Margaret with her to Dr Peele's gathering and could see that the two women took to one another immediately, not because they were of the same class but because they were both rather unconventional at heart and not willing to put up with things they didn't like.

It was easy to have that confidence when you had money behind you, she thought wistfully.

When Margaret returned home to Lancashire, Mr Farran and Mrs Upton asked Mary Ann to come into the office and her heart sank at the thought that they were going to send her back to being a chambermaid. However, as she realised what they were offering her, she felt a surge of joy.

'Oh, I'd *love* to continue working as your assistant! It's much more interesting.'

Mr Farran leaned back in his chair, smiling. 'Good. I'll leave it to Mrs Upton to sort things out with you, then.'

'You'll need some better clothes,' the housekeeper said without preamble when they were alone in her office. 'Something smart but businesslike. Navy is always suitable for a woman, I think. Black looks too much like mourning. We could go into town and choose something tomorrow afternoon. Can you afford it or shall I lend you the money?'

'I've money saved, thank you.'

'And we'll give you your own bedroom from now on, too. It wouldn't be right for you to share with a chambermaid. The end room in your corridor is vacant so you may as well move into that.'

When she got back to the room she shared with Colleen, Mary Ann plumped down on the bed, unable to stop smiling. She couldn't believe her luck.

Even the other chambermaids' jealousy didn't dim her happiness. Nor did the way Mr Preston kept looking at her.

She felt she had taken an important step in her life. Agnes and Margaret would both be proud of her.

14

March 1914

Mary Ann hummed as she ran lightly down the back stairs with the list Mrs Upton had asked for. As she reached the landing, Mr Preston stepped forward and barred her way.

'How about walking into town with me this afternoon?'

His smile made her shiver. 'No, thank you. I'm meeting a friend.' Only she wasn't. The assistant porter was attending a family funeral, so Bob couldn't get away.

'You're not, you know. Hall's busy this afternoon.'

She drew back, annoyed that he had been watching her so closely. 'The answer is still no.'

'If you're being so generous with others, it's unfair not to share your favours around. Makes for bad feeling around the place.'

'I'm not being generous with anyone,' she snapped, fury surging through her in a hot tide. 'I have more respect for myself.'

Mrs Upton called from partway down the stairs: 'Mary Ann, could you please hurry up?'

With a sigh of relief she moved forward, but she still had to push past him, touch him, go close enough to feel his hot breath on her face.

The housekeeper gestured to her to be quiet until they reached the bottom of the stairs when she asked in a low voice, 'Is that man giving you trouble?'

'Yes. He's giving a few of us trouble, actually.'

'I know. I asked him to stop annoying my maids, but he pretended not to understand me. I'll have to have a word with Mr Farran about him.' She stepped back and studied Mary Ann's appearance. 'You're looking very smart in your new outfit, my dear, and I'm pleased with your work. Try not to let him upset you.'

'I won't.' Mary Ann sighed as she went on her way. It was all right to say that, but Mr Preston simply wouldn't take no for an answer. And how could she not be upset by his touching, fumbling ways?

When she left the hotel that afternoon he was waiting for her at the gate.

Her heart sank but she walked past him with her head in the air, ready to start running if he so much as laid one finger on her. She heard footsteps behind her and when she glanced back saw him following, still smiling. Her next glance showed that he was speeding up and her heart gave a funny little jump of anxiety. The cliff path was very quiet at this time of year. She hoped she could outrun him.

But fortunately some women began walking up the path towards them and when she looked round, Preston had dropped back a little.

She walked on as quickly as she could but he continued to follow her for the next half-hour, no matter where she went in town. She didn't fancy going back up the cliff path on her own so could think of nothing to do but head for Dr Peele's house.

She was relieved to catch her friend at home and blurted out as the door was closed behind her, 'I'm sorry to be a nuisance, but there's a man following me.'

'You're not a nuisance. Show me.'

They looked out of the window, but there was now no sign of him.

'Oh! He's gone. He was there, though, I promise you.'

'I believe you, my dear. Do you know him?'

'Yes, it's the assistant manager from the hotel, actually. Mr Preston. And he's – well, being rather a nuisance at work too, pestering me, touching me.' Mary Ann could feel herself flushing. 'I didn't know what to do because if I walked back up East Cliff on my own, he'd catch up with me and – well, there aren't many people about in winter.'

Constance looked at her thoughtfully. 'Well, stay and have a cup of tea with me and then I'll drive you back to the hotel. I have to go out in that direction anyway.'

There was no sign of Preston at the hotel, so Mary Ann hurried inside and made her way up to her bedroom, which was not where she wanted to spend her time. Let alone it was cold there, she preferred to be out and about when she wasn't working. Locking the door, she went to stare wistfully through the window at the sea and the pier.

It was a shame when you couldn't even enjoy your afternoon off.

In the middle of the night she woke to hear a key in her bedroom door, which she'd locked carefully before getting into bed. The key on her side fell out.

Her heart started to pound. Only the managers and Mrs Upton had access to the spare keys. Surely it couldn't be Preston? Did he really think she'd keep quiet if he tried to creep into her bed? Grim-faced, she slid from under the covers and picked up her candlestick to use as a weapon, wishing they'd put in electricity up here as well as down in the guests' areas!

As the door opened she screamed at the top of her voice, then leaped forward and hit out at the intruder.

There was a muttered curse and Preston staggered to one side, by which time there were two girls outside in the corridor, one of them carrying the lighted candle that always stood near the bathroom.

He tried to push past them, but Mary Ann grabbed his clothing from behind and shouted, 'Hold on to him! Don't let him get away!'

He fought furiously but there were three of them. Mrs Upton and Mr Farran arrived on the scene before he could get away.

'What is going on here?' roared Mr Farran.

'He broke into my room,' Mary Ann said, pointing.

'She invited me,' Preston said, 'then changed her mind. She's no better than she should be.'

'I had my door locked. He must have taken one of the spare keys to get in.'

Mr Farran stepped forward and quickly felt in his assistant's dressing-gown pocket, pulling out a key. 'Let's try this.' It fitted the door lock. He looked down and saw Mary Ann's key on the floor. Turning to his assistant he said coldly, 'I can see no reason for you to have this key in your possession, and if she'd invited you, you wouldn't have needed an extra key.'

Preston glared at the manager, but said nothing.

The other maids had gathered outside, watching everything in fascination, nudging one another and exchanging quick glances of delight to see their tormentor caught out.

Mary Ann's hair had tumbled round her shoulders and as she pushed it back, she realised suddenly that she was wearing only her nightdress, so snatched up her dressing gown from the bedside chair and wrapped it hastily round her.

'We'll discuss this in my office,' Mr Farran said. 'Go back to bed, everyone. Mrs Upton, would you and Mary Ann get dressed and join me downstairs, please? Preston, we'll go and wait for the ladies.'

'Ladies!' he scoffed. 'That one's nothing but a whore.'

'Mind your language in front of me!' Mrs Upton snapped then turned to Mary Ann. 'I'll go and get dressed, dear, and wait for you in my room.'

When the two women met again, Mary Ann said pleadingly, 'You do believe me, don't you?'

'Yes.' The housekeeper hesitated then added, 'But I fear it won't do much good. Which is why I haven't made a fuss before now about him.'

'What do you mean?'

The older woman sighed. 'As you know, he's a nephew of our major shareholder and I doubt we'll be allowed to dismiss him. They're more likely to ask you to leave. However, I shall certainly speak up on your behalf.'

Mary Ann gaped at her. 'You mean, Mr Farran might sack me for something that's not my fault?'

'It's a possibility that you'll be asked to leave, which is different from sacking. I've seen it happen before, I'm afraid, in similar circumstances. I just wanted to warn you.'

'But that's not fair!'

'Life isn't fair. Haven't you discovered that yet?'

'Yes,' Mary Ann whispered, closing her eyes as memories rushed back at her in a dark tide. After a few seconds she drew herself up and looked at the older woman. 'We'd better go down, I suppose.'

'Whatever happens, I shall provide you with an excellent reference and I don't think you'll find it hard to get another job.'

'I already have a job I enjoy. I'd rather keep that.'

Mrs Upton's hand rested on her shoulder for a minute and squeezed. 'I know. And I *will* do my best for you.'

Mr Farran was sitting behind his desk and Preston was standing to one side, arms folded, still in his dressing gown.

'She looks like butter wouldn't melt in her mouth now, doesn't she?' he sneered as they went in.

'Do take a seat, ladies.' The manager looked sideways. 'You've already told me your side of things, so kindly keep quiet now, Preston. Mary Ann, please tell me exactly what happened?'

She went through the day's events, describing the way the assistant manager had followed her around the town.

Mr Farran turned to the housekeeper. 'Have you anything to add?'

'Only that I believe Mary Ann, because I've had complaints about Mr Preston from other maids.'

'I've seen one or two incidents myself. I spoke to him and thought he'd mended his ways.'

'Now look here!' Preston blustered.

Mr Farran turned an icy stare on him. 'I am, in any case, dissatisfied with your general performance in this job. You are dismissed and I'd be obliged if you'd leave as soon as it's light.'

Mary Ann sagged in relief. She'd be able to keep her job.

Preston strode towards the door, turned and stopped for a moment. 'My uncle won't like this.'

'In which case he is at liberty to deal with me. Now, kindly leave.'

When the door had slammed behind him, Mr Farran turned to Mary Ann. 'Unfortunately, his uncle *is* very influential. I think it'd be better, my dear, if you found other employment. Harris won't countenance his nephew being sacked and you staying on.'

'That's hardly fair,' Mrs Upton said.

'I know.' Mr Farran sat with his head bowed for a minute or two. 'Look, I have a friend who owns a few businesses and a couple of tea rooms. He owes me a favour and I know he's just lost one of his lady clerks. He may be able to find you a job in the office, Mary Ann. Will that help?'

She could only look at him reproachfully.

'You can stay here until you've found yourself some lodgings, but please do it quickly. I'll give you two weeks' pay in lieu of notice and I'm sure Mrs Upton will join me in providing you with glowing references.' He shook his head sadly and added, 'I'm afraid that's the best I can do for you.'

'I'm sorry,' Mrs Upton said as she went into her own bedroom.

Mary Ann said nothing. She felt both furiously angry and depressed by this turn of events. Were things never to go right for her?

In the morning Dr Peele was called in to see a sick guest and afterwards asked to speak to Mary Ann: 'She was a bit upset yesterday.'

Mrs Upton, hearing this, hesitated then told the doctor what had happened the previous night. 'She's out searching for lodgings at the moment.'

'It's shameful that she's been asked to leave!'

'Sadly, it's what usually happens in such cases. At least this time we can ensure that she has another job to go to.'

The doctor frowned in thought. 'I think I might be able to help her with finding some lodgings. Ask her to come and see me.'

Within a week, Mary Ann had started work in a new job and

taken a room with one of the doctor's other protégées, Helen Charters. She was able to lodge there free in return for helping her friend with the housework and care of her elderly parents, for the mother was very frail now though Mary Ann quickly realised that the father was exaggerating his ill health.

She might have found a new job easily enough but still felt angry at the way she had been treated. She felt even angrier when she met Bob one evening and he told her that Preston had been found a position in another of the company's hotels.

Bob laid his hand on hers. 'I'm sorry, lass. Just thought you'd better know. The uncle tried first to send him back here but Mr Farran wouldn't have him, not for anything, threatened to resign if they tried to foist him on us again. I – um – happened to overhear him talking on the telephone.'

She nodded, knowing that the porters were always aware of what was going on in the hotel. 'Well, it's no use crying over spilt milk and at least I've found another job and somewhere to live. But it isn't very interesting work.' In fact, the two lady clerks were treated like children and strictly supervised at all times.

She hated that and had already decided she wasn't going to stay there any longer than she had to. She'd keep her eyes open for another job, something more interesting.

Margaret showed Mary Ann's letter to the Garbutts and they were shocked to think of an employee of the hotel group being treated like that.

'I always feel sorry for young women who have to earn their own living,' Angela added. 'But I suppose, given the circumstances, your friend wouldn't easily have found a man to marry her.'

'Do you mean, because of the baby?' Margaret asked, trying not to sound too sharp.

'Well, yes.'

'That wasn't her fault. She was forced by her stepfather.'

Angela blushed.

'No need to go into details,' Papa Garbutt said hastily. 'But she couldn't have been kept on after what happened. Harris would have been very upset if she had.'

'But *she* did nothing wrong!'

He looked at her pityingly. 'There's no smoke without fire. Maybe she didn't realise she was encouraging him.'

Margaret had to bite her tongue so as not to argue with him. She was only too conscious of how much she owed to them and he was already upset by her intention of not only buying a motor car, but learning to drive it. She didn't want him to put his foot down and forbid it outright. A car would give her a degree of independence and mobility without the Garbutts' chauffeur or second chauffeur reporting back to his employer on where she had been or who she had seen, for they had a second motor car for the lady of the house's use as well as the master's vehicle.

She investigated electric cars because they were easier to start and drive. But they could only go for about fifty miles without recharging the batteries. This meant the batteries had to be taken away and she would have to have two sets, which would be very inconvenient. In the end she settled on the Morris-Oxford light car, a two-seater which went about fifty to fifty-five miles on one gallon of petrol. That was good because she'd already seen how awkward it was to pour it into the fuel tank from the square cans in which it was sold by hardware stores.

'The car goes up to fifty-five miles an hour in top gear,' she said enthusiastically over dinner.

'I hope you won't drive it that fast!' Angela exclaimed. 'It *can't* be safe.'

'No, no. Of course I won't.' Margaret glanced sideways to see Papa Garbutt frowning and added quickly, 'I'd be afraid to go so fast. I was just telling you about the car's capabilities.'

'I think you should stick to twenty miles an hour at most,' he said firmly.

She made a non-committal noise, and to her relief he took it for agreement.

When the Morris-Oxford was delivered, the hardest thing was learning to start it because she found the crank handle difficult to turn. But Margaret was determined to conquer it and she did. The Garbutts' chauffeur-mechanic taught her to drive and, finding her an enthusiastic pupil, also taught her some of the simpler procedures needed to maintain a car, just in case it broke down on her.

When his chauffeur assured him that Miss Pensham had taken to driving like a duck to water, Papa Garbutt agreed to come out with her for a drive one day, but Angela refused and they both advised against taking little Johnny.

'Not till the summer,' Margaret agreed. 'It's quite cold at present, even with the hood up. But on a fine summer's day, I shall definitely take him out.' She saw the dismay on their faces and added gently, 'I shall be very careful indeed, I promise you. He's the centre of my life as well as yours.'

The car was a small step towards independence but she decided to wait a while before starting to learn about first aid, which was the next item on her list. Once she had some useful skills, she could do voluntary work, meet people and get out a bit more. She was hoping that interesting herself in charity work would lead to wider social acceptance.

Mary Ann didn't get any fonder of working in an office, especially one whose window looked out only on to a blank wall and where the paintwork was a drab brown to shoulder height and a dingy cream above that. Her job was to act as general dogsbody to Mr Jenks, the owner, and Miss Marshall, his secretary. She had to open letters, sorting them into various categories such as receipts and invoices, and also to file various documents. She brought up morning and afternoon tea for the three of them from the tea room below, which at least got her out and gave her a minute or two to chat to Ruby, the cheerful woman in charge there.

The task Mary Ann hated most was making handwritten copies of letters and documents. It was worse than being back at school. One day Miss Marshall, who always seemed to be looking down her nose at her, said Mary Ann would have to go to night school to learn to type. What, spend all day shut up in an office, then spend the evening shut up with a typewriter? She wouldn't do it!

'Idling again, Miss Baillie?' said the voice of her employer one afternoon.

'I'm sorry, Mr Jenks. The sunlight distracted my attention for a moment.'

'Don't let it happen again. You're not paid to stare out of the window.'

'No, sir.' She wondered whether to apply for a chambermaid's job in another hotel. It had to be better than this. Only she'd enjoyed being Mrs Upton's assistant so much it had spoiled her for chambermaiding.

Miss Marshall came in. 'Ruby has just sent word that one of the assistants in the tea room has fainted and been sent home, and the other didn't turn up for work. She wondered if we could find someone to help her out over the lunchtime rush. Would you mind doing that, Mary Ann?'

She stood up at once. 'Not at all.' She ran down the stairs and slipped into the tea room by the back door, delighted to get out of that dreary office for a few hours.

There were people waiting to be served and looking annoyed, while Ruby was trying to do everything on her own and looked distinctly hot and bothered.

Mary Ann slipped behind the counter. 'What can I do?'

'Thanks for coming down, love. Hope you don't mind? Here's an apron. If you could take orders and carry stuff out to the tables, I'll make up the trays.' She smiled at the people on the nearest table. 'Soon sort you out now. One of my girls was taken sick, you see, but the replacement has arrived.'

Mary Ann soon felt at home with the work and was able to be of more use to Ruby. At one stage she saw Mr Jenks standing in the doorway and wondered if he'd come to fetch her back, but he just continued to watch so she decided he was checking up on her. Well, she supposed he had a right to do that, since he was paying her wages, but he should know her better than to suppose she'd not do her best, whatever the circumstances.

When the rush eased Ruby insisted they get themselves a cup of tea and have a sandwich. 'The bread only goes stale and we don't want you fainting on me as well, do we? I wonder why Susan didn't turn up? I hope she isn't expecting. She's turned into a real flighty piece lately, man mad. How long did Mr Jenks say you could stay and help?'

'He didn't say anything.'

'Why don't you nip up and ask if you can stay for the rest of the afternoon? There's the teas for the various offices to do soon. I really can't manage on my own.'

Mary Ann went back upstairs. 'I came to ask if I could stay and help Ruby for the rest of the afternoon?'

'Well, that's not up to me, is it?' With a sniff Miss Marshall turned back to her typewriter.

Mr Jenks looked up when she knocked on his office door. 'Ah, Mary Ann, there you are. Come in and sit down for a minute, will you?'

Mary Ann did so, wondering what she had done wrong.

'I looked in on you a couple of times downstairs. You appeared to be enjoying yourself.'

She blinked in surprise. Where was this leading? Suddenly she was fed up of trying to fit in. 'I was. I like to meet people.'

'You seemed to be coping well.'

She shrugged. 'It isn't hard work if you know how to organise things.'

'You're not enjoying office work, though, are you?'

He was going to sack her, she knew it! 'Am I not giving satisfaction?' she asked cautiously.

'You're doing the work adequately but you don't seem happy to be here. I – um – know why you had to leave the Charrington. It was very unfortunate. But seeing you today has given me an idea.'

She waited, puzzled.

'How would you like to be in charge of the tea rooms?'

'I can't take Ruby's job!'

'She would still be in charge of the practical work there, but she'd be the first to admit she hates the paperwork. The lady who formerly organised everything retired a few months ago, you see. I have two other tea rooms in the town and you would do the paperwork and ordering for all three.' He smiled suddenly. 'Ruby has been with us a long time, so we didn't like to sack her, but there have to be changes made as she's simply not coping. Besides I think she's taken to you.'

'What would it entail, sir?' Mary Ann asked cautiously. 'And how much would it pay?'

'It would mean you doing anything that was needed. Book work, serving at the counter when there's a rush on, ordering food, organising the services we provide to nearby firms, checking on cleaners, making sure there are enough staff in each place and organising their rosters – that sort of thing.'

Mary Ann beamed at him. 'It sounds wonderful.'

He leaned back, looking more relaxed, and smiled at her. 'That's settled, then. As to money, we'll start you on five shillings a week more than you earn as a clerk and see how you go. Can you take over below for a few minutes and send Ruby up to see me?'

'Yes, sir.'

Beaming at the world she ran back down the stairs. Things were looking up again. And to think she'd been considering giving notice!

15

June – September 1914

A few days later Lady Bingram walked into the tea room and Mary Ann hurried forward to usher her to the table in the window.

'I thought you were working at the Charrington?'

'I had to leave.'

'Problems?'

Mary Ann hesitated.

'Tell me.'

And because she was a trusted friend, Mary Ann explained briefly why she had had to leave the hotel.

'And you say this sort of thing often happens to women?' Lady Bingram said in astonishment.

Mary Ann shrugged. 'Not all that often, but some men have difficulty working with women – don't respect them, if you like.'

'If I catch any chaps messing about with my girls, there'll be trouble! I'm putting together a corps of capable women who are able to help out in emergencies in case it comes to war.'

There it was again, people expecting war and planning for it. Mary Ann hated to hear it.

From then on she saw Lady Bingram regularly because she came into town to meet the young women who were arriving from all over the country to join her volunteer corps.

Bob popped in occasionally for a cup of tea on his day off or invited Mary Ann to go for a walk with him when they could both get time off together, which was not often because her new role was very demanding.

Sometimes he would bring her magazines which guests had left behind at the hotel. Like her, he was frugal in his ways and spoke wistfully of the cottage he had inherited from his grandfather where he would really like to live.

She got ready to lock up the tea room on the evening of 29 June, feeling pleasantly tired and looking forward to a lazy evening. When she saw a big crowd gathering round the lad who sold evening newspapers just outside the station, she was curious enough to walk across to find out what the fuss was about.

'What's happened?' she asked the man next to her. 'Has there been an accident or something?'

'Haven't you heard? The Archduke Franz Ferdinand has been assassinated at Sarajevo. I'd just like to see anyone try that with *our* royal family, but you can't trust foreigners. Ah, here we are!' He handed over his money and took a newspaper eagerly from the lad, scanning the front page as he walked off down the street.

Mary Ann went on her way, not bothering to buy a paper because Mr Charters had one delivered and she'd be able to read it later. It looked like Dr Peele was right. At their last meeting she had warned them that things were very unstable in Bosnia and Serbia, and she kept insisting that any trouble in Europe would inevitably affect Britain. Mary Ann couldn't really understand why the actions of foreigners should affect her, though, or send her country into war.

The following day at their meeting Constance Peele looked very solemn and clapped her hands for their attention as soon as they were all assembled. 'My dear friends, I think it won't be long now until we're facing war.'

There was a chorus of gasps and protests from the women gathered there.

'Don't forget that Germany has been arming itself for a while and a country doesn't do that if it has no intention of using those weapons.'

'You know, I just can't imagine us being at war,' Helen said in a hushed, shocked voice as she and Mary Ann walked home together later.

'I can't either. I still can't believe it'll come to that.'

'Constance seems very sure and you can see she's upset by it

205

all. She's a clever woman and understands these things better than you or I.'

'Do you ever wish you were better educated?' Mary Ann asked wistfully. 'I feel so ignorant sometimes.'

'Oh, yes, definitely. But I went to a small private school for young ladies and we did more embroidery than history. At least you're out in the workforce earning a living and meeting people, while I'm stuck at home looking after Mother and Father. Sometimes I think I'll go mad with frustration.' Helen's voice grew bitter. 'I know it's my duty to look after them, but Father in particular pretends to be worse than he is and they could easily have afforded to pay someone else and let me—' She broke off for a moment, then confided in a muffled voice, 'There was a young man once, you see. He began courting me and – and I liked him, too. Only Father threatened to have him dismissed if he didn't stay away from me. I'm not supposed to know that, but I overheard my parents talking about it afterwards. They were *pleased* at what they'd done!'

Mary Ann reached out to link arms, feeling the tension radiating from her friend. 'That's a terrible thing to do to your own daughter.'

'Yes. And there was nothing I could do to prevent it, nothing at all. Because he – Bill – had already been frightened away and Father *would* have had him dismissed. Bill's employer was one of his best friends, you see, and Father can be very – well, spiteful.' She sighed and walked on for a few steps in silence. 'Now my life is just housework and cooking and running round after the two of them. I get money every week for the housekeeping but only two shillings for myself. *Two shillings!* Even the dress allowance Father gives me is mean and I have to scrimp and save to look decent.' She stared down at her clothes. 'I buy material like this when it's going cheap because no one likes the colour. Who is there to care whether it flatters me or not?' Her voice broke on the last few words.

'Oh, Helen, you poor thing.'

She lowered her voice to a whisper even though there was

no one nearby. 'I sometimes manage to save a bit from the housekeeping, though, and keep it for myself. Do you think that's wrong?'

'Of course not. You've more than earned it.' Mary Ann's heart went out to her friend, who was plain, thirty and the youngest daughter of four. She had seen for herself how demanding Helen's parents were and how scornful her three married sisters were of her unmarried status.

'I'm saving up just in case – well, they might not leave me any money, you know, and then what would I do? I've heard Father say more than once that women don't have the intelligence to manage money, and that he's glad three of his daughters will have husbands to guide them after he's gone.' She gave a stifled sob and pressed the back of one hand to her mouth, as if to hold her pain in. 'I don't know why I'm telling you this, Mary Ann, only you've been so kind.'

'That's what friends are for.'

'I sometimes think I'll *burst* with frustration. I've never had a real friend before and they only let me go to Dr Peele's meetings because they knew her mother and think she'll be good for me. They see *you* as a cheap extra servant, so you don't count in their eyes. And – well, I've been meaning to apologise for how brusquely they speak to you, not to mention Father telling you what time to come home by.'

'It doesn't matter. I get the room free and I enjoy your company. I wouldn't want to stay out late anyway. Come and look out over the water for a few minutes. We don't have to hurry back.' As they stood on the promenade, Mary Ann suggested, 'Perhaps we could go out to the picture house together one evening?'

'They'll find some way to prevent it.'

'Then don't tell them till just before we leave.'

'Father will still forbid me to go out.'

Mary Ann thought about it and then said slowly, 'How can he stop you, though? He has trouble walking. You could just – go.'

Helen stared at her, round-eyed. 'I couldn't *disobey* him!'

'Why not?'

'He'd be furious.'

'You wouldn't be there to see it. You'd be watching the films with me.'

'He'd be furious for days afterwards. I'd be there to see that.'

'Then you should get angry with him, too. Helen, you have a *right* to go out sometimes. You must make it clear that you won't put up with being kept in like a prisoner. You're over thirty, after all, not a giddy young girl.'

'What if Father threw me out?'

Mary Ann gave a sudden chuckle. 'What, get rid of his free servant? Not him. And if he even threatens it, tell him you'd *prefer* to get a job and go into lodgings where someone else does the housework, and have only stayed with them because you felt it your duty. Then mark some jobs in the paper and leave it for him to find.'

'Oh.' Helen let out a gurgle of shocked laughter, then they started walking again. 'Dare I?'

'You have to, unless you want to go on like this for ever. And what's more, you should *demand* more money from him.'

'He won't give it to me.'

'Then cut down the food you give them and take it openly.' She looked at the other woman. 'I know it's easy for me to tell you, but I have another friend and she'd say the same thing exactly. She taught me that if you want something, you have to find ways of getting it – even if that means taking risks.'

Helen gave Mary Ann a sudden hug. 'I'm so glad you came to stay with us. I can't tell you what a difference it's made to me to have someone to talk to every day. I thought I was being unreasonable and selfish – at least, that's what my sister Georgina said.'

Mary Ann had met Georgina and thought *her* the selfish one. 'I'm happy to have a friend, too.'

But she was still missing Agnes's liveliness dreadfully. Helen was quiet and docile in comparison, though tonight's revelations had brought them closer. 'Come on,' Mary Ann said at last. 'We'll walk past the picture house and see what's showing. Give you something to look forward to.'

'I've never even been to one. Father says it's only a fad and won't last.'

'He's wrong. It's fun and I love going. And I'm not the only one. The place is always crowded. Anyway, it's only threepence, so it won't break the bank.'

In Lancashire Gabriel was keeping an eye on events in Europe. He bought newspapers more often, reading them carefully, thinking about the latest happenings while he did his work. When first Austria then Russia mobilised, he began to look grave and forecast that it would come to war.

Ivy refused to believe this and mocked him for his preoccupation, feeling grateful that Dan didn't bore on and on about German military might or instability in the Balkans. She felt she would go mad if she didn't have him to talk to once a week.

When Germany declared war on Russia on 2 August, Gabriel said, 'It'll definitely come to war now.'

'Are you sure, son?' Jassy asked.

'Yes. Germany's demanding passage through Belgium, you see. That'll tip the scales.'

On 4 August the German Army invaded Belgium and Britain delivered an ultimatum calling upon them to withdraw.

The Cloughs were woken on Wednesday 5 August by Maurice Greeson hammering on their door to announce that Germany had failed to answer Britain's ultimatum and the country was now at war. He thrust a newspaper into Gabriel's hand. 'See! I got one for you.'

When he had gone Jassy busied herself getting the fire burning and Gabriel sat devouring the newspaper.

Ivy went to sit opposite him. 'Dan says even if it does come to war, it'll all be over by Christmas. You surely don't think those nasty Germans can defeat Britain?'

He could not hold back a scornful sound. He was getting tired of the words 'Dan says' and was convinced now that his wife had stronger feelings for that fellow than she would admit. What he didn't know was whether he cared about that or not – and whether she intended to do anything about it. 'That just shows how little Dan Barworth knows. Germany's been rearming for a while and we're a long way behind them, so I reckon we'll have trouble holding them off.'

'You always were a pessimist.' Ivy tossed her head and refused to discuss the war, but could not help hearing Gabriel reading out the article to his mother.

On market day she was first shocked then grew sullen as she found even Dan obsessed by the latest war news.

In mid-August she came home in a foul mood because Dan had been absorbed in a new publication called *The Penny War Weekly* and had hardly talked about anything else all day, reading and re-reading it, showing her pictures of the Huns and of the much superior British soldiers.

She didn't want to see pictures of men fighting and dying, didn't want even to think about war. All she wanted was to find a way to escape from Gabriel and tending stinking hens day after day.

As August passed and the German Army continued its inexorable progress across northern France right to the gates of Paris, the British Government began to commandeer people's horses and recruiting posters appeared on walls saying, 'Your King and Country Need You'.

Young men flocked to volunteer and women took their places behind the stalls at the market.

Ivy felt she couldn't escape from war talk whatever she did and was grateful that their pony was considered too old and puny for war service or she didn't know what she'd have done about getting into town.

Gabriel began meeting regularly with a few like-minded men at the local pub to discuss the war. The group included his cousin Tom. They argued one night about who should volunteer, and most felt war was for single men and professional soldiers. Married men had responsibilities, people depending on them. But some of the men in the group, married or not, were eager to enlist and do their bit for the country. It seemed to Gabriel that they wanted an adventure and hadn't thought about what war would really be like.

When they were walking home, Tom said abruptly, 'I can't go. I'd not pass the medical with my bad leg.'

'I'd forgotten about that.'

'So had I. But I had a fall a few months ago and it started me limping again when I'm tired. The doctor says there's nowt else they can do.'

'Do you wish you could go?'

'I do and I don't. I've never left Lancashire and I'd like to see summat of the rest of the world, but I don't know whether I *could* kill anyone. What about you?'

'I'm torn both ways, too.'

As Gabriel drove home he wondered why he had this urge to enlist. Patriotism, he supposed. It wasn't something you talked about, but it was there. What it boiled down to was: you were proud you were an Englishman and would defend your country to your last breath.

But he had Ivy and the girls to look after. He couldn't just up and leave them – especially now with Dan Barworth and his wife so cosy.

At the next market Dan announced his intention of joining the Army. Ivy gaped at him. 'You must be mad!'

He shrugged. 'Mebbe. But I'm going down to the recruiting office tomorrow.'

She was so furious with him she refused to go for their usual cup of tea after the market closed, though she regretted that all evening, feeling she might have been able to talk a bit of sense into him if she hadn't flown into a temper. What if he were whisked off somewhere to do his Army training and she never saw him again?

How would she bear that?

The following week, however, he turned up at the market looking so unhappy she went across to him even before she set up her stall. 'What's wrong, Dan love?'

'They wouldn't have me in the Army. Said I can't see well enough without my glasses and there's something wrong with my lungs. That doesn't stop me working hard, does it? I've no one dependent on me now, so it's fellows like me who should be signing up. I could do *something* to help, I know I could, even if it was only a desk job.'

Relief coursed through her. 'Well, I'm thrilled that you'll not be going away.'

He clasped her hand briefly. 'It was partly because of you I wanted to join.'

'What on earth do you mean? *I* never egged you on to volunteer.'

He glanced round to make sure no one was close enough to overhear what they were saying. 'I can't go on like this, seeing you only once a week, thinking about you the rest of the time. I go home to an empty house every Thursday, knowing you don't love him,' his voice lowered still further, 'and don't even share a bed with him. Eh, Ivy lass, I love you so much.'

'Oh, Dan! You never said how you felt.'

'Didn't you guess?'

She nodded. 'And hoped I wasn't fooling myself. But you should have *said*.'

'What good would it have done? You're married.' He looked her in the eyes, his own haunted. 'I can't go on like this. If I'm not allowed to join up, I'm going out to join my cousin in Australia. He's asked me several times and the doctor says it'll be good for my lungs to live in a warmer climate. Maybe there I'll be able to forget you.'

Someone passed by and called a cheerful greeting.

Ivy waved one hand in response but her eyes never left Dan's. 'If it wasn't for the children, I'd leave Gabriel today and come with you.'

'*You would?*'

'Yes. I love you too, you know.'

'Oh, Ivy, I can't imagine owt I'd like better than for us to be together.' After another pause, he said slowly, 'If it's the girls who're stopping you, you could bring them too. I like kids.'

She shook her head. 'I couldn't take them away from Gabriel.

He loves them both and he's a wonderful father, even though Frances isn't his. I feel so indebted to him, but do I owe him the rest of my life? Oh, Dan, there must be some way to—'

Her voice had risen and he grasped her arm, shaking it and saying gently, 'Shhh, love. Keep your voice down.' As they looked at one another he said huskily, 'It's hell not even being able to touch you.'

Another long silence then he added, 'Would you think about it anyway, Ivy love? Coming with me to Australia, I mean? We'd have to leave quickly, before the war stops us. I'd always love and respect you, treat you as my wife, you know that, don't you?'

She nodded, a smile lighting up her face suddenly. 'Yes, I do know it. I'll – think about it. I'm very tempted.'

A woman called over, 'You all right, Ivy love?'

She glanced round. 'Yes. I'm fine.' She was behind in setting up and everyone was staring at them. 'We'll talk afterwards.'

She went back to the stall, her mind in turmoil.

Could she? Dare she?

The following few days were rainy and the hen houses seemed to smell worse than ever. The children grizzled because they couldn't play out and Ivy knew she was being sharp with everyone.

At night she lay awake for hours thinking of Dan, trying to work out what to do.

Every evening she stared across at Gabriel, lost in his reading, or Jassy, placidly sewing, and knew she couldn't face a lifetime of this.

The following Thursday she walked across to Dan before she lost the courage and said, 'I'll come.'

He dropped his bundle of blankets and stood like a man frozen for a few minutes, then a smile dawned on his face. 'Eh, Ivy love, you've made me the happiest man on earth.'

'Well, keep your voice down because I don't want folk guessing.' She sighed and looked at him, realising she'd spoken as sharply as ever. 'Are you sure you want a woman who'll speak to you like that?'

'Very sure. And Ivy . . .'

'What?'

'I've already been making inquiries. We'll have to leave before the end of September or we might not get a passage.'

'So soon?'

'Aye.'

She swallowed hard. 'Then you'd better book, hadn't you? Two adults, two children. Dan, what are you doing?'

'Going off to book.'

'But your stall!'

'To hell with that!' He began cramming things back into boxes.

When the market finished, he turned up again and came across to her. 'Let's go to the café.'

As they sat sipping their tea, he asked, 'Is there any way you can get away during the week? We need to make proper plans.'

'Monday,' she said without hesitation. 'I'll come into town on Monday to your house.'

'You know where I live?'

'Yes. I'll come in the back way.'

Jassy was suspicious when Ivy insisted she had to go into town on the Monday. She couldn't have said why, but she was. She watched Ivy harness the pony and take the girls to school, then stood hesitating in the kitchen before going up to her daughter-in-law's bedroom. She had never been one to pry but something was wrong, she knew it, and she didn't want her Gabriel getting hurt any more. He'd grown so quiet these days, only showing his old sense of fun with the girls.

At first glance there seemed nothing wrong with the room, then she saw something sticking out from beneath the bed and pulled out Ivy's suitcase. What was that doing down here? It was usually stored in the attics.

She opened it and stared in surprise at some neatly folded clothes, Ivy's winter things, all carefully packed.

Closing it she pushed it back under the bed, leaving the corner sticking out just a bit, exactly as it had been, then went downstairs to make herself a cup of tea and try to work out what this might mean.

Well, it could only mean one thing. Her daughter-in-law was leaving.

But where was she going?

When Ivy came back that evening Jassy could see that she was full of suppressed excitement, unable to settle to anything. After the girls were in bed, she fidgeted around for a while, then said casually, 'Eh, I'm a bit tired tonight. I think I'll go up early.'

Only she didn't go to bed. Jassy heard her footsteps moving to and fro because however quietly you walked the old floorboards creaked.

She looked across at Gabriel, lost in a book as usual. When the girls went to bed, it was as if you'd turned down a lamp inside him and he hardly said another word. She wasn't sure whether he'd noticed anything, so didn't comment on Ivy's strange behaviour.

Not yet.

On the last Thursday in August Jassy heard a motor car chugging along the lane to the farm. Nasty smelly thing, she thought. Must be someone for the Greesons.

Since they were now on holiday from school for the summer, the girls were playing in the back garden, running a shop with their dolls, selling each other little bunches of wildflowers they'd gathered, using small pebbles as money. They were good little lasses, she thought fondly, devoted to one another.

When the car stopped outside the farm Jassy went to the front door, surprised to see Ivy getting out of it. Her daughter-in-law was supposed to be at the market. What was she doing home? She was accompanied by Dan Barworth, though he stayed in the car.

'Is summat wrong?' Jassy asked.

'No. Summat's very right,' Ivy answered. 'Where's Gabriel?'

'You know where he is, gone over to Burnley to deliver them sheep.'

'Good.' Ivy hesitated then said brusquely, 'I'm leaving him, Mrs Clough. I've come to fetch my things.' Another hesitation, then she added, 'And I'm taking the girls with me.'

'Tha'll never! Eh, I won't let thee do it.'

'How can you stop me? I'm their mother.'

Jassy watched her go inside, calling out for the girls, then it came to her what she should do and she ran round the side to where they were playing. 'Your mam's going to take you away from here,' she said. 'You'll never see your daddy again if she does.'

Two faces puckered up as this sank in and tears welled in their eyes.

'If you run away up on the moors, to the fairy circle, she'll not be able to find you. Your daddy will come to fetch you later and—'

Ivy's voice rang out behind her. 'Ah, there you are! Frances, Christina, come and wash your faces. We're going for a ride in a motor car.'

'Run!' Jassy shouted. 'Run as fast as you can.'

But Ivy grabbed hold of the girls and began dragging them towards the house.

As they started to cry, Jassy knew she had to act. She ran at Ivy from behind and knocked her over, yelling, 'Run!'

Ivy was so shocked by the attack it took her a moment to realise what was happening and struggle to her feet, by which time the two little girls were partway up the hill.

'Come back at once,' Ivy roared.

They stopped, looking back at her, but Jassy made shooing noises and called again, 'Run away, quick!' They set off again, nimble as mountain goats.

Ivy ran a few steps, ricked her ankle and stopped to yell, 'Dan! Come and help me.'

The girls were now in the top field and vanished over the brow of the hill soon afterwards.

'How *dare* you do this to me?' Ivy yelled at Jassy, taking her shoulders and shaking her hard.

Dan appeared round the corner and rushed towards them. 'Nay, love! What are you doing?'

Ivy turned to him. 'She's sent the girls off somewhere.'

He stepped between them and looked at Jassy. 'Why did you do that?'

'Because my Gabriel's heart would be broken if he lost them lasses. I don't know where you were thinking of taking them, but it wouldn't be fair. He's their father.'

Dan bowed his head for a moment.

'Where are you going?' Jassy asked. 'Where did you intend to take my grandchilder?'

There was a long silence then he said quietly, 'Australia.'

'Nay, never! Eh, that's wicked, that is.' She turned to her daugher-in-law. 'I didn't think it of you, Ivy Clough. He fathered that child of yours and saved your good name. How could you repay him by taking t'lasses so far away that he'd never see them again?'

Ivy flushed a dull red. 'Because they're my daughters, too.'

'Tha loves only thysen,' Jassy said scornfully, falling back instinctively into the language of her childhood. She folded her arms and scowled at Ivy. 'Well, tha'll not find 'em now afore my Gabriel gets back.'

'But *you* know where they are.'

'Aye. But I'm not tellin'.'

'Please, Jassy, fetch them back.'

The older woman shook her head, her features set in stubborn lines, every inch of her scrawny body radiating defiance.

Ivy looked at Dan, who put his arm round her shoulders. 'We have to leave today,' he murmured. 'Our passage is booked.'

'How can I, now?'

He looked at her steadily. 'Only you can make that decision, but I'm going. It's too late to change my mind now, and any road I don't want to.'

She began to weep against him, great racking sobs.

Jassy watched her, unmoved. Tears meant nowt. It was what folk did as made you respect them and Ivy hadn't even had the courage to tell Gabriel to his face that she was leaving.

Dan looked across at Jassy. 'She's not been happy here.'

'What's happy got to do with it? Her *duty* lies here.'

'That's cold comfort for a loving woman like Ivy.'

He really meant that, Jassy realised, which showed what a fool he was. 'Take her away, then, and make her happy. I can look after them lasses. She'll know they're in good hands.'

Ivy stopped sobbing. 'How can you ask me to leave them?'

'I'm not asking you to do anything. You can stay with them if you want and I'll say nowt about this to our Gabriel.'

Ivy looked round. From the runs round the hen houses came the steady clucking of the fowls. The smells that wafted across on the breeze made her shudder. Every time she had to go into those hen houses she felt sick. She sagged against Dan and looked at him, lips quivering. 'I can't stay.'

He put his arm round her shoulders. 'Come and get your things then, love.'

Jassy watched them walk towards the hosue. She didn't go inside until they'd left, then she went up to Ivy's room. It had an empty feel to it. One of the drawers wasn't closed properly and she pushed it in carefully. She wandered next door to the girls' rooms and found two suitcases standing open on the beds, full of clothes crammed in anyhow.

A piece of paper fluttered to the floor and she picked it up automatically. A list of the girls' clothes. There were no toys listed. Had Ivy not intended to take any? All those weeks on a ship and nowt of their own to comfort them lasses. How could she even consider taking them to Australia, going so far away that Gabriel would never have seen them childer again?

Feeling suddenly shaky, Jassy sat down on the bed. What if the girls hadn't done as she'd told them? What if they hadn't run away? Eh, it didn't bear thinking of.

Never mind Gabriel, it'd have torn her own heart in two to lose her granddaughters.

She'd never considered Ivy cruel before, but she did now.

Just to be safe Jassy didn't go up to the top field until later that afternoon. When she began calling she saw two heads bob up and beckoned to them. The girls came running towards her.

'We're hungry,' Christina said.

'Well, you come with me and I'll mek you a nice jam butty.' She put one arm round each girl and they walked slowly down the field together.

As they got to the farm Gabriel came out of the barn, looking pleased with himself. 'I got good prices!' he called. Then he saw the girls' tearstained faces and his mother's grim expression. 'What's wrong?'

So she told him, watched him shudder and take both girls into his arms, hugging them convulsively. He looked up and said simply, 'Thanks, Mum.'

And she couldn't help weeping, she who never cried, because it was a terrible thing she had done, keeping children away from their mother. She knew that. She was a mother too.

Her son's arms were strong and for a moment she leaned against him, but for a moment only. Seeing the two girls watching her fearfully, she pulled herself together with a brisk, 'Well, then. Let's get you that jam butty.'

Only when the girls had gone to bed did Jassy tell her son all the details. He nodded and then sat staring into the fire all evening, not even pretending to read. His face was sad, his whole body drooping.

Eh, you never stopped hurting for them, even when they were grown men, Jassy thought as she got ready for bed.

16

September 1914 – January 1915

Everyone talked of 'business as usual' in spite of the war, but Mary Ann didn't see how that would be possible. Ordinary customers at the tea rooms were fewer, though groups of men came in from time to time, complaining about poor Army food and the fact that they were being trained by old men who had retired from the services decades ago and should have bloody well stayed retired. Many of them also grumbled about the lack of proper uniforms and having to live in tents.

When some of the male porters and railway clerks enlisted, the station master had to take on women to replace them. This caused a lot of amusement in some quarters, with men saying women wouldn't be able to handle the heavy luggage let alone the commercial goods that were being transported.

Ruby sniffed when she overheard them mocking. 'Just listen to them fools! Women have been carrying children and heavy shopping bags since time began. No one says children are too heavy for them, do they? Those idiots don't know what they're talking about and I've a good mind to tell them so.'

'It's not worth it. They'll get used to seeing women doing men's jobs, whether they like it or not.' Mary Ann straightened the last tablecloth and looked round with satisfaction. She liked to have the place looking its best.

'Will they, though? Everyone says it'll all be over by Christmas.'

'Dr Peele doesn't agree. She thinks it'll last longer – years even.'

Ruby laughed comfortably. 'I can't see that.'

Mary Ann didn't bother to argue with her. She hated the thought of a prolonged war, but Dr Peele had been right before and was probably right now. Already English soldiers and sailors were being killed over in France or at sea – and for what? Simply because their leaders had quarrelled, as far as she could work out. Dr Peele called it 'entrenched arrogance and stupidity'.

Well, whatever the reasons, it wouldn't prevent Mary Ann from doing her bit, and she suspected that Constance Peele would feel the same.

Three weeks later Lady Bingram came bustling into the tea room. 'Ah, there you are Mary Ann! Can you take a few minutes off? I want to ask you something.'

'I can see to things,' Ruby whispered, giving her colleague a push, then raising her voice to add, 'I'll bring you over a pot of tea, your ladyship.'

Mary Ann led the way to a table in the corner and took a chair, wondering what her visitor could want.

Daphne came straight to the point, as usual. 'You know I've been forming a corps of volunteers to help in the war effort? Well, I've been asked to get together a group of women who can drive the top brass around. It'll save soldiers doing it. I wondered if you'd like to join us?'

Mary Ann could only stare at her. 'Me? But I can't drive.'

'We'll soon teach you. It's not all that difficult. But we need strong women who can start cars and aren't afraid to be out on their own.'

'I – don't know what to say.'

'Say yes. As Lord Kitchener tells us, your King and country need you.'

But still Mary Ann hesitated, trying to think it through. 'I'd like to try it, but does it pay wages? I have to earn my living, you see.'

'What are you getting here?'

'Twenty-five shillings a week.'

'I'll give you a pound a week, all found, plus your uniform. I can't give you more than the others are getting.' Daphne leaned back to allow Ruby to set the tea things down on the table, nodded her thanks and began to pour. 'So it's settled? Good. Shall we say you'll join us a week today?'

Bemused, Mary Ann nodded. She didn't mind getting a little less money if she could help the war effort. Besides – learning to drive would be wonderful, she was sure.

'Good girl. I'll send you your train ticket and directions to our London house where some of the motor corps will be living because we can park the cars in the mews behind. Give me your address.' Daphne devoured two scones and poured a second cup of tea, stirring in three spoonfuls of sugar. 'Before I go back, I'd better speak to Jenks and tell him you're needed for the war effort and he's to give you your job back afterwards.' She grinned. 'That's if you're not married by then or wanting to stay in London.'

Mary Ann gave her usual answer, 'I don't intend to get married.' Then she realised something else and added, 'And I wouldn't want to live permanently away from the sea.'

'M'husband's the same about the country. Until the war started he hardly ever went up to town.' Daphne drank the second cup of tea with the same enthusiasm she seemed to turn to everything in life.

When she had left, Mary Ann cleared the table and took the dishes back to the kitchen.

'Well?' Ruby asked at once.

'She wants me to join her volunteer corps as a driver. I'm to go and live in London and they'll teach me how to drive.' Suddenly excitement surged through her. 'I can't believe it's happening to me.'

Ruby's face crumpled. 'But what'll I do without you? I can't manage the paperwork, I just can't do that sort of thing.'

'I've got an idea about that, but I can't tell you till I've spoken to Mr Jenks and someone else.'

That night she suggested Helen take over her job. After a stunned silence her friend said bitterly, 'How can I? I still have Mother and Father to look after.'

'You know as well as I do that they're not as helpless as they pretend to be. Tell them it's your contribution to the war effort and they won't dare refuse. Suggest your daily help comes in more often. That's if you want to do it?'

'Oh, Mary Ann, I'd love to.' Helen began fiddling with her cuff. 'Only – what if I can't manage?'

'Of course you can. It's not hard. You can come in to work with me tomorrow and I'll start showing you what to do.'

When he was told Mr Charters turned bright red and forbade his daughter even to think of such a thing.

For once Helen stood up for herself. 'I'm doing it.'

'I'll turn you out then. See how you manage without anywhere to live.'

'I can find myself lodgings like others do, but I'm determined to do my bit, Father.'

Surprisingly her mother said, 'She's right. We can't be selfish when the country needs women like her, Thomas.'

He rounded on his wife. 'It's not her country she'll be serving, she'll be working in tea rooms! Our daughter, waiting on any common person with the price of a cup of tea in his pocket!'

'Soldiers use the tea rooms all the time,' Helen said softly. 'And my doing the job will allow Mary Ann to go and work in London. So it *is* helping the country.'

There was a long, pregnant silence then her father said pettishly, 'I don't know what's got into you lately, I really don't.'

'The same thing as has *got into* everyone else. There's a war on. I can make a difference.'

When she went to her room, Helen sat down on the bed, feeling shaky but triumphant. She had done it! Stood up for herself.

And would continue to do so.

A few days later Mary Ann set off for London. The train journey inevitably made her think of Agnes, but there were so many soldiers travelling now that her thoughts soon turned to the war and the opportunities it was providing for her to learn new things. It didn't seem right that she was benefiting from other people's suffering.

Well, I'll repay them, she vowed. Whatever they ask of me, I'll do, and do it well. If men can give their lives for their country, then we women can cope with whatever needs doing at home.

It seemed to her in later years that this vow was another major turning point in her life.

Like many other women involved in war work, Lady Bingram's Aides were kitted out in a smart uniform, supplied by the Bingrams, consisting of boots and trousers with a long tunic coat over them and a very smart cap, all in dark brown.

'You girls may as well look good,' said Daphne with one of her irrepressible grins. 'It'll cheer the soldiers up to see you.'

The women from the drivers' corps were lodged in the old servants' quarters at the Bingrams' London house, a ramshackle place which had been allowed to run down. To Mary Ann's surprise there were quite a few girls from Lancashire there and she found that Daphne's family came from the north, though she'd never have guessed it from her friend's accent.

The drivers' corps were to take it in turns to help with the cooking though their food would be provided. When nobody else did it, Mary Ann worked out a roster for this and pinned it to the notice board that had been provided for them.

Daphne found the piece of paper, asked who'd drawn the roster up and looked thoughtfully at Mary Ann. 'Good, good.' They were to find that this was her main form of praise. She judged her 'girls' on how they worked, not their family backgrounds, and those who'd been tossed the curt, 'Good, good,' soon learned to feel proud of themselves, for her ladyship didn't praise you unless you'd earned it.

One other thing Daphne did early on was bring in an old army sergeant to teach the girls some self-defence tactics. 'You'll be out at night on your own,' she said in her abrupt way. 'It's best to

avoid trouble but sometimes you can't, so you should know how
to defend yourselves.'

There was much giggling at first, but what Sarge taught them
made sense to Mary Ann. She had been unable to defend herself
against Jeff Powling when she was fourteen, but if she met him
now, she'd give a better account of herself. She was not only
bigger and stronger but most important of all, more confident
– and Sarge said it was often lack of confidence that prevented
weaker people from fighting back.

Sometimes, on the evenings when Lord Bingram was out,
Daphne ate with them, for she was not one to stand on ceremony.
At first the class differences made for stiffness between the girls,
but she wouldn't allow that. 'We're all of equal worth here,' she
insisted, 'because we're helping our country in its hour of need.
So from now on I'll be Daphne, not "my lady", and we'll have
no more fussing about rank or class.'

By the time they'd all worked together for a few weeks, the
stiffness vanished, especially when it was found that some of the
working-class women, Mary Ann for one, were quicker to learn
the new skills required of them.

They were all nervous when they had their first lessons in
driving, but Mary Ann found her height and strength an advantage
and soon mastered the new skill. One girl who was very slight
simply couldn't turn the crank handle to start the cars and had
to leave the group.

'Knew you'd do well,' Daphne said smugly to Mary Ann one
day when she was driving her to a meeting.

'Did you?'

'Yes. You're a very capable sort of woman.'

Capable or not, the first time Mary Ann took a car out on her
own she was terrified. But nothing went wrong and soon she built
up confidence, the main problem being to learn her way about
central London.

One day she'd be driving Lady Bingram, the next some high-
ranking officer or foreign dignitary. It was wonderful not knowing
what she'd be doing from one day to the next. And even waiting

around for one's passenger wasn't so bad because Daphne had told them to borrow books from the library in her house any time they wanted.

Gabriel refused to discuss his wife's disappearance with anyone outside the family, though he did tell his cousin what had happened.

Most difficult of all was trying to explain to the girls why Ivy had gone away, and he wasn't sure he'd done it well. Both of them had clearly been hurt by their mother's actions and Christina had occasional nightmares, waking them all up by screaming for her mother.

Ivy's actions had hurt Gabriel, too, though he tried not to show it. Not even to say goodbye after all they'd shared!

If he didn't have his daughters and mother to consider, he'd have joined up immediately. It seemed wrong that he could be doing the same old things day after day, his life almost unchanged, while other men were away fighting for their country. He'd led too sheltered a life, he knew, which was why he'd so easily fallen prey to Ivy.

'You want to join up, don't you?' his mother asked abruptly one day.

He hesitated, then nodded.

'We could manage if you did. Tom would keep an eye on us and you know I'd look after the girls.'

'It wouldn't be fair to lay such a burden on you.'

'Burden? Those girls aren't a burden, they're a joy to me.'

He had never heard her express her love so openly and it seemed to him that she was mellowing as she grew older.

'Doris and I can see to the hens,' Jassy went on, 'and she likes going to market, but you'd have to do something about the livestock. We couldn't manage that.'

'It wouldn't be fair.' But he could hear how half-hearted his protest sounded.

She gave a dry laugh. 'Fair! When was life ever fair?'

'I'll think about it.'

A few days later Gabriel came to stand next to his mother as she pegged out the washing. 'I'll not do anything till after Christmas. If it looks like the war's going to be over quickly, they won't need me, though I suspect it'll continue for longer than that.'

'I reckon it will, too. With all them men traipsing to and fro across Europe, I can't see how it'll ever be over quickly. Nor I don't think much of that Lord Kitchener everyone's so fond of. I never did like men with moustaches.'

Gabriel chuckled and risked giving her a quick hug.

Jassy looked up at him with one of her rare smiles. 'Eh, you're a good lad.' Then she moved away and began fussing over the washing.

Just after Christmas, Daphne got a message which made her look grave and gather her girls together.

'They need three extra stewardesses to help bring Belgian refugees across the Channel and have asked if some of you would help out temporarily.'

'What would it entail?' a girl called Virginia asked.

'You'd have to go across on the ferry and help look after the refugees on the way back. You'd be doing whatever was necessary: serving food, cleaning up after those who're seasick, comforting folk who're upset. Oh, and they said they prefer people who're good sailors.'

Virginia pulled a face. 'I don't think I'd do, then. I'm always dreadfully seasick.'

'I'd like to give it a try,' Mary Ann offered. 'There were paddle steamers running from the North Pier in Blackpool. Agnes and I went to Southport a few times, and to Llandudno once. I loved it.'

Two other aides called Patricia and Ellen volunteered to help the refugees as well, so Lady Bingram told them to be packed and ready to leave first thing in the morning.

The three of them got together to discuss what to take.

'It sounds jolly exciting,' Patricia said.

'It'll be dangerous, though,' Mary Ann warned her.

Patricia shrugged. 'If it wasn't for the war, I'd probably be married to Tim Wiskill-Carpe and now that I've seen a bit more of life, I know he'd have bored me stupid.' She stared into the fire. 'I was brought up to marry well, you know. Everything led back to that for people like my family. Not marrying for love, but for money and position.'

'I wouldn't have minded a family with more money,' Ellen said frankly. 'We never had any choice. It was get a job and bring in wages as soon as I was thirteen.'

'When I left school I worked for my mother in our boarding house,' Mary Ann said. 'She didn't even give me proper wages. I've always resented that.'

'Whatever happens to us,' Patricia said softly, 'I think we're all learning a lot about ourselves and our abilities, and that can only be good.'

The three young women were driven to Parkstone Quay by one of their colleagues. When she left them at the waterside they confessed to one another that they were nervous. After a brief interview with a woman who seemed incapable of smiling, they were each sent to a different ship.

Bridie, the head stewardess of *The Grey Lady*, looked suspiciously at Mary Ann. 'Have you had any experience looking after people?'

'I've worked in boarding houses, been a chambermaid in a big hotel and helped run some tea rooms.'

'Sounds more promising than the last volunteer they sent me. Spoiled little rich girl, she was, too proud to clean up after people. And at least you look strong.'

'I am. I'm never ill.'

'Good. Let me show you the ropes, then.'

They had to prepare the cabins for the first-class passengers, help with the simple refreshments that would be served, and get ready for passengers who were seasick.

'There's always someone sick, however calm the day,' Bridie warned her. 'And if it's rough, we're run off our feet helping them.

You'll get used to clearing up the mess. Just make sure any time you empty a bucket over the side, you do it with the wind at your back. If you face into it everything will blow back all over you.'

Mary Ann nodded.

'It's important to learn where everything goes and then to stow things carefully in their proper places. We don't have much room, you see, so we have to be very well organised. We won't have many passengers on the trip across, just a few soldiers and officers going back to the Front, but we'll be crowded on the way back.'

They left the following morning, pulling slowly away from Parkstone Quay beneath a lowering sky that threatened rain. Mary Ann was thankful the sea was reasonably calm. As the ship made its way down the river to the open sea, she noticed Bridie watching her. 'I'm fine.'

'There are some as get sick the minute the ship sails.'

'Not me.'

Suddenly, just off Landguard, there was a gentle bump and a jarring feeling.

'Oh, mercy, we've run aground on a sandbank!' Bridie exclaimed.

Mary Ann looked at her in shock. 'Run aground?'

The head stewardess grinned. 'It happens sometimes. They'll get us off, but we might as well serve the breakfasts while we can. It'll be a lot choppier later.'

It seemed strange to be serving bacon and eggs, then eating some herself, but Mary Ann found that she was ravenous. By the time she had finished eating the ship had started off once more.

'There, we're moving again,' Bridie said. 'Come on! There's still a lot to do.'

Mary Ann trailed about after her like a shadow, winning praise for her speed in learning as she gradually got used to the various tasks.

At one stage she was given a lesson in emergency procedures and it was stressed that any ship could be sunk and several had been, so she was to learn where every single piece of lifesaving equipment was as a matter of urgency. That brought home to her once again the danger of this new job of hers. Well, so be it. Men were facing danger every day and dying for their country.

'Are we losing many ships?' she asked. 'I heard about HMS *Formidable* being sunk, of course, but I hadn't heard of any others.'

'There have been a couple that I know of sunk,' Bridie admitted. 'We think it was mines, but we're not sure. The German Navy doesn't usually attack us in the Channel, but there's always a first time, isn't there?' She shrugged. 'I try not to think of it. But do learn the emergency procedures, dear. Just to be safe.'

When they gave her a ten-minute break and told her to get some fresh air, Mary Ann went to stand on deck, enjoying the bracing air and the sight of the vast expanse of grey water. Out here it was noticeably choppier than it had been in the Thames and she was glad she had a good sense of balance.

An older officer whose uniform was unfamiliar to her came up to stand at the rail next to her, saying in heavily accented English, 'You are new.'

'Yes. I usually drive people around London, but they asked for volunteers to help bring refugees back, so I thought I'd give it a go.'

'I'm here to keep an eye on my compatriots.' He pulled a rueful face. 'Not all of them are as grateful to our allies as we would wish. And many speak no English.'

'You're Belgian?'

He nodded. 'And you're English – very English indeed.'

His gaze was warm and friendly, but there was nothing at all objectionable in it. Well, he was considerably older than she was, after all, old enough to be her father. It was strange how comfortable she felt with him. Bridie came to join them and it seemed that the older woman also considered the Belgian officer a friend.

'Ah, Captain Lepuy. I see you've met our new stewardess. Mary Ann, if you need an interpreter, you call for the Captain's help. Or if anyone is being troublesome.'

He gave them both a mocking bow, flourishing one hand. 'At your service always, ladies.'

'I'll remember that.' Mary Ann looked at the fob watch pinned to her lapel. It was part of her uniform these days, though she'd never carried a watch previously, just relied on the sun and the nearest clock. 'Well, I'd better get back to my job.'

Bridie lingered for a moment. 'I like that one,' she told Georges after the younger woman had left.

'My older daughter would have been her age if she'd lived,' he said quietly, 'and she had hair of just that colour.'

Bridie patted his arm. This was his third voyage with them and they all knew the tragic tale of how his wife and two daughters had been killed in their own home by a German shell at the very beginning of the war. She must, she decided, tell Mary Ann about it so there weren't any awkward questions. You could see the sadness in Captain Lepuy's eyes at times, though he didn't dwell on his personal tragedy, just got on with things.

Which was all anyone could do.

The ferry arrived at the Hook of Holland at about four-thirty in the afternoon and when Mary Ann confessed that she'd never before set foot on foreign soil, Bridie laughed and insisted on rectifying that. She and another stewardess took their new colleague for a short walk, stopping in a dockside café for a drink of red wine.

Mary Ann sipped hers cautiously because she didn't usually drink alcohol, trying not to grimace at the taste.

Bridie laughed. 'It'll grow on you, girl. Get it down.'

But Mary Ann found the wine went straight to her head and didn't like the woozy feeling, so left half the glass. It was nice to be in a foreign country, though, and this place was very different from the ones where she'd worked, halfway between a pub and a café as far as she could tell.

The following morning they all got up early and started preparing for the refugees who were expected to come on board about ten o'clock. However, a message arrived to say they'd been delayed.

'They were delayed last time, too,' Bridie grumbled. 'Foreigners just can't organise things properly, though don't tell Captain Lepuy I said that.'

At two-thirty the refugees began to arrive on the quay and the stewardesses had to go and help put labels on each person. This took so long they were unable to get them all on the ship until seven o'clock.

A meal of Irish stew and potatoes was served then and Mary Ann was pleased to see everyone tucking in. Some of the cabin passengers pulled a face at the simplicity of the food, but it didn't stop them eating it, she noticed.

The refugees seemed pleasant enough and those who could speak English asked her anxiously when they would be setting off, seeming very anxious about the crossing and keen to reach the safety of England.

She didn't get to bed until past eleven, so tired that she fell straight asleep in spite of the hardness of her narrow bunk. In the morning Bridie had to shake her awake.

They left the Hook of Holland at seven-thirty in the morning and the sea was much rougher than it had been on the way across from England. Mary Ann felt a slight queasiness for a few minutes when they first hit open water, but that soon passed, probably because she was too busy to heed it.

They served only dry biscuits and coffee. 'Safer,' Bridie said. 'Don't like to waste good food.'

A lot of people were sick during the morning but in the afternoon the wind seemed to abate a little and some of the passengers were able to eat a few sandwiches.

As soon as they'd got into the quieter water of the Thames, they served a hot dinner of ham, pease pudding and potatoes, to which about half the passengers did justice.

When they reached Tilbury at quarter to eight, Mary Ann stood for a moment on deck watching the ship dock, feeling pleased with how she'd coped with her first trip abroad.

'Well, now we've got rid of the passengers,' Bridie said later, 'let's clear up and go to bed. I'm tired even if you young ones aren't. Oh, and Mary Ann . . .'

'Yes?'

'You did well. I hope you'll stay with us till this crisis is over.'

'I'd love to.' She went to bed feeling proud that she was contributing even more directly than before to the war effort.

The following day she was allowed to go back to base and rushed across London to find she had the place to herself except for the housekeeper, as all the other girls were out on jobs.

She also found a letter waiting for her from Bob, telling her the news at the Charrington and Bournemouth and saying he was thinking of volunteering.

Already her life at the hotel seemed far in the past, but she had warm memories of Bob, so she did a little washing, wrote a reply and posted the letter on her way back to the ship.

The next trip was uneventful until a pilot boat signalled to them to stop as they were nearing the Hook of Holland because they'd found and sunk a mine and were still checking the area for others.

Captain Lepuy came to stand at the rail with Mary Ann and watch what was happening. 'I don't think we're in much danger.'

'To tell you the truth,' she confided, 'I forget about the danger when I'm busy.'

Looking at her sparkling eyes and rosy face, he said impulsively, 'You remind me very much of my older daughter, though she was a much smaller woman. But she had your zest for life, and her hair was very similar.' He touched it briefly.

'I was sorry to hear about your family.'

'They usually tell new crew members about it so that they won't upset me by asking, but sometimes I like to talk about Marie and the girls. If I don't, it's as if they never existed, isn't it?'

'I never knew my father,' she said, offering confidence for confidence, 'and I haven't seen my mother since I was fifteen because I didn't get on with my stepfather. At least you had your family for all those years.'

'Yes. And I shall always have them here.' He tapped his chest.

After docking at the Hook of Holland they had a quiet evening on the ship, Mary Ann declining to go out and drink more wine with Bridie. Nasty sour stuff, it was, if you asked her. So she again found herself at the rail, warmly wrapped and chatting quietly to Captain Lepuy, heedless of the chill night air.

As they were turning to go down to their quarters, he said abruptly, 'I've enjoyed your company, my dear. I have no daughter now and you have no father, so maybe we can become friends?' He cocked one eyebrow at her, waiting with his usual quiet dignity for her answer.

'I'd be honoured.'

She had tears in her eyes as she undressed and lay down. Meeting Captain Lepuy and hearing his story had brought home to her far more than the stories in the newspapers did the personal losses that were the price people paid for fighting a war.

It made her wish she could see her mother again, for some strange reason. It was so sad to be estranged from her only relative. But not if it meant seeing Jeff Powling too. His face still haunted her nightmares, as did her dead baby's.

No one in her present life knew anything about the baby and she understood exactly what the Captain had meant. Sometimes she wished quite desperately that she could talk about Elizabeth and share her feelings of loss with someone.

17

December 1914 – late 1915

Margaret heard regularly from Mary Ann, letters bubbling with excitement about her new life, and felt very jealous. The bombing of Scarborough and Hartlepool in December 1914, with the loss of over a hundred lives, further convinced her that civilians simply could not sit and wait for the armed forces to win the war. They had to play their part, too. And there was no sign of the conflict being over by Christmas.

After agonising for days she went to talk to Angela. 'I don't feel I'm doing enough for the war effort. Oh, we knit and roll bandages, but I want to do *more*. And – I want to be with people who don't look down their noses at me while I'm doing it.'

Angela looked at her with a wry smile. 'I've been wondering how long it would be before you decided that.'

'You have?'

'Yes. I was young once and full of energy like you. There was no war to give me a reason to leave home so I married, and after that, well – Edward would never have let his wife do half the things you do, even if there had been cars for me to drive in those days.' Her smile twisted into sadness for a minute. 'I never even managed to have the large family I wanted.'

Margaret truly understood for the first time why she had such a staunch ally in the older woman. 'Will Papa Garbutt let *me* do something more, do you think? And most important of all, will you look after Johnny for me if I have to go away?'

'Of course I'll look after Johnny. It's something I adore doing.' Angela's smile this time wasn't forced. 'And I think Edward will throw a fit at first, but if we both talk to him, he'll come round eventually. Best to have something definite in mind first, though. It's much easier to dismiss a vague plan out of hand.'

So Margaret wrote to Lady Bingram offering her services.

She didn't receive a reply for several days and found it hard to conceal her anxiety about this from Angela, even Edward commenting on how fidgety she was and asking if she felt all right. Then the letter arrived, a curt few lines asking her to come to London for an interview because her ladyship never took on anyone without meeting them first.

Margaret broached the idea to Edward that evening. He bristled and interrupted before she had even finished the reasoned arguments she had rehearsed.

'What's happening to you young women nowadays? You're always wanting to go off gallivanting about the country. Well, I'm not having my womenfolk traipsing round London until the war is over. The place is full of soldiers and it's no longer safe for a lady.'

'I'd not be going there for pleasure,' Margaret snapped, annoyed that he hadn't even given her suggestion fair consideration. 'I'd be helping with the war effort. And anyway, I'd be living with Lady Bingram so I'd be perfectly safe.'

'She might not take you on, dear,' Angela put in.

Margaret turned in surprise, feeling this was no way of supporting her.

'Not take her on!' Edward spluttered. 'That woman would be hard pressed to find anyone as clever as our Margaret.'

'Then at least let her go and meet Lady Bingram, dear. Margaret's been with us since she was twenty-one and it's time she got more experience of the world.'

'But she's no need to go! There are things she can do *here* to help. We all play our part by carrying on.'

'I wonder if you'd leave us alone, dear? I need to talk to Edward privately.'

Margaret went to pace up and down the conservatory, wondering what Angela was saying to him. When he came into the conservatory a few minutes later he was still grumpy but gave her permission to go and meet her ladyship. 'After that, we'll see. She may not even offer you a place in her group. And you're definitely not going if you can't live in her house.'

Joyfully Margaret wrote to both Mary Ann and Lady Bingram to say she'd be coming down to London in two days' time.

'What did you say to make Papa Garbutt change his mind?' she asked Angela who had come to help her pack for a short stay at the London Charrington.

'I told him your doing war work would go a long way towards reinstating you in people's good graces and that we had no right to deprive you of this opportunity, both for your own and for Johnny's sake.'

'You cunning creature!'

'It's true.'

Margaret looked at her wistfully. 'Do you really think so?'

'Yes, I do.'

Margaret went across to give her a cracking hug. 'I'm lucky to have you and don't think I don't appreciate what you do for me! Johnny's lucky in his grandmother too.'

Angela's face softened. 'He's so like John was at that age.'

Margaret left Overdale for London very early on 21 January. She bought a newspaper at the station, only to discover that the previous day German Zeppelins had flown over Yarmouth, Cromer and Sheringham, dropping about twenty bombs and killing four people. If Papa Garbutt had known about that, he'd have stopped her going, she was sure.

London was full of uniformed men and there were quite a few women in roles Margaret hadn't seen before: at the station working as porters, directing traffic, delivering mail, working as conductors on omnibuses. The sight of them made her even more keen to be part of these sweeping changes – a truly modern woman – and she wondered for the first time how it would have been if John had lived and they'd married. Would he have been as over-protective as his father and would she, like Angela, have had secret regrets?

She went to the hotel then took a cab to Lady Bingram's house. To her disappointment, she found that Mary Ann wasn't there as she was helping bring back more refugees from Belgium and was not expected home for two days.

'She speaks very highly of you, Mrs Pensham,' Daphne observed.

Margaret looked her in the eye. 'It's *Miss* Pensham. Sadly, my fiancé died before he even knew I was carrying our baby. I now live with his parents, but some people can't forgive me for bearing a child out of wedlock. I thought you should know that before you decide whether to take me on.'

The older woman pursed her lips and studied Margaret. 'Strange. You look just like any other young woman to me. You haven't got two heads or a tail.'

Margaret felt tears of relief well in her eyes.

'Don't turn weepy on me. Your circumstances don't concern me, though I'm glad you told me the truth. You can drive already, so that's in your favour, and you say you're not afraid of menial work?'

'I'm not. What I am afraid of is doing nothing worthwhile with my time and energy.'

'Hmm. Since you're a friend of Mary Ann's, I'm already half inclined to take you on. That young woman has a shrewd head on her shoulders and I can't see her being close friends with a fool. I'm thinking of making her my deputy when she's finished helping with those refugees.'

'Mary Ann?'

'Yes. She may not be of our class, but when she notices something needs doing, she goes ahead and does it without needing telling. She's a very capable organiser, though I'll have to take her in hand a bit because she lacks confidence and experience of the world. But I think she'll repay the effort.' Daphne Bingram smiled as she added wryly, 'There are more ways of helping women play a full part in our society than by fighting for the vote, you know.'

Margaret felt a swift twinge of jealousy of the friend who had forged so far ahead of her, but banished it resolutely.

Daphne leaned back. 'Very well, then. I'll take you on as an aide. Go back to Overdale and sort out the arrangements for your son's care then come to me. You can live here, if you like, though you'll have to share a bedroom with several other girls. Oh, and you'd better get measured for your uniform before you leave. I'll give you a chitty for the tailor who makes them.'

'Thank you so much. And – would you like me to bring my car, add it to the pool?'

'That's jolly decent of you.'

Joy filled Margaret as she strolled back to her hotel after visiting the tailor. She passed many people in uniform, some of them soldiers recovering from wounds, but even the civilians had found a variety of uniforms to don as if to demonstrate that they were doing their bit. Soon she would be joining them.

When Gabriel and his mother were sitting by the fire after tea one night he said in his usual quiet way, 'The war isn't going to end quickly so I'd like to volunteer, Mum. Is that still all right with you?'

She sighed but didn't hesitate. 'Aye, son.'

'I've spoken to Maurice Greeson. He'll look after the stock, use our fields, and share the profits with us. Can you and Doris see to the hens like you said? People will still need feeding. And Tom will look in on you regularly, of course. Will you be all right for getting into town? Thank goodness they didn't take our horse.'

'Poor old thing. She ought to be put out to grass.'

'We need her too much to do that, I'm afraid.'

Jassy sat frowning into the fire. 'I think I'll ask my friend Carrie to come and live with me, if you don't mind. She's good company and I know she's been lonely since her Frank died.'

'That's an excellent idea.'

'I'll move upstairs with the childer and she can have my bedroom.' After a pause his mother added, 'Your room will allus be waiting for you for when you get leave, son, and I'll pray every day for your safety.'

She shed a few fierce tears in bed that night but didn't let

Gabriel see how upset she was to think of her only son going out to face death and danger. Other mothers coped. She would, too.

The war seemed to Mary Ann to have been going on for ever, though it had only been a few months. In February it was reported in the newspapers that over a hundred thousand men had been killed already. She went to bed and lay awake for a long time, thinking of the families of those men and how they must have suffered from their loss.

When the rush of Belgian refugees eased, she went back to working with Daphne Bingram, only now she found herself promoted to her ladyship's deputy, something that almost overwhelmed her at first because the job would inevitably involve dealing with top brass.

'Don't be silly,' Daphne said sharply. 'I wouldn't offer you the job if you couldn't do it. And those men are only human like the rest of us, for all their gold braid.'

So Mary Ann not only went back to driving but to managing the other girls, including Margaret, drawing up rosters, assigning jobs. She found in herself a talent for doing all these things, and also for settling quarrels and comforting those who'd suffered the loss of family members.

Although Britain imposed a naval blockade on Germany, it didn't stop the enemy sinking a ship off Scotland in March with two hundred casualties. Later that month Mary Ann found it hard to join in the general jubilation when the Royal Navy sank the German battleship *Dresden*, because she realised, after getting to know Captain Lepuy, that foreigners were not much different from English folk and cared just as deeply about their loved ones. She kept thoughts like that to herself, however, knowing they wouldn't be popular. To many folk there the enemy were evil and deserved to be killed, while all foreigners, even non-hostile ones, were inferior to the British.

In April everyone was horrified when the Germans used poison gas at Ypres. It seemed such a dreadful, cowardly weapon.

The news kept getting worse and she couldn't believe they'd

all been naïve enough to believe that the war would be over in a few months, a year at most.

In May the liner *Lusitania* was sunk with the loss of over a thousand lives. What harm had those civilians ever done to be killed so ruthlessly? Mary Ann wondered. Some of them were Americans, too, who weren't even at war with Germany.

Everyday life was getting more difficult on the Home Front and food was rising in price all the time, some items becoming scarce so that you had to queue for them. Mary Ann was now in charge of purchasing food for the aides and also had to roster the others on for the tedious task of queuing for groceries. She did her best to see that they ate reasonably, and when some of the girls grumbled about what they were being served, scolded them for it. 'Just be thankful we're not living in muddy trenches like the men. There are more important things than food. If you don't believe that, what are you doing here?'

Daphne, who had accidentally overheard this, grinned as she moved quietly away. Mary Ann would have made a good officer. They would have to see that she found a job worthy of her talents after the war.

Bob Hall joined the Army at about the same time as Gabriel and managed to get to London before he went overseas. Mary Ann spent an afternoon with him and found him as good company as ever.

'Will you write to me?' he asked as she walked with him to the station. 'I don't have any family left, not close relatives anyway.'

'Of course I will.'

He set down his bag and captured her hands. 'Are you still as determined as ever not to marry?'

She nodded.

'That's a pity, because I can think of nothing I'd like better than to make you my wife.'

She stared at him, mouth open in shock at this unexpected proposal, trying to think how to refuse tactfully.

He gave her a wry grin. 'I wouldn't normally have spoken out, but with a war going on you don't waste time because you never know if you'll come back or not.'

'I'm so busy I don't – well, think of marriage and things like that,' she stammered.

'You should. You're a fine woman and it'll be a waste if you don't have your own family one day.'

She shook her head, relieved when he let the subject drop.

Other men had shown an interest in her as well, but she hadn't been attracted to any of them. What was wrong with her? Had Jeff Powling ruined her for marriage? It was beginning to seem like it. Bob's words made her realise with some surprise that she would like to have other children, though. Not now, of course, while there was a war on, but one day.

After Bob went to France she wrote to him regularly, even though she never knew whether her letters would get through or not, because you had to do your best to keep up the morale of those fighting for you. As the weeks passed she began to worry about him. From his letters she could tell things were grim for the troops, with appalling living conditions and a high mortality rate. It wasn't that Bob went into details or asked for pity, but he did occasionally mention that a mate had copped it, or that he'd give a week's wages for a home-cooked meal, or that after this he never wanted to see mud or lice again.

In June he was wounded and sent back to England. She managed to visit him in hospital and found him thinner, with a grim expression. But his whole face lit up at the sight of her and once again she felt guilty that she couldn't return his regard.

'I didn't think you'd come,' he said, keeping hold of her hand.

'Of course I wanted to come.' She didn't say that it had taken her three hours to get here, which included two half-hour waits for a change of train. 'Are they looking after you properly? Is there anything I can get you for next week?' She looked at his left leg, which was heavily bandaged.

He followed her gaze and tried to make light of his injury. 'At the moment my leg has as many craters in it as the moon, but they say it'll heal enough for me to go back. And the nurses are very kind.' He stared into the distance and then said in a low voice, 'It's bad out there, Mary Ann. I never thought anything could be that bad. They're all dead now, the lads I went out with. Every single one except me.'

She clasped his nearest hand in both hers. When he didn't speak again, she started telling him about her experiences bringing Belgian refugees back, and about Georges Lepuy who had been to visit her several times since.

'I'm jealous of the way you speak about that fellow,' Bob said in a hard, bitter voice.

'*Jealous?* Oh, Bob, he's old enough to be my father – and feels more like a father, too.'

He flushed and began to run his forefinger along the wrinkles in the bedspread. 'I'm jealous of every man who spends time with you, if you must know.'

'There's nothing to be jealous of. Nothing.'

Sometimes she wished there were, wished she could fall as madly in love with a fellow as some of her colleagues had done.

She was planning to see Bob again the following weekend but got a message that he'd been moved to a convalescent home in the country. After wondering what she could do to cheer him up she hit on the idea of taking him out for a picnic, so telephoned the home and asked if they'd allow this. The Sister in charge of his ward said it'd do him a world of good and she would make sure he was ready for an outing the following Sunday.

Mary Ann then begged the loan of a car from Daphne who agreed immediately when she learned what it was for.

'Got to keep up our lads' morale.'

When Mary Ann arrived at the home, Bob was waiting for her in the hall. 'Could a couple of the other lads come with us? We're all a bit down-hearted, stuck here like this.'

'Of course they can. I can fit two in the back and you in the front. Do you think the hospital would give us some more food?'

A kind nurse rustled up some sandwiches and apples and they went for a drive, picnicking by the banks of a small river. None of the men said much, but they turned up their faces to the sun, smiling and relaxing visibly.

Bob and Mary Ann sat a little apart and she felt embarrassed as she saw how the other men, who both had upper body wounds, tried to give them some privacy by going for a stroll along the river. As soon as they were out of sight Bob took hold of her hand and she didn't have the heart to pull away. When he bent to kiss her, his eyes pleading for this privilege, she let him do so, her heart pounding with sudden fear that subsided quickly as his kiss proved nothing like the way Jeff Powling had ground his mouth into hers. Bob's kiss was hesitant and gentle, clumsy even. She found herself kissing him back just as gently. It didn't stir any great emotion in her, but it didn't stir any disgust either.

When they got back to the home the other men thanked her profusely for their treat and left. She and Bob sat talking for a while longer.

'That was a wonderful outing,' he said. 'I wish there was more of that simple sort of thing to do on leave. I don't like sitting drinking in pubs, and when you haven't any family nearby there's only tea rooms and such to fill the time. You get to miss the company of women, too – decent women, that is.'

'We'll do it again before you leave,' Mary Ann promised.

'Thank her ladyship for us, won't you?' Again he pulled her to him and kissed her, this time less hesitantly but still gently.

On the way back she was thoughtful. She didn't know what to do about Bob. She wasn't in love with him, though he was clearly very fond of her. But how could you tell a man likely to die that you doubted you'd ever return his regard?

However, his kisses had healed something inside her, she realised, something that had been damaged every since Jeff Powling. She no longer feared a man touching her, and for that she was truly grateful to Bob.

After some thought she went to see Daphne. 'I think there's something else we could do for the lads.'

'Oh?'

'When enlisted men come to England on leave they can't always get home and some of them don't have families anyway. They haven't a lot of money to spend and not all of them want to sit and booze. I think they deserve somewhere decent to go. Officers have clubs and I think enlisted men need them too.' She looked round. 'There are rooms still not being used here. Maybe we could use them to start a sort of club for enlisted men? Several of us girls could sit with them and chat when we're not on duty. Bob said they really miss the company of decent women.' She held her breath as she waited for an answer.

'I think that's a damned fine idea. I'll speak to a friend of mine about how best to arrange it. You start planning which rooms to use and how to provide tea and sandwiches.'

'Dancing too, perhaps, if we had a gramophone?'

Daphne smiled as she watched Mary Ann leave. It was deeply satisfying to watch her young friend grow in confidence and ability. Others of her 'girls' were showing similar development, both in the drivers' and the general corps.

Gabriel found it hard at first, living with so many other men. Since he had no choice but to get on with his companions in arms, he tried not to let his discomfort show. He coped easily enough with the physical training because he was far fitter than most of the others. A few of them were clearly under eighteen, but no one else seemed to bother about that so he didn't comment either, though it made him feel sad to see such youngsters trying valiantly to play a man's role.

He wrote to his mother and daughters every week and received terse letters from her and neatly printed messages from the girls, illustrated with little crayon drawings.

After a brief period of training his group was sent to France, crossing the Channel on a dirty tramp steamer, crammed together on the rusty plates of the deck as the vessel rolled and heaved like an ailing sea monster. Some men were sick, but Gabriel found he was a good sailor. He smiled wryly. Even in these lousy conditions he still liked being near or on the sea.

Although it was almost spring it seemed bitterly cold to him and he didn't feel as though he had been truly warm for a long time. He remembered the lazy evenings at home reading in front of a glowing fire, with his mother sewing tranquilly opposite him, and longed quite acutely to be back with her. What the hell had he volunteered for? He must have been mad.

He carried some of his daughters' letters around with him, feeling as if they gave him some sort of protection, which was silly when so many were dying. Two of the men with whom he'd trained were killed within the first week, poor sods. He had seen animals die many a time, yes, and slaughtered them himself, but still found it hard to point a gun at his fellow human beings, even if they were Huns and trying to kill him. And he found it even harder to kneel by a dying comrade, whose body was shredded and torn, and take down the final whispered message to his loved ones. Gabriel hoped if he was killed it would happen quickly and he'd not be aware of it.

Within three months he was promoted to corporal, which gave him added responsibility but he didn't mind that as it helped pass the time. In between periods of fighting life was very boring and he entertained himself by scribbling little stories and poems, or descriptions of the fighting and what it did to the countryside around, which must have been beautiful once.

Other men sat staring into space or played cards with grimy tattered packs or just talked quietly to one another. When they realised what Gabriel was doing, they begged to read the stories and somehow he couldn't deny them. The crumpled and mud-smeared bits of paper were passed from one to the other eagerly, and to his astonishment the men clapped him on the back and paid him gruff compliments.

Of course the sergeant found out and had to read them too, after which the captain overheard his men talking and demanded a sight of these little tales.

Two nights later he summoned Gabriel to his quarters, offered him a tot of whisky and said, 'Those stories of yours are damned good.'

Gabriel was puzzled by that. He knew they weren't particularly well written. He'd read enough good authors to understand that. However, you didn't contradict a captain, so he made a non-committal sound in his throat and waited to see where this was leading.

But this captain was an educated man. 'I know they're not perfectly written, but you've still managed to capture something, call it the essence of what it's like out here. If you like, I can help you improve them. I used to be an English teacher.'

'Thank you, sir. If you think it's worth your while, I'd appreciate that.'

'I do. Someone should record what's happening to ordinary chaps. And also – we could print a few and pass them round the lads of our own Division to read. Good for morale. I've seen one or two printing presses among the ruins. Wouldn't take much to get one of them operational. Division will provide the paper.'

Stunned, Gabriel could only nod. But the way the men received the first of 'their' stories made him realise it was a worthwhile thing to do, so he continued to write in the occasional lulls. And when one of his companions proved to have a gift for joking, he let him add little 'adverts' to the stories, or 'sports reports'.

Owing to the rain and muddy conditions, last weekend's sporting events had to be cancelled. We're still short of men to take part in tossing the grenade or mud running, since some of our other runners failed to return.

Room to let: no roof, floor of finest Belgian mud, wood-panelled walls. Apply Private Tommy Bates, Trench 72.

Next time you fancy an outing, try our new tour of Belgium. All transport provided. Guides will meet your train and supply food and suitable clothing. Picturesque scenery, changing daily, with interesting underground tunnels and barbed wire mazes to explore.

He sent copies of the finished stories home to his mother because if he survived he knew he'd like to keep them. And if he didn't, his daughters might be glad to have them when they grew older. Funny how desperate men got to leave their families something to remember them by.

And through it all he continued to fight as ordered, pushing to the back of his mind the thought of how much danger he was in, of what he was doing to others.

It came as something of a surprise when he was injured because it happened out of the blue. A sunny day made him lift up his face to the warmth and then suddenly there was a searing pain in his arm and he was staggering backwards.

Since his life wasn't threatened he lay in the field hospital for several hours waiting to be tended to and listening to other men dying.

'You'll be sent home to recover because if this gets infected you'll lose the arm,' a doctor told him brusquely as he dressed and sewed up the wound.

Gabriel bit back a groan and held on to the thought of a few weeks' relief from trench life as pain stabbed through him.

18

Late 1915 – mid-1916

Once his arm was on the mend, Gabriel was given two days' leave. Since there wasn't time to visit his mother and daughters in Lancashire, he chose to spend those days in London, a city he had never spent time in before. One of his fellow patients joined him and, knowing a bit more about the city, took him to a club that had been opened for rankers.

The first person Gabriel saw as he walked through the door was Mary Ann. There was no mistaking her. He stood watching her for a moment, smiling at how capable she looked, a woman now, not a child, and an attractive one at that.

Sensing someone staring at her, she turned to see who it was. As she looked across the room she saw Gabriel Clough, looking thinner than before, but still one of the tallest men there and with that same air of quiet assurance she remembered so well.

She was too busy to join him straight away, but waved and mouthed the word, 'Later'.

'Do you know that young woman?' Dennis asked as they made themselves comfortable. 'The tall one, I mean.'

'Yes. Well, I used to know her when she was younger.' He concentrated on putting sugar in his tea, amazed at the rush of feeling the sight of Mary Ann had roused in him.

A little later Dennis said, 'She's coming across.'

As he looked up, Gabriel's hand jerked and sent sugar all over the tablecloth.

His friend looked from one face to the other and pushed back his chair with a smile. 'I've just seen a chap I know.'

They were left staring at one another, then Gabriel tried to pull himself together and gestured to a chair.

Mary Ann sat down, her eyes devouring him. He was just as she'd remembered, though there was a light frosting of grey in his hair now and he had a sad expression in his eyes. 'How's your family?'

'Mum and the girls are all right.'

'And Ivy?'

'I neither know nor care. She left me last year.' He picked up the spoon and began stirring his tea round and round as he gave the bare details of what had happened.

Mary Ann listened in silence, as she had listened to so many soldiers' stories, then reached out to stop him slopping the tea all over the table in his agitation. She had wondered how this gentle man who had been so kind to her would cope with the horrors of war, but he had a strength behind that gentleness and like many others he'd survived. So far. His hand felt warm under hers, but that didn't explain why she suddenly felt heat spreading through her own body and found it hard to breathe evenly. There might have been only the two of them in the room.

He was looking at their hands now and twisted his round to grasp hers properly. 'Eh, lass, it's grand to see you.'

She wondered whether to pull her hand away, only she didn't want to let go of him. All her wits seemed to be scattered and she could only say his name, 'Gabriel!' surprised at how soft her voice was.

He shrugged. 'At least I've got the children. I love both my daughters, you know.'

Her voice was soft and honey-warm. 'That's good.'

Silence hung between them for a moment, then he smiled at her. 'You've grown up since I last saw you. Tell me about yourself. What's happened to you these past few years and what are you doing in London? Have you been happy?'

She nodded and shared details of her own life with him, her eyes lighting up as she described the happy times and her voice breaking on a near sob as she told him about Agnes.

Across the room Margaret stopped several times to watch them, thinking how comfortable they looked with one another. In fact, she'd never seen Mary Ann look at any man as she was looking at Gabriel Clough. She didn't go across to join them, not wanting to interrupt anything, so contented herself with a wave. She kept the other girls away from that table as well and made sure none of the men who knew Mary Ann tried to join them, either.

When Mary Ann realised the aides were preparing for the evening and the room was nearly empty, she looked at her watch and gasped. 'Gabriel! We've been talking for nearly two hours!'

'It feels like two minutes. Look, are you doing anything tonight? Would you come and see a show with me or even just go for a walk?'

'I can't tonight. I have to drive a general round and the other girls are all busy, so I can't swap.' She did some quick calculations. 'But I can spend the whole day with you tomorrow – if you'd like, that is? We could take a picnic and drive out into the countryside. Daphne will let me borrow one of the cars, I'm sure.'

'I'd love that.' He grinned. 'Are you a good driver, then?'

'Very good. I hope you don't have prejudices against women drivers?'

'Not after seeing them drive ambulances and save lives in France.'

They stood up, each reluctant to leave the other, then he smiled and reached out to touch her cheek before walking quickly towards the door. He stopped for a quick word with Margaret then strode out, whistling cheerfully.

Margaret came hurrying across then. 'He's still a good-looking fellow, Gabriel Clough.'

'Yes.' Mary Ann ran her finger round the rim of the cup he'd used. 'I – Margaret, I've never felt this way about a fellow before. He's married but she's left him, gone to Australia. What should I do about it? I don't know what to do.' She felt disoriented as well as bewildered by the way Gabriel had affected her. 'He was wounded but they're sending him back to France soon.' And then she would worry about him – far more than she had ever worried about Bob, she knew that already.

Margaret gave her a hug. 'You don't have to do anything at

the moment but get to know him again. And Mary Ann – don't waste a chance of happiness if you see one. Life is too short. I sometimes think of all the things I wish I'd said to John and didn't – and I regret it.' For a moment she looked into the distance, her eyes welling with tears.

Mary Ann nodded and gave her friend's arm a quick squeeze.

She spent the rest of the day trying to come to terms with her own feelings. She was twenty-four and it was the first time a fellow had affected her like this. Was she a fool to think so warmly of Gabriel Clough? She didn't know. But from the look in his eyes, he was attracted to her, too. Anyway, she couldn't stop the feelings, didn't want to try.

Even the weather conspired to give Mary Ann and Gabriel a golden time together. The sun shone all day long, birds twittered and swooped around them, and flowers seemed to be blooming everywhere they looked. She drove them out towards Watford, turning off the main road and stopping to picnic near a little village that seemed particularly pretty. Even here there was a man in khaki walking across the green with a young woman holding his arm and looking up at him adoringly.

'It's everywhere, the war, isn't it?' Mary Ann said, her eyes following the other couple.

'Not today. We won't let it spoil today. We're just two people out to enjoy ourselves.'

They sat under a tree to eat their sandwiches and drink luke-warm lemonade.

'Why do I feel so comfortable with you?' Gabriel asked suddenly, his smile warm and relaxed.

She wasn't going to pretend. 'I feel the same with you, always did.'

He searched her face and what he saw there seemed to reassure him. 'Eh, Mary Ann, why didn't I wait for you? Why did I rush into marriage with Ivy like that?'

'Perhaps the sea and the holiday happiness went to your head. It does with some people. I've seen it many a time.'

His voice had an edge to it as he said, 'Ivy must have thought me stupid to fall into her trap so easily.'

Mary Ann found herself touching him, wanting to comfort him. He was so bitter about his marriage, and with reason. When he pulled her into his arms and bent his head to kiss her, she didn't try to stop him. It began as gently as Bob's kiss had, with Gabriel's lips soft on hers. But soon it turned into a passionate exchange that left her gasping and tingling all over.

He drew away and stared at her, breathing rather heavily. 'I'm sorry. I didn't mean it to – to . . . Oh, Mary Ann, I wish I was free, but I'm not, so I had no right to kiss you.'

She kept hold of his good arm and leaned her head against his shoulder. 'I'm glad you did. Never mind about the future or anything else, Gabriel. Let's just enjoy today.'

'Are you sure?'

'Very.' She looked at him shyly. 'I've never felt quite like this before, you see, and I don't want to stop. It makes me feel – normal. Like other girls.'

Instant understanding showed in his face, then pity. 'Did what that man did affect you for this long?'

'Yes.'

So he had to kiss her again, and cuddle her closely, and try to hide how that affected him. It had been a long time since he'd touched a woman's soft body.

Later they went for a stroll, then he bought them another bottle of lemonade to share as they sat under a tree in the lazy warmth of the afternoon.

Inevitably the shadows lengthened and began to creep across the ground towards them. 'I don't want this afternoon to end,' Mary Ann said.

'Everything comes to an end.' Gabriel pulled out his watch. 'Time to go back, I'm afraid, love.'

'I suppose so. Will you come and see me again?'

'Of course I will.' He watched her get out the crank handle. 'I wish I could start the car for you. I feel so useless.'

'I like to do everything myself.'

He smiled fondly as he watched her swing the crank handle and then drive him back competently. 'You seem quite at home doing all this.'

'I love it.'

He began to look grim, however, as they drove through the streets of London and came to a halt at the rear of Lady Bingram's house. 'Mary Ann—'

'Yes?'

'I ought to stay away from you, for your sake, but I don't want to. They're sending me on a training course, so I might be able to get up to London a few times.'

'Good.'

'And do you think you could write to me after I go back?'

'Of course I will.'

She managed to see him four more times and by then felt utterly at ease with him. Just before he returned to France, they walked along the Embankment together, this time on a windy day with clouds casting occasional patches of shadow over them, though it didn't rain.

As the afternoon drew to a close the happiness vanished completely from Gabriel's face and even his body seemed tenser. 'It's hard to go back to the trenches.' He couldn't stop the shudder that ran through him at the mere thought of it.

She'd seen other men look like that, heard them speak of the appalling conditions under which they lived and died. 'I'm sorry.'

'Thank you for the times we've spent together. I shall treasure the memories. And I'll write.'

'I shall too.'

'I'd better go now.'

'Kiss me first, Gabriel.' She stepped into his arms.

With a groan he drew her closer and kissed her until the world spun around them. Then he stepped back, gave her a salute and hurried away, not even turning at the corner to look back.

She watched till he had vanished from sight, but still couldn't move. She wanted him in a way she had never expected to want a man. A tender smile crept across her face. She wasn't going to let absent wives or his scruples or anything else come between them. In war you seized what happiness you could – and gave it, too. Next time she would do something about it.

That night she lay awake for a long time, pondering on the irony of it all. There was Bob, who loved her and was free to marry her. Why couldn't she have accepted his offer? Why had she fallen in love with Gabriel Clough so quickly and completely?

Letters continued to arrive every week from Bob, sometimes twice a week. Mary Ann wrote back on Sundays usually, trying to sound cheerful and interested in what he was doing. But her heart didn't lift at the sight of one of his letters as it did when she saw Gabriel's scrawl. He wrote so vividly she felt she was there with him as she read, sharing his humorous observations about the other men and their foibles. And when he sent her one of his short stories, she was amazed by how good it was. The poignant tale of comradeship brought tears to her eyes.

Then Gabriel's letters stopped. For weeks she kept hoping to hear from him, but there wasn't a word. At first she continued writing, then she stopped because she didn't want the letters going to some stranger to open. She grew more and more worried, lying awake praying desperately that he was all right.

In the end, after two months had passed, she wrote to his mother. A few days later she received a terse little missive to say that Gabriel was 'missing, presumed dead'.

Mary Ann stared at the letter in horror. It couldn't be true! It couldn't!

She didn't realise she was weeping until Margaret led her out of the drivers' kitchen and took her into the men's club, deserted at this time of day.

'What's happened?'

'Gabriel. Missing presumed dead.' She couldn't hold back the harsh, racking sobs.

'Oh, no. Oh, Mary Ann, you poor thing.' Margaret sat rubbing her shoulders, patting her, making soothing noises. She stayed with her until she had wept herself out, then took her up to the little attic bedroom and tucked her in with a hot water bottle.

'Stay there. I'll bring your tea up. Just rest.'

After an hour or so, however, Mary Ann got up and dressed again. She wasn't the sort to lie abed. She'd cope better if she kept busy.

But it was a long time before she could do more than plod through the days, feeling as if each one was grey and savourless.

The other girls were sympathetic, because many of them had lost someone, but it was Georges Lepuy who was the most comfort to her. He didn't force her to talk or try to cheer her up, just took her out walking or for tea in one of the large hotels and spoke of inconsequential things. It was the fact that he was there which comforted her most. She was hardly aware of what he said.

19

1917

In March 1917 Baghdad fell to the Allies and morale improved in Britain. The same month Mary Ann received a letter from Bob to say he was coming back on leave and looking forward to spending some time with her.

'I don't want to see him!' she told Margaret. 'Let alone go out with him.'

'You have to start living for yourself again. You can't dwell on what happened to Gabriel for ever. It's what you've said to others who've lost their men. Now I'm saying it to you.'

Mary Ann sighed.

'Bob's fighting for us. You're not letting him down. Anyway, it'll do you good to get out a bit.'

To Mary Ann's relief Bob was no more inclined to chat than she was.

'Sorry if I'm a bit quiet-like,' he said on the first evening. 'It's just that I lost my best mate a week ago and – well, it makes you think.'

'I lost a good friend last year as well,' she said. 'I understand how you feel.'

On their last afternoon he held her hand and asked gruffly, 'Couldn't you think again about marrying me, Mary Ann? I love you so much. If I didn't have you, I don't know how I'd stay sane.'

That jolted her out of her own apathy and she looked at him, really looked. He was pale and shrunken, nothing like the robust man she had first met. She suddenly realised that she could help him greatly. 'We could get engaged, if you like.'

His face lit up and suddenly the old Bob was there, beaming at her. She knew then that she was doing the right thing.

'Do you mean that?' he asked.

'Yes.'

He pulled her to her feet and kissed her long and hard. Why didn't it excite her as Gabriel's kisses had? She tried to respond and hoped she hadn't disappointed him, but he didn't seem to notice her reserve.

'Right, then. We're going to buy an engagement ring this very afternoon,' he said firmly. 'Before I go back I want to know that the world can see you're spoken for.'

When Margaret saw the ring, she told Mary Ann roundly she was a fool. 'I said, go out with him, not marry him.'

'He needs me.'

'You don't need him!'

'Maybe I do.'

Georges was equally disapproving. '*Chérie*, this won't work. One day you'll come to life again and you'll be tied to a man you don't love.'

She gave him the same answer she had Margaret. 'He needs me.'

'You need things too. And if Bob could give them to you, you'd not have fallen in love with Gabriel.'

She shook her head obstinately. She'd agreed to marry Bob, she liked him a great deal and she wasn't going back on her word. Gabriel was gone. If she married, she could still hope for children and a normal family life. That meant a great deal to her.

They arranged to get married on Bob's next leave. Daphne said they could use a bedroom on the next floor until the war ended so that Mary Ann could continue to work for her – unless she started a baby, of course.

The wedding day was showery and cool, though it was June. Mary Ann had bought a new outfit, a smart dark grey suit with a skirt of the new shorter length, slightly above the ankles, and over it a three-quarter-length coat. Underneath she wore a blouse in cornflower blue, and had a matching ribbon and bow on her hat, a simple affair with a low round crown and downturned brim.

Georges came to drive her to the church and give her away. He nodded his approval of her appearance. 'You look charming, *chérie*. I don't think I've ever seen you look so elegant.'

They found Bob pacing up and down outside the church, looking very smart in his dress uniform.

Mary Ann hesitated as she got out of the car.

'If you have any doubts, *chérie*,' Georges said in a low voice, 'it'd be kinder in the long run to stop this now.'

She shook her head. She couldn't possibly do that to Bob.

After the ceremony they found another couple waiting outside to get married, the man also in uniform. They wished them well and went out to a café for a meal with Margaret and Georges, then Mary Ann and Bob went to the hotel where he'd booked a room.

Suddenly she felt nervous and it must have shown.

'No need to be frightened of me, lass,' Bob said quietly. 'We needn't do anything tonight if you don't want to.'

She gave him a nervous smile. 'I'm sorry. I think my – other experience left me – a bit afraid of that sort of thing. I'll be all right, though.' She had, of course, told him about her stepfather and the baby.

But it was he who couldn't manage to complete the marital act, he who wept tears of shame on her shoulder in the darkness.

'Shh, don't. Bob, this must happen to a lot of men. When this horrible war is over, you'll be all right again, you'll see.' As he lay there, rigid, she could feel his tears on her bare arm. She began to stroke his shoulder and with a sigh he cuddled up to her. He didn't attempt to touch her in an intimate way again.

When he'd fallen asleep she lay awake for a long time. She was glad he hadn't been able to do it and that was very wrong. Most of the time she felt comfortable enough with him, but in bed he wasn't Gabriel and she froze at his touch.

When he went back the next day, she returned to her duties.

They called her Mrs Hall now, which took her a bit of getting used to, but apart from that life went on as usual.

Not even to Margaret did she admit what had happened on their wedding night. That was Bob's secret and she wouldn't shame him by telling anyone.

Bob went back straight into the Battle of Messines and wrote jubilantly to his wife from the Western Front boasting of the Allies' success. He was slightly wounded a month later, not seriously enough to be invalided out, but enough to need a couple of weeks in hospital then several more in a convalescent home in England.

Mary Ann visited him regularly, but their relationship still seemed very strange to her. She didn't *feel* like anyone's wife.

But even though they had not yet consummated their marriage, *he* was the epitome of the loving husband, beaming at her with pride in every line of his body, delighted to show her off to his fellow patients.

So she was making him happy. That was something, at least.

While Mary Ann was away visiting Bob, Gabriel Clough turned up at the club. Margaret saw him in the doorway and gasped in shock, hurrying across to him and guiding him out quickly before anyone else noticed him and told Mary Ann.

'We thought you were dead!'

'I was hit on the head, lost my memory for a while.' He fingered the scar which still ached at times. 'Is Mary Ann here? I should have written to her, but things have been – hectic.' He'd even wondered if it'd be kinder to let her believe he was dead. She deserved better than a liaison with a married man. But in the end he had not been able to resist trying to see her.

'She's not here. Look, let me get my coat and we'll have a chat. There's something I need to tell you.'

They found a small park and sat on a bench.

Margaret couldn't think how to begin.

He watched her fidget, then said abruptly, 'What is it? Just tell me.'

'Mary Ann's married.' She heard him suck in his breath and when she glanced sideways, saw the pain on his face.

'Who to?'

'Bob Hall. She's known him for ages.'

'Oh. Well, I'm happy for her then.' But he wasn't. He felt like weeping – or cursing – or thumping his fist into the nearest wall.

'She doesn't love him, she loved you. But your mother said you were missing, presumed dead, and when we heard nothing more, we all assumed – well, it usually means the person *is* dead. No one told us anything different.'

After a few minutes she asked, 'What are you going to do about it?'

Gabriel turned his head slowly to stare at her as he asked, 'What do you mean?'

'Her husband's been wounded and is still convalescent. He loves her deeply. She's – comfortable with him. If you tell her you're alive . . .'

'. . . it'll upset her all over again.'

'I'm afraid it will.'

'And I still might be killed. And I still can't marry her.'

He stood up suddenly and began walking as if he couldn't bear to sit. She had to run to catch up with him. She didn't say anything, just stayed beside him.

After a while he slowed down and looked at her, misery on his face. 'Don't tell her you saw me. And – you can go back now. I'd prefer to be by myself.'

She could have wept for him. And for Mary Ann.

Gabriel did weep when he was alone.

For all the good it did him.

The war continued, everyone weary of it now and enduring what they had to grimly. In November British tanks were successful in pushing the enemy back at Cambrai and bells were rung in

London, which made some people think the war had ended – a short-lived hope.

In early December Mary Ann received a cheerful letter from her husband, wishing he could be with her for Christmas but telling her it was unlikely. Then the very next day she received an official letter from the military authorities. Her first thought was: *Not a telegram, thank goodness*. Everyone dreaded those. She hesitated then opened it, hoping Bob hadn't been badly injured this time.

It took a while for the words to sink in.

*It is my painful duty to inform you that a report has been
received from the War Office notifying the death of Robert
James Hall which occurred in the field on the eighteenth of
November, 1917.*

The report is to the effect that he was killed in action.

*By His Majesty's command I am to forward the enclosed
message of sympathy from their Gracious Majesties the King and
Queen. I am at the same time to express the regret of the Army
Council at the soldier's death in his country's service.*

Officer in Charge of Records

The enclosed letter was on behalf of the King and Queen.

*The King commands me to assure you of the true sympathy of
His Majesty and The Queen in your sorrow.*

*He whose loss you mourn died in the noblest of causes. His
Country will be ever grateful to him for the sacrifice he has made
for Freedom and Justice.*

Secretary of State for War

She re-read the first letter and then went instinctively to find Margaret. But she bumped into Daphne first.

'What's wrong?'

Mary Ann could only proffer the letters, couldn't even form any words.

'Oh, Mary Ann!' Daphne put her arms round the young woman automatically. There was nothing you could say or do to ease this sort of loss, only hold the person and stay with them.

'I lose everyone I love,' Mary Ann said in a muffled voice against her friend's shoulder. 'Everyone!'

'We all lose people.'

'Most people have family, friends, quite a few others who belong to them. I didn't. Now I only have you and Margaret left who know and care about me. *Even my baby died!*'

The older woman blinked. Baby? What baby? But the anguish in her companion's voice made her keep her arm round Mary Ann's shoulders and urge, 'Come and sit in my room. We'll send for Margaret, if you like.'

When they were sitting down, Mary Ann stared into the low fire that was always kept burning there because it was the place people went when they were in trouble, all sorts of people, not just the aides. 'I didn't love Bob, you know,' she said at last. 'Well, not in the way I should have. Oh, I was fond of him, but I didn't love him as a husband deserves.'

'There are many sorts of love. He was happy and proud of you. I could see that for myself.'

'Then why could he never – make me his wife properly? I think something inside him sensed I didn't want him and I'll always regret that.' She looked up and confessed, 'I loved someone else, you see, but he was killed.'

Daphne blinked in shock. Whose baby was it who had died, then? And when?

Margaret came in and knelt beside Mary Ann. 'Oh, love, I'm so sorry.'

'I'm sorry too.' She looked at her friend in sheer bewilderment. 'Why am I not crying? I don't understand why I'm not crying my eyes out. Bob deserves that of me at least.'

'I didn't cry for ages when I heard about John being killed. Then one day, for no reason, I suddenly started weeping. We all react differently to painful events.'

Mary Ann stared back into the fire, unable to think what to say or do next.

Daphne said in a low voice, 'She feels she's losing everyone she loves. She mentioned a baby who died. Do you know anything about that?'

Margaret nodded, glanced at the rigid figure of her friend and explained quickly how they'd met.

Daphne didn't mince her words. 'Men like her stepfather should be taken out and shot. I had an uncle once who tried to pester me like that, but my father found out and beat him senseless. The cur never came to our house again!'

'Mary Ann never had a father.' Then Margaret looked suddenly thoughtful. 'But she thinks of Captain Lepuy as one. I think we should send for him if he's still in London.'

Later she wondered whether she should tell her friend that Gabriel was still alive, but quickly decided not to. His circumstances hadn't changed and she knew better than anyone how you could suffer if you broke society's rules.

Georges Lepuy came that evening and sat with Mary Ann, talking quietly.

At one stage she looked at him and managed a faint smile. 'What would I have done without you during the past few years?'

'I feel the same. When I lost my family, I felt so cold and distant. Then I met you and came to life again. It's as if you are my family, *chérie*.' He hesitated, then said, 'But you do have a mother left. Don't you think it's time you contacted her?'

'I would if it weren't for her husband. I've thought of doing it several times since the war began.'

He looked thoughtful. 'I could go and see her first for you, if you like, to find out how things are. If he's still alive.' When she said nothing, he asked, 'Was she a bad mother? Unkind?'

'No. Not really. A bit sharp-tempered, but no one is perfect. Give me time to think about it, will you?'

Mary Ann worked as usual the next day. She was touched by the way all the girls went out of their way to be kind to her, how

Daphne stopped her in the corridor later in the afternoon to ask if she was sure she should be working, and how even an elderly general whom she drove quite often when he was in London took the trouble to offer her his sympathy on her loss.

The next time she saw Georges she said, 'After the war is over I'll go and find my mother. And I'd be grateful for your support in that.'

'*Très bien, chérie. J'y serai.*'

One evening just before Christmas Margaret drove Daphne to a meeting with some other women who were all contributing to the war effort. She sat waiting in the car enjoying the peace of an unusually mild evening for that time of year and watching the driver of the next car smoking a cigarette, blowing the smoke slowly and carefully into rings. When he had finished, he got out and ambled across to her.

'It gets a bit boring hanging around, don't you think?'

'Sometimes.'

'I'm Dick Holroyd.' He stuck out his right hand and studied her openly as she shook it.

'Margaret Pensham.'

'Miss or Mrs?'

His expression was admiring and she usually discouraged that sort of attention from men, but with this one she hesitated. 'It's Miss.'

'I don't suppose you'd be fancy-free?'

'Why do you ask?'

'Because you have a nice smile and I'd like to see you again.'

She didn't know what to make of him. He was obviously from a working-class background, someone the Garbutts would consider 'unsuitable' to be her friend, and yet there was something very attractive about him.

'Well?' he prompted.

'I'm absolutely fancy-free.'

'Then can I see you again, when we're not tied to these?' He flapped one hand towards the vehicle he was driving.

'Are you based in London?' she asked.

'At present.'

'And afterwards?'

He shrugged. 'Wherever the War Office and my colonel send me. I'm not his regular driver. I do other little jobs for him.'

'All right.'

She gave him her address and agreed to see him the following evening. She didn't know why she was doing this when she usually had a strict rule about no involvements. But there was something special about Dick Holroyd. She liked his cheeky grin, his directness. And it didn't hurt that he was quite good-looking, with curly hair and bright blue eyes.

To her surprise Mary Ann received a letter from a solicitor in Bournemouth early in January, saying that her husband had left her everything in his will. She wasn't sure what 'everything' meant – the cottage, she supposed – nor did she feel she deserved it, but she took two days' leave and went to sort things out with Mr Peaburn.

An elderly clerk led her in to see an even more elderly man. 'Ah, Mrs Hall. Do come in. I'm sorry for your loss.'

She murmured something. People never seemed to notice what you said as long as you made some sort of response to their expression of sympathy.

He seated her on one side of a vast oak desk, then went to sit in a worn leather chair on the other side, getting straight down to business. 'Now, your husband's estate was small but useful. The main item is a cottage in Stanstone, near Poole. We've been collecting the rents for him for some time now and putting the money into his savings account.'

'What's the cottage like?'

'Small. Two rooms and a scullery on the ground floor, two bedrooms above. There's not much land, only about half an acre, but it's nicely situated in the heart of the village. The tenants have been there for some years. Do you wish to give them notice and move in yourself?'

'Oh, no. I have a job in London for the duration of the war. But I would like to see the cottage.'

'Very well. We'll arrange that for tomorrow if you like. One of my clerks can take you out there.' He tapped the paper in front of him with one fingertip. 'Now, the second item is your late husband's bank account. It contains nearly four hundred pounds. A frugal man, Mr Hall, saved his money carefully. Very praiseworthy. He did well for tips at the Charrington, he told me.'

Mary Ann swallowed hard. They'd never got round to discussing finances or even what they'd do after the war. They'd only had short periods together, and their time together after they married had been clouded by his inability to consummate their marriage.

A clerk who was only slightly younger than the solicitor drove her out to the cottage in a pony and trap.

The place looked very picturesque from outside, but inside Mary Ann found it cramped, with low ceilings and tiny rooms. She knew almost immediately that she would never want to live here. The tenants were obviously looking after it well, so she instructed the solicitor's clerk to continue collecting the rents, then went with him to the bank to transfer Bob's account into her name.

It had been a day charged with deep regrets. All Bob's careful saving over the years, and for what? He had never benefited from the money he'd earned. She sat on the train to London, lost in thought.

The club was still open when she arrived back and she went to look for Margaret. But something about the way her friend was looking at the man she was with stopped Mary Ann interrupting them. They were chatting in a corner and seemed oblivious to everything and everyone else.

Mary Ann had never seen Margaret remotely interested in any man, though they were always inviting her to go out with them. She herself didn't feel like talking to soldiers tonight, wasn't sure she could stay cheerful for them, so went quietly up to her bedroom. But it was a long time before she fell asleep.

20

1918

As the new year began people seemed war-weary and not at all optimistic. Mary Ann couldn't help thinking back over the previous year, so momentous for her personally. Married and widowed all within a few months!

On New Year's Eve she sat in the club and spoke as cheerfully as she could to the men who had nowhere else to go for comfort. After it closed she still didn't feel sleepy and sat on drinking a cup of cocoa with some of the other aides.

Daphne joined them. 'You're all looking tired,' she said abruptly.

'Tired of the war,' one woman said. 'It feels like it's been going on for ever.'

'The darkest hour is always before the dawn,' Daphne said bracingly. 'We'll win in the end, you'll see.'

'We'd better,' someone muttered. 'Look at all the men who've died defending us.'

But for civilians and soldiers alike, times were hard. Food was increasingly limited, and even when you could find it, you paid more dearly for it, about half as much again as before the war. By official decree they all had regular meatless days but sometimes they had extra ones without meat or fish simply because they couldn't find any on sale.

Mary Ann drew the most comfort from immersing herself in her work. If she wasn't driving, she was talking to 'the lads' at the club, and she knew that helped them. She rarely took a day off now, didn't want to sit and think about poor Bob, or about the other sadnesses in her life.

Margaret was still seeing Dick Holroyd and the two of them

looked like a couple, somehow. One evening, feeling tired and out of sorts after seeing her friend's happiness, Mary Ann went to bed. There in the darkness it happened. She began to weep for Bob, muffling her tears in her pillow but weeping for a long time.

Such a waste of a decent man's life! And she wasn't even sure if she'd made him happy.

But at least she'd wept for him now. That eased something inside her.

Margaret and Dick strolled along the street the next day, not noticing much about their surroundings, simply happy to be together and out in the fresh air. She felt as if she had known him for years, not days.

'What shall you do after the war?' It was a question she asked herself often but had never been able to answer satisfactorily.

'Something to do with radios,' he said at once.

'Radios? You mean Morse telegraphy?'

'No.' He stared at her in surprise. 'Surely you've heard of Marconi and what he was doing before the war?' He saw that she hadn't and added quickly, 'Sorry, didn't mean to be rude. I forget most people aren't interested in radio.'

'I might be if I knew more about it.'

'Well, Marconi's been working out ways to send messages without wires – *wireless* they call it. Why, as early as 1901 he sent a message across the Atlantic to Newfoundland from Cornwall. Well, not a message, just the letter S in Morse code, but it was a start. I was in a wireless club at home before the war. We made our own transmitter and receiver.'

She could see his eyes gleaming in the moonlight and enthusiasm showing in every line of his bony body, so different from John's but already dear to her.

'The war's made a big difference,' he went on. 'They've got valves now, so they can send speech – we call it telephony.' He broke off suddenly and looked at her a bit sheepishly. 'I'd better not go too deeply into that sort of thing. It's what I work on and I'm not supposed to talk about it.'

'I won't tell anyone. And if this telephony stuff makes as much of a difference to people's lives as gas and electricity have, I hope they'll carry on with it after the war. Papa Garbutt bought a Decca gramophone just before the war and we used to listen to it a lot. It's wonderful to be able to listen to an orchestra just by winding up a machine and putting on a recording.'

'Wait till you can switch on an electric wireless machine and listen to concerts from London as they're played,' Dick said. They walked along in silence for a while then he said wistfully, 'Anyway, that's the sort of thing I want to get involved with after the war.'

Margaret began seeing Dick so regularly that the other girls began to tease her. 'I don't know what to make of him,' she confessed to Mary Ann. 'He's a ranker and I know the Garbutts wouldn't approve, only – he's fun to be with, and intelligent too, and I feel really comfortable with him. He says the war has done him good, shaken him out of his rut and he's never crawling back into it.' She blushed. 'I'm getting quite fond of him, actually.'

So fond that the next time she saw him she was determined to tell him about her son. He had planned to take her to the cinema, but instead she borrowed her own car back and they sat in it talking for most of the evening. It was one of the few ways they had of getting some privacy.

'I need to tell you something,' Margaret said as she had planned. She felt so nervous her voice cracked as she spoke.

'Oh? That sounds ominous.'

'I hope it won't be.' She explained her situation.

He looked thoughtful and it was a while before he spoke. 'I'd promised myself not to get interested in a woman until the war was over and I'd made something of myself.' He took her hand and looked at her as he said, 'Trouble is, I've grown fond of you, Margaret. And I think you wouldn't have told me about your son if you weren't fond of me. Am I right?'

She nodded.

'There are quite a few things against us, though, aren't there?'

'Are there?'

'You know there are. Oh, not your son. I don't mind about him. My cousin had a son before she got married and he's a lovely kid. No, what's against us is the difference in our backgrounds. Listen to us! We don't even talk the same way. And those Garbutts of yours have got money. Real money. They won't approve of me, will they?'

'No. But that doesn't matter to me, Dick. It's whether *I* approve of you that counts.'

He grinned suddenly. 'Eh, my mam would throw a fit at the thought of me associating with a lady like you.' He pulled her closer and bent his head towards her as he said huskily, 'But I don't give a damn about the rest of the world.'

His kiss was that of a man who knew what he wanted and who was experienced with women, unlike John's shy kisses. And yet, there was a tenderness to the way Dick held her, pushed a strand of hair out of her eyes with one fingertip and used that same fingertip to trace a line round her face. 'You're pretty, but that's not what I love about you. It's your determination, the way you took on a man's job, the way you smile at the world however grey things seem. Will you marry me, Margaret Pensham?'

'Yes.'

'When?'

'As soon as you like. Only – I should like to tell the Garbutts first, not spring it on them.'

'You want to take me home and introduce me to the family, is that it?'

She nodded.

'And what if they don't approve?'

'I'll marry you just the same.' She looked at her watch. 'Unfortunately I have to get back now.'

'I'll see you on Saturday then and we'll make more plans.'

She dropped him at his lodgings and drove back to the house feeling as if she were floating. But he turned up the very next day at the club, looking unhappy.

'What's wrong?' she asked at once.

'My colonel's going off to France tomorrow and taking me with him.'

'Oh, Dick, no!'

'Aye. And I only have an hour so I've written down the address for you to write to. I lay awake half the night thinking and I reckon it's not worth saying anything about us to the Garbutts until the war is over and we know I've survived.'

She clasped his hand tightly. What did you say to a remark like that? So many men didn't survive, like Mary Ann's husband, or they came back maimed. 'I shall miss you dreadfully.'

'I'll miss you, too.' He hesitated then said, 'After the war I want to start my own business selling gramophones, and later radio sets. I know there's a future in such things and I want to be one of the pioneers. I have some money saved already and, whatever else it takes, I'll do it.' He thrust a big envelope into her hand. 'Read these and you'll see what I'm thinking of. And if you're any good at figures, check mine out. No one in my family has ever done owt but work in factories so that other blokes make money out of their labour. One of the lads was helping me with this, but he was killed a few months ago. I think I can make summat of myself. If you want to risk it, then we'll get wed as soon as the war is over.'

Then he was gone, as quick and decisive as ever, leaving his proposal floating behind in the air. She smiled as she watched him walk away and turn to wave to her from the corner. He was only her height and had a thin, cheeky face. She was definitely going to marry him if he survived. Her smile faded and she shivered. It was a hard time to be in love.

She went to put the papers away. Dick wasn't the only one who could make plans. She'd already decided to pave the way with the Garbutts – and find out all she could about how she could help Dick with his business.

Wireless. Telephony. She said the words often as a sort of litany, praying he'd still be there after the war to make his dreams come true.

She didn't think she could marry someone who didn't have dreams.

Memories of the last few months of the war were always associated with food for Mary Ann. In late 1917 and early 1918 the food crisis worsened and shopping became a time-consuming affair, not always rewarded by success. Getting something to eat seemed to vie with the war as a topic of conversation. Butter and cheese were extremely hard to obtain and even margarine, which only the poorest people ate willingly, was in short supply. If a rumour went round that a shop had some butter, it'd be rushed by crowds and there were some nasty scenes when people wouldn't believe the shopkeeper's insistence that he had none.

At the end of January, the Ministry of Food announced new and more stringent rules for public meals, which included the sandwiches and cakes served at the club. There would be two meatless days a week, and in the London area they were to be Tuesday and Friday. Fats were rationed for the first time and milk could only be served in other beverages like tea and coffee, unless it was for a child under ten years of age. Even the amount of bread, cake, scone or biscuit served with afternoon tea was limited to one and a half ounces.

Mary Ann drew up new rosters for queuing and the aides struggled to find things to offer to 'the boys', knowing how it cheered the men up to come to the club.

'They're setting up a rationing system,' Daphne announced in February. 'What next?'

Once people got used to it, however, rationing made life easier. The queues and rushes on food were over and everyone had the same entitlement.

'Isn't it wonderful not to queue so much?' one of the girls said to Mary Ann. 'It's bad enough in summer, but you nearly freeze in winter.'

To make sure the rationing system wasn't abused, the Enforcement Branch of the Ministry of Food prosecuted those acting unlawfully and trying to obtain more than their allotted share of meat or other prized foods. The punishment was usually a fine but occasionally imprisonment, and lists of offenders were published. It stopped the worst cases but there was still a black market supplying food to those who had the money.

The year seemed to drag for Mary Ann. She felt as if she was in limbo, waiting for something to happen, for her own life to start again – only it couldn't till the war was over. Her happiest hours were spent with Georges, who insisted on taking her out for a meal at his favourite hotel to celebrate her birthday and presented her with a pretty bracelet.

'You shouldn't have!'

'It was my wife's. I wanted you to have it, *chérie*.'

'I'll wear it with pride.' She let him fasten it round her wrist and held out her arm to admire it.

The outings cheered her up and, indeed, she had regained her old vigour. Although the war news wasn't always good, she found enough inner strength to hold on to a belief that Britain simply could not lose. Even when the British Commander-in-Chief, Field Marshal Sir Douglas Haig, was quoted as saying they had their 'backs to the wall' she would not let any of the girls speak pessimistically.

Bob and Gabriel had given their lives to save them. She was not going to let down the two men she had cared about by losing faith in her country and its defenders.

The Great War, which had begun in the summer of 1914, ended at eleven o'clock on the eleventh day of the eleventh month of 1918.

When she heard the news Mary Ann stood stock still, unable to take it in.

Then the world went mad around her and some of the girls whirled one another round in clumsy dances. The rejoicing spilled out on to the streets and although Mary Ann declined to leave the house, she stood on the doorstep and watched the younger aides skipping and shouting as they ran to join the happy throngs.

A hand on her shoulder made her turn round to see Daphne standing beside her.

'I shan't be needed now. And do you know what? I'm delighted the war is over, of course I am, but I don't want to go back to being just an old lady with servants doing all the work for me and boredom dogging my footsteps.'

'There will still be plenty of work for people like you,' Mary Ann said warmly. 'There'll be injured men to look after, families to support, all sorts of things will need doing. If you want useful work, there's always something available. After all, you didn't just sit around before the war, did you? I remember you helping at that train crash.'

Daphne looked at her, mouth working, then for the first and only time Mary Ann saw tears run down her friend's wrinkled face.

'Bless you for saying that, Mary Ann. I was being selfish and that won't do.' She hugged the younger woman suddenly, a tiny figure against her tall sturdy friend.

'I hadn't realised how small you are,' Mary Ann said, bemused. 'You always seem so magnificently powerful.'

For which she got a second hug.

'Come and have a sip of brandy with me,' Daphne said. 'I've been saving my last bottle for the day Victory was announced.'

Mary Ann accepted a tiny amount of brandy to keep her companion happy. She had never developed a taste for alcoholic beverages.

'What shall you do with yourself now?' Daphne asked, smacking her lips in a distinctly impolite way.

'That depends.' Mary Ann saw the steady gaze Daphne had levelled on her and knew she wouldn't get away without offering more details. 'First, I'm going to see if my mother is still alive. Georges is coming with me. I don't want to meet my stepfather alone, you see.'

'If I were you, I'd want to meet that fellow with a cudgel in my hand.' Daphne poured herself another hefty tot of brandy and sighed with pleasure as she took another sip. 'And what if she isn't alive?'

'I can't seem to think beyond seeing her again. I haven't since I was fifteen.'

'She produced a fine daughter.' Daphne looked at her over the top of her glass. 'You've made a difference to the war effort, Mary Ann. You're a hard worker and you have an ability to organise and manage people. No, don't blush and shake your head. It's quite true. I wouldn't say it otherwise. Don't settle for some boring job afterwards. Find something worth doing, eh?'

'We'll both make a bargain to do that, shall we?' Mary Ann asked.

They clinked glasses.

When they heard people coming back, Daphne said, 'If you ever need a reference, you can give my name.'

Then a group of young women erupted into the room and insisted they join the party. No one got to bed until after midnight because the impromptu celebration spread to the club. Mary Ann found herself dancing with one man after the other: tall men, short ones, thin ones or beefy ones, it didn't matter. They all had one thing in common, they were smiling. They had been reprieved. None of them had to go back and face the daily possibility of death.

Margaret came up to link one arm in her friend's. 'Now I can plan to get married.'

'I hope you and Dick will be very happy.'

'No one's happy all the time, but I feel right when I'm with him. It's the Garbutts who'll have doubts, not me. When you've seen your mother, why don't you come and settle in the north so that we can see one another often?'

'I'm definitely coming to the north, but I have a hankering for Blackpool and the sea. I loved living there.'

'Then I shall come and spend my holidays with you every year.'

Other women were making similar promises to keep in touch. Mary Ann wondered how many of Lady Bingram's Aides really would do that. They'd come from so many different backgrounds. She didn't think somehow that the war would do away with all the barriers of class and money.

PART THREE

Late 1918–1922

21

November 1918 – April 1919

Just before the war ended people had begun falling ill with influenza – and not only falling ill, but dying too, in such numbers as to cause concern to the authorities. The epidemic began in October and as soon as peace was certain, Daphne Bingram swung into action with her usual willingness to serve a need. Mary Ann watched her in admiration, hoping that if she lived to be seventy she would still be as useful and capable as the splendid woman she regarded as her friend.

After the Peace celebrations the club changed almost overnight into a hospital annexe for those who had no one to look after them. The worst medical cases went to proper hospitals, but for those who were recovering but still too weak to look after themselves, her ladyship found beds, obtained food supplies and set up a home visiting service once they were well enough to leave.

Mary Ann didn't enjoy nursing duties so dealt mostly with the administrative details, though she also helped in any way needed. Once a man died during the night, and she and another girl carried his corpse out quickly so that the other patients wouldn't be upset.

Some of the aides inevitably contracted influenza, including Margaret and two quiet girls called Nancy and Ellen who both came from the north. Fortunately Mary Ann and her ladyship enjoyed superb health and that didn't fail them even now.

Christmas passed very quietly, with the big club room full of partitions and wheezing, coughing patients. There were still severe food shortages but her ladyship managed to obtain a few chickens, which were a real treat in such lean times.

Because of all this, Mary Ann couldn't immediately fulfil her

promise to Georges to go and see her mother once the war
ended. She wasn't even sure now that she wanted to do this,
but he remained insistent that you could not simply abandon
your family – if you were lucky enough to have one.

Margaret found it harder than she had expected to recover from
influenza, and to make matters worse she hadn't heard from Dick
for two or three weeks and was worried in case he was ill as well.
Mary Ann and the other girls were very kind to her, but she wanted
to see him. Daphne suggested she go home now, since they were
going to disband the aides gradually, but she didn't want to go
home until Dick could come with her.

When one day he walked into the shabby sitting-room used by
the young women she burst into tears at the mere sight of him,
something that was very unlike her. He came to sit beside her on
the sofa and put his arm round her. 'Mary Ann told me you'd
been ill.'

'Influenza. I was so sure I wouldn't get it. Where have you *been*?
I haven't heard a word from you.'

He gave her his lop-sided grin. 'I've been arranging to be
demobbed as quickly as possible.' The grin faded. 'My dad's
ill and if I don't get back tonight I may not see him again, but
I had to nip over and see you before the train leaves.' He held
her at arm's length and said with mock severity, 'What do you
mean by getting ill, woman? I can't let you out of my sight for
a minute.'

'I don't *want* to be out of your sight.' Margaret clung to his
warm, firm hand. 'And I'm not going home until you can come
with me.'

'Bit of a shock for them, don't you think, if I just turn up
unannounced? I think you need to prepare the way, love. I'll
come to Overdale as soon as I can, I promise.'

'Dick, about the money for your business – I have some of my
own and I could maybe help you a bit.'

His face grew still. 'I'm not intending to sponge off you, love.'

'But—'

'And your Papa Garbutt won't think much of me if that's how we start off together, will he?'

'He won't think much of you anyway. His family have always had money. So have mine. It doesn't bring you happiness, though. Or love.'

'Well, my family may not have money but we've always had love – and happiness too most of the time. Wait till you meet my mother. She'll be a bit upset about our marrying, but only because she'll be frightened you'll look down on her and keep me away from my family.'

'I'd never do that,' Margaret said softly.

He kissed her cheek, saw one of the other occupants of the room giggling and winked at her in the mirror. Then he noticed the time and stood up. 'I have to go, love. Walk out with me?'

At the door he thrust a piece of paper into her hands. 'Here. That's my address.' He pulled out a stump of pencil and held it ready over the little notebook he always carried. 'Now, what's yours in Overdale? Right. I'll come and see you as soon as I can.'

When Mary Ann came in for a break, Margaret was sitting smiling dreamily.

'You look better. Everything all right between you and Dick?'

'Yes. Except I now have to tell the Garbutts about him which won't be easy.' She sighed. 'I don't want to hurt them, but I intend to marry Dick whatever they say.'

'And Johnny?'

'I don't know. How can I take him away from Angela when she's been more of a mother to him than I have? Anyway, he'll be twelve in December. Old enough to have views of his own on what he wants – or to dislike the thought of a stepfather.'

'I'm sure he won't do that, love. He sounds to be a lovely lad, from all you've told me about him.'

Margaret left London the next day, driving her by now rather battered car.

Her going left a big hole in Mary Ann's life after their four years of working closely together. In fact the disbanding of Lady

Bingram's Aides was going to leave a big hole in many of the young women's lives and, though they'd all exchanged addresses, Mary Ann knew it was inevitable they'd drift apart gradually. The closeness they'd known had been forced on them by the demands of the war. What peace would do to them all remained to be seen.

Two days later Margaret arrived back in Overdale, having stopped overnight en route. She turned into the drive and drove slowly towards the house. Before she had pulled up, the front door opened and Johnny came rushing out, stopping suddenly a yard away from her as if he didn't know whether to throw himself at her or not.

She spread out her arms and pulled him into a hug. 'Heavens, you're nearly as tall as I am, darling!' She'd come back regularly during the past few years, but he seemed to have shot up again and was all arms and legs, like a young colt.

He grinned proudly. 'Granny says my father was the same. Did you drive all the way back from London by yourself?'

'Yes.'

'Nobody else's mother would do that.'

Some people didn't even approve of a woman driving, she knew. 'Angela!' She went to hug the older woman, thinking how tired she was looking. 'Are you all right?'

'Edward has influenza now and he's a dreadful patient, always complaining and fussing.' She looked at the loaded car. 'Are you back to stay?'

'Yes, and I'll be able to help you nurse Papa Garbutt. I've had plenty of practice in the past month or two. Johnny dear, will you help me with my luggage?'

'Thomas can bring your things in, dear.' Angela's tone was disapproving.

Margaret had forgotten how the Garbutts expected to be waited on hand and foot and knew she could never return to that sort of life – even if she hadn't met Dick. 'I've grown used to doing things for myself,' she said gently. 'Come on, Johnny. You can carry one of my bags.'

When they had taken everything upstairs, she let her son sit in the car with her as she drove it round to the back of the house.

'You won't leave me again, will you?' he asked suddenly. 'I've kept all your letters but it isn't the same and–' he shrugged and avoided her eyes '– Grandad is getting very fussy lately. He won't let me go out at weekends now, just because I got into a couple of fights.'

'What about?'

He wriggled uncomfortably.

'Me?'

'He nodded.

'Thanks for defending me, love.'

Would it ever stop? she wondered as they walked into the house. Her son began telling her about a new friend of his that Grandad didn't approve of because his family weren't rich and she suppressed a sigh.

Angela was waiting for her in the hall. 'Just pop your head in and say hello to Edward when you get upstairs, will you? Then you can change for dinner.'

It wasn't until the following morning that Margaret managed to get her son alone. She took him for a walk, enjoying his chatter about school, and his friends, and desire for a dog of his own which Grandad wouldn't allow. When they found a secluded spot in the park, she plumped herself down on the grass.

'Gran would throw a fit to see you do that,' Johnny said with relish as he sprawled beside her.

'She'll throw a fit anyway when I tell her my news, but I wanted to tell you first. Darling, I've met a man and want – no, *intend* – to marry him. He's called Dick Holroyd and he's not at all *suitable*.'

Wide-eyed, her son listened to her. 'He doesn't mind about me?'

'Of course not. He comes from a big family and he's used to lads of your age. He's very lively.' She smiled even as she thought of Dick. 'I'm sure you'll like him.'

'What if I don't?'

'We'll cross that bridge when we come to it. It's your grand-parents I'm most worried about. Dick has very little money, you see, and wants to open a shop and sell gramophones and radio receivers. He thinks we'll be having public radio broadcasts within a year or two and then he'll be able to sell lots of them. He's been in the Signals Corps and knows all about things like that.'

Johnny looked interested, but not upset.

'If you lived with us, there wouldn't be any servants apart from a daily char,' his mother added.

'Could I leave Northstones?'

'Your school? Don't you like it?'

'I hate it. They look down their noses at me. Why else do you think I get into fights?'

'We'll have to see. I'll certainly consider it.'

'I don't mind meeting this chap. I'd like a more interesting life.' The boy hesitated then added, 'Especially if he makes you happy. It's been a long time since my father died, hasn't it? I wish I'd known him.'

'I wish you had, too.'

She tackled Angela next, explaining about Dick and asking if he could come to visit them.

Angela became stiffer with each second that passed. 'I didn't think you'd ever forget John!'

'It's been twelve years. I haven't exactly rushed into marriage, have I?'

'No, but – things will change if you marry this man. We were hoping everything would settle down again now that the war is over.'

'I don't think things will ever be the same again. Too much has changed. Women have been out in the world doing what used to be men's jobs, and doing them well. Some may be content to stay at home again, but some of us won't.'

'You mean yourself?'

'Yes. Even if I hadn't met Dick, I'd not have returned to my old life. I have to have something to *do*. I've loved being so busy and useful these past few years.'

'Well, I don't know what Edward is going to say to this . . .'

'I need to know if you'll receive Dick here?'

'We'll certainly have to meet him, see if he's suitable.'

'He isn't by your standards, I already know that. He's from a working-class background. But he's very clever, and my standards must have changed because I find him,' Margaret could feel herself smiling, 'just right for me.'

'Obviously. But there's not only you to think of, there's Johnny as well. How shall you tell him?'

'I've told him already.'

'Well, I think you might have waited to do that! Children always let things out.'

Margaret closed her eyes and prayed for patience. She needed it. Angela went up to Papa Garbutt's room to prepare him, then came to summon her.

'He's not pleased,' she said on her return.

That was putting it mildly. Edward Garbutt was furious.

'This is what comes of letting you go off to London! I should have stuck to my guns and kept you here.'

'I needed to do my bit, and feel I've benefited greatly from my stay with Lady Bingram.'

'What does she think about this fellow?'

'She likes him. Thinks he'll go far.'

'Then let him think about marrying you when he's made his way in the world.'

'No. I'm thirty-three now. If Dick and I want a family – and we do! – we don't have much time. Besides, I can help him with his business. I *intend* to help him.'

'Don't you tell me what you'll do and not do, young woman. I can stop that allowance of yours and then where would you be?'

'Earning my own living like many other women. I'm not afraid of hard work.' And she had some savings, because Lady Bingram had insisted on paying them all a wage though Margaret had never told the Garbutts that or they'd have had a fit.

'I'd have thought you'd have grown out of that selfish, stubborn streak now, after all your *experience*,' Edward said sarcastically. As she would have spoken he held up one finger. 'I'll meet this fellow, see what he has to say for himself, but he's not staying here and giving people ideas and you're definitely not marrying him yet.'

He began to cough and the coughing fit lasted so long that Angela gestured to her to leave. He didn't come down to dinner that evening, but Angela joined Margaret and Johnny, as immaculately dressed as if she were going out to a dinner party. She said very little and excused herself immediately afterwards to return to her husband.

The next day a letter arrived from Dick who had got back in time to see his father die. He would be arriving in three days' time on the two o'clock train.

Margaret went to show the letter to Angela first because Edward still wasn't well enough to do more than get out of his bed and lie on a sofa looking out of the window.

'Oh, dear.'

'I'll go and book a room for Dick in town. I'm sorry Papa Garbutt doesn't feel he can offer my fiancé a room.'

'He's *not* your fiancé! If Edward decides to forbid the connection—'

Margaret had had enough. 'He *can't* forbid me to marry. I'm thirty-three years old.'

Angela stared at her in horror. 'You mean, you'd go against Edward's wishes, after all he's done for you?'

'Reluctantly, yes. I love Dick and intend to marry him, with or without your approval. I'm not doing this to hurt anyone, but because I've met the man I want to spend the rest of my life with.' Which made her think of Gabriel and Mary Ann, for some strange reason but as usual she decided to leave things as they were.

When she went to meet Dick's train, she walked right into his arms, not caring who saw them and reported back.

He hugged her close, then held her at arm's length. 'You look frazzled, love.'

'I am.'

'Are they kicking up a fuss about me?'

She nodded.

'Well, let's get the first battle over with, then.'

She drove him back to the house. 'You'd better leave your bag in the car.'

He looked up at the house and back at her, then grinned. 'They can't even find me a spare sofa to sleep on?'

She blinked away a tear, feeling very emotional. 'I'm ashamed of that.'

He set his hands on her shoulders. 'It's not your fault. Now, chin up and let's face the dragons.'

She led him into the house and along to Angela's sitting-room, finding Papa Garbutt there, the first time he had come downstairs. He was lying on a sofa looking very washed out. When he would have stood up, Angela went to stop him, then turned to face the newcomer. Their hostility was palpable.

'This is Dick Holroyd.'

He stepped forward to shake hands then Angela asked him to sit down and take a cup of tea with them. A stilted conversation followed in which Dick made no secret of the fact that his father had been employed in an engineering works, and not in a skilled capacity, and his mother took in sewing.

'They worked hard all their lives, raised their children decently, and I'm very proud of them,' he ended.

He managed a teacup and ate a piece of cake without showing himself up by their standards.

Margaret watched them closely observing the way Dick behaved. She would have smiled if this had been anyone else. Did they not realise that people from all walks of life had lived and worked together during the War?

Afterwards, Angela said, 'I think we should leave the men together, Margaret dear.'

Dick winked at her and went to open the door for them, then came back to face Edward.

'We're not happy about this relationship, you know,' he said.

'I didn't expect you to be, sir. Margaret's a wonderful woman, though, and I'll look after her, I promise you.'

'By selling gramophones?' Edward asked sarcastically.

'Selling and repairing them, also radios – they're the coming thing and I mean to be in on the ground floor.'

'Make your money first, then marry Margaret if you must. That's the decent thing to do.'

Dick sighed. This conversation was getting them nowhere. 'You're trying to treat her like a girl, sir, and she's not. She's a woman who's seen death and heard stories that would chill anyone's blood. She's served her country just as much as if she'd fought at the Front, believe me. Lady Bingram's Aides were very well thought of by the top brass.'

When the older man continued to scowl at him, he added, 'It'll upset Margaret greatly if we have to marry without your blessing, sir. I think for her sake you and I should set our differences aside.'

'Oh, you do, do you? Well, I think—' A prolonged coughing fit left him gasping for air and Dick slipped out to find Mrs Garbutt.

When she had rushed to help her husband, Dick looked sadly at Margaret. 'They're not even going to give me a chance.'

'I know. But it won't make any difference to me. Now, I want you to meet my son.'

And this meeting, the one she had dreaded most, went really well, with Johnny and Dick finding common ground in cars and machinery.

A month later Margaret and Johnny left the Garbutts' luxurious home and went to Bilsden where she was to marry and they would both live near Dick's family. They were received with such love and kindness it made her weep in bed that night to think how badly the Garbutts had treated Dick.

They were married a few days later, with Mary Ann and Daphne coming up to Bilsden for the wedding. But even in her busy new life Margaret continued to fret about the rift with the Garbutts. She had agreed that Johnny would go to Overdale regularly to visit them, would have done almost anything to heal the breach.

Surely, now that her marriage was a *fait accompli*, they would start to accept her husband?

22

May 1919

In early May, with her help for the influenza patients no longer crucial, Mary Ann requested a few days' leave to go and look for her mother. She took the train to Brighton, accompanied by Georges and feeling almost sick with nerves. Would her mother want to see her? Would Jeff Powling still be there? Other men had died in the war, why not him?

Mary Ann caught herself up on this thought, horrified that he could still affect her so strongly or that she could wish for anyone's death. When they got off the train she looked at Georges, suddenly afraid to take another step.

'*Chérie*, you are not alone today.'

He tucked her arm under his and patted her hand, but his words couldn't take away the dread that sat leaden in her belly or the remembrance of how badly hurt she'd been by Powling – and her mother.

Was it too late to change her mind about this reunion? No. If she acted the coward now, she'd never forgive herself.

Georges left her sitting in a small café while he went to her mother's house to prepare the way. She kept glancing at the clock on the wall to find that only two or three minutes had passed, and couldn't eat a single mouthful of the small cake he had ordered for her with a pot of tea.

When the café doorbell tinkled she looked up to see him smiling at her and pushed her chair back at once to hurry across to him. 'Well?'

'There's a lot to explain, *chérie*. Shall we walk along the sea front?'

When he told her what had happened, Mary Ann looked at him

with tears in her eyes. 'You mean – I could have gone home after I left Birtley?'

'You could, but—' he hesitated, then said '—I think probably you're better for having made your own way in the world. Your mother has a very – strong personality, does she not?'

'Yes, I suppose so. Does she want to see me?'

'Very much. But she still thinks of you as a child, *her* child to mould and command. And you're not. You're twenty-eight, used to managing people and situations. The meeting will not be easy for you, I know, but I shall be disappointed if you give in to her in any way.'

'You didn't like her, did you?'

Another hesitation, then, 'I didn't dislike her exactly, but I feel she's a very bitter woman and is thinking more of herself than of you. I don't want her to hurt you again. Now that I've met her, I'm not even sure I was right to bring you here. Perhaps we should have left sleeping dragons to their dreams.'

'No. You were quite right. I need to – to sort things out with her, because what happened still upsets me. I should have well and truly got over it by now, don't you think?'

'Perhaps. But I think bad experiences scar us for life. We can learn from them, but I doubt we ever forget them.'

She could tell from his sad expression that he was thinking of his own lost family.

Georges shook his head as if to rid it of memories. 'Well, then, I shall take you to your mother's house and come back for you at four o'clock. Don't agree to anything today, whatever she says.' He gave her a wry smile. 'I'm talking as if I'm your father, which I have no right to do, but I care for you very much, my dear girl.'

She stopped walking to look him in the eyes and say, 'As far as I'm concerned, you *are* my father – in every way that matters.'

He swallowed hard and his own eyes were bright as he inclined his head, too full of emotion to answer. He left her at the front door, which opened before she had even knocked, and stood on the pavement outside for a moment or two, observing the meeting before he moved away.

The two women stared at one another, each shocked by what she saw.

'You're so like your father!' Dinah whispered, one hand pressed against her chest. 'I didn't expect you to have grown so *tall!*'

Mary Ann didn't say it, but she thought her mother looked lined and shrunken, much older than her years. 'Who else should I be like?' she asked, trying to keep her voice light.

'Me.' Dinah made one of her impatient gestures. 'Well, come in, do. We're letting all the warm air out.'

Mary Ann watched in surprise as her mother carefully locked the door behind them. There was not only the normal door lock, but bolts at the top and bottom, plus a ball and chain gadget for opening the door to strangers. What had happened to make her so nervous? As Mary Ann followed her along the corridor she noticed something else. 'You're limping. Have you hurt your foot?'

'I had an accident some years ago. It doesn't worry me now. I'm used to it.' Dinah opened the door of her small parlour and led the way inside, gesturing to an easy chair near the fire. She sat down and continued to stare at her daughter.

It was then that Mary Ann realised her mother hadn't attempted to hug her or even take her hand. She'd grown used to people touching one another, because Margaret and most of the aides hugged one another often. Even Daphne put her arm round you when something was wrong. 'Georges told me what had happened – with Jeff, I mean. I'm so sorry, Mother.'

Dinah's mouth pulled down at the corners and she turned to stare into the fire. 'He stole a lot of my money as well as being a bigamist. He hurt me badly.'

'He hurt *me*, too.' Surely her mother should have mentioned that? Apologised even? No, Dinah Baillie never apologised to people. Why should that have changed?

But her mother surprised her by saying, 'I hate even to think of what he did to you. Such things are best forgotten. At least *you* weren't burdened with a baby.'

Like you were burdened with me, Mary Ann thought. She didn't say how much she'd wanted Elizabeth. Her mother would never understand. And it hurt Mary Ann to be considered a burden.

After a moment during which the only sound was the ticking of the clock on the mantelpiece and a motor car chugging past outside, Dinah said, 'You look well and you're smartly dressed, so you must have made a decent life for yourself. *That man* said you were well thought of.'

'Georges, do you mean?'

'Yes. He's too old for you, you know. It won't work.'

'There's nothing like that between us. He lost all his family in the war and I thought I'd lost mine. He's been like a father to me. He even gave me away at my wedding.'

'*You're married?*'

'Not any more. Bob was killed in '17.'

Dinah's face looked as sour as if she'd sucked a lemon. 'I've never been married and I never shall be now.'

This meeting was proving even harder than Mary Ann had expected. How could she have forgotten her mother's way of selfishly relating everything to her own needs?

'I was sorry at first to lose you, then glad you were out of Jeff's reach. He did this, you know.' Dinah pointed to her injured leg. 'Came back one day and tried to kill me. He threw me down the stairs, and if Maisie hadn't come back just then, I wouldn't be alive today.'

Mary Ann gaped at her in shock, then realised something. 'Is that why you have all the locks on the front door?'

Dinah nodded. 'I've seen him a couple of times since then, staring at the house, but not since the war started. Which doesn't mean he won't come back one day and kill me.'

'Surely not?'

'You didn't see his face when we threw him out.' She breathed in shakily, then clicked her tongue in exasperation. 'That's enough about *him*. Just make sure that you never leave an outside door unlatched. You *are* coming back to live with me, aren't you?'

Mary Ann tried to be diplomatic. 'I don't know what my plans are yet.'

'But you have to come back or what's my life for?' Dinah waved one hand around. 'It'll all be yours one day, you know. I always knew I'd see you again, I just knew it. And besides, I could do with your help.'

'I don't think I want to work as a housemaid again. I've grown used to organising things and being in charge. I'm thinking of starting a small business of my own. I'd prefer to move back to the north, actually. You couldn't sell up here and move to Blackpool, could you?'

Dinah shook her head. 'No. I swore I'd never go back to the north and I meant it.'

'Even to be near me?'

'Not even for that.'

Her tone was so flat and emphatic that Mary Ann knew better than to think she'd be persuaded so said with a sigh, 'Then I'll have to come and live in Brighton, for a time at least. You're my only relative and I don't want to lose touch with you again – if you want me to, that is?'

Dinah's eyes filled with tears. 'Of course I want you to.' She took out a handkerchief and dabbed at her eyes. 'Look at me being silly when it's something to be glad about.'

Well, thought Mary Ann, surprised by her own offer, at least if she came to live here she'd be close enough to go and visit Georges in London or for him to visit her. She didn't even need to ask whether he'd keep in touch. She knew he would.

But she intended, once she'd gained her mother's confidence, to insist on being told at last who her father was. That was very important to her.

As they sat on the train returning to London, Georges looked at Mary Ann quizzically. 'Well? You're very quiet. And you don't exactly look happy.'

'I'd forgotten how very selfish and – and intractable my mother is. She wanted me to go back and work for her, but I refused. I intend to do something more interesting than clean up after lodgers.'

'And have you thought any more about what we discussed?'

'Yes. But if I do start a business, I think I'd like to do it myself, Georges. Please don't be offended, but I've grown rather independent. I've asked the lawyer to sell Bob's cottage, and with that and my savings I'll easily have enough money. The only thing is – I think it had better be in Brighton, for a few years at any rate. My mother doesn't look well and I'll need to keep an eye on her.'

'She doesn't deserve a daughter like you.'

'We don't always get what we deserve.' For some reason she suddenly thought of Gabriel Clough. Another good man killed. And even before that, he hadn't been doing what he wanted with his life. She had never met anyone who affected her like he did, still thought of him fondly and had now resigned herself to remaining a widow.

A widow who had never really been a wife.

So it was particularly important to her that she find some satisfying way of earning her living.

When Gabriel was demobbed he passed through London and almost went to check that Mary Ann was all right. For all he knew she might be a widow now. But he didn't go because *he* was still married and had nothing to offer a woman. As Margaret had pointed out, that wouldn't be fair to Mary Ann.

He couldn't ask a woman like that to live in sin, especially knowing how Margaret had suffered because of her fall from grace. He had seen other ladies walk past her in Overdale as if she didn't exist, even her own father. No, he couldn't bear the thought of putting Mary Ann in the same position, an outcast from society.

It was strange, he mused, as the train rattled its way north, how much he thought of her when they hadn't really spent much time together. He still had all her letters, with their round, childish handwriting and honest warmth. He still remembered their few kisses, dreamed of her at night, thought of things to tell her.

Oh, he was a fool!

When he arrived in Overdale, the town looked small and dirty. He took a motor taxi out to the farm and this was the first change to strike him. Even Overdale was losing its reliance on the horse. The second change was in the farm itself. There were two more large hen houses and although he had known about them, had even chosen the sites and seen them started, he hadn't seen them finished, so it all looked – different.

As the motor car drew up at the house, the girls rushed out, shrieking, 'He's here! He's here!'

Christina had shot up since the last time he'd seen her and now was taller than Frances. Neither of them was a 'little girl' now. The war had robbed him of the pleasure of seeing them grow, of being with them, of teaching them the things that all fathers do their daughters. His throat felt thick with tears as he dropped his bag and simply gathered them into his arms, hugging them and rocking them to and fro till he heard the driver clear his throat.

They were both his, he thought as he pushed them gently away and turned to pay the man – his because he'd made them his own.

Only then did he notice his mother and Carrie standing on the doorstep, also smiling at him. He waved to them and quickly finished paying the driver. Before the girls could clutch him again, he strode across to his mother and took her in his arms, lifting her off the ground and swinging her round to shrieks of, 'Gabriel! Now stop that!' But he swung her round a few times more before setting her down again and planting a kiss on one wrinkled cheek, then the other.

'Give over with thee!' Jassy said, flapping her hand at him, though her eyes were bright with tears of joy.

'You look well,' he said, his eyes searching her face and body for signs of ill health and finding none. She looked no different to him, as if she had stopped ageing years ago.

'I keep going,' she said in her abrupt way. 'Thou'st getten thin, though, son. Didn't they feed thee in th' Army?'

'Not half as well as you do.' He turned to smile at Carrie and ask, 'How are you, Mrs Anders?'

'I'm well, lad.'

She hesitated, then leaned forward to peck quickly at his cheek as if she feared a rebuff, but he took hold of her shoulders and kissed her right back. 'I can't thank you enough for keeping my mother company while I was away, and I hope you're going to stay on with us?' His mother had already written to ask him if he'd mind. Of course he didn't. The more people his daughters had round them, the more normal their life would seem. And Carrie was as near family now as made no difference.

Then shouts made him turn to see the girls pushing and shoving one another for the honour of carrying his kit bag. He strode over to take it from them, yelling over his shoulder, 'I hope that kettle's boiling, Mum!'

He was home again.

As he sipped a cup of strong tea, he admitted to himself that although he was delighted to be back with his family, he was not delighted to be here in Birtley again. He'd seen enough of the sea during his military service to know that it still held a fascination for him that the moors never would.

As she got ready to leave London, Mary Ann felt like soldiers must have when they were demobbed. She had worn the Aides' uniform for so long that her own clothes felt strange on a working day. Until now she had had an aim in life and enough work to fill every hour, not to mention the companionship and support of other women.

Now she had only herself, because Georges had gone over to Belgium to see what he could retrieve there. He would soon be leaving the forces and had promised to return to England.

'I wish you were settling in Bournemouth,' Daphne said, shaking her hand then retaining it in hers for a few seconds. 'I shall miss you greatly, Mary Ann.'

'I need to be near my mother. She's my only surviving relative and she doesn't look at all well.'

Daphne knew the story. 'I'm not sure you owe the woman anything, but you must do as your conscience dictates.'

'I suggested Mum move to the north. I prefer it there, actually, especially Blackpool. It has such firm sandy beaches, you can walk for miles along them. I've missed that. Pebbly beaches just aren't the same to me. But Mum wouldn't even consider a move.'

'You're going to live with her?'

'No. Well, only temporarily anyway.'

Daphne raised one eyebrow quizzically.

'I mean it. I'll find myself somewhere else to live once I've decided what I want to do with my life.'

She spent the first few days in Brighton going for long walks, revisiting the scenes of her childhood and taking in all the changes. Her friend Sheila had moved away and there was no one else she knew well enough to call on. In Blackpool there would have been several people to see because she'd kept in touch with Miss Thursby and Agnes's family.

Mary Ann helped her mother when she was in the house but made sure she got out in the morning and didn't come back until she was ready to because she didn't intend to be treated like an unpaid maid.

She first noticed the café during her second week in Brighton. She'd been looking at businesses for sale, or at places which might be turned into businesses, but had come to the conclusion that it'd be easier to buy an established place. This one had a FOR SALE sign in the window, a dog-eared thing, and the whole place looked run down, with dull windows and a dark, unappealing interior behind them. She walked up and down the street, noting that the café was in a good position, with lots of people walking past. If she was running it, she'd have found ways to tempt them inside.

On that thought she went in and ordered a cup of tea. It was sloppily served by a thin man who wheezed every time he moved. Gassed, Mary Ann thought immediately, having seen men like that before.

'Where did you serve?' she asked.

'France. Got gassed at Ypres in '15.'

'My husband was killed in '17,' she said.

297

'I sometimes wish I had been, too,' he muttered, and slouched off to the door that presumably led to the kitchen.

Definitely not a place that made you welcome, she thought. And the tea was cheap stuff, stewed and horrible.

She left the cup on the table and walked round the café, finding an open doorway at the other side that led to a second room where the furniture was stacked haphazardly and covered in dust. Why was this one not in use as well?

'Did you want something else?' a voice asked behind her.

This time it was a woman. She looked almost as tired and dispirited as the man had.

'I was interested in the café. It is for sale, isn't it?'

The woman's face brightened. 'Yes. Do you want to look round?'

'If you don't mind.'

The kitchen was quite big but very old-fashioned. It was immaculately clean, though there wasn't much evidence of food.

'You can't get decent stuff these days,' the man said. 'It's hardly worth opening.'

The woman dug him in the ribs and continued to show Mary Ann the cupboards and the equipment. Then she took her upstairs to a small flat where they lived.

That made it even more attractive to Mary Ann because it would give her an excellent excuse for not living with her mother. 'How much are you asking?'

They told her and she shook her head at once. 'It's not worth that.'

'It's in a good position, got a long lease,' the woman protested.

'But it's run down.'

'We can't take less,' the man said, scowling at her.

'Then I'd better look elsewhere.' She turned as if to leave.

The woman stepped forward. 'Hold on a minute. How much were you thinking of offering?'

By the time Mary Ann left, they had agreed a price, subject to her checking a few things. She was sure she could turn the business around and make it much more valuable for the day when she could sell it and move back to the north.

She'd give her mother a year or two then, if Dinah still refused to move, she would move to Blackpool without her.

Mary Ann had the café painted a cream colour, with new red-checked tablecloths and electric lighting. She put two pots of flowers outside the door and found people stopping to stare inside even before it was finished.

Dinah came along a couple of times to see what she was doing, but shook her head over the money being spent. 'You should have waited till you got going to make improvements.'

'It won't get going while the place looks so gloomy. Anyway, the holiday season is upon us, so I think I'll soon recoup what I've spent.' She looked round with great satisfaction. The café now had a bright, cheerful air, as did the waitress she'd hired. Jane was a widow with no experience, but she had a warm friendly smile which Mary Ann believed important. Anyway, she wanted to train her staff herself.

Now that she'd put in electricity and modernised the kitchens, she was going to hire a cook as well.

Soon the café was so busy she could only visit her mother in the evening. One night, as she was about to go home, Dinah said abruptly, 'Be careful. I saw Jeff standing outside last night. I told you he'd be back.'

'Are you sure it was him?'

'Of course I am! I went to bed early and glanced out of the window – and there he was! Standing across the road, watching this house. He saw me and waved.' She shuddered. 'I couldn't sleep after that and I'm sure I heard someone prowling round the back. But he won't find a door or window open on the ground floor, and there are plenty of people in the house, so I'm safe enough at night.'

Mary Ann wasn't sure whether to believe her about Jeff Powling, but as she was walking home she heard footsteps behind her. She stopped and they stopped. She started walking and the footsteps began again. Swinging round suddenly, she saw a man dodge into a shop doorway. From her years in London she knew how to take care of herself and her height always made her feel more confident, but she quickened her pace because it was better not to let trouble start.

The man following her also quickened his pace and low laughter floated towards her as she turned a corner. He wasn't even trying to hide now, but it was too dark to see him clearly because he was walking on the side of the street without lamps. But it had sounded like Jeff's laugh. You didn't forget a man like that.

To her great relief Mary Ann bumped into a policeman round the next corner. 'Oh, thank goodness! Constable, there's a man following me. I wonder – are you going anywhere near the Tudor Café?'

He escorted her home and warned her not to go out so late on her own again, also promising to walk past the café a couple of times during the night.

She locked the front door but as she looked round she realised the big windows made it easy to break into. Upstairs she also walked round, assessing her little home in a way she'd never felt the need to before.

Suddenly there was a crash of breaking glass from downstairs. Someone must have broken one of the windows. She went and got the rolling pin but didn't venture downstairs because she'd be too vulnerable there. When she peeped out of the sitting-room window, she saw a man standing on the other side of the road. Definitely Jeff Powling. He threw back his head and laughed, shouting, 'I'll be back.' Then he walked away.

Nothing else happened and there was no further sound from below, but Mary Ann knew she'd not be able to sleep so sat up on guard.

Half an hour later there was a knocking on the café door and she looked out of the window again to see the policeman standing there, his face a pale blur in the moonlight. She went downstairs then.

'Looks like you were right, miss,' he said.

She stared round at the mess, feeling anger boil up inside her again.

'Have you any idea who did this?'

'It's probably a man called Jeff Powling.' She explained the situation but the constable frowned at her as if her story sounded far-fetched.

'You'd better come to the police station tomorrow and make a statement, miss. In the meantime, if you'll be all right on your own for a while, I can fetch a fellow who'll come and stay with you until the morning for five bob. Do you want me to fetch him?'

'Yes, please.'

The next day she called in a glazier and a carpenter, asking the latter to fit a heavy door and locks at the top of the stairs, so that her flat would be more secure.

The day after that she turned round to see Georges standing in the doorway watching the men working.

'What happened, *chérie*?'

When she had finished explaining, he sat frowning. 'It's hard to believe that this man would bear a grudge for so long. Do you think he still lives in the area?'

'I doubt it. My mother thinks he comes back for the sheer pleasure of tormenting her because it only happens once in a while. And he does enjoy upsetting people, I saw that myself.'

'You should not walk home alone after dark from now on.'

She could feel her anger rising again. 'I'll not be stopped from doing what I want. I'm going to buy myself a weighted walking stick. If he attacks me, he'll regret it.'

But no more attacks occurred. Her mother shrugged when asked her opinion. 'Jeff won't be back for a while, unless he's changed. It's just an amusement for him. He always did enjoy playing cruel jokes.'

She looked so bleak that Mary Ann put an arm round her and gave her a hug.

Dinah stiffened for a moment, then smiled and patted her hand, a rare concession. 'You're a good daughter. And kind. I know you don't want to live in the south, but I can't *bear* to go back to the north.'

'I know. Mother, don't you think it's time you told me something about my father? I don't even know his name and I long to.'

'Why? He's dead, died years ago, so you can't go back and see him.'

'He might have – other children. They'd be my half-brothers and -sisters.'

'And they'd look down their noses at you. No, it's best you and I make our own life.' Dinah's mouth set into that tight bloodless line and she said, 'I'll never tell you, so it's no use asking me.'

Mary Ann couldn't prevent tears from coming into her eyes.

'Weeping won't win me over, either.'

'No. It never did.' She got up and left the house then, knowing that the next time she visited her mother this incident would be completely ignored.

If only there was some way of finding out about her father!

Margaret looked round the small house they were renting and sighed. She loved being married to Dick, and Johnny loved the freedom of going to the local grammar school in Bilsden, but she found this place very claustrophobic.

She had gone back to Overdale several times to visit the Garbutts since her marriage, usually taking Johnny as well. At first they'd been stiff with her, but now Angela at least had come round and was her old self. But Margaret never took Dick with them, just drove herself across from Bilsden because she didn't see why he should put up with being patronised.

As her allowance was still being paid into the bank, she had decided to keep the car because it was so useful to them both. Dick was annoyed about the allowance and said she should give it back, but she wouldn't. She didn't spend it, just added it to her savings account because it was good to have something behind you.

When someone knocked on the door just as she was about to

go out and help Jeff in the shop, she sighed and hoped it wasn't going to delay her.

It was a telegram. She stared at the proffered envelope, reluctant to take it from the lad. After the war you always felt that telegrams meant bad news.

She opened it.

COME AT ONCE STOP EDWARD VERY ILL STOP ANGELA

'Any reply?' the lad asked.

'Yes.' She scribbled down: DRIVING OVER AT ONCE STOP MARGARET and gave it to him with the money, then went upstairs to pack. Leaving a note for Johnny to find after school, she drove down to the shop and told Dick what had happened.

'Eh, I hope Mr Garbutt is all right, love.'

'It doesn't sound like it. Angela would only have sent that telegram if she was desperate. Shall you be able to manage without me?'

'Aye. My mother will cook for us, or we'll go to the fish and chip shop, and I'll get my nephew in to help mind the shop. He's a smart lad.' Dick gave her a hug. 'Drive carefully, love. I'll miss you.'

She arrived in Overdale to find the doctor at the house and Edward Garbutt sinking fast.

'Oh, thank goodness!' Angela said. 'Come up at once. He wants to see you.'

Edward stared at her from the bed, his eyes pleading for something. He'd had a stroke and was unable to speak.

'Thank you for all you've done for me,' Margaret said softly, taking his hand and raising it to her lips. 'You can be sure we'll look after Angela. You might not approve of Dick, but he's a kind man.'

His expression lightened and he turned to look at his wife, all his love for her showing in his eyes, then with a last sigh he died.

Angela burst into tears and Margaret took her away, keeping an arm round her shoulders.

'I've made my life round Edward. I've nothing left now, nothing!' Angela wept.

'You've got us – if you'll have us? Dick won't hold a grudge.'

'That's all very well, but who's to look after the business? Things haven't been easy since the war and I know Edward's been a bit worried, but I know nothing about running a business. Nothing.'

'We could help.'

Angela stared at her. 'But what about your shop?'

'It's doing as well as can be expected, but it's a bit ahead of its time, I think, and Dick's bored to tell you the truth. He likes fiddling with radios better than selling them. If *you* need our help, we could put in his nephew as manager and come back here for a while. Dick's turned into a whizz with figures.'

'Would he do that, after the way we treated him?'

'Of course he would. He's a lovely fellow, my Dick.'

Margaret hesitated. This wasn't really the time, but perhaps it would give Angela more hope for the future. 'Besides, I'm expecting a child and I'd like it to be born here. I still feel that Overdale is home, you know.'

Angela hugged her close. 'Oh, *please* come back, then!'

23

November 1921

Mary Ann was worried about her mother, who seemed to be getting thinner all the time and had a drawn look to her. She went round to see her one afternoon during the quiet time at the café, leaving Jane in charge. She entered the house at the rear, knowing the front door would be locked, and found Dinah's maid in the kitchen washing some dishes.

When she tapped on the window, Gertie looked up and brightened when she saw who it was. She wiped her hands on the roller towel and came to open the back door, locking it automatically behind the visitor.

'Come in. I was just thinking of sending for you.'

'Is something wrong?'

'Yes. *She* isn't well and should be in bed, but she's up in the attics doing something. You should hear her coughing in all that dust, and it's freezing cold up there. But will she be told? No. Well, you know what she's like.'

Gertie had been with her mother for years and was a sensible woman with a heart of gold. If she was worried about Dinah's health, then Mary Ann was sure something was really wrong.

'I'll go up and see her. Maybe I can do whatever it is for her.'

Mary Ann made plenty of noise on the stairs to the attics, knowing how nervous her mother was. When she got to the top she called, 'Where are you, Mum?'

'Here. At the back.' The words were croaked out and followed by a paroxysm of coughing.

Mary Ann hurried through the attics and found her mother kneeling on the floor, surrounded by boxes and papers. 'What on earth are you doing?' she demanded. 'You should be in bed with that cold.'

'Don't you start. I've had – enough of that from Gertie.' Dinah gestured round her. 'I just – wanted to set my things in order. There are old papers – need burning.' Two huge sneezes took her by surprise.

Mary Ann reached down and pulled her to her feet. 'Come on. You're going to bed if I have to tie you down to keep you there.' Had her mother always been so thin? she wondered.

'Maybe I'll just lie down for an hour. A rest can work wonders.'

But Dinah stumbled as she stood up and swayed dizzily, so Mary Ann picked her up like a child and carried her down to her bedroom. 'You get undressed and I'll fill you a hot water bottle.'

By the time she got back Dinah was clad in a flannel nightgown that looked too big for her shrunken body and was lying in bed shivering.

Mary Ann gave her the earthenware hot-water bottle in its quilted flannel cosy and Dinah sighed as she first hugged it to her chest then pushed it down to her feet. 'Eh, that's better.'

'Can I get you anything else?'

'Handkerchiefs. Top drawer.'

Mary Ann put a few by the bed, then hovered near the door. Her mother had closed her eyes, was still shivering slightly and yet had red fever spots burning on her cheekbones. After a moment Mary Ann left the room and walked slowly downstairs, working out what to do.

'Gertie, I'll have to go back to the café to arrange for Jane to look after things there, but I'll be straight back. My mother's not well at all and we may have to send for the doctor. Do you know anyone who could come in to help you do the housework and cooking?'

'She'll hate that.'

'Do you, though?'

'Yes. My sister.'

'When I get back, you can go and fetch her.'

On her return she peeped in at her mother and found that Dinah had thrown the covers off and was now complaining about being too hot, even though it was a bitterly cold day.

Mary Ann ran back down to tell Gertie to call in the doctor then took up the makings of a fire, lighting it before her mother realised what she was doing.

'There's no need for that!'

'I think there is.'

'I never have a fire up here. It makes such a mess in a bedroom.'

'Well, you've got one now. And I've sent for the doctor, too. That looks like the influenza to me.'

It took a minute or two for that to sink in, then Dinah's eyes flew open and she glared at her daughter. 'I'm not seeing any doctor.'

'Oh, yes, you are. I'm stronger than you and for once you'll do as you're told. I was involved in nursing during the influenza epidemic just after the war and if you think I don't know when to call in a doctor, you're wrong. We don't want this turning to pneumonia, do we?'

Dinah stared at her, then shivered and snuggled down under the covers. 'You always were obstinate.'

'I take after you there, then.' She saw a faint smile cross her mother's face, but Dinah didn't speak and soon her breathing showed that she was sleeping, though the wheeziness of her breathing worried Mary Ann.

The doctor arrived two hours later and Dinah woke with a start to scowl at him.

'I didn't send for you.'

'No, your daughter did and rightly so.' He took her pulse and listened to her chest, shaking his head as he did so. 'My dear woman, how long have you been dragging yourself around for?'

'Don't believe in – giving in to illness.'

'With the influenza, you don't have much choice.' He looked at Mary Ann. 'She'll need careful nursing.'

'I can do that.'

As she walked him to the front door, he asked in a low voice, 'Has she always been so thin?'

'No, though she was always on the slight side.'

'When this is over we'll have to check her for TB. In the meantime, keep all her things separate from yours, even her eating utensils.'

Mary Ann stared at him in shock then walked slowly through to the kitchen where Gertie and her sister were enjoying a cup of tea and a savoury-smelling stew was bubbling on the stove for the guests' evening meal. 'Can you manage? I'll have to go and make arrangements at the café. I think I'm going to be needed here for a few days.'

Gertie looked at her in dismay. 'Is she that bad?'

'Influenza, and the doctor's concerned she might have TB so we have to keep her things separate from everyone else's.'

'We can manage here, dear. You go and do what you need to.'

Mary Ann flung on her coat and strode along the streets to the café to find Georges sitting there waiting for her.

'I didn't know you were coming!' she exclaimed, kissing his cheek and giving him a hug.

'A sudden impulse. You looked worried when you came in. Is something wrong?'

When she explained, he clasped her hand in his. 'Be careful, *chérie*. TB is a dangerous illness and can spread from one person to another very quickly.'

'I will, I promise you. But I'm afraid I can't stay with you. I have to make arrangements for running the café and then get back to my mother.'

'After you've made your arrangements, I'll oversee things here, if you like. In fact, if you're going to be sleeping at your mother's, why don't I stay here? I don't like to think of you leaving the place empty at night, not after what you've told me.'

She looked at him gratefully. 'You're always helping me, Georges.'

Our Mary Ann

'We help one another.' He hesitated, then said, 'I've sold everything in Belgium. If you can bear to have me around, I thought I'd settle somewhere near you.'

'I'd love to have you around, you know that, but I'll be moving back to the north within a year or two whether my mother comes or not, so don't buy anything down here. I may not have been born in Lancashire, but I feel at home there. And I don't know why I hanker to live in Blackpool, but I do. I went there for a quick visit earlier this year and I felt so well, saw all my old friends, walked along the beach and sat on the pier. Locals insist the air is stronger there. I don't know about that, but it certainly suits me.' She pulled herself to her feet. 'Well, I'd better go and talk to Jane, then I'll pack my things and change the sheets for you.'

She was gone within the half-hour. He smiled as he watched her leave. No woman he'd ever met could organise things so quickly. He loved to see that brisk, alert expression on her face. What a pity it was that she had never found anyone to replace Gabriel Clough in her heart. She'd have made a wonderful wife and mother.

Dinah was a fretful and ungrateful patient, complaining about everything. The room was too hot, then too cold. The bed was lumpy. There was a draught from the window. She didn't fancy anything to eat and nothing her daughter said or did would persuade her to eat more than a mouthful or two, so if she'd been thin before she was skeletal now.

When Mary Ann sent for the doctor again, he could only say that Mrs Baillie was barely holding her own. They should be prepared for the worst, though it might not come to that, he had seen more serious cases recover – but not usually.

After he'd left Mary Ann went to stand in the front parlour looking out at the street through a blur of tears. She was so glad she'd come back, would never have anything to reproach herself with now – but it was hard to lose your mother when she was your only relative in the whole world.

It was as if Dinah had given up caring about living and didn't

want to be saved. She seemed to be worried about something, though, and yet refused to say what.

The following night Mary Ann was woken by a thud and hurried to the bedroom next door, to find her mother lying on the floor near the door, weeping. She lifted her up and laid her back in bed, tucking the covers warmly around her.

'What on earth were you doing getting out of bed like that?'

'I need to sort some things out in the attic – in case I die.'

'Of course you're not going to die. I won't let you. But you can't possibly go up there! It's freezing cold and you're too weak. You know the doctor said you have to keep warm.' She sat down beside the bed. 'Is there something *I* can do for you?'

'No! I don't want anyone seeing my private papers, not even you.' Dinah grasped her arm and said, 'Promise me – promise faithfully – that if I die – you'll burn – *all* those old papers. You won't – let anyone see them. You won't – look at them.'

Mary Ann hesitated, guessing that somewhere in those papers would be the secret of who her father was, but her mother continued to weep and she could not deny her what she asked. 'I promise. *If* anything happens to you – though I'm going to make sure it doesn't – I'll burn your papers.'

Dinah sighed and mopped her eyes, then looked at her daughter. 'You're a good girl. Your father would have been proud of you.'

Within a few minutes she was asleep.

As the days passed, it became obvious to everyone that Dinah was weakening. She couldn't even cough up the fluid on her chest and the slightest movement brought sweat to her brow. The doctor shook his head and spoke about getting her into hospital.

Dinah overheard and fell into such a passion of mingled weeping and fury at the mere thought that Mary Ann promised her they wouldn't take her to hospital.

As she walked downstairs with the doctor, she asked, 'Would it make much difference, taking her to hospital?' He looked at her doubtfully and she said quietly, 'Please tell me the truth.'

'I don't think we have any chance of saving her, whatever we do. Some of them get a certain look on their faces when it's hopeless – and you've seen for yourself how she's struggling for breath, heard her chest bubbling and rattling when she tries to cough. She has pneumonia now, and I doubt she'll last more than a day or two.'

Mary Ann walked back up to her mother's room and sat beside the bed. Dinah's breathing was indeed very laboured and the sound of it seemed to fill the room. They had her propped up on pillows but she wasn't comfortable whatever they did.

Mary Ann was going to lose her mother and had promised to burn the papers that might tell her who her father had been.

She had always prided herself on keeping her promises.

Could she bear to keep this one?

Gabriel bought himself a small motor lorry for the farm, or rather had one built specially. His friend Paul had come back from the war talking enthusiastically about manufacturing motor vehicles. Not cars, but lorries and vans for farmers and businesses. After all, Ford had built a truck from a Model T and Paul was sure he could do the same from an English car. So Gabriel let him make a small hybrid vehicle, which looked like a truncated passenger car at the front but had a longer, heavier frame at the back and stronger rear suspension. And very useful it was too, he had to admit. He turned their poor old horse out to pasture. She'd more than earned her retirement by her hard work during the war.

Like his friend, a lot of men had come back from their military service with new skills and were looking to make better lives for themselves. Small businesses had opened up everywhere and a spirit of optimism had at first prevailed. They'd won the war, hadn't they? Now they could win better lives for themselves and their families as well.

But many ex-soldiers were still unemployed and the financial situation seem to be getting worse. Gabriel kept reading the employment figures in the newspapers and worrying about them. Lads who'd fought for their country didn't deserve this.

Although Overdale wasn't affected, he kept reading about riots and disturbances in other parts of the country. Race riots took place at several seaports in May and June, aimed at the West Indians who'd been brought in as sailors to fill shortages in the Merchant Navy. He thought it a shame to treat them like that when those same people had helped save the country.

Disturbances erupted at Luton in July. He shook his head sadly as he read about them.

And then to crown it all there were terrible riots in Liverpool and Birkenhead in August following strikes by the Liverpool Police. Hundreds of shops were looted and the troops had to be called in. What was the world coming to when Englishmen behaved like savages?

He bumped into Margaret one day on his way back from the library, which his mother sarcastically called, 'thy second home', and stopped to talk to her. She was pushing a baby carriage and looked to be in blooming health.

'How is the little fellow?' He peered in at the sleeping infant and smiled fondly. 'Eh, he's getting quite big now, isn't he?'

She beamed at her son Edward, then looked at Gabriel. 'How are you keeping? I haven't seen you for a while.'

He shrugged. 'Same as ever. Up to my ears in hens and sheep.' He hesitated, then asked, 'How's Mary Ann? Do you still keep in touch?'

'Yes, we write often, though I'm due a letter at the moment. She's doing well, her café is successful and she seems to be getting on all right with her mother.' He always asked about Mary Ann and Margaret always felt guilty that she'd never told her friend he was still alive. 'Have you heard from your wife?'

'No. And I don't suppose I shall now, either.'

But to his surprise he received a letter from Ivy the very next week, sent from Newcastle. At first he thought she'd come back to England, then he realised there was a town of the same name in New South Wales.

Dear Gabriel,
I hope you're all well. Dan and I have settled in very happily
here. If you have any photos of the girls, I'd love to have them. I
do miss them.
*   I'm writing because the only thing that mars our happiness is*
the fact that we can't marry. We were wondering if you would
consider providing us with grounds for divorce? You'd have
to go to a hotel and be caught in bed with another woman, but
apparently that sort of thing can be arranged. Dan says to tell
you we'd pay all the expenses.

Gabriel stopped reading to mutter angrily, 'Not bloody likely!
Why should I?'

I know this is a lot to ask, but surely you want to remarry as
well? I hope you find someone who suits you more than I did.
Girls of Frances' and Christina's age need a mother.
*   Please let me know what you think.*
*   Ivy*

He took the letter and showed it to his mother, who was even
angrier than he was. 'We've never had divorce in our family and
I hope we never shall. The fact that *she* has broken her marriage
vows doesn't mean you have to as well.'

'I might want to marry again one day myself.'

'Who would you marry? You never look at a woman twice.'

He sighed. His mother was right. He didn't. He compared them
all to Mary Ann and they didn't come off well. 'Don't tell the girls
Ivy wrote.'

'Dost think I'm stupid?'

'Anything but.' He was thoughtful as he put the letter away. His
initial anger had died down now. Maybe he should think about
doing as Ivy asked, whatever his mother said.

Only what was the point? Mary Ann would probably have met
someone else by now. At the thought of her he sighed. Such a kind,
bonny woman deserved to be happy. Maybe he'd ask Margaret
next time he saw her whether Mary Ann had a fellow or not.

If she hadn't, perhaps he could get in touch with her, even go down to Brighton to see her – and if they still got on well then he'd definitely do something about a divorce.

Or was he just building false hopes for himself?

Mary Ann sat by her mother's bed and watched her struggle for breath. Gertie had gone to bed, assuring her that she only had to knock on her bedroom door and she'd be down to help. But Mary Ann didn't want that. She wanted to spend this time with her mother. Not that Dinah could talk much – or had changed her mind about naming Mary Ann's father – but she seemed to enjoy hearing about her daughter's work during the war and even about her life in Blackpool before that.

Dinah grew suddenly agitated, twisting feebly about in the bed and clutching her throat. Her breath whined in and out with a huge effort and she looked quite terrified.

Mary Ann bent over the bed and clasped her mother's hand. 'I'm here. Shh! Calm down. You're making it worse.'

Dinah looked up at her. 'Sorry – not been good – mother.'

'You did your best, I'm sure.'

She nodded, fighting to say something else. 'Your – baby . . .'

Her grasp on Mary Ann's hands tightened for a minute, then slackened, and the dreadful noise of someone struggling for breath stopped so abruptly that it came as a shock to Mary Ann, even though it was expected.

Not yet! she thought, tears filling her eyes. *I didn't want you to go yet.*

She closed her mother's staring eyes and straightened the painfully thin body that hardly made a bump under the sheets.

Now I have no one of my own blood, she thought suddenly, then scolded herself for giving in to her unhappiness. She had Georges and lots of friends who were as good as family.

After standing there for a few minutes, she straightened her back and went to wake Gertie. It was nearly dawn. As soon as it was light, Gertie must go and fetch the doctor to certify the cause of death.

The next few days were very busy indeed. There was the funeral to prepare for, paperwork to be submitted to the authorities, and the lodgers to get rid of. Most of the women left within a day or two, not finding it difficult to obtain new lodgings at this time of year. One or two of them seemed surprised that Mary Ann wasn't going to take over the boarding house, for her mother had assured them several times that if anything happened to her, her daughter would run the place.

As they left, Georges moved into the house to help and was at Mary Ann's side whenever she needed him, while Jane took over the flat above the shop.

'He's a lovely fellow, isn't he, Moosoor Lepwee?' Gertie said one day. 'Even if he is a foreigner. You could do worse for yourself.'

'Georges has been like a father to me,' Mary Ann said firmly, because Gertie was of a romantic turn of mind. 'Don't go reading anything more into our relationship. Now, can you stay on until we sell the place? I'll suggest whoever buys it continues to employ you. But if not, I'll give you excellent references.'

'Of course I can stay. You'll need me to help clear the place out.'

'If there are any of my mother's things you want, you have only to say. Clothes, for instance. You're not much different in size.'

'Well, that's very handsome of you. I will have a look, if you don't mind.'

'Take what you want.'

The funeral was a simple affair because her mother hadn't had any real friends. Gertie attended, of course, and so did a couple of the lodgers, but otherwise there were only Mary Ann and Georges at the graveside.

It seemed very sad that so few cared about the passing of Dinah Baillie.

It was a week before Mary Ann found time to attend to the

papers in the attic. She had thought about them several times, very tempted to go through them and try to find out who her father was. But she had given her word to a dying woman, and in the end decided to keep it.

She picked up the cardboard box in which the loose papers had been stored, intending to carry it down and burn everything in the back yard. As she lifted it up, however, the bottom fell out and papers cascaded everywhere.

'Oh, drat!' She knelt down and began picking them up.

You couldn't help seeing what was written on some of them and the words 'your daughter's baby' seemed to leap out at her. She spread the letter out with fingers that trembled and began to read:

Dear Jeff
As you requested, I have arranged for your daughter's baby to be adopted and this is to inform you that last night the infant went to her new home.

Since Mary Ann was very determined to keep the child, I had to tell her that it had died during the night. I'd be greatful if you'd keep up this pretence, for both our sakes, so that she won't pine for it.

Mary Ann should be ready to leave here within a week or so. I'll confirm that once I'm sure she's recovered from the birth.

Yours
Jane

Mary Ann read Jane Greeson's letter three times before it sank in, then closed her eyes and let the tears drip down her face. All these years she'd carried a weight of guilt and grief for killing her own baby – and it had been a lie! Why had Jane Greeson thought it necessary to tell her that? It was one of the cruellest things she'd ever heard of.

She answered that question for herself almost immediately. To pay her back, of course, for helping Margaret to escape!

'I didn't do it,' she whispered. 'I didn't kill her.' Then she began to weep, great racking sobs that shook her whole body.

Gertie heard and came running. She brought Monsieur Lepuy, but they couldn't stop Mary Ann from weeping for a very long time.

24

February 1922

Mary Ann signed the final document the lawyer pushed towards her and sighed in relief. It had taken three months to sell her mother's house, which everyone said was quick but which had seemed interminable to her. She hated living there now, couldn't wait to leave Brighton; even the café didn't seem like hers any more.

As she strolled home she took a detour along the sea front, feeling as if she had shed a heavy burden.

Georges was waiting at the house and cocked one eyebrow at her. 'Happy now? No regrets?'

'None whatsoever. This place holds a lot of bad memories for me.' She still shuddered if she went into the attic room where Jeff Powling had abused her so shamefully and where they had kept her a prisoner until they'd taken her to Overdale.

'So – what can I do to help you? I'm sure you're already making plans.'

'I still have to find a buyer for the café, though I can always leave Jane to run it. I shall finish clearing up this house, then sell my mother's furniture and knick-knacks. What I can't sell, I'll give to charity.'

He was surprised. 'All of it?'

'Yes. Every single thing. I want to start afresh in Blackpool.'

'It's still to be Blackpool?'

A smile softened the determined expression on her face. 'Oh, yes. I do hope you'll like it there, Georges.'

'I shall like anywhere if you're there, chérie. It's people who matter most to me.'

She worked like a whirlwind from then onwards because there was no more need to keep the house looking tidy. She should have started clearing things out before but she'd had a superstitious feel that it would be bad luck. Which wasn't like her. But then, she hadn't felt like herself since she'd found out about her daughter, and only by exercising all her willpower had she prevented herself from rushing up to Overdale and demanding that Jane Greeson tell her what had happened to her baby.

Now the waiting was almost over. With Gertie's help she moved from one room to the next in a methodical way, emptying drawers, making piles of clothes and table linen, putting things that she could sell to one side, keeping nothing. Heavens, her mother had hoarded table linen that was nearly in rags. Had Dinah never thrown anything away?

'I shall miss this place,' Gertie sniffled as they cleared the last room.

'You have a good job to go to and I'm sure you'll soon settle in with Mrs Bender,' Mary Ann said bracingly.

She waved Gertie off the next day, feeling that this was another milestone passed.

The last place to be cleared was the attic. At her request no one had touched the papers scattered on the floor up there and they had lain gathering dust ever since she had found out about her baby. But now she could no longer avoid the task of clearing them up.

Sitting with a brightly lit oil lamp on the floor to either side of her, she took a deep breath and began to read and sort out the papers. Letters from a long time ago, from this relative or that, receipts, postcards. Why had her mother saved the monthly letters from Jane Greeson reporting on Mary Ann's health and pregnancy? She didn't want those and after a cursory glance ripped them to pieces, keeping only the one which told of her daughter being alive.

When she had cleared all the scattered papers, she found another box which contained photographs of her mother's family with their names and relationships written on the back, some from seventy years ago, the men with long beards and the women in very full skirts and with unflattering centre partings to their hair.

They all had solemn expressions on their faces, even the children. She scanned her grandparents' faces and decided she looked like her grandfather. These she would keep. She wondered why her mother hadn't even shown her them and whether any of her family were alive. They couldn't all have died, surely?

At the bottom of the box of photographs was another package, small and wrapped in tattered brown paper. In it was a letter from a man called Stanley Kershaw and a cracked and worn photograph of him. Mary Ann gasped and pressed one hand to her mouth as it became obvious from the letter that he was her father. Her mother must have written to him to let him know he had a daughter and he had written back to wish Dinah well, sending money to buy the baby a present. At the same time he reported the birth of a son by his wife, a lad they'd called Percy. The letter ended with a request to Dinah not to write again. It would only stir up old troubles and they both had new lives and responsibilities now.

When she looked at the dates of birth she realised she was only a month or so older than Percy. What did that say about her father? Had he been fickle-hearted? Was that why her mother would never talk about him?

She took the photograph across to the window to study it more carefully, then found a dusty old mirror with a cracked frame and studied her own face. Was she fooling herself or was there a resemblance? Yes, there definitely was.

As well as the letter there was a wallet, empty but with the name 'Stanley Kershaw' written in black ink on the tan leather. How had her mother obtained this? And why had she kept it? Had she loved him so much?

Mary Ann felt desperately sad to think she would never know.

Three mementoes of her father. Not much of an inheritance, but at least she knew his name now and had a photo of him.

And she had a half-brother!

Well, she did if Percy Kershaw was still alive. He might have been killed in the war. How did you approach a man and tell him you were his half-sister? He might not even believe her tale. Her emotions were fluctuating between tears and the faintest fluttering of hope, but she would not let herself cry. She had believed she'd no one of her own blood left, but it seemed she was wrong. There were at least two people related to her – her daughter and Percy. And he might have sisters, children.

Before she settled in Blackpool she would go to Overdale and look for her brother and daughter. With the money from her mother's house behind her she could afford to do this and take as much time as necessary. She would face the demons of her girlhood, too, and if she was very lucky see her daughter again. Elizabeth would be fourteen now. Nearly a woman. If she had a good life, was happy, Mary Ann didn't intend to spoil that by introducing herself. Why, the girl might not even know she was adopted.

But to see her, ah, that at least Mary Ann could hope for. She began to sob in spite of her resolve. She had wept a lot since finding out that her daughter was alive, but she had not had the dreadful nightmare about killing her baby since. Jane Greeson had a lot to answer for. Mary Ann intended to face her too because she would be the person most likely to know what had happened to the baby.

Only then would she feel ready to start a new life for herself.

Georges insisted on driving them up to Overdale in his new ten horse-power Riley tourer, saying she shouldn't do this alone. He went by easy stages, refusing to be hurried in spite of the draughtiness of the vehicle, even with the hood up.

As they drove into the town Mary Ann stared round her. She didn't recognise much except for the station because she had been a prisoner at the Greesons' farm for most of her time here. She couldn't even remember the way out to Birtley.

They booked into a pleasant hotel opposite the station and then went for a walk along nearby High Street together. It was cold, but both felt the need for some exercise. On one corner a man stood playing a fiddle, with an upended cap in front of him and a sign saying 'Injured at Paschaendale. Wife and family to support'.

Georges moved across to slip some coins into the cap and the man's face brightened.

'You often give generously to these men,' Mary Ann said as they walked on.

'I can afford it. When we settle down again, I'll find a better way of helping former soldiers.'

At that moment Gabriel saw them smiling at one another and stopped dead in his tracks to stare. Then he realised how shocked Mary Ann would be to see a man she believed to be dead and dodged back round a corner, incurring surprised glances over their shoulders from two elderly ladies walking sedately along arm-in-arm.

He couldn't resist peeping round the corner and watching Mary Ann and her companion as they walked away. What the hell was she doing in Overdale and who was that man? He was much older than she was and not as tall, but when she looked at him it was with patent affection.

As Gabriel leaned back against the wall, his eyes closed, trying to work out what to do about her, a man's voice asked, 'Are you all right?'

He jerked upright and nodded. 'Aye. Just a dizzy turn.' He went to find his lorry, forgetting completely about going to the library.

All his old feelings for Mary Ann surged up. She looked as bonny as ever, with that clear, bright-eyed gaze. There was no woman to compare with her. Not for him, anyway.

Damn Ivy! She had ruined his whole life. Left him in limbo. And damn Margaret for persuading him not to see Mary Ann again.

How could he avoid seeing her if she was staying in Overdale?

Did he even want to?

No, of course he didn't.

When they got back to the hotel, Mary Ann telephoned Margaret and smiled as her friend complained about their going to a hotel.

'You're to pack up and come straight round here!' she insisted.

'I'll come and see you tomorrow. We'll discuss it then.'

'You're still as stubborn as ever.'

'I'm afraid so.'

'Tomorrow morning, then. Come on your own. I want to hear about everything with no interruptions.'

'Very well.'

The next day it was pouring down. Mary Ann wouldn't let Georges, who had a slight cold, drive her round to her friend's but took a taxi. She didn't want anyone interrupting their tête-à-tête.

The Sycamores was bigger even than she'd expected. Much bigger. A rich man's house. Once it would have overawed her; now she counted a titled lady among her closest friends and wrote to Daphne regularly. She had lived in a house even grander than this one and that made her smile as she thought of how she had been changed by her experiences during the war.

The front door was flung open before she had even knocked and Margaret swept her into a twirling hug, let her go, then hugged her again for good measure.

'Angela is looking after my little Neddy and I've given orders that you and I are not to be disturbed. I want to hear about everything that's been going on, including all your plans for the future. Every single thing, mind! You've been so mysterious about why you've come back to Overdale. I thought you were never going to come back here. What's changed your mind?' Margaret giggled suddenly. 'If I don't stop asking you questions, you'll never be able to answer them, will you?'

Mary Ann found it difficult to start her tale, then even more difficult to keep her emotions in check as she confided in her friend. When she told Margaret that her baby hadn't died, her friend stared at her in horror then burst into tears.

'I can't bear what they did to you! Stealing your baby was bad enough, but making you believe you'd killed her . . . It's downright wicked, that's what it is. If someone took Johnny away from me or little Neddy, I'd go out of my mind.' She snapped her fingers suddenly. 'Is that what caused those nightmares where you whimpered and wept?'

Anna Jacobs

'Mmm.'

Margaret immediately hugged her friend again, wondering if this was the right time to tell her that Gabriel was still alive, yet reluctant to do so in case Mary Ann was angry with her.

When she pulled away, Mary Ann found it easier to talk. 'There's more. I think I have a half-brother here – if he's still alive, that is. I found out my father's name when I cleared the house, you see. There was a letter from him to my mother, written just after I was born. So—' she took a deep, shaky breath '—I have a lot of things to do and it didn't seem right to come and stay with you when I'd be in and out all the time.'

'On the contrary, this is the best place to work from and I intend to help you in your search. I'm sure Angela will agree with me.'

So Georges and Mary Ann moved across from the hotel and met Angela Garbutt, whose beauty was faded but still evident in the elegant lines of bones and flesh, enhanced by clothes so flattering as to make Mary Ann look down at her own serviceable garments and grimace.

When she glanced sideways during the evening meal she found Georges and Angela talking earnestly, so turned her own attention to Margaret and her husband. Dick was managing Garbutt's now and had learned a lot about finance and investments.

'What happened to your interest in radio?' Mary Ann asked to be polite.

'It's still there. I'm going to open a chain of shops selling radios and gramophones eventually. The first one is managing to hold its own, even in these times, because there are still a few folk with money to spare. They're talking about founding a national company for broadcasting radio programmes instead of all these little radio stations that just broadcast locally. Think of that. Wouldn't it be grand? We could . . .'

Margaret leaned across and put her hand across his mouth. 'That's enough, darling.'

Dick gave Mary Ann a sheepish grin. 'Sorry. I get carried away. It's so exciting! You wait and see. A few years and everyone will have a radio set to listen to, concerts, readings, all sorts of things.'

324

Mary Ann nodded politely, but she couldn't see that. Why, they'd get no work done if they sat around listening to music all evening!

When they went up to bed, Margaret came to make sure that everything was all right in her friend's room, having steeled herself to tell her that Gabriel was alive. But Mary Ann looked absolutely exhausted, so she postponed her confession until the following day.

In the morning Mary Ann woke at six o'clock as usual. She had been told that there would be a leisurely breakfast at nine o'clock, but she could ring for a tea tray before then if she was hungry. She couldn't bear to wait until what seemed to her like mid-morning to start her investigations, so got dressed quickly, pushed a note under Georges' bedroom door and went to beg a cup of tea and a piece of toast in the kitchen.

Afterwards she left the house and borrowed Georges' car, cranking it up efficiently under the disapproving gaze of Mrs Garbutt's chauffeur and driving off without even noticing him.

She sighed with relief as she drove towards Birtley. She didn't want anyone going with her. This was something she wanted – no, *needed!* – to do on her own. Farmers began their work early, so Jane Greeson was bound to be up by now, and if not, she'd wake her up. Or wait. Whatever was necessary.

As the car chugged its way up to the small hamlet on the edge of the moors, Mary Ann gazed across the rolling green landscape and remembered how much the permanence and beauty of it had comforted her over those long weeks of waiting for her baby to be born. She had stood in the top field many a time, staring out across the moors and breathing deeply.

She drove more slowly down the lane from Birtley village, passing the Cloughs' farm with a pang and wondering who was running it now. She was glad not to see any sign of a strange man working in the fields because the place was so linked in her mind with Gabriel.

Putting him firmly from her thoughts she drew up outside

Redvale and got out of the car. The place seemed totally unchanged and she hesitated for a moment, remembering the young girl who had been brought here willy-nilly and left to face alone the consequences of *his* actions. Strange how she had never connected Jeff Powling with the child after it had moved inside her. It had become *her* child then; still was as far as she was concerned.

Banishing those memories and reminding herself that she was a woman of thirty-two not a child now, she quelled her nervousness and walked across to the front door to ring the bell, ringing it again when no one answered.

There was the sound of footsteps, a bolt being drawn back, then Jane Greeson opened the door. She looked older, with lines of unhappiness graven down the sides of her mouth. She frowned and then stared in shock as she realised who her caller was. 'What do *you* want?'

'To speak to you.'

'Hmm. You'd better come in, I suppose. But I can't spare long, I'm busy.' She led the way to the room where Mary Ann had done so much plain sewing. 'Well, sit down.'

Mary Ann took a chair opposite her. 'I want to know what happened to my daughter.'

Jane's expression tightened. 'I told you: she died.'

'I have a letter from you saying otherwise.'

There was a pause, then, 'Your mother shouldn't have told you that.'

'She didn't. I found the letter after she died.' Mary Ann waited a minute then repeated, 'What happened to my daughter?'

Jane stared at her, then shrugged. 'What do you think? She was adopted.'

'Who by? I want to see her.'

Jane shrugged. 'I don't know. I deliberately didn't get involved in that part of it. Dr Browning-Baker took care of everything.' She gave her visitor a sneering smile. 'And he's dead now, so you can't ask him.'

Mary Ann thought about this for a moment. 'There must be records.'

'In some lawyer's office. I can't see them letting you go through their clients' private papers.' After a pause, she added, 'Any road, it's long past and would only cause trouble. I don't know why you're even bothering. You had your pleasure and you paid for it.'

'I had no pleasure. I was forced by my stepfather.'

Jane shrugged.

The words were out before Mary Ann could stop them. 'You're a hard woman.'

'It's a hard world.' She stood up. 'Now, I have work to do. Don't come back here again. I shan't let you in and I can't tell you anything else.'

Mary Ann left the house. The trouble was, she believed Mrs Greeson. The woman had looked so triumphant when she'd said she didn't know that her words had rung true, somehow.

But Mary Ann wasn't going to let that stop her. She'd find her daughter. There must be lots of ways. Parish records of christenings, school records. She knew her daughter's birth date, knew she was dark-haired, could guess that she'd be tall. She'd find her if it took years.

She had to, had to be sure Elizabeth was all right before she could settle to anything else.

When the door closed behind Mary Ann, Jane called, 'You can come out now. I know you've been eavesdropping. I saw your shadow under the door.'

Jeff Downham, who had once been known as Powling, came to join his cousin in the front sitting room and watched through the window as Mary Ann drove away. 'Funny, her turning up here just now. She looks well, better than she ever did as a girl.'

'Her mother's dead, so's your real wife, and maybe now you can stop playing your stupid little games. I don't know why you boast about them. It's a daft way to behave.'

'Well, it amuses me to torment those who've upset me. Maybe

I'll transfer my "little games" to the daughter now.' He chuckled. 'Don't try to spoil my fun, Jane. You know you hate her as much as I do.'

'I used to. But I don't waste my time on old quarrels. With Maurice ailing I have enough on my plate. And if you cause me any trouble, it'll be the last time you stay here.'

'I'm always very careful and you can't deny having me as a lodger helps you financially at the moment.' He smiled at her, holding her eyes until the hard expression softened. 'Well, I'd better go and finish off my paperwork. The trouble with being a sales rep is that there's too much writing things up involved.'

He went to his bedroom, but it was a while before he started work. As he sat at the battered little table he used as a desk, staring out of the window, he remembered various episodes in a life whose lack of success he blamed on other people. He'd always got his own back on them, though. Well, more or less. The biggest disappointment had been Mary Ann's mother. He'd been so close to getting her house, which had been worth a packet, and hadn't dared work in the south after Dinah threw him out because the Brighton police had made inquiries about him and he didn't want to risk being caught.

He smiled as he thought of Mary Ann, who had actually come back to Overdale just when he was feeling bored with life. It would be fun to torment her a bit. She'd probably be just as easy to hoodwink as she'd been before. You could see what other folk called openness still written on her face. Well, he called it stupidity and he particularly enjoyed removing expressions like that.

And who was there to care about her now that her mother had died? No one. So it'd be quite safe to indulge himself. He wondered suddenly if she'd inherited the house and, if so, might it still be possible to get his hands on the money it'd bring?

Might be worth a try.

Maybe this time he'd get lucky.

Mary Ann started up the car and drove slowly back along the lane.

A man came out of the front door of Clough Farm and turned to look at the vehicle.

The world spun round her and she was so shocked she let the car swerve towards the stone wall. She hauled on the brake, but it was no good. The car hit the wall with a thump and the world turned black around her as her head hit the windscreen.

Gabriel rushed towards the car as the front door of the house opened behind him, horrified to see Mary Ann unconscious with blood pouring from a wound on her scalp. He was already easing her from behind the steering wheel when his mother and Carrie joined him.

'Eh, what happened, son?'

'It's Mary Ann. She thought I was dead and when she saw me, she was so shocked she ran into the wall.'

'Here, let's give you a hand.'

The two elderly women helped carry Mary Ann inside the house.

The sofa was far too small for such a tall woman. 'My bed,' Gabriel said.

'I'll fetch some boiled water,' Carrie told them. 'We'll need to wash that wound.'

As Mary Ann stirred, he looked at his mother. 'Could you give us a minute or two alone first?'

Jassy pursed her lips, but didn't voice her disapproval.

He picked up Mary Ann's hand as he waited for her to regain consciousness and glanced down at it. The same as it had always been, a large capable hand with short, well-kept nails.

Her eyes flickered open and for a moment or two they simply looked at one another.

'I thought you were dead,' she said at last.

'Missing, presumed dead. I'd been hit on the head and it scattered my wits for a few weeks. Couldn't even remember who I was at first.'

'Why didn't you let me know you were alive?'

'You'd got married. I thought – leave her to be happy.'

'I've grieved for you. You should have let me know you were alive, Gabriel.' It was a pleasure even to say his name.

'I wanted to, but I had nothing to offer you. Margaret thought – and I agreed with her – that it was best I stay away.'

'Well, it wasn't best! Didn't either of you think to ask *me*? Had I no say?' She felt furious at her friend for interfering like that and would tell her so when she got back.

There was a knock on the door and Carrie came in with a steaming bowl, followed by Jassy with some clean cloths.

'We need to look at that head,' Carrie said firmly. 'You two can talk as much as you want later.'

When the two women had ministered to her, they left again, Jassy turning at the door to say, 'You need to rest for a bit before you leave, lass.'

'I know. I feel a bit shaky still. Thanks for your help.'

Gabriel closed the door behind his mother and came back to sit on the edge of the bed. 'Is your head hurting?'

'It's throbbing a bit. That'll pass. I was knocked out once before in a train crash. I lost a good friend then.' Her lips quivered and she scanned his face intently. 'Maybe this time I've found one.'

'I've still nothing to offer you.'

'Yourself would be enough.'

He closed his eyes, then opened them again. 'I never forgot you, lass.'

'Nor I you.'

'Who was the fellow you were with in town, the one you seemed so fond of?'

'Georges Lepuy. I've adopted him as a father. I needed one and he'd lost his whole family in the war.'

Relief surged through him. 'Poor fellow. What brought you back to Overdale?'

She hesitated then said, 'They told me years ago that my daughter was dead, but she wasn't. It was all lies. I've come back to find her. Mrs Greeson won't help, says she doesn't even know what happened to the babies, but there must be some way

of finding out where my daughter is now.' Oh, the joy of saying
the words *my daughter*!

'She might not be living in Overdale.'

'I'll still find her. I don't want to spoil her life, but I have to
see her, Gabriel. I have to know that she's all right.'

Mary Ann's voice rang with so much anguish that he took her
in his arms and held her close, his breath warm on her cheek. She
clung to him, breathing in the smell of fresh air and soap. The
mere fact that he was alive set a glow of joy in her heart.

And a warm feeling of hope, too.

On the other side of Overdale, Mrs Ethel Bawton, widow, smacked
her daughter hard across the face. 'You will go and dust the sitting
room – *properly* this time. And if you ever miss the mantelpiece
again, you'll also miss your evening meal. *I* saw Mrs Garbutt
staring at it when she called on me this morning.'

Beatrice bit her lip, determined not to cry again. Since her
father's death her mother had become very strange, not just strict
but cruel. Apparently her father had not left as much money as
they had expected so she'd had to leave her little private school
last year. Her mother had sacked the maids and now Beatrice had
to do their jobs as well as she could. Cook wasn't pleased to have
such an inexpert helper and her mother was never satisfied with
how she cleaned the house, though she laboured hard all day.

Her mother did very little to help, saying she hadn't been
brought up to do housework and wasn't going to start now,
always adding that it was only fair that Beatrice should pay them
back after all they'd done for her.

That made no sense. All parents looked after their daughters,
didn't they? What was so special about what they'd done for
her? When she compared her life with those of her friends,
she'd realised hers weren't loving parents and they'd both been
extremely strict with her. It was as if they'd *expected* her to
misbehave, and sometimes she had done so out of a spirit of
pure defiance.

In the past few months Beatrice had thought seriously about

running away, but there was simply nowhere to go. Her father had apparently quarrelled with most of his relatives and hadn't communicated with them for many years. Her mother had come from another town and said relatives were nothing but a nuisance, always wanting something or gossiping about you.

But if things got any worse Beatrice would definitely leave. If she went as a maid to someone else she'd get paid, at least, and have a roof over her head. Only – employers would want references and of course she had none. Besides, she was barely sixteen. Were you allowed to leave home at that age without your mother's permission or would the police bring you back again?

The bell from the sitting room rang, then rang again.

'Well, aren't you going to answer it?' Cook demanded. 'She always comes down to the kitchen if she wants to see me.'

Heart sinking, the girl made her way to the front of the house. What had she done wrong now?

'I have some errands for you,' her mother announced. Ethel produced a list then the small leather purse she used for house-keeping because she no longer had accounts with any of the shops. 'Go to Dearden's. They have the best tea and their shop is the cleanest in town.'

'Yes, Mother.'

'And, for goodness' sake, change your dress and do something with that hair of yours before you leave. You look like a housemaid in that thing and you're so tall people can't help noticing you. I shall not allow slovenly habits to creep in just because your poor dear father is dead.'

It was only by a supreme effort that Beatrice held back the retort that she was doing a housemaid's work so it was no wonder she looked like one. She answered back in her head all the time now but didn't dare do it aloud. Somehow, when she tried, the words froze on her lips. She'd felt like hitting her mother back this morning, which would have been a dreadful thing to do. Or at least, so she'd been taught.

The Bible said, *Honour thy father and thy mother* – but what if they didn't deserve it?

When she was dressed to her mother's satisfaction, in an old-fashioned outfit that was getting a big skimpy and short because she'd grown again, Beatrice let herself out of the house. She felt better once she was in the fresh air and didn't hurry to the shops as she'd been ordered.

Dearden's was full so she waited her turn, enjoying the peace of simply standing around and listening to the various conversations.

Mrs Dearden herself served her, which was always best. Mrs Dearden was about ten years older than her, she supposed, slim and lively with a lovely smile that made you feel warm inside.

As she looked at Beatrice today, the smile slipped a little. 'Have you hurt your cheek, dear?'

Startled, Beatrice glanced into the mirror behind the counter, the one with Tate & Lyle's Sugar printed along the bottom, and saw that her cheek looked bruised. 'Oh, no. I – um – bumped into a door.'

'Have you a minute to come through to the back, love?' Lizzie Dearden said.

'Yes, of course.'

When they were in the packing room, where the sugar, currants and other dry goods were weighed and put into packets, Lizzie said bluntly, 'I know your mother's hitting you, love, and I just wanted to say, if things get too bad, you can always come round here for a bit of comfort.'

Beatrice swallowed hard. This sympathy made her want to weep, but she mustn't start that or she'd never stop. 'She doesn't let me out except to go to the shops.'

'I understand because my mother used to hit me a lot,' Lizzie went on. 'Not because I behaved badly but because she took against me after my father died.'

'Oh. It was the same for me – though she's never been very loving.' Beatrice looked at Mrs Dearden and said, 'There's nothing you can do about something like that, though, is there? I'm too young to leave home, but I will one day.'

'Don't make my mistake and marry the wrong man to get away. My first husband was as bad as my mother.'

'That must have been awful.'

'Yes. But he's dead now, so it's over and done with. I just wanted you to understand that a hasty marriage is no way to escape.' She patted Beatrice on the shoulder. 'Other people aren't supposed to do anything when they see this sort of thing happening, but I can't stand by. So remember: if you need help, you can come to me. Any time, day or night.' She looked up at the girl, who was taller than her, and said wryly, 'You're getting big enough to hit her back, you know.'

Tears threatened again and Beatrice turned to go, fighting for self-control. 'I can't – talk about it any more.'

'No, of course you can't. Look, I've got some arnica. Let me put it on your cheek. It does help the bruising. I'm always using it on my little monsters.'

Beatrice shook her head. 'She'll smell it and then I'll be in trouble again. But thank you anyway, Mrs Dearden – for everything.'

Lizzie waited a minute to be sure no more tears threatened then said, 'Here, have a sweet. These are really nice ones.' As she received a wobbly smile she said briskly, 'Well, we'd better get back into the shop, hadn't we? It's quite busy today.' But not as busy as it had been before the war. She and Peter had to work much harder nowadays to make a living and employed fewer staff.

After she had served the girl, Lizzie watched Beatrice walk out. When Peter came across and put his arm round her, she looked up at him. 'Her mother is beating her.'

'That's fairly obvious. But you can't interfere, love.'

Oh, can't I? Lizzie thought. I can't *not* interfere if it gets any worse. She turned round as the shop doorbell tinkled and stared in shock as a woman paused in the doorway. Goodness, for a minute the stranger had reminded her of . . . She'd better pull herself together. Whatever had got into her today to be so fanciful? She moved forward. 'Can I help you, madam?' There was a big bruise on this woman's forehead as well and before Lizzie could stop herself the words were out. 'Eh, that must have been a nasty bang on the head.'

'Yes. I had an accident in the car. I'd like a box of chocolates, please, a nice big one. It's a present for someone who helped me.'

As she handed back the change, Lizzie thought the woman was going to ask her something, but just then two children erupted into the shop, laughing and pushing one another, followed by their mother, so the moment was lost. Strangers in town sometimes did ask for information as they tried to settle in.

This woman looked very pleasant, tall and with a healthy complexion. Lizzie often wished she herself were taller like her father, instead of short and skinny like her mother. Not that wishing did much good, but everyone was entitled to a dream or two.

25

Late February 1922

Mary Ann borrowed Georges' car again and drove out to Clough Farm, using the excuse of giving Gabriel's mother and Mrs Anders the chocolates for helping her after her accident. The vehicle looked a bit battered on one front wing, but Georges said accidents happened all the time and as long as she was all right that was all that mattered to him. He could always buy another car.

She found Gabriel mucking out one of the many hen houses. It had a hinged side for easy cleaning and he was surrounded by squawking birds who didn't seem to appreciate what he was doing. She watched for a minute or two as he finished the task then lowered the side. He wasn't as thin as he had been when she first knew him and she thought him a fine figure of a man now.

He worked rhythmically, his thoughts clearly elsewhere, and didn't become aware of her until he turned round. When he did he stopped short, then spread his arms and pulled a wry face at himself. 'You've chosen a bad moment if you want to speak to me, lass.'

'I'm sorry to interrupt your work, but I wanted to thank you all for helping me and . . .' She let the words trail away, unable to pretend with him, 'No, what I really wanted was to see *you* again, Gabriel.'

He stopped to lean on his shovel. What he wanted to say was, *And I wanted to see you again,* but for her sake he changed it to, 'We both know that road leads nowhere, Mary Ann.'

'It leads nowhere only if we allow it to end. We've both seen a lot of people die or be injured so that for them there's no chance of proper lives again. We don't have that burden, at least. I thought I'd lost everyone who mattered to me, but now I've been given a second chance and I'm not going to waste it, any of it. I still love you, Gabriel, and always have. I only married Bob because I thought you were dead and he wanted it so much. I tried to make him happy, but I didn't succeed.' She flushed slightly, but was determined that there should be no lies between them. 'He couldn't even play a man's part and I've always wondered if he realised my heart was elsewhere.'

Gabriel set the shovel against the side of the hen house and rubbed his mucky hands down his overalls. 'I'm going to get a good wash and change my clothes. We need to talk without interruptions.' As he drew level with her, he said softly, 'I never stopped caring about you either, love. But I care too much to ruin your life.'

'You wouldn't do that.'

'I saw how folk treated your friend Margaret when she had a child out of wedlock.'

'She's happy now, which is what matters most. You can't be happy with the wrong person, Gabriel. We've both found that out.'

'Come into the house and wait while I make myself decent, then we'll take a picnic up on the tops. I've got a sheepskin jerkin that'll fit you, because the wind can cut like a knife up there.' He glanced down and smiled. 'You always did wear sensible shoes.'

'Is that a compliment?' she asked ruefully, looking down at her feet. 'I have trouble even finding shoes that are big enough. Women are supposed to have dainty feet.'

'It's definitely a compliment. I don't like women who mince about, dressed like dolls, with shoes that stop them walking properly. I like women who stride out beside you and face up to all that life has to offer.' His expression softened again and he added, 'Women like you.'

She sat in the kitchen and waited for him, repeating those words inside her head, hope burning brightly in her now. As she listened to the splashing sounds from the scullery, she remembered how it had felt to regain consciousness and see Gabriel by the side of the bed, feel his hand holding hers. She wanted him beside her always and didn't intend to let anyone or anything stop them being together – as long as he wanted her too.

When they were out of sight of everyone, he set down the bag of food he'd put together hastily and took her hand to pull her towards him. 'May I kiss you?'

'I'll be angry if you don't.'

His lips were warm, his skin a little chilled by the wind and his body felt as solid as a rock. She was almost as tall as he was, a comfortable size for an embrace. As she melted into the kiss, she offered him her love with every fibre of her body. They were both breathing deeply when he pulled away and instinctively she made a tiny noise of protest in her throat.

He spoke first. 'Not yet, love. This is a day for talking – and for decisions. Tell me everything that's happened to you since we last met. Every single thing.'

'If you'll do the same.'

'I don't like to talk about the war, but I'll tell you the rest.'

They found a tumble of rocks in a place sheltered from the wind and sat on a flat one looking down at the valley and the small town. The sun shone on them, still lacking real warmth, but the jerkins kept the worst of the wind off. She'd have sat there in a snowstorm to be with him!

'What are your plans now?' he asked when they had finished talking about the years they'd been apart.

'I had intended to move to Blackpool, buy a business there, perhaps a café, and settle down. Georges wants to settle near me. He's like a father to me now and he has no one else.'

'If he's a good father, he'll tell me to stay away from you.'

'He's the most tolerant man I've ever met. You'll like him, I'm sure. And I don't think he'll tell me to run away from love.'

'*Had intended* to move to Blackpool?'

She looked at him, making no pretence. 'What I do now depends on you.'

He laughed. 'Eh, I love your honesty and lack of pretence. I love you so much, Mary Ann.'

'And I love you.' She gazed at him, feeling as if she was glowing with the warmth of her feelings for him. 'When you see a chance of happiness, I think you should take it.'

'People will talk, spurn you – as they've spurned your friend Margaret.' He hesitated. 'And I have the girls to think about as well.'

'As long as they don't take a dislike to me, it might be better if we all left Overdale and you and I pretended to be married. I have to confess, I'm a little nervous of what your daughters will say, though. They're old enough now to resent me. And there's your mother, too. Will she come with us?'

'She's always refused to leave Birtley.'

'Would you go without her?'

'And come to you penniless? That wouldn't sit well with me.'

'What use is my money if I'm unhappy? Besides, if we bought a business, we could work in it together.' She grinned suddenly. 'You'd earn your way, I promise you. I'm a real slave-driver. Ask Margaret. I was in charge of her during the war.'

He smiled. 'I can't believe this is happening. I never dared hope I'd find love again.'

'Nor I,' she echoed softly.

At that he muttered something beneath his breath and pulled her into his arms, kissing her eyelids, her cheeks, and finally her lips until they were both breathless.

As he drew his head away, she clasped her arms round his neck and said, 'Well? Are we to be together?'

'Yes, we are. I should say no, but I can't. But if I'm ever free to marry you, I promise I shall. Come on! If we stay here I shall lose what little self-control I've got left.' He took hold of her hand and pulled her to her feet. They walked back at a cracking pace through a world that seemed filled with new brightness.

They arrived back at the farm to find Jassy sitting in the kitchen peeling potatoes. She nodded to Mary Ann.

'We need to talk to you, Mam,' Gabriel said. 'Where's Carrie?'

'Out at a birthing.' She looked from one to the other and pressed her lips tightly together, praying that this wasn't what she suspected.

Gabriel waited until Mary Ann had sat down then said bluntly, 'Our feelings for one another haven't changed, Mam.'

'And something else hasn't changed, either. You're still married to Ivy.'

'It's only a paper marriage now. Shall I let that ruin my life?'

Jassy hesitated. She wanted to say this wouldn't do but there was an indefinable connection between the two of them. They were as easy together as if they'd been married for years and there was no doubt the lass cared for him. She sighed. 'It's not me but other folk who'll ruin your lives – and your daughters' too.'

'They might if we stayed in Overdale, but not if we moved away.'

She stilled and closed her eyes as if in pain.

'I'm sorry, Mam. I've done my best to settle here. I know you love it, but I don't and I never will. The stink of those hens seems to fill my nostrils every hour of the day. What I want is to live near the sea and breathe in clean, fresh air.'

'It's just a novelty. It'd wear off.'

'No, it's not. I saw enough of the sea during the war for that to happen, but my liking for it didn't change. I could watch it for hours. I love the way the air smells near the water.'

'I'm the same.' Mary Ann hadn't meant to speak out and tensed as the older woman looked at her and sighed. She expected recriminations but Jassy remained silent, staring down at her lap now and pleating the fabric of the pinafore she always wore in the house.

In the end she looked up and asked quietly, 'Can you wait a bit, let me get to know you, Mary Ann, see how you get on with the lasses?'

'Of course.'

Jassy looked at her son. 'Is that all right with you as well, our Gabriel?'

'Yes. Though our feelings won't change.'

'Then say nowt to the girls. Just give us all time to shake down together. Happen summat will come of it.'

As she drove back into Overdale, Mary Ann felt joy bubbling through her. She couldn't remember feeling this happy in her whole life. She knew it wouldn't last, because happiness never did, but with Gabriel by her side, she felt she could weather anything life threw at her now. She smiled at the thought of him. He was a quiet man, gentle and yet strong in himself. Other men might attract more attention but he suited her perfectly.

Then, as she was driving down the street to Margaret's house, she saw a man standing in the shadow of some trees. He lifted his hat and smiled. Recognition jolted through her.

Jeff Powling!

She slowed at once, but by the time she had stopped the car he had vanished down a narrow snicket between two houses. It couldn't be *him!* Surely it couldn't? No, it had to be her imagination playing tricks on her.

But she finally admitted to herself that it wasn't. She would never mistake that man.

What was he doing in Overdale?

Well, whatever it was, she vowed grimly, he would never get the better of her again. Never.

Later that day, Mary Ann went to the parish church and asked to see the register of christenings.

The minister frowned at her. 'Is there some reason for this?'

She had worked out a story and hoped it sounded good enough. 'Yes. I'm trying to trace a missing relative. I know she got married and had a baby at the same time as I had mine, but I can't remember her married name.'

She went through all the christenings of little girls for 1907, but found no child with a birth date within even a month of her daughter's. The minister came in a couple of times and frowned at her, as if he wasn't quite sure he believed her. While he was out, she also checked for the name Percy Kershaw in 1891, the year they had both been born, but that wasn't there, either.

When she left the church she was thoughtful, wondering where to turn to for help in tracing the Kershaws. As she passed

Dearden's grocery shop, she saw that there were no customers inside, hesitated, then entered. There was something kind and welcoming about Mrs Dearden. Surely she wouldn't mind if Mary Ann asked her a few questions?

Lizzie looked up and smiled as the doorbell tinkled.

Mary Ann marched up to the counter and came straight to the point. 'I wonder – do you know a family called Kershaw, Mrs Dearden? I believe there is a Percy Kershaw and perhaps others.'

It was the last thing Lizzie had expected to hear. She gaped at the other woman. 'Why are you asking?'

'I found the name Percy Kershaw in my mother's things when I cleared the house. I – um – think we may be related. My mother had lost touch with her relatives, but I'd like to find them.'

'You'd better come up to the sitting room,' Lizzie said, raising her voice to call, 'Peter love, can you take over for a bit?'

He poked his head round the rear door, nodded a greeting to Mary Ann and said, 'All right, love.'

When they were seated in the shabby but comfortable sitting-room upstairs, Lizzie looked at her visitor. 'Why do you think you're related to the Kershaws?'

After a moment's hesitation, Mary Ann dipped into her hand-bag and offered her the photo. 'I found this in my mother's things, and a letter.'

Lizzie gasped at the sight of the photo, recognising it instantly, then looked back at Mary Ann in puzzlement. 'What did the letter say?'

'I think that's something I ought only to discuss with Percy – or any other Kershaws. It's – well, rather private.'

'Percy's my brother.'

Mary Ann felt as if the floor were rocking beneath her feet. For a moment she could not speak and a lump rose in her throat. She had to swallow several times before she managed to say in a tight, scratchy voice, 'Then I think you may be my half-sister.'

It was Lizzie's turn to gape. '*Half-sister!*' Then she realised what had been teasing at the back of her mind ever since the first time she'd seen this woman: a resemblance to her father. He'd died when she was twelve, but she remembered him so clearly. She picked up the photo and stared from it to her visitor. Yes, you couldn't mistake the resemblance. 'I don't even know your name.'

'Mary Ann. My maiden name was Baillie, but it's Hall now.' She fumbled in her bag, her hands shaking so much she had difficulty extracting Stanley's letter. When she held it out she realised her companion's hand was shaking too. 'I'm sorry. This must be a terrible shock to you. Are you all right?'

'Yes.' Lizzie unfolded the letter, which was as worn as the photograph, and read it carefully. Then she stood up and pulled Mary Ann to her feet, giving her a big hug. 'I believe you.' Tears were running down her face and she couldn't form any more words.

There were footsteps on the stairs that led up from the shop and Peter appeared. He looked from one weeping woman to the other and stopped. 'Shall I leave you alone?'

'No, you shan't,' Lizzie said, wiping her face with the back of her hand. 'Come and meet my half-sister, Peter love. This is Mary Ann.'

They explained the situation to him, interrupting one another in their excitement.

He was more suspicious than his wife. 'How can you be sure it's true? I'm not saying your father might not have had a bas – er, child by another woman, but how do you know this woman's the one? No offence meant, Mrs Hall.'

Lizzie gave a laugh that turned into a sob. 'Because she looks like Dad. I can still remember him quite clearly. You wait till our Percy sees her. He'll say the same. Eh, I'll nip round to see them tonight. They'll all want to meet her.' She turned back to Mary Ann and said with a smile, 'You'll be sorry you started this. There's not only Percy and me, but Eva and Polly and our Johnny, the youngest. Eh, what's the matter, love?'

Mary Ann was sobbing harder than ever. 'I'm so h-happy! Not

long ago I thought I had no one left in the world, and now – now I've got brothers and sisters. Well, half-sisters.'

'We'll not bother about the half. As far as I'm concerned you're enough of a Kershaw to count as one of us.'

It was a while before Mary Ann could calm down and Lizzie wondered what sort of life she'd led. It must have been lonely. Lizzie couldn't imagine life without her brothers and sisters. She might not see them very often, but they were there, part of her. Just as this woman was part of her now. She wanted to find out everything she could about Mary Ann's background, but this wasn't the time to ask. For the moment, she'd just accept whatever this new sister told her.

She studied the other woman, who was so much taller than her and sturdily built. No matter what she ate, Lizzie stayed scrawny. Polly and Eva were more rounded, a mix of both their parents. But they all three had the same dark brown hair, whether straight like Lizzie's or wavy like Eva's – and like this woman's, too.

'Eh, isn't it lovely? Fancy getting another sister!'

'I was so worried you wouldn't want to know me.'

'There's always room for another in our family. More people to love. You'll see. They'll all be happy you've found us.'

'Can I just – start with you? I have a few things to tell you, not now but before I meet the others.'

'Life's not been kind to you, has it?' Lizzie said softly, seeing the pain in her new sister's eyes.

'Not always. I wished I had a proper family, but there was just Mother and me and she wasn't very – affectionate. And for years I didn't even see her.' As they heard the shop doorbell tinkle again Mary Ann looked at her watch. 'Can we talk another time? I have to get back and you're busy. I'm staying with my friend Margaret at The Sycamores, by the way.'

'I know the house. We deliver to them. Look, I'm sorry if I'm rushing things. Why don't you come round tomorrow afternoon and I'll take an hour off to talk? Then you can come to tea on Sunday and meet Percy and Johnny. There are the children, as well. I've got two and Polly's got one, and a stepdaughter – eh, and our Eva's got two stepdaughters now as well.'

'That'd be wonderful. Just—' Mary Ann's voice broke again, '—wonderful.'

She walked slowly back to The Sycamores and to her relief when she got there no one else was around. What she needed now was some quiet time to get used to the fact that she had a real family. It was so wonderful a thought that tears welled in her eyes each time she dwelled on it.

Her expression softened into a smile as she thought about Lizzie. What a warm loving woman! Mary Ann hoped the rest of the family were like her and would want to recognise a new half-sister. In spite of Lizzie's assurances that they would, she wouldn't truly believe it until she experienced it herself.

Beatrice's mother studied her with a disapproving expression on her face as she set the table for dinner. 'You've grown again. That dress is far too short. You'll have to let the hem down.'

'There isn't anything to let.'

'There must be.' She stepped forward and picked up the hem, making a sound of irritation in her throat. 'No, I remember, you let it down two months ago – and a very poor job you made of it, too. I suppose we'll have to buy some more material and let you make yourself another dress.'

Beatrice looked at her in dismay. 'But you know how bad I am at sewing.' And besides, when did she have time for sewing? 'Couldn't you help me? Please. You're so good at dressmaking.'

'No, I can't! I have far too many other calls upon my time. I'll buy some material while I'm in town and you can make a pattern from one of your old dresses. Something simple will do, just so you don't disgrace me when you go to the shops.'

When her mother had left to call on her friends and continue the pretence that she still led a life of leisure, Beatrice went out into the garden. There were plenty of jobs to do around the house, but Cook was getting so bad-tempered lately that she wanted a few minutes to herself before she started on them.

Without consciously taking any decision to disobey her mother, she found her steps turning towards the park. The sun was shining and it felt very spring-like today. She turned her face up to the warmth and strolled along the paths, admiring the new growth on the bushes and the fine display of snowdrops just starting to come into bloom.

Little children were running about playing and she smiled. She loved to watch them, though she'd never had much to do with other children as her parents didn't like her playing out after school and *getting into mischief* as they'd put it.

She was later getting back than she'd intended and was greeted by her mother at the back door, arms akimbo and an angry expression on her face.

'*Where have you been?*'

'Just to the park.'

'Who with?'

'No one. By myself.'

'Without a hat or gloves? You look like a hoyden. What will people think?'

As Ethel raised her hand to administer a slap, Beatrice stepped back to avoid the blow.

'Stand still and take your punishment!' screeched her mother.

Suddenly Beatrice's own anger boiled up. 'No. You've done nothing but hit me since Father died and it's not fair. I work as hard as I can and never get any time off. I'm not going to put up with it any more. Even hired servants get time off and wages.'

But her mother darted forward so quickly that Beatrice didn't have time to dodge the slap on the cheek. That was the final straw! Cheek stinging from the violence of the blow, she held her mother's arm to prevent her from doing it again and her mother screamed so loudly that Cook came running.

'What are you doing?' she cried, seeing the girl struggling with the mistress.

'She's not right – to keep hitting me,' Beatrice panted.

'She has every right. She's your mother.'

'Help me hold her down,' Ethel ordered. 'I'll teach her to cheek me!' The two women held the struggling Beatrice in a corner near the back door and her mother grabbed a walking stick from the stand and used that to such good effect that Beatrice was soon screaming to her to stop.

In the end Cook stepped back, sickened by the gloating expression on her mistress's face, and the girl tore herself out of their grasp, fleeing down the garden sobbing loudly. It was always the same. She vowed to stand up for herself, but somehow her mother always got the better of her.

When she got to the wall, she looked round and saw her mother coming after her, so clambered over it, ripping her skirt in the process. She ran off down the back lane, trying not to sob aloud.

She went and hid in a shrubbery in the park until dusk fell, enduring an hour of intermittent rain and hardly noticing that her clothes were wet through because the moisture felt so cooling on her battered face.

As it grew darker she made her way to the only person who had ever offered to help her.

Dearden's was still brightly lit. Beatrice waited outside, shivering, until it was clear of customers then went inside, stumbling to a halt as the warmth hit her.

Lizzie looked up as the doorbell tinkled and gaped at the apparition that stood there. Beatrice was soaking wet, her clothes torn and her face in a shocking state, with one eye swollen and the upper lip cut and puffy. Other blows had left weals on her arms which were bare in spite of the chilly weather. She didn't speak, only stood there, shivering.

'Dear God, what have they done to you?' Lizzie whispered. It was like looking back at herself when she'd been married to her first husband.

'Mother and Cook h-held me down. She used Father's walking cane on me.' Beatrice began sobbing.

Lizzie caught a glimpse of someone walking towards the door. 'Go through to the back quickly!'

Beatrice went into the rear of the shop, closed the door and leaned against it, trying to hold back her sobs.

'Hey, are you all right?'

A man's voice made her jump in shock. She flinched as he came towards her and he stopped in shock at the sight of her battered face.

The door pushed against Beatrice's back and Lizzie came into the packing area. 'Oh, Mr Downham, are you still here?' She looked from him to the girl, biting her lip and wondering what to say. He wasn't her favourite sales rep, too smarmy, and she usually got Peter to deal with him. 'This is – a young friend of ours. She's – um – been in an accident. I'd be grateful if you'd not mention seeing her here.'

'Of course not.' But he studied Beatrice again, frowning and wondering who she reminded him of.

Peter came bustling from the office at the rear of the yard carrying the order book, but stopped dead at the sight of the fugitive. He looked quickly at Lizzie.

'I'm just taking *Jenny* upstairs to see to her cuts,' she said loudly, putting her arm round the girl, who was much taller than her, and shepherding her towards the stairs. 'Can you mind the shop for me, love?'

'Yes. We've just finished making up our order. I'll see you out, Mr Downham.'

Jeff nodded, intrigued by this scene. Someone had really laced into the girl. Must have been someone in her family. It was usually the father. But what had she done to get him so angry? She didn't have a cheeky sort of face.

He was glad he'd never allowed himself to be lumbered with kids. They were more trouble than they were worth, from what he'd seen of other people's. Whistling, he walked out of the shop and strode along the street, soon forgetting the battered girl and wondering what he could do next to upset dear Mary Ann.

He intended to have some fun before he moved on to the next town after the weekend. And if he could, he intended to get some money out of her, too.

26

March 1922

Mary Ann woke up feeling as if something wonderful was about to happen and smiled as she remembered the events of yesterday. She'd found a sister and there were other sisters and brothers still to meet. She lay in bed for much longer than usual, reciting their names like a litany and wondering what they looked like: Percy, Lizzie, Eva, Polly and Johnny. Were any of them tall like her? If they were half as nice as Lizzie she knew she would like them.

It was almost enough to persuade her to stay in Overdale, but no, both she and Gabriel shared the same dream of settling near the sea. And anyway, although her two half-brothers and Lizzie lived here, Polly lived on the coast near Fleetwood and Eva lived a bit further north, in a small town right on the edge of the moors.

When she got up she found Georges waiting for her in the dining room with the news that Margaret had gone out already and wouldn't be back until afternoon. Mrs Garbutt rarely joined them for breakfast, so there were just the two of them.

'What shall we do today, *chérie*?'

'Find the other churches and look at their records of christenings – if they'll let us. And Lizzie's asked me to go round there this afternoon for an hour, just to chat.'

But the errand boy from Dearden's turned up as they were finishing breakfast with a message from Lizzie cancelling the afternoon's meeting, due to a 'small domestic crisis'.

Mary Ann looked at Georges. 'You don't suppose she's – changed her mind about me, do you?'

'I doubt it. Why should she? Come on. Let's get started.'

They found a Methodist church and a Baptist one, and

managed to catch the minister of the former and the care-
taker of the latter. But the records didn't show any girls being
christened with birth dates matching or near that of Mary Ann's
daughter. The nearest in all three registers was a girl who had
been christened two months after Mary Ann's daughter was
born.

'What if your child was adopted by a couple who lived in
another town or moved away?' Georges asked gently.

'I can't even bear to think of that. I'm going to start on the
schools next.'

But the local primary schools refused to show her their records,
though one headmaster did check his rolls and assured her that
they'd had no girl pupils of that birth date, or even that month.

'She was probably adopted by people who could afford to send
her to a private school,' Mary Ann said as they walked back to The
Sycamores. She could see Georges purse his lips and consider this,
but he said nothing.

That evening she was somewhat nervous because she was
going to meet Gabriel's daughters and it was crucial that they
liked her.

When she drove up in the car, he came to the door, smiling
at the sight of her. Two young women came to stand beside
him and watched as she parked the car and switched off the
ignition.

'I told you she drove herself everywhere,' he said as he moved
forward to greet Mary Ann. Clasping her hand, he gave her a
smile that lit up his whole face and made him handsome in spite
of the light sprinkling of grey hairs at his temples and the fine
lines around his eyes.

The girls allowed themselves to be introduced, staring at her
with curiosity but not, thank goodness, hostility.

'Can I watch when you crank the engine before you leave?'
Frances asked. 'I've never seen a woman start a motor car. Dad
says it's really hard to start them up.'

'It's a good thing I'm not a small woman then, isn't it?'

Christina, who was slightly taller now than her older sister, looked up at her. 'Do you mind being so tall? I used to be the tallest in my class at school and I hated it.'

Frances gasped and dug her elbow into her sister's ribs, hissing, 'That's rude!'

'I'm happy to answer,' Mary Ann said mildly, remembering what it had been like as a girl. 'I did mind being tall when I was younger, but it's come in useful since and now I'm glad. For one thing I was able to be a driver during the war and I enjoyed the work.'

'Dad was over in France. How did you two meet?'

'I visited London when I had short leaves,' Gabriel said. 'Mary Ann worked at a servicemen's club I used to go to in the evenings. Now, let's go in and talk to your Grandma and Mrs Anders, shall we? I'm cold out here even if you two aren't.'

Jassy was standing by the fire and Mary Ann saw at a glance that efforts had been made for her refreshment, with a couple of plates set on the dresser, covered by cloths, and a pretty tea set standing ready next to them. 'It's nice to meet you again, Mrs Clough.'

'You're looking better, but that's a nasty bruise still.'

'That'll teach me not to get distracted when I'm driving.' Jassy indicated a comfortable chair in front of the fire and she took it. The girls pulled out stools and sat near their father but kept gazing at the visitor.

'Have you had many accidents in the car?' Christina asked.

'That was the only one, though I had a couple of near misses during the war.'

'Mr Downham's had lots of bumps in his van,' Frances said. 'He says you can't help it when you're driving because people sometimes don't realise how fast you're going. Much faster than a horse.'

'Who's Mr Downham?'

'Mrs Greeson's lodger. He was talking to us over the wall of the top field on Sunday.'

Her father frowned. 'He must be a careless driver, then. I've not had any accidents at all in my truck. And you keep away from Mrs Greeson's lodgers.'

Frances giggled suddenly. 'Mr Downham was probably talking to someone when he had the accident. I reckon he really could talk the hind leg off a donkey, that one. He came into the village shop to take Mr Butterby's order for stock and you should have seen him flirting with Mrs Butterby! She got all flushed with a soppy look on her face.'

'I wish I worked in a shop,' Christina said. 'It's boring in an office. I thought I'd like it, but I don't.'

Mary Ann could see that Gabriel wasn't happy about this statement and she knew you had to take any job you could these days. 'I worked in an office for a while. It didn't suit me either, I must admit. I moved on to managing some tea rooms and – enjoyed that much more. But I have used my office skills since then, so the time there wasn't wasted. Just learn as much as you can while you're there and look for something else later on.'

Gabriel flashed her a quick glance of approval and changed the subject firmly to a discussion of Blackpool and what it was like living at the seaside.

Jassy and her friend contributed little, but Mary Ann was aware that both the older women were studying her and listening intently to what she said.

When Gabriel walked her out to the car, she smiled at him. 'How did I do?'

'Really well.'

'Your mother didn't say much.'

'She never does. She notices everything, though.'

'I like your daughters.'

'Strictly speaking Frances isn't mine, as I told you, but she feels like mine now. I hope she never finds out. How are you doing in your search for Elizabeth?'

Her smile faded. 'Not well at all. Georges is wondering whether she was adopted by people who left town, but I still feel she's here in Overdale somewhere. After all, this doctor who handled the adoptions worked at the local hospital, didn't he? It was surely more likely that he'd know people here who wanted babies.'

She hesitated, then changed the subject. 'Would you like us to

take the girls out for a drive on Sunday? I could bring Georges
as well.'

'I'll ask them. It sounds like a lovely idea to me.'

When Jeff saw *her* standing talking to Clough in the lighted
doorway of the farm next door, he averted his face quickly as
he drove past and parked his van out of sight of the neighbouring
farm. He'd taken particular care not to be seen by Clough since
he came to stay at Jane's. Going to the corner of the house, he
peered down the lane and saw Clough pull her into his arms then
give her a lingering kiss.

It was a while since Jeff had had a woman and he was feeling
the need. He scowled as he watched the two of them embracing.
Didn't that stupid fellow know how to handle a woman? Fancy
getting her excited then letting her go. He should have taken her
into the barn and had his way with her while she was still roused.
Jeff had had a few interesting experiences in barns in his time,
and in his van since his company had supplied him with it. Vans
were better than motor cars because it was harder for people to
see into the back and there was room to stretch out.

Perhaps if he played his cards right, he could use the van to
good purpose with Mary Ann. He'd have to plan it carefully, but
she had been easy enough to subdue before and would be again.
Once you'd trained a woman to fear you, you could do what you
wanted with her, he'd found.

He went inside, seething with frustration, but when he put his
arm round Jane and asked if she didn't miss her bed games, she
shook him off and fixed him with a cold stare.

'No. And what's more, I never did think much to that sort of
thing so I'm glad to be done with it. You'd have got on better in
life if you'd kept your private parts buttoned away where they
belong.'

'Ah, Jane love—'

'Don't "Jane love" me, Jeff Downham! Your supper's in the
kitchen. I'm having an early night. Make sure you side away the
plate and cup afterwards.'

But it was a long time before he could sleep. He would definitely have to do something about getting himself a woman.

The next time Mary Ann went round to the Cloughs' the girls were out practising for a concert the church was putting on, so there were just the two old women and Gabriel.

Jassy pulled out the box of chocolates. 'We're making them last, just one every now and then. You pick first, Mary Ann.'

It was the first time she had addressed their guest by her first name.

When they had all finished their treat, Gabriel glanced at his guest. 'All right if I tell Mum and Mrs Anders about your search, love?'

She nodded.

'Mary Ann's been looking for her daughter, but Jane Greeson says she doesn't know anything about who adopted her.' He looked at Carrie. 'Jane told her at the time that the baby died and she didn't find out it'd lived till after her own mother passed away. She didn't want to have it adopted, you see, but they tricked her.'

'I called her Elizabeth,' Mary Ann said, feeling suddenly sad as she thought about her baby. 'I've never forgotten what she looked like. She had dark hair like mine and blue eyes, with a little birthmark on her upper right arm. She was born on the tenth of March, 1907. I've searched all the church and chapel records and can't find any sign of a girl born in March.'

'Would this be another of Dr Browning-Baker's adoptions?' Carrie asked.

'So Mrs Greeson says.'

'I've worked in Overdale as a midwife since 1890 and I've seen that man do a few things I didn't reckon were right. I know you shouldn't speak ill of the dead but he wasn't a good man, doctor or not.' She made a scornful noise to show what she thought of him. 'Let me have a think.' After a minute or two, she stood up. 'I might look in my diary for that year. I've got a feeling that . . .'

But as she stood up there was the sound of a horse and trap

clopping to a halt outside then someone pounded along the path and banged on the front door.

'Can you come quick, Mrs Anders?' a man's voice called. 'Our Betsy's having t'child early and it's comin' reet fast.'

Carrie stood up. 'There! What did I tell you, Jassy? She *was* further on than the doctor reckoned. She must have got her dates wrong.' She bustled into her bedroom, saying as she came out with her bag, 'I'll have a look in my diaries tomorrow for you, love.'

Mary Ann nodded and watched her go, sighing in frustration.

Jassy looked across at her. 'It's hard to lose a child, however it happens. I lost a little lad once. Eh, I skriked like a babby.'

'I've cried many a time,' Mary Ann said in a low voice, 'and had nightmares about it. Mrs Greeson told me I'd lain on the baby and killed it, you see.'

'Eh, never!' Jassy reached out to give the younger woman's hand a quick pat. 'That's downright cruel. She's a nasty one, her, for all her smiles and fancy ways.'

When they walked out to the motor car, Gabriel pulled Mary Ann into his arms and said into her hair, 'My mother's coming round to the idea of us being together.'

She leaned against him, taking comfort from his strong, warm body. 'Good.'

He spoke into her hair. 'You've had a hard life, love. It's a wonder it hasn't soured you.'

'I've been lucky, had some wonderful friends. That's helped. I'd like you to meet Georges and get to know him. Would you come and visit us tomorrow evening?' She wondered if she was pushing too hard but Gabriel smiled and nodded without hesitation.

'I don't like to think of you driving home on your own in the dark,' he said as he started the car for her.

'Well, it could break down, I suppose, but I maintain it carefully and I've only a few miles to go, so I could walk if I had to.' When he still looked unconvinced she chuckled. 'I used to drive all over London after dark, Gabriel. It doesn't worry me. There are advantages to being tall and strong.' She brandished a mock fist in the air and made him chuckle.

At home she found a message from Lizzie saying Percy and Johnny had been told about their new sister and both were eager to meet her.

Mary Ann shared this news with Margaret and Georges, then went happily to bed. Things were coming together well for her on every front except the search for her daughter. There was such a hunger in her to find out what had happened to the girl. No matter how many other relatives she found, she needed to know that her daughter was happy. If she were very lucky indeed, maybe she could get to know Elizabeth. She sighed. She didn't even know what the girl's name was now. Didn't know anything. It was so frustrating.

She hoped desperately that Mrs Anders would be able to shed some new light on the situation.

Georges had tried to tell her that she must be prepared not to find her daughter and even Margaret had warned her about setting her hopes too high, but Gabriel seemed to understand her desperate need better and had assured her that he would help her in any way he could. Mary Ann couldn't believe how easy it was to be with him, how they seemed to understand each other without words, how even a glance from him across a room could make her feel warmly loved and cherished.

It couldn't be wrong for them to be together, whether they were legally married or not. It just couldn't.

Only when the car had chugged away into the distance did Gabriel go back inside. 'The girls are late back. If Tom wasn't bringing them home, I'd be worried.'

He accepted another cup of tea. 'Mum – if Carrie can't help Mary Ann, I'm going over to see Jane Greeson again myself.'

'She'll not tell you owt. Allus were close as an oyster, that one.'

'I have to try. It's tearing Mary Ann apart not knowing.' He hesitated, then asked, 'Do you like her better now you're getting to know her a bit?'

She looked at him, nodding slowly. 'Aye. You cannot help but like her because she's an honest soul. I value that, and if things were different I'd welcome her as a wife for you. But it doesn't sit well with me for you two to live in sin. And if you think those girls of yours can keep a secret, you're far and out.'

'Then we'll have to concoct a tale for them, say Ivy got a divorce in Australia. They'll never know different. Will you back me up if I do that?'

Jassy was silent, then said grudgingly, 'You're set on it, aren't you, son?'

'Yes. I love Mary Ann and – well, I just I feel right with her.' He went to stand beside her and put one hand on his mother's shoulder. 'We'd both like you to live with us in Blackpool. It's a wonderful place. You could at least come and look at it.'

She sighed and looked round, suddenly accepting her coming loss. 'If we did, me and Carrie would want a little place of our own, mind. I'm not going to live in another woman's house after being used to my own.' Her lad's face was such a blaze of joy she was touched to the core to see it. He'd been such a good son to her, worked so hard. At that moment she vowed she'd never let him know how much she would miss Birtley and the moors.

Realising he'd spoken and was waiting for an answer, she asked, 'What did you say again, our Gabriel?'

'I said, "You mean, you'll come with us?" because I couldn't believe my own ears.'

She smiled. 'I never say owt I don't mean, as you should know by now. Yes, I'll sell the farm and come with you. I'd not like to be away from my only son and my grandchilder.' She busied herself then with redding up the fire because she could see how near to tears he was.

When he'd regained control of his emotions, he told her about Mary Ann having quite a lot of money and how they wanted to buy a business together, maybe a café.

'What dost know about cafés, lad?'

'Nothing, but I can learn, can't I? Mary Ann knows a lot. Or I can do something else and maybe the girls would like to work in the café with her. I don't know. There suddenly seem to be so many possibilities. If only we could find out what happened to the child. Mary Ann won't settle till she knows.'

Ethel Bawton was angry that the police hadn't managed to find her daughter. On the Friday of that week she dressed very carefully, walked to the police station and insisted on seeing the sergeant in charge.

He stood there stolidly as she harangued him, his face expressionless against her rudeness. He was sick of folk like her who thought themselves better than you and spoke to you like dirt, but you couldn't upset them because they always had friends in high places. When he was sure she'd finished, he said mildly, 'If you can point out any other avenues for us to explore, madam, we shall be happy to pursue them, but according to our notes your daughter has no friends, goes nowhere and has no relatives to whom she can turn. It leaves us very little to investigate.'

Ethel stood there considering this. 'Have you questioned all the shopkeepers? One of them might have seen her. She does do my shopping regularly, at Dearden's mostly.'

'The constable did call there while he was doing his rounds, madam. No one had seen her.'

'Perhaps *you* could go and ask them? They'll pay a lot more attention to you than to a mere constable.'

Mere constable! He thought the world of his men. There was nothing *mere* about his lads. His dislike for this arrogant woman grew even stronger. He wasn't surprised the girl had run away. When a lass of that age was allowed no friends and no outings, life could be pretty bleak. And what he hadn't told the mother was that one of the shopkeepers had hinted to the constable that someone was beating the girl, who was always turning up with a bruised face or arms.

'Well?' Ethel prompted. 'Are you going to do that or are you just going to leave things? Because if so I shall speak to the Chief Constable who was a friend of my late husband.'

'I shall, of course, do as you ask, Mrs Bawton.'

He went along to Dearden's later that afternoon, sure he was on a wild goose chase but determined to give that harridan no reason to complain.

Beatrice saw Sergeant Carswell coming along High Street from Mrs Dearden's bedroom window, that being the safest place for her to hide in the daytime until her kind hostess could help her escape. Her heart started thumping at the mere sight of a police uniform, and when he turned into the shop she gasped in dismay.

He mustn't find her here! She would do anything rather than get the Deardens into trouble. Last night she'd heard Mr Dearden urging his wife to give her up to the authorities, but Mrs Dearden had refused, saying if he knew what it was like to face beating after beating he'd never even suggest that.

The deep voice of Sergeant Carswell boomed up from the shop. Beatrice crept out on to the landing.

'. . . and just so that I can satisfy Mrs Bawton that her daughter isn't here, I wonder if you'd let me search the premises, Mrs Dearden? It's not that we doubt your word, but you have several sheds and storerooms and she might be hiding there without your knowledge.'

Beatrice felt panic-stricken. She couldn't stay and get them into trouble. She just couldn't! She crept downstairs, thankful the Sergeant's voice was so loud that she'd know if he started to come towards the back of the shop. In the yard was a van making deliveries. A man unloading boxes shoved the back door of the van shut with his foot and vanished into the store room.

The van door didn't catch and stayed slightly open. The girl glanced round, took a deep breath and darted across to it. This would get her away from Dearden's and later she supposed she'd have to go home, though she'd never tell her mother where she'd been. She found to her relief that the van was half empty and wedged herself between two large cartons containing lots of small boxes. Each bore the name of a local shop scrawled on the side.

When Jeff came out he slammed the back door properly shut and got into the van, relieved that he had only a couple more deliveries to make. He never even noticed his passenger as he drove along to the next shop, but when he came round to the rear of the van for one of the deliveries, he found himself face to face with a young woman.

'What are you doing here?'

'I'm sorry. I needed to leave somewhere quickly.' Beatrice moved as if to get out of the van.

He barred the way, eyes narrowed, then it suddenly clicked. 'You wouldn't be that girl they're searching for, would you? I ought to drive you straight to the police station and hand you over.'

She gasped and looked at him pleadingly. 'Please don't. It'll get the Deardens in trouble and they've been so kind to me.'

Jeff looked at her more closely. 'That's a nasty bruise you've got there.'

'My mother hits me. She *likes* hitting me. That's why I ran away.'

'Where were you going today?'

She shrugged. 'I don't know. Anywhere, just – away from the shop.'

'I'm driving over the tops to Bilsden after I've made my deliveries. I could take you with me, if you like. It'd make a nice little outing.'

Hope flared in her eyes, then died just as quickly. 'I'll still have to return home.'

'Then you might as well enjoy a day out before you go back. It's a pretty road over the tops and I'll buy you tea in Bilsden.'

She looked at him dubiously. Why would a complete stranger – and an older man at that – want her company? 'Why are you doing this?'

He spread his arms wide. 'I know what it's like to be beaten. When I was a lad my dad had a very heavy hand.'

Beatrice frowned, knowing she shouldn't go off with a strange man, then shrugged. Her mother had hurt her more than any stranger ever could. 'All right. And thanks. The longer I can put off going back the better as far as I'm concerned. I wish I need never go home.'

'Good. Make yourself comfortable.' Whistling, he picked up one of the boxes, winked at her and closed the van door. She sagged against the side of the van and sighed. She was being a coward, she knew, but she was sure her mother would go mad at her when she returned – and would probably beat her again. Why not delay it?

Jeff stopped the van on the top of the moors, wondering if his passenger could be tempted into a bit of kissing and cuddling. He took out the cakes and bottle of pop he'd bought at the last shop and went to open the back door of the van. 'Thought you might like to join me in a snack.'

They sat in the lee of a wall looking out across the moors but she didn't show much appetite and kept sighing. He felt sorry for the poor little bitch, if truth be told. When she reached out for something he saw the mark of a blow on her lower arm. He must be getting soft in his old age.

After they'd finished eating he picked up her hand. 'You feel cold.'

She pulled it away. 'I am.'

'Here, put my jacket round you.' As he was settling it round her shoulders, he touched her hair. 'Pretty hair you've got.'

She stiffened and gave him a suspicious look, jerking her head away from him. 'My mother says it's a common colour.'

He suddenly remembered another young woman with hair that colour. 'I don't think so. I always did like dark hair.'

She stood up, shrugging off the jacket. 'Don't you think it's time we started again?'

He hid his irritation. So she wasn't going to be easy to seduce. Well, there were ways of dealing with that.

On the way to Bilsden, he delivered the final box then drove into the little town. 'I've just got someone to see then we'll go and find a nice café, eh?'

But when he got back to the van she wasn't there. He waited a few minutes, which turned into half an hour, then realised the stupid bitch had run away. Furious at himself, worried that he was losing his touch, he went to the depot to pick up the next batch of deliveries. This was the worst job he'd ever had, offering the least money and the most boring work.

Oh, well, the girl had only been a diversion. When he got back to Overdale he'd do something about Mary Ann Baillie. His present troubles were all her fault – hers and her stupid mother's.

Lizzie and Peter searched everywhere in the house, the back warehouses and even the store cupboards. No sign of Beatrice. She looked at her husband in dismay. 'She must have run away when she heard Sergeant Carswell talking to me. Where could she have gone?'

'Home, probably. You said she had no money.'

'But if she does that, her mother will beat her again.'

He took his wife in his arms and raised her chin so that she had to look at him. 'Lizzie darling, you can't save everyone in the world. And in one sense I'm relieved. I think you'd have been in serious trouble if you'd been caught harbouring her. After all, she is only – what – fifteen? Sixteen?'

'I'm going round to her house later to see if she's there.'

'We'll go out for a walk together,' he corrected, 'and if it's safe, I'll go and peep through the windows. I'm not having you getting into trouble.'

'So you'll get into trouble instead of me?' She gave him a hug. 'You're a right old love, Peter Dearden.'

But the Bawtons' house was quiet and Peter reported that Beatrice's mother was in her sitting-room alone, staring into the fire. Nor were there any lights on in the rest of the house, apart from the kitchen where the cook was also sitting alone, toasting herself in front of a fire.

27

March 1922

Gabriel drove round to The Sycamores that evening in the lorry, feeling absurdly nervous. Mary Ann thought so highly of this Georges Lepuy that it was a very important meeting. It gave him some idea of how nervous she must have been feeling before meeting his daughters. Well, she'd charmed everyone by being herself and he hoped he could make an equally good impression tonight. He had no intention of pretending to be something he wasn't, though.

Being himself meant going openly in the little lorry. No luxurious cars for him. The clumsy vehicle looked incongruous in front of the elegant house, but at least it didn't smell of the farm because he'd given it a thorough cleaning.

A maid showed him in, took his trilby and overcoat and led him into a drawing room where everyone was waiting for him. He tripped over a rug, but that didn't matter because Mary Ann came forward, beaming at him, her love showing clearly. Did he look at her in the same way? He hoped so. He wanted the whole world to see how he felt about her.

'Come and meet everyone, Gabriel. This is Mrs Garbutt.'

He shook hands, horribly conscious of a graze on the back of his hand as it clasped the older woman's soft white skin.

'I remember that you were the one who helped Margaret escape from *that woman*,' Angela said quietly. 'My late husband and I were so grateful.'

He relaxed a little. 'I was happy to be of use.'

'He helped me to escape as well,' Mary Ann said, linking her arm in his and smiling at him. 'You know Margaret already, but you haven't met Georges yet, have you?'

As they shook hands, Gabriel studied the other man, whom he'd only seen in the distance. He was shorter than Gabriel and very well-dressed, clearly not lacking money. Well, none of these people were. He felt very conscious of his cheap suit and well-polished but clumsy boots.

'Tell us about your farm, Mr Clough,' Mrs Garbutt said, patting a space on the sofa next to her.

He sat down and did his best to comply. The conversation limped on for a while, then Angela and Margaret excused themselves with murmurs of 'tired' and 'early night'.

'Now we can talk properly,' Mary Ann said. 'Mrs Garbutt always makes me feel I have to be on my best behaviour.'

'She is very much a woman of her class and time, *chérie*.' Georges said. He looked across at Gabriel. 'You will excuse me if I say that I am not happy at the prospect of you and Mary Ann living together without being married.'

'I'd marry her tomorrow if I could.'

Mary Ann grimaced at Georges. She knew he was upset because his accent had become stronger than usual, but she wished he hadn't said that. 'We don't have much choice, do we?'

'There is the possibility of your obtaining a divorce, Mr Clough, and I would be happy to pay the expenses for this.'

Gabriel looked at him sharply but saw nothing on the other man's face save concern for Mary Ann. 'My wife wrote recently to ask me to provide evidence for one. She too wishes to remarry,' he admitted.

'Then will you allow me to discuss it with a lawyer?' Georges asked. 'We could at least find out what it would entail.'

Gabriel hesitated. 'What stopped me doing anything was that I didn't want to upset my daughters. Wouldn't it get into the newspapers?'

'That too I shall enquire about, *mon ami*.' Georges hesitated then said, 'Nor do either of you seem sure of what you want to do with your lives. Would it not be better to find a business first and then settle down together later when it becomes legally possible?'

Mary Ann had not expected Georges to keep suggesting things which would delay her and Gabriel being together. 'That could take years and I'm not prepared to wait. I'm nearly thirty-two, so if we want to have children we daren't delay.'

Georges gave a very Gallic shrug. '*Chérie*, you are rushing into this. It's so unlike you.'

Mary Ann smiled. 'Gabriel's the only man I've ever wanted to marry, Georges dear. I feel right with him and have done since I was fifteen.'

Gabriel went to sit on the arm of her chair and put his arm round her. 'We both want to rush into it, sir, and I can think of nothing more wonderful than our having a child together. But I'd be grateful if you could make enquiries about getting a divorce. If it doesn't cause trouble for my daughters, I'll do whatever is necessary.'

Georges inclined his head.

When Mary Ann walked outside with Gabriel afterwards she said thoughtfully, 'We're just going to have to stick to our plans and not *let* anyone stop us, you know.'

He pulled her to him. 'You're a brave lass.'

She shook her head. 'Most of us who've fought or helped out in the war have realised how fragile life is. You have to seize your chance of happiness while you can.' She looked at him, no guile in her beautiful grey eyes. 'And I'm quite sure my best chance of happiness lies with you.'

Deeply touched, he drew her to him and kissed her. Only as he was getting into the lorry did he remember the message he'd been charged with. 'Oh – if you have time to come round and talk to Carrie tomorrow evening, she thinks she may be able to help you find your daughter.'

She jumped up on the running board, her whole face alight with eagerness. 'If she really has found something, I'm coming round first thing in the morning.'

He chuckled. 'That's my Mary Ann.'

She jumped down again and stepped back, to stand watching him drive away. Only when the sound of the motor had died completely away did she go inside and say accusingly to Georges, 'You didn't sound as if you were on our side tonight.'

'I am on your side. Very much so. But I don't like the idea of your not being properly married.' He gave her a twisted smile. 'If you adopt me as a father, I must be allowed to play a father's role.'

Her annoyance softened. 'As long as you realise that no one and nothing is going to stop me from being with Gabriel, whether as his wife or his mistress.' She watched him shake his head and added, 'You haven't even said if you like him.'

'I do, actually. He has a steady look to him and his love for you is very obvious. If life had been kind to you, you'd have married a man like him many years ago and have a family of your own by now.'

'Life has been kind to me in many ways. It's brought me good friends – and you.'

But after she went to bed, she forgot even Gabriel because she lay awake for a long time, hoping desperately that Carrie Anders would be able to shed some light on the fate of her daughter the following day.

Surely the midwife wouldn't have sent that message if she hadn't found something out?

Beatrice wandered round Bilsden until dusk, then found shelter for the night in a church where someone had left a side door unlocked. It was eerie inside the big, echoing building, and at first she jumped at every noise. But it was far warmer than outside, especially after she found a rug and an old coat in the vestry to wrap herself in. It was a long time before she got to sleep, though, because she was ravenously hungry and was worrying about what she was going to do in the morning. She hated the thought of returning to her mother, knowing it would mean another beating. Although she kept vowing to stand up to her mother, sometimes she just froze when confronted with the woman who had controlled all her actions since she was a child.

She was woken by someone shaking her shoulder and found

herself staring up into the faces of two men, one of them a clergyman with a gentle expression on his narrow face, the other a burly, white-haired man who looked extremely disapproving.

'What are you doing here, young woman?' the clergyman asked.

She scrambled to her feet. 'I had nowhere to go and the side door was open. I haven't done any damage.' She bent to spread out the rug then hung up the coat on the door. 'I'll leave now. I'm sorry.'

'Are you hungry?' he asked, putting out one arm to bar the way.

She paused, then nodded.

'Then come and have breakfast with me and my wife. You can tell us what's happened to you, why you aren't with your family.'

She hesitated, then nodded and walked away with him.

His wife was a plump woman who showed her guest into a chilly bathroom to have a wash, then sat her at the kitchen table and put toast and plum jam in front of her. She didn't ask any questions, but somehow, as she drank two cups of strong tea, Beatrice found herself telling them about her mother and the beatings. 'I can show you the rest of the marks, if you don't believe me.'

Her hostess nodded, took her into the scullery and studied the marks on her back and shoulders in silence. 'You must let me dress those,' was all she said.

But Beatrice had noticed through the window the clergyman leaving the house and was suspicious that he might be going to call the police, so when her hostess bustled off to get some ointment, she put her clothes back on and slipped out of the front door, running off down the street heedless of the people who stopped to stare at her headlong flight.

She might have to go home, but she didn't intend to be taken back by the police. Somehow it seemed important that she get there under her own steam and that once she was there she continue to stand up to her mother. Who was it who had said to her, 'You're big enough to fight back?' She couldn't remember, was too tired to think clearly this morning.

As she walked through the busy streets, shivering in the cool morning air in her short-sleeved dress covered only by Lizzie's old cardigan which was a bit skimpy on her, that phrase kept coming back to her. She must learn to fight back, to overcome this paralysing fear of her mother's wrath.

With that decision made, she felt something shift inside her. Most people would say she ought to obey her mother in all things, and she would if her mother didn't treat her so badly. But she didn't deserve the beatings, she knew she didn't.

Her father hadn't been exactly loving, either, but he had treated her fairly, at least, protecting her, she now realised, from her mother's easily aroused irritation.

She asked a passer-by the way to Overdale and went in the direction he indicated. When she saw a signpost saying *Overdale 10 miles* she set off along the road, walking slowly up towards the moors. She tried to enjoy the views, which were splendid, but could not ignore the leaden feeling of apprehension in her belly, and in spite of the brisk exercise she was soon feeling the cold.

She was dreading going home.

At eight o'clock that same morning Mary Ann borrowed Georges' car again and drove out to Birtley, unable to wait another minute. There was no sign of Gabriel working around the place, but when she knocked on the front door, Mrs Clough opened it and gestured her inside.

'He said you'd be here early.' She raised her voice. 'Carrie, she's come.'

Mrs Anders came out of the bedroom on the other side of the kitchen carrying a notebook. She smiled and sat down at the table, gesturing to a chair beside her. 'I've always kept diaries, ever since I was thirteen.'

'Did you find something?' Mary Ann asked, her voice coming out a bit breathless because she felt so wound up inside.

'Yes, I did, love. Only whether it'll help you, I can't tell. I was working for Dr Browning-Baker the year you came here – as a midwife, you know – when I heard that Mrs Bawton was expecting. Only he never sent me to see her, said he was keeping an eye on her himself. He'd done that once or twice before, especially with better-off patients, so I never thought much about it. Then one day I saw her in town – and she didn't look as if she was carrying a child. Oh, she had a belly jutting out all right, but she didn't walk like pregnant women do, or so it seemed to me. And she didn't have that look of soft fullness on her face, either.' She sighed and shook her head. 'It sounds daft when I put it into words, doesn't it?'

'No. I'm sure you know what you're talking about.' Mary Ann waited for her to continue.

'Well, Mrs Bawton had the child in due course, but who attended her I don't know. *He* didn't usually deliver babies without a nurse to do the dirty work. And they never told anyone for ages that she'd had the child. A couple of months later I saw her pushing it in a pram and if that babby was three months old, then I know nowt about babbies. It was a month old, if that.'

They looked at one another.

'You mean, it could have been my baby?' Mary Ann let out a long, shuddering breath. Dare she even hope on such slender evidence?

Carrie patted her hand. 'There's no saying it is, love, so don't get your hopes too high, but it'd be worth looking into, eh? I've seen the daughter since and she doesn't look at all like the Bawtons. Ethel is a narrow-minded woman with a thin face and body, as mean as they come and spiteful with it. She has fair hair and is of medium height only. The daughter is tall. Well, the father was tall, so there might be nothing suspicious in that, but he had red hair afore it turned grey. The daughter has hair about the colour of yours, now I come to think of it. I'd like to see the two of you together. A resemblance might show up.'

Mary Ann swallowed hard and tried to hold on to her self-control. What she wanted to do was leap up and rush off to see the Bawtons' daughter this very minute. Surely she'd recognise her own child?'

'There's more. The father died a year or so ago and the widow's apparently a bit short of money.' Mrs Anders smiled complacently. 'Folk tell me all sorts, though I'm no gossip and I don't usually pass tales on. If I were you, I'd go into Dearden's and wait for the lass to come in. She does all the shopping for her mother now and I've seen her there myself many a time, usually just before midday.'

'Does she look – happy?'

Carrie hesitated then shook her head. 'No, I'm afraid not. She allus were quiet. Ethel's a strict sort of woman, pillar of the church, no breaking the sabbath, that sort of thing. But since the father died, the lass has looked downright miserable.'

Mary Ann's heart clenched in a spasm of pain. 'I'll go to Dearden's now. They'll let me wait in the back room. I know Mrs Dearden. In fact, she's my half-sister.'

The two elderly women gaped at her.

'My mother was called Dinah Baillie and used to live in Overdale, but I only found out Stanley Kershaw was my father when I was clearing the house out after she died. She would never tell me.'

'*That's* who you remind me of! Stanley Kershaw. I can see it now, though I couldn't think who it was afore,' Carrie exclaimed. 'Eh, I brought most of them Kershaws into the world. Do the rest of 'em know about you?'

'Lizzie does and I think she's told all the others. I'm supposed to be having tea with them on Sunday.'

'It's a small world, it is that.' Carrie smiled reminiscently. 'Eh, I took a fancy to Stanley Kershaw myself when I were young – he was a lovely fellow and kind with it – but of course he never looked at me because I was nothing special, allus plump and a bit shy. That wife of his was very pretty but her looks didn't last. Was your mother pretty?'

'I suppose so. I don't take after her, though.'

'Nay, you're a bonny woman and don't let anyone tell you

different. Any road, you don't have to be pretty to be happy. I've done all right without. Anders never gave me any trouble even though he never gave me any childer – strange that, isn't it? – and he dropped dead at forty, but we were happy enough together and I missed him after he died.'

Mary Ann waited but Mrs Anders didn't offer any more information, so she stood up. 'I think I'd better get back. I want to go and see Lizzie straight away.' On a sudden impulse she went and gave Mrs Anders a hug. 'Thank you so much for your help. I can't tell you how grateful I am.'

'She's a nice lass, that,' Carrie said after the car had driven away.

'Aye, I've no problem with her. It's our Gabriel being wed to the other that sticks in my gullet,' Jassy said with a sigh. 'Are you sure you won't mind moving to Blackpool?'

'I think it'll be just the thing for us. Eh, to think we've neither of us ever seen the sea.'

Beatrice trudged along the road, shivering slightly. Ten miles was a long way to walk, but she wasn't in a hurry to get back to Overdale. At least it wasn't raining and when a woman working in a garden passed the time of day with her, then offered her a cup of milk, she accepted. It seemed like an omen, somehow, that the future wasn't all black.

A man driving a cart stopped to offer her a lift but she shook her head. 'I'm enjoying my tramp over the tops, thank you very much.'

'Suit thysen, lass.' With a cheery wave he drove on.

She stood watching him, feeling very alone, and as a chill wind blew around her she wondered whether she should have accepted his offer. No. 'Suit thysen,' he'd said to her. That was what she was doing: suiting herself – and enjoying her final hours of freedom. She was sure her mother would be even stricter with her when she got back.

Although she didn't see any wildflowers, there were patches of bright new growth of a more tender green and sheep were grazing peacefully in the fields. When she got right up on the tops there were no fields or houses, just herself and the rolling miles of moor, with a breeze lifting her hair and filling her lungs with good clean air. She even forgot that she was cold.

The morning after his débâcle with the girl, Jeff started off at Dearden's, delivering the box of bits and pieces they'd ordered the day before. His present company dealt in all sorts of small items connected with baking and prided itself on delivering orders within two days. He'd preferred it when he'd sold larger, more profitable items which had to be delivered by other people, but it was convenient to work in this area of the country and live at Jane's so he'd carry on as he was for a while.

Peter Dearden wasn't anywhere to be seen, so Jeff put down the box on one of the packing tables. He'd have lit up a cigarette while he waited but Mrs Dearden didn't allow smoking on the premises, saying it made the shop smell stale, and she wasn't the sort you crossed, for all her friendliness. He went round to use the outside lavatory that delivery folk were allowed access to and when he came back, paused at the corner as he heard two women talking in the packing area.

'. . . and Mrs Anders thought Beatrice Bawton might be my daughter.' Mary Ann explained exactly why.

Lizzie studied her, lips pursed. 'She could be if looks are anything to go by. She's got your build and colour of hair. Well, all us Kershaw women have dark hair like Dad's.'

'What was he like, your – our father?'

'A big man, fun, hard-working, proud of his strength. He used to toss us children up in the air, and though we shrieked and pretended to be afraid, we loved it. He'd sit with us on his knee sometimes in the evening and tell us silly stories. Mam used to get vexed with him because she liked to get us to bed early and have him to herself, but he could always jolly her out of it.'

Mary Ann fumbled in her handbag to produce her precious photograph. 'Is this a good photo of him?'

Lizzie studied the tattered piece of card. 'Yes. He grew a bit heavier as he got older, though.'

After a moment's silence Mary Ann asked, 'Can I wait here in case Beatrice comes in to do the shopping?' Beatrice! She'd never liked that name.

'I don't think she will. I hear she's run away from home. But you're welcome to stay as long as you like, love. You know that.'

'I'll come every day till I do see her, and I'll go and watch her house as well if there's no sign of her coming here. I'm not leaving Overdale till I've seen her. If she comes in, will you tell me it's her?'

Lizzie looked at her in sympathy. Fancy not even knowing what your own daughter looked like. 'Of course I will. Come upstairs and have a cup of tea with me first, though. The shop's fairly quiet still.'

Jeff heard the two women climb the stairs and when Peter came through to the back he strolled round the corner and got through the formalities of the delivery as quickly as he could.

Once outside he sat in the van feeling shocked and bewildered. The girl he'd given a lift to might be his daughter. *His daughter!* He knew he'd fathered a child or two, but he'd never seen any of them, so they weren't real to him. But he had not only seen Beatrice, he'd talked to her. Hell, he'd tried to seduce her. He grinned, relieved he hadn't succeeded, then grew thoughtful. Mary Ann had sounded desperate to see the girl. This might be the key to getting his own back on her and her bloody mother. Not to mention getting some money out of her and obtaining a bit of relief from the constant need for a woman that had driven him all his adult life.

He made the rest of his deliveries more quickly than ever before, then instead of going out to start on the trail of little village shops he was due to visit, he made some purchases and drove out along the Bilsden road again. He'd have to make sure no one from the company's depot saw him, but if he could find out what had happened to that girl he might be able to persuade her to come back with him.

Luck was smiling on him because halfway to Bilsden he saw her sitting on a stone wall staring out across the moors. He pulled up and got out of the van. As she turned her head and stiffened, he smiled. 'What happened to you yesterday?'

'I decided not to bother you any more.'

'I wasn't bothered. I enjoyed your company. And I was a bit worried about what had happened to you. Where did you spend the night?' She looked like she'd slept in her clothes.

She threw him a cynical glance. 'Why should you worry about me?'

'I've a daughter of my own and I didn't like to think of a lass your age having nowhere to sleep and, if I'm not mistaken, no money. Have you eaten today?'

Beatrice flushed, then frowned. He sounded different today, she couldn't work out why and for some reason she didn't feel as nervous of him as she had before. 'Someone gave me breakfast. I've had nothing since except a glass of milk.'

'Want a cream bun? I bought two in case I found you.'

'Oh. Well, yes. Thanks. That'd be nice.'

'Come and sit in the front of the van then. That wind's getting up a bit. I think it's going to rain before nightfall.'

After visible hesitation she did that, but left the van door open. He handed over her bun and ate a little of his own, chatting about this and that as he waited for the powder he'd used once or twice before to take effect. Sure enough she began to yawn and then fell asleep in mid-sentence.

He waited a minute or two then got out and lifted her into the back of the van, staggering under her weight because she was a tall girl. Like her father, he thought complacently, staring down at her. She was thin, though, and looked as if she hadn't been eating properly. And those bruises upset him. He'd make that woman who'd adopted her sorry for treating *his daughter* like this.

After he'd dealt with Mary Ann.

Covering Beatrice with some packing paper so that even if

374

anyone looked through the rear windows they'd not see her, he turned the van round and drove back to Overdale, this time going straight to the farm.

Luck was with him again. There was a note from Jane prominently displayed on the kitchen table: *Maurice taken ill. Heart attack. Gabriel Clough is taking us to the hospital.*

Jeff rubbed his hands together in delight and went to fetch the girl in. She was starting to regain consciousness because he hadn't used a large dose, stumbling along with his support, half-asleep and only partly aware of her surroundings. He took her up to the attics Jane had used to house the young women who were having babies until her husband fell ill and she had to stop doing that to nurse him.

He found a room with a lock on the door. A bit of bustling around and he had food and water up there, plus a chamber pot. The lass wouldn't get out because there were bars on the windows and a good strong door, but she would come to no harm. And no one was going to beat her here, at least. That Bawton woman was going to regret beating *his* daughter.

Getting into the van he drove back into town, whistling cheerfully. Now to find Mary Ann.

28

Gabriel could not shake off a sense of unease, though he couldn't work out why. Things were going well between him and Mary Ann. The girls seemed to have taken to her and his mother had agreed to move to Blackpool. Even Monsieur Lepuy wasn't hostile to him personally, only to the fact that he was still married to Ivy – and you couldn't really blame the old chap for that.

So why was something hovering at the back of his mind, making him feel slightly anxious? It felt like a presentiment of trouble to come and yet he normally scoffed at such things.

He was working in the back garden when he heard a van pass the front of the house. The Greesons' lodger, that'd be. You got used to the different sounds of various motors. Funny, but now Gabriel came to think of it – he rested his hands on his spade and frowned as he searched his memories – no, he'd never actually seen the man's face. Downham always parked the van behind the farm and went in the back way.

But the girls had apparently chatted to the fellow several times. Suddenly Gabriel wanted to see the face of the man who took time to chat to his daughters across the back wall but kept out of sight of his other neighbours. Maybe this was being overly suspicious, but you couldn't be too careful where girls of that age were concerned, and his were bonny lasses, everyone said so. Leaving the spade standing upright in the moist earth, he ran across the narrow stretch of field behind the back garden to stand behind a tree and peer over the wall at the next farm.

He recognised the man who got out of the van at once – Jeff Powling, the fellow who had once ravished Mary Ann then had the cheek to pretend concern for her when she ran away! So why was he calling himself Downham now? And what was he doing back in Overdale? Gabriel growled in anger as he watched the man go into the house. He would give his daughters strict instructions to keep away from their neighbour from now on, by hell he would!

He was about to turn away when the back door opened again and Powling came out. The fellow looked round as if afraid of being seen before going to the passenger side of the van and opening the door. A lass nearly tumbled out. Gabriel screwed up his eyes, wishing he were just a bit closer and could see them properly.

What was going on here?

The lass seemed half-asleep – or drunk even from the way she walked, though it was a bit early in the day for anyone to be drinking. She had to be helped into the house and leaned against Powling as she stumbled along, but she wasn't being coerced to move.

Eh, was she a whore? She was a bit young to be doing this sort of work, but what else could she be? Some of them started walking the streets young and Gabriel always felt sad when he saw them. With a sigh he turned away, thinking, *When the cat's away, the mice will play*. It wasn't often Jane Greeson left the farm these days, but she'd said she would be staying with Maurice at the hospital.

Which made him wonder how Greeson was going on. The poor sod had looked in a terrible state this morning, grey-faced and breathing shallowly as if every breath were an effort. Gabriel had driven him to hospital in Overdale in the lorry which had set him back on his day's work, but you were a poor sort of human being if you couldn't help your neighbours when they were in trouble.

Jane would be furious if she found out Powling had brought a loose woman home with him in her absence and he didn't envy the man if she did. She could be a real shrew when she was angry.

Beatrice didn't appear at Dearden's that morning, but her mother came in to buy a few items and complain about the inferior quality of the last packet of Dearden's Own Blend tea she'd purchased. Mary Ann was peering through the small glass window in the storeroom through which you could see everything that was going on in the shop and when she heard Lizzie greet the customer by name, she studied the woman who had mothered her daughter. She was bitterly disappointed by the thin face with its downturned mouth and the fretful whining voice. There was no sign of a capacity for love in that face. Had Mrs Bawton always been like that or had widowhood turned her sour?

Anguish ran through Mary Ann, as it had many times before. How she would have cherished her daughter had she been allowed to keep her! She had often daydreamed about the baby, imagining her growing up, thinking she'd have been five, ten, twelve, whatever – *if she'd lived*. She'd wept time and again over her loss. It was galling to think that they'd not only stolen her daughter from her, but had placed the child with a woman like this!

How could she ever make that up to Beatrice?

Would the girl even be found? She had run away, Lizzie said, after being beaten, and Lizzie for one hoped she never came back to such treatment.

If Mary Ann had come so close to finding her daughter, only to lose her again, she did not know how she would bear it.

When Lizzie was free from customers, Mary Ann went into the shop and said goodbye. No use hanging around now. The girl wouldn't be coming in today if her mother had done the shopping. She started walking up the street towards the area where the Bawtons lived, lost in thought.

Suddenly a hand grasped her arm and she was pulled into a side street before she knew what was happening. She used her elbow to good purpose and pulled free from her attacker, who stood rubbing his arm and scowling. As she stared at him she realised with a shudder that her worst nightmare had reappeared. '*You!*'

Jeff stopped rubbing his arm and studied her, running his eyes up and down her body in a very offensive way. 'You've grown up – and you look better than I'd have expected. I didn't manage to catch sight of you in daylight in Brighton last time.'

His skin was deeply engraved with lines which gave him a cynical, debauched air, and on that ageing face his smile made him look like a caricature of the charmer who had courted her mother so successfully all those years ago. 'So it *was* you following me!'

'Of course it was. Your mother must have told you I was in Brighton. I always made sure she knew.'

Mary Ann wondered why he was accosting her now?

'Would you like to meet our daughter?' he asked casually.

She could not move for a moment or two, so shocked was she by this. As the implications sank in she felt anger begin to rise in her as well as dismay. 'Where is she?'

He tapped his nose and winked. 'That's for me to show you, isn't it? As long as you behave yourself, that is.'

'I don't believe you.' What did he mean, *behave herself* ? Surely he didn't intend to rape her again? If so he'd find her a different proposition now. But she said nothing, because he might, he just might, really know where their daughter was.

'Her name's Beatrice and she's very unhappy. The so-called mother keeps beating her, so she's run away – and I'll make sure the woman pays for that, believe me. No one attacks *my* daughter with impunity and . . .'

Mary Ann listened to him ranting for a minute. He seemed to hold a grudge against the entire world and something about him made her feel even more uneasy than she had as a child. It was as if his nature had warped further, if that was possible. A young woman walked past and automatically he flashed her a dazzling smile, the sort of smile a charming young man might offer a member of the opposite sex, but not a man who looked every year of his age. The young woman moved on quickly, casting a nervous glance over her shoulder, but Jeff didn't appear to notice that.

'If you want to see Beatrice, I'll take you to her,' he repeated.

'I'm not going anywhere with you.'

He shrugged. 'Suit yourself. But I'm going to take her away from Overdale, and if you behave yourself I'll take you with us,

too. You might never find her again if you don't join us. I'm on
my way to her right now.'

As Mary Ann hesitated, wondering what to do, he turned and
walked along the street to a van, swinging the starting handle
without another glance in her direction. Then he got in and the
vehicle began to roll slowly forward.

'Wait!' She ran after it, grasped the door handle and tried to
open it.

He stopped, put on the brake and came round to help her in.
'The door sticks sometimes. There's a trick to opening it from
outside.'

She hesitated, hating even to stand next to him let alone get into
a small enclosed space with him. 'Don't try any funny business
with me this time!'

'You enjoyed it last time,' he said confidently. 'I know how to
please a woman.'

She stared at him in shock. Surely he didn't believe that? But
his smug expression didn't change. *Did he really believe that!*

He drove out of town towards Birtley and she wondered where
they were going. As they turned down the lane that led to Gabriel's
farm she could not believe her luck. Jeff must be staying at the
Greesons' farm. She could jump out and fetch Gabriel to help
her. They'd break into the other house if they had to.

But as they got near the farm and she snatched at the door
handle she found it wouldn't open.

'Thought you'd try that,' Jeff said complacently. 'There's a trick
to it opening it from the inside too. It can be very useful at times,
that door.'

She decided then that when he stopped she'd kick him where
it hurt most and run for Gabriel. But as Jeff came round to
open her door, he fumbled in his pocket and produced what
looked like a piece of carved wood but turned suddenly into
a small but wicked-looking knife. Only then did he open the
door and the way he held the knife showed he knew how to
use it. The blade flashed in the sunlight as he waved it to
and fro.

'Don't try anything or I might have to hurt you,' he said, his smile not altering at all.

She accompanied him inside, thinking it might be better not to try to escape until she saw whether he really did have their daughter here. But even if she got hurt, she wasn't giving in to him. She doubted he'd go as far as murder.

He led the way through the kitchen to the front hall and made a mocking gesture with one hand. 'Ladies first. Up two flights of stairs, then stop. I'll be right behind you. This isn't a big knife, but it's nice and sharp.' Again he brandished the thing.

Grimly determined to foil him, she started up the stairs.

When Beatrice regained consciousness she stared round, thinking for a moment she was in her own bed, then realising this was a strange room and she was still fully dressed. She sat up in panic, but her head spun and she had to clutch the bed head and lean back against it.

She felt dreadfully thirsty and when she saw the jug of water and cup, poured herself some. As she was lifting it to her lips, however, she paused and stared down at it. The last thing she remembered was sitting in the van with *him* eating a cream bun. Had he drugged her? The cup trembled in her hand and in spite of her thirst she set it down, afraid it might contain something to put her to sleep again.

She got up, steadying herself on the ugly metal cabinet beside the bed and moving two paces beyond it to look out of the window. Bare meadows sloped up towards the moors. Nothing seemed familiar, though. Where was she?

Trying to move quietly, she walked across to the door and turned the handle. It was locked and she stared at it in panic, wanting to scream and call for help, but not knowing if that would bring *him* back again. Grown-ups frightened girls with tales of kidnappers. They'd all laughed about it at school, only this wasn't a made-up tale, it was really happening to her.

She heard footsteps and voices in the distance but couldn't make out what they were saying so moved hastily back to the bed and lay down. If she pretended to be only half-conscious, it might give her an advantage.

There was the sound of a key in the lock and she saw through her eyelashes a woman walk in, followed by *him*.

'She's a bit slow to wake up. I must have given her more than I intended,' Jeff said.

Beatrice let her eyes roll open and took in the scene, then groaned and shut them again. *He had a knife!* And he was threatening the woman with it. Who was she? And why was he kidnapping people? He must be a madman.

Then he said something which shocked her so much she could not have moved or spoken even if she'd wanted to.

'Well, how do you like the looks of our daughter? This is Beatrice. I'd introduce you formally, but I doubt she'll remember anything we do or say until she's fully conscious.'

It couldn't be true. Could it?

Footsteps. Beatrice risked another roll of the eyes as the woman came to stand by the bed and look down at her.

'She looks like you,' he said, then as silence followed, added, 'Well, aren't you going to say something?'

'I bore her in this very room,' the woman said. 'The furniture hasn't changed since. She was so beautiful – and when they told me she'd died, I wanted to die, too.'

'You should never believe my cousin Jane. She'll do anything for money, even sell babies to rich people who can't have their own. She did that several times, apparently, and they paid her well for it. She must have plenty of money stashed away, but the fool still lives like a poor woman.' He laughed. 'You don't think she ran a home for unmarried mothers in order to help *them*, do you? It was just for the money.'

Beatrice let out a choking sound as this information sank in and tried to disguise it with another groan. She felt a hand on her forehead and then it brushed her hair back gently from her face. It must be the woman – the one he said was her mother! She dared to open her eyes again and stare at the face hovering over her, but closed them again with another sigh.

This woman had a kind face, unlike the one who had brought her up. If it was true, if *she* was Beatrice's real mother, it would explain so much. And suddenly she wanted it to be true, wanted it quite desperately.

'She'll be thirsty,' he said. 'Better pour her a cup of water.'

Beatrice stiffened, knowing there was already a cup poured out which would betray that she had recovered more than she was letting on.

Mary Ann walked round to the other side of the bed, stared at the half-full cup, shot a quick glance sideways at the girl then pretended to pour more water. Beatrice must be awake, she decided, and instead of putting the jug of water down she dashed it into Jeff Powling's face, yelling, 'Get up, Beatrice! Help me!' and ran towards him, brandishing the jug for protection against that knife.

But he darted out of the room and slammed the shut before she could reach him, turning the key in the lock and yelling, 'You stupid bitch! What do you think you're doing?'

'Keeping you away from us.' Mary Ann picked up the only chair, glad it was a solid one as she wedged it under the door handle. Then she took a deep breath and turned to face her daughter. 'I'm sorry you had to find out like this. Did you even know you were adopted?' She ached to go and cuddle the girl, who was shivering now and looked huge-eyed as well as exhausted.

Beatrice shook her head. 'No.' She stared at Mary Ann. 'How do I know you're telling the truth?'

Mary Ann walked across to a mirror on the wall and stood in front of it. 'Come and look at us together.'

Beatrice joined her. As she stared into the mirror, tears welled in her eyes and she raised one hand to press it against her mouth before turning to stare at the tall woman beside her. 'We do look alike,' she whispered. Then she grew angry. 'Why did you give me away? Why did you give me to *her*?'

'I didn't. They told me you were dead, and I've mourned that every day of my life since. You don't forget a child you've held in your arms, kissed, loved.'

After another silence, Beatrice whispered, 'Is *he* really my father?'

'Yes.'

'How *could you* go with a man like him?'

'He raped me. I was fifteen at the time. He was my step-father.'

Beatrice stood with her head bowed as if trying to take this in, then muttered, 'If that's true, I can't see how you'd want me, let alone love me.'

Mary Ann smiled. 'You were all I had because my mother sent me away. I loved you long before you were born, talked to you, even sang to you when no one could hear. But I had you in my arms for such a short time.' A sob escaped her and she had to swallow hard before she could continue. 'You had dark hair even then and a tiny birthmark at the top of your right arm.'

The young woman reached up instinctively to clutch her arm. 'There's no way you could have known that. No one knows about it except my moth—*her*. And she always kept it hidden, said people didn't like girls who had blemishes.'

'She was wrong. We all have blemishes and we love one another in spite of them.'

There was the sound of the door handle rattling, then a voice yelled, 'Open it, you fool! What good does it do you to barricade the door? You can't get away.'

'It keeps you out,' Mary Ann yelled back. 'That seems very worthwhile to me.' She studied the door as he thumped and kicked it, making it shake and rattle. 'Let's shove the bed behind the chair. We might even be able to wedge it in place with the cabinet. I don't want him coming in with that knife of his.'

Beatrice helped her but asked in puzzlement. 'He's right. What good does it do?'

Mary Ann went to the window. 'It lets us call out for help.'

'But there's no one to hear us.'

'There's a farm nearby. Someone is bound to hear us if we keep calling. Have you got a loud voice?' For the first time she dared put an arm round her daughter's shoulders and guide her to the window, but didn't dare keep her arm there, didn't dare push things along too quickly. Beatrice had had a shock. She needed time to get used to the idea that Mary Ann was her mother.

And Mary Ann needed time to get used to a daughter who was nearly as tall as she was.

Oh, the years she'd missed! Agony pierced her to the core.

'Help!' she yelled at the top of her voice. 'Gabriel, help us!'

'Help!' Beatrice echoed, then grinned at her mother and proved there was nothing wrong with her lungs.

Jassy was cleaning the upstairs bedroom windows when she saw the van draw up again outside the house next door. What was that fellow doing coming back twice in the middle of the day? She stopped work to watch as he pulled something out of his pocket, something that flashed in the sunlight. When he opened the door of the van, a woman stepped out.

The old woman's eyes weren't as good as they had once been, but she was better at seeing things in the distance than she was at reading her own newspaper, for which she needed her dratted spectacles. She recognised Mary Ann at a glance and watched as if it were a puppet show as he gestured and threatened while Mary Ann obeyed, keeping her distance as they walked towards the house, looking nervous.

What was it that had flashed? There it went again! Metal. Was it – could it be a knife? Jassy wondered with a shiver.

He wasn't trying to hurt Mary Ann, was he?

She watched until the two of them had gone into the house, then hurried downstairs. She knew Gabriel was working in the top field, so she ran up the hill, stumbling and gasping for breath until she had to slow down. When she saw him she waved and shouted.

He turned round and immediately set off running towards her.

'That fellow next door – Downham,' she gasped for breath, 'he's got Mary Ann and I don't think – she went with him willingly. There was something flashing – in the sun. Could have been a knife.'

'You're sure of this?'

She nodded.

'He's not Downham, he's Jeff Powling. I saw him this morning. The cunning devil kept out of sight of you and me, but was happy enough to chat to our girls. Did he think he'd use them as he did Mary Ann? I'd have killed him if he had.' He looked towards the farm next door, his expression grim. 'Will you be all right if I go and see what's happening?'

'Aye. You go after her, son. But be careful.'

Gabriel set off running, vaulting over the stone wall between the farms but slowing down as he got close to the Greesons' house. Then he heard women's voices yelling for help.

The front door was locked so he went round the rear, only to find the back door locked as well. Growling in anger, he picked up one of the rocks edging the path and used it to smash the window in the top half of the door before reaching carefully through the jagged hole to unbolt the door.

Once inside he stood and listened, hearing the calls for help still coming from upstairs. He began to walk through the house, moving cautiously. In the front hall he heard the sound of a man's angry voice also coming from upstairs and went towards it with a grim smile, his footsteps muffled by a thin piece of worn carpet in the middle of the stairs.

At the top of the first flight he paused to listen again, which saved him from discovery, because someone was just starting to come down the next flight of stairs. Swiftly he stepped into the nearest bedroom, leaving the door slightly ajar so that he could see who it was.

It was Jeff Powling, his face twisted by anger. Gabriel let the fellow continue downstairs to the ground floor then tiptoed up to the attic floor.

Most of the doors stood open, except for two. The women's voices were coming from behind the nearest one. He tapped on it, thinking, In for a penny, in for a pound.

The calls stopped abruptly. 'Who's that?' asked a voice from inside.

'Is that you, Mary Ann?'

'Gabriel! Oh, thank heavens. Where's Powling?'

'Downstairs.'

'Has he left the key in the lock?'

'No.' He glanced round. 'I'll try the keys from the other doors.'

But they didn't work.

'You'd better go and fetch help,' she said. 'We'll be all right. We can keep him out of here.'

'Who's "we"?'

'Me and my daughter. He kidnapped her then blackmailed me into coming here.'

'I'm not leaving you alone with him. Has the man gone mad? Who does he think he is, kidnapping people?'

Earlier, as the van pulled away to take Mary Ann to her daughter, Sergeant Carswell squinted at it from across the road. He knew who the van belonged to because there weren't all that many people with motor vehicles and besides it had the company's name on each side in fancy letters. But he had been too far away to make out who the woman was, and truth to tell, his eyesight wasn't as good as it had been. It had looked like the missing girl to him, definitely a tall, dark-haired female. Pursing his lips, wondering if he dared take the risk of following them, he walked briskly back to the police station.

His heart sank when he saw Mrs Bawton walking towards him from the other direction.

'Ah, Sergeant,' she said in that penetrating voice of hers. 'Have you found my daughter yet? Shouldn't you be out looking for her?'

He drew himself upright. 'I've just been following up a lead.'

'What lead? I insist you tell me.'

He'd have refused, but the chief constable walked out of the building just then and Ethel Bawton turned to him with relief. 'Mr Savernoy, I can't tell you how glad I am to see you. This man of yours is being most unhelpful.'

The sergeant spluttered in annoyance, but didn't dare protest too vehemently, not while the chief constable was folding Mrs Bawton's arm in his, smiling down at her and leading the way inside again.

She was offered a comfortable chair in Savernoy's office and the chief constable sat down behind his desk while Sergeant Carswell was left standing to one side of them like a naughty schoolboy. Which didn't improve his temper.

'Perhaps you'll tell us what progress you've made, Sergeant?' his superior asked.

'I'm following up some leads, sir. Don't like to discuss them until I see which ones have any substance. Don't like to raise false hopes.'

'My God, don't you realise how anxious I am?' the harridan exclaimed, rolling her eyes and clamping one bony hand against her withered breast.

Carswell winced at the strident edge to her voice and looked appealingly at his superior.

'Tell us about your most promising lead, Sergeant,' Savernoy ordered.

Sighing, the sergeant explained about seeing a dark-haired female get into the sales rep's van driven by the fellow who lodged out in Birtley at the Greesons' farm. 'I was on my way to make enquiries about this when Mrs Bawton stopped me, sir.'

Savernoy looked at Ethel Bawton, who was now sobbing quietly into a lace-edged handkerchief. The stupid woman was a friend of his wife's and he'd never hear the last of it at home if he didn't show her they were doing something. 'We'll all drive out to the farm, I think, and see if you were right. We can go in my Humber.'

Sergeant Carswell breathed very deeply as he went to summon a constable to accompany them. The last thing he wanted was a stupid woman like that getting in the way if the man turned out to be violent, which you couldn't always predict in advance.

*   *   *

Gabriel shook the door, but it was a very solid, old-fashioned one and hardly budged. 'I'm going to have to find something to break it down with,' he called. 'I won't be long.'

Inside the room Beatrice looked at Mary Ann. 'Who is that?'

'Gabriel Clough.' She hesitated, then added, 'I'm going to marry him when all this is over. He lives at the next farm. Come on. We'd better move these pieces of furniture. We'll want to get away quickly once the door's open.'

Gabriel was just about to go downstairs when he heard footsteps coming up. Once again he darted into the nearest room. When Powling had passed he peered out and saw to his horror that the fellow was carrying a big axe.

'Are you going to move those things away from the door or must I break it down?' Powling yelled.

'I'm not letting you get your hands on her again,' Mary Ann yelled back. 'I know what you're like with young women.'

'She's my *daughter*, for heaven's sake.'

'I still don't trust you.'

Powling slipped the key into the lock and turned it. He rattled the door, but the chair jammed on the other side held firm. 'Right! We'll see about that.' He swung the axe and it splintered the panel. He swung again and again, grunting with the effort. Chips of wood flew in every direction.

Gabriel moved forward as quietly as he could but something must have warned Powling that he wasn't alone, because he turned suddenly.

Gabriel leaped forward, taking him by surprise so that he had no time to swing the axe and the two men began to struggle for possession of it.

'What's happening?' Mary Ann yelled from inside the room, but no one answered.

Beatrice bent to peer through a slit in the door. 'There's a man fighting with *him*.'

'I'm going to open the door. Gabriel may need our help.' Mary Ann removed the chair and swung the door open, hissing in shock as she saw the two men locked in a struggle. She had to act quickly before that axe sliced into someone. Pushing Beatrice aside, she grabbed the chair and moved forward purposefully.

As the two men swayed to and fro near the top of the stairs, she jabbed the chair leg into Powling's back and kicked his nearest leg for good measure.

He howled in pain and his grip loosened on the axe. Gabriel seized the opportunity to snatch it from him and toss it down the stairs.

But Powling wasn't finished yet. He pulled out the flick knife and lunged towards Mary Ann who was closest to him.

With a scream of, 'No!' Beatrice ran forward. The knife glanced off her arm and as blood welled up, Powling yelled, 'Why did you do that?' and lowered the blade.

Gabriel seized the opportunity and kicked the knife out of his hand, then punched him on the jaw as hard as he could.

Powling went flying backwards to slam against the wall and slide down on to the floor.

As Mary Ann went to put an arm round her daughter a voice yelled, 'What's going on up there?'

They all turned to see two policemen.

After a quick glance to make sure Powling wasn't in any condition to attack them again, Mary Ann hurried her daughter into the bedroom and pulled off a pillowcase, using it to staunch the blood.

'How are you feeling?' she asked.

'A bit – dizzy.'

A man's deep voice behind her said, 'Don't try to escape.'

Mary Ann glanced round in exasperation at the policeman. 'Do I look like I'm trying to escape?'

29

'What's that woman doing with my daughter?' Ethel Bawton demanded from the doorway. 'Come here at once, Beatrice, and let me see what you've done to your arm. You always were careless.'

The girl pressed against Mary Ann.

'Do as you're told!'

'I never want to go near you again,' Beatrice said. 'All you do is hit me and use me as a slave.'

'Mind how you speak to your mother, young lady,' the chief constable snapped.

'She's *not* my mother.'

Ethel gasped and turned white.

'This is my mother.' Beatrice moved closer to Mary Ann. 'We even look alike.'

Everyone stared at them.

'Don't be stupid!' Ethel said. 'Everyone saw me carrying you. You're *my* daughter.'

'I don't know what tales you've been spinning her, madam,' the chief constable said to Mary Ann, 'but although you're both tall and dark-haired, I can vouch for the fact that this lady is the mother of the girl. My wife and I have known her for many years and I saw her regularly when she was carrying the child.'

'She only pretended to be pregnant,' Mary Ann insisted. 'They took my baby away from me and gave her to the Bawtons, telling me she was dead. Then I found a letter from Mrs Greeson saying she'd tricked me and the child had been adopted.'

'That doesn't mean Beatrice is your child. I must say, madam, you're not thinking clearly about this and if you persist in obstructing us, I shall have to arrest you.'

'I'm *not* going back to her,' Beatrice insisted. 'I hate her.'

'I shall not tell you again, young woman,' he thundered. 'Carswell, take her out to the car. She can ride back with us.'

'No!'

Gabriel stepped forward. 'Just a minute, if you please, sir. This will be much easier if we don't have to use force.' As Beatrice shrank back behind her real mother, he moved forward and said in a low voice to Mary Ann, 'We need to see a lawyer about this, love. These folk have the police on their side at the moment. We can do nothing if they lock us up – and we do want to do something. Beatrice, you understand, don't you?'

She searched his face with eyes that held fear as well as hope.

'I can't let her go now!' Mary Ann said, her voice breaking on the words. 'That woman's been ill-treating her.'

Gabriel's voice was gentle. 'You don't have a choice.'

The chief constable cleared his throat. 'Let the girl go now, madam, or I'll definitely arrest you.'

Shoulders drooping Beatrice looked from one to the other, then across at Ethel Bawton. As Sergeant Carswell took her arm, she shook him off, wincing. 'Mind my arm!'

'She needs to see a doctor,' Mary Ann said. 'That cut on her arm is quite bad and will need stitching.'

'She always makes a fuss about nothing,' Ethel declared. 'I have some sticking plaster at home which will do perfectly well.'

Sergeant Carswell turned to Beatrice. 'Let me see.' He clucked his tongue at the sight of the long, deep gash and shot a scowling glance at Powling, who was groaning and starting to regain consciousness. 'She definitely needs to see a doctor, sir. This cut does need stitching. I can take her to the hospital if you like. She'd still be under our care and you can be sure she won't escape from me.'

The chief constable looked at the deep gash still oozing blood. 'Good idea, Carswell. We'll take you to the hospital then you can escort the young lady home after she's been treated. Ethel, my dear, if you look you'll see that it's a very nasty cut and needs attending to as soon as possible.'

She breathed in so deeply she swelled visibly and the look she threw at Beatrice boded no good for the girl.

Mary Ann hugged her daughter, whispering, 'We'll find a way to rescue you, I promise you, love.'

Beatrice looked at her, misery in every line of her face and body.

'Let go of my daughter, you imposter!' Ethel screeched.

The sergeant cleared his throat. 'Better come along now, young lady, or you'll get these people into trouble.' He led Beatrice down the stairs, leaving Savernoy and the young constable to haul Powling to his feet.

'Those two attacked me!' he said, pointing to Gabriel and Mary Ann. 'I wish to charge them with assault.'

'You two had better come down to the police station as well, then,' Savernoy said. 'Give the constable here your name and address, and you too, madam. You'll have to make your own way but see you're there within the hour.'

'Er – I know Mr Clough already, sir,' the young constable said. 'He lives on the next farm to this one and his family's been in the district for years.' He turned to Mary Ann. 'If I could have your name and address, madam?' He pulled out a notebook and a stub of pencil.

When she said where she was living, the chief constable stared at her in surprise.

'You know Mrs Garbutt?'

'Yes, of course, though it's Margaret who's my friend.'

'They're a pair of whores then,' Ethel snapped.

The chief constable said nothing, but his tone was much politer as he said to Mary Ann, 'If you'd go downstairs now, madam?'

She and Gabriel stood outside the house and watched the others drive off in the big motor car, then he put his arms round her and she leaned against him. 'That woman will hurt her, I know she will. Did you see the fury in her eyes? I can't bear it, Gabriel.'

'Let's go home and get the lorry.'

They walked along hand in hand and when they got there, found the two old women waiting to see what had happened. Quickly they explained and when they'd told all they knew, Jassy looked at them.

'Seems to me you two aren't thinking clearly. You need to get Jane Greeson on your side, for one thing, and it sounds like you need Mrs Garbutt supporting you, too. Do you think she'd go to the police station with you, Mary Ann?'

'I can't ask her to do that!'

'You can ask help of anyone if you want to save that lass of yours. I never heard any ill of the Garbutts. She keeps her servants a long time, which says a lot to me. The Bawtons' servants never stay for long.' She turned her attention to Gabriel. 'Now, son, get yoursen a clean shirt afore you go into town, and change into your suit and Sunday shoes.'

When Mary Ann and Gabriel reached the Garbutts' house, they found Angela sitting with Georges. Both exclaimed in shock at Mary Ann's dishevelled appearance and explanations were again necessary.

'I can't believe that even Ethel Bawton would behave so badly towards a girl,' Angela said in astonishment.

'I've seen the marks of her beatings myself,' Mary Ann said, 'and so has Lizzie Dearden.'

Angela opened her mouth to say something, then closed it again, looking thoughtful. 'Go and change your clothes, my dear. Wear something smart and pretty.' She bounced to her feet. 'In fact, I'll come and help you choose what to wear, then accompany you to the police station.'

Left alone the two men discussed the situation, faces grim.

'I can't think what to do,' Gabriel admitted.

'I don't think there's much you can do, *mon ami*,' Georges said.

'Do you know any lawyers? At least we can consult one, see if he could help in any way. I have some savings.'

Georges looked thoughtful. 'Angela will know who to see. I'll get her to take us round to her lawyer after we've been to the police station. Do not underestimate the help you can gain from a woman in her position in a small town like this one.'

'I'd rather be the one to help Mary Ann.'

'Naturally. I'm looking forward to meeting Mary Ann's daughter myself.'

But when they got to the police station, they found that Mrs Bawton had returned home.

'I must caution you against going anywhere near her from now on, Mrs Hall,' the chief constable warned Mary Ann. 'I know *you* believe Beatrice is your daughter, but I'm afraid I saw Ethel carrying that child and I know better. Now, about this Downham fellow . . .'

'I knew him as Powling and he's wanted for bigamy,' Mary Ann said. 'It happened in Brighton.' She gave him the relevant years and her mother's details.

'You realise we shall check this out?' he said, clearly doubting what she'd said.

'I'm not in the habit of lying,' she retorted. 'About anything!'

Angela laid one hand on her arm and smiled at the chief constable. 'You must make allowances for my young friend. She's been threatened at knife point and imprisoned today by that man. I'll take her home now if you don't need her any more, Charles.'

When they left the police station, she said, 'We'd better go and see my lawyer first. Mr Clough, I think you should go home. Your mother will be anxious about you.'

He couldn't resist driving past the Bawton house before he left town and was in time to see the sergeant bring Beatrice back. The girl was hanging back as he escorted her up the path to the front door.

'Damnation!' Gabriel muttered. 'Can't they see what that harridan's like?'

When the door opened Mrs Bawton and her cook bundled Beatrice inside and slammed the door on the policeman.

Gabriel had a sick feeling that Beatrice was about to pay dearly for what had happened. He decided to see if he could get close to the house at the rear. If he heard any sound of her being beaten then he'd go to her aid, even if they threw him in jail for it. He could never abide cruelty in any form.

Inside the house Beatrice stood by the door, trying not to show how frightened she felt. Her arm was throbbing and painful, and she felt utterly exhausted.

'Go into the sitting-room,' Ethel said coldly.

After a moment's hesitation, Beatrice did as she was asked.

Ethel followed her. 'Bend over the chair and raise your skirt. I intend to teach you a lesson you won't forget.'

'No.'

Ethel rang the bell. When Cook came in, she said, 'Help me hold her down.'

'Ma'am, I think she's in no fit state for a beating.'

'*Do as you're told or you'll be dismissed.*'

Cook hesitated, then looked at Beatrice. 'Best get it over with.'

'I shan't do it. I shall never let her beat me again without fighting back.'

Ethel looked at Cook. 'Well?'

Cook looked at the girl's bandaged arm and took a step backwards. 'I can't do it, ma'am. I'm sorry, but I just can't. Not when she's injured.'

'Then go and pack your things.'

As Cook left, Ethel moved quickly to lock the door and went to get her husband's walking cane from the mantelpiece. 'Bend over, I said.'

'No.' Beatrice moved behind an armchair. She had never seen her so-called mother in quite such a fury and was feeling terrified. The cane gave the other woman an advantage and a longer reach, while she already had an injured arm.

Ethel darted forward suddenly and began lashing out at the girl, and for a few moments Beatrice froze again, unable to strike back at the woman who had brought her up. But the pain of the blows made her start fighting and she pulled back, trying to get behind a chair, throwing ornaments at the woman who had totally lost control and was hitting out blindly time after time.

However as she moved to dodge the cane again, her foot caught in a rug and she fell over, unable to defend herself against the blows that rained down.

Gabriel was standing at the end of the back garden, watching the house and listening. He turned as he heard footsteps coming along the back alley and his heart sank as he saw Sergeant Carswell approaching.

'I thought you might be here, Clough. It won't do any good. You'll not be allowed near the girl. Neither you nor that woman has any legal right to see her.'

'You've seen how much she resembles her real mother. You know this isn't fair.'

'We both have to abide by the law and the law says Mrs Bawton is the girl's mother.'

'We're both afraid she'll beat the girl.'

'All children are beaten from time to time. Never did me any harm.'

'That woman goes beyond reason.'

'Can you prove that?'

Suddenly there was the sound of screaming from the house. Gabriel stiffened. 'She's hurting Beatrice again. What'll happen to that arm now?'

The sergeant stood there, biting his lower lip and listening.

The screaming grew louder, not only Beatrice's voice but a woman's shrieking at the top of her voice.

The kitchen door opened and Cook came out, creeping round the side of the house.

'What's *she* doing?' the sergeant muttered.

'Only one way to find out.' Before the other man could stop him, Gabriel vaulted over the wall and began to run up the garden.

'Hoy!' Muttering in annoyance, the sergeant followed.

As Gabriel turned the corner of the house, Cook took a step back from the window. 'No!' she moaned. 'Oh, no! She's run mad.' She began to weep loudly and turned to go back to the kitchen.

Gabriel pushed her aside to see for himself what was going on and through the window saw Beatrice lying on the floor, her arms up to protect her face as a woman with a face that was a mask of fury sliced the cane through the air and raised it for another blow.

'Dear God!' Sergeant Carswell breathed beside him. 'That woman really has gone mad. We have to stop this before she kills the girl.'

Gabriel looked at the windows which had strong wooden frames and small panes. No possibility of breaking in that way. He ran round to the back and burst into the kitchen, running through to the front of the house, yelling, 'Get out of my way!' to Cook. He had no difficulty finding the door from behind which the screaming was coming.

As he flung the door open, Carswell pushed him aside and ordered, 'Leave it to me now.' He ran across the room more quickly than Gabriel would have believed possible from such a portly man.

Ethel hadn't even noticed them come in but was still screaming vituperations at the girl she called her daughter and lashing out at her.

Carswell grabbed the cane as it rose for another cutting blow and wrenched it out of Mrs Bawton's hand.

Gabriel moved to stand protectively in front of the girl, shocked by what he saw. The back of her thin dress was spattered with blood in places where the cane had cut right through material and skin. She clung to him, sobbing and distraught.

At first Ethel fought against the sergeant, still trying to attack the girl, but he was stronger than she was and dragged her backwards. When she realised she could not fight him, she gave way to a full-scale bout of hysterics.

'Get the girl to a doctor and make sure he's prepared to testify in court about this,' the sergeant muttered, having to shout over the screams of the woman rolling about on the floor. 'You're doing this at my request, remember, if anyone asks, because I'm having to restrain Mrs Bawton.'

'Thanks.' Gabriel turned to the girl leaning against him, who was dazed and so white he feared she might faint on him. 'Come on, love, let's get those cuts seen to, then we'll take you to Mary Ann.'

Only the sound of that name seemed to penetrate her daze. 'I want my real mother,' she wailed suddenly.

When they reached his lorry he decided to take her to the Garbutt house, not the hospital, and get them to send for a doctor. It was only a few streets away, but as he jolted along his companion moaned at every bump and seemed unable to respond coherently to his questions. He stopped the lorry in front of the house and jumped out to open the passenger door.

As he helped Beatrice out, Mary Ann ran out of the front door and across to them. 'Dear Lord, what's happened?'

'I followed the Bawton woman home and kept watch from the back garden. She went mad. There's only one word to describe it.' He broke off as they entered the house and Angela came out of a sitting-room. 'Could you please telephone your doctor and tell him to get here quickly? Beatrice is in a bad state.'

One look was all it took then their hostess ran across to the telephone and made the call.

By that time Mary Ann and Gabriel had helped Beatrice up the stairs to her mother's bedroom. He left her to undress the girl and went downstairs, where he found Georges and Angela waiting. 'How long will the doctor be?'

'He said he'd come over straight away.'

Gabriel explained what had happened and Angela bustled away to get hot water and clean cloths.

The doctor arrived at the same time as Sergeant Carswell.

'The chief constable's kicking up a fuss, Mr Clough. Says we had no right to intervene.'

Angela said, 'I had better speak to Mr Savernoy, then. Use the telephone and get him for me.' She waved one hand towards the apparatus.

With a smile Carswell picked up the earpiece.

The doctor still had not come downstairs by the time the chief constable arrived, but maids had gone up several times with hot water and old sheets for bandages.

When the doctor eventually did come down he was grave-faced. He entered the drawing-room and glanced round. 'I hope you're not going to send that girl back? The woman might kill her next time. I've left her with her real mother. She needs the reassurance.'

'It's not yet been proved that Mrs Hall is the mother,' the chief constable said stiffly.

'You only have to look at the pair of them to see they're related, not just the face but the very bones of their hands – they've both got a twisted little finger, for instance.'

'But legally—'

'I shall be writing a report. My advice is to keep the girl here, quiet and safe. It'll be several weeks before she fully recovers. If you allow her to be injured again, I shall write to the coroner to state that I warned you and you didn't heed my advice.'

The sergeant cleared his throat. 'Mrs Bawton's been taken to hospital anyway, sir. She had to be sedated. They said it was a complete nervous breakdown. Even if we wanted to, we couldn't send the girl back to her.'

'Thank goodness,' Gabriel muttered under his breath.

The following day, Angela took Mary Ann to see her lawyer. He listened carefully to what she had to tell him, then shook his head. 'Unless you can prove you really are the mother – prove it to the full satisfaction of a court of law – then Mrs Bawton will continue to be regarded as the legal guardian of that girl. If the woman makes a full recovery, she will still have the right to do as she pleases with her daughter until the young woman is twenty-one. I'm sorry. I'd like to help, and from your tale I sincerely pity the girl, but I cannot work miracles. If you do gain any more information to support your claims, come back and see me. But I don't believe in raising false hopes.'

Mary Ann let Georges and Angela take her home, refused all offers of food and went to sit in her daughter's bedroom, her heart heavy.

Beatrice looked up at her. 'What did he say?'

Mary Ann hesitated.

'I'd rather know the truth.'

'That unless we can prove our claim, she remains your legal mother.'

'I'll kill myself before I go back to her.'

'You'll do no such thing! If we can't keep you with the blessing of the law, you and I will book passages to Australia under false names and I'll keep you illegally.'

Only if she did that, she mustn't involve Gabriel. It would break her heart to leave him, but she wasn't letting her daughter fall into that woman's hands again.

Beatrice was staring at her. 'What about Gabriel?'

'He has two daughters of his own and an elderly mother. He couldn't leave them.'

There was silence, then, 'You'd do that for me?'

'Yes.' Mary Ann saw the tears on her daughter's cheeks and leaned forward. 'Why are you crying?'

'Because I love you.' She sniffled and managed a watery smile. 'No wonder you have so many friends who care for you. I wish I'd been able to grow up with you.'

Mary Ann smiled at her. 'If I've learned one thing in life, it's that it's no use regretting what can't be altered. We have to make the most of what we do have. I never even met my own father, you know, but always longed to know him. Then I met Georges, who became like a father to me. He'll help us escape, if necessary. So chin up, darling.'

Beatrice nodded, took her mother's hand and held it to her cheek, nestling against it. 'As long as we can be together.'

30

Sergeant Carswell frowned at the woman who was waiting at the front desk in the police station, insisting on seeing him. Then he realised she was the cook from the Bawton house and took her into a small room they used for private interviews.

'What can I do for you?'

'I want to give notice, only the people at the hospital won't let me see Mrs Bawton. I need my wages paying, and then someone will have to lock up the house and keep an eye on it. Nor I won't be persuaded to stay on, not for nothing. I'm still having nightmares about what she did to that girl.' The woman paused, then said, '*She* keeps money in her desk. I've seen it. Couldn't you get me what's owed?'

'I'll have to consult the chief constable. I'll come round to the house later and tell you what he says.'

'I'm packing my things as soon as I get back, whatever. You won't persuade me to stay, even if I don't get my money.'

He arrived at the house later in the afternoon, armed with a magistrate's warrant to do what was necessary in consultation with a lawyer while Mrs Bawton continued to receive medical treatment. He found money in the desk and used it to pay Cook, who left the house almost immediately.

But in the desk he also found a stack of bills and demands for payment and it seemed to his inexpert eye that Mrs Bawton had been sinking deeper and deeper into debt since her husband's death.

Of his own accord he went round to Mrs Garbutt's house and asked if he could speak to Beatrice. He was shown through into the conservatory where he found her lying on her side on a cushioned rattan couch with her head on her mother's lap, laughing at something Mary Ann was telling her, while Georges watched them from a nearby armchair with a fond smile.

Beatrice already looked like a different girl from the one the sergeant had helped rescue in spite of the weals that still showed here and there. It did his heart good to see it. In fact, he had to blow his nose before he could compose himself and explain why he had come.

But the girl knew nothing about Ethel Bawton's finances, only that she had been acting strangely ever since her husband died.

When the sergeant left, Georges came with him to the front door. 'It could be this which has driven Mrs Bawton to act so strangely. I wonder – would it be possible for me to see her? Is she in a fit state to talk?'

'I could find out, sir. It might take a while. She's not been very rational, apparently. They've had to commit her.'

'Please do your best.'

Lizzie came several times to visit Mary Ann and meet her niece. She watched with approval as Beatrice gained weight and began to look like a normal, happy young woman.

'Is it time for that Kershaw family reunion now?' she asked as she got ready to leave one day.

Mary Ann hesitated. 'Could you – would the others mind if we waited till I know what's going to happen about Beatrice? I can't seem to settle to anything till then.' Not even planning her own pretend wedding or meeting her family.

'Of course not. Anyway, she's included in the invitation. She's a Kershaw too, isn't she?'

Beatrice beamed at her as she said that. It had thrilled her to find that Mrs Dearden was really her Auntie Lizzie and that she had several other relatives scattered about the north, both young and old.

A week later Georges left the house without saying where he was going. He drove to the hospital to meet Sergeant Carswell and speak to Mrs Bawton, who was sitting up in bed waiting for them looking terrified.

'Are you feeling better now, ma'am,' the sergeant asked politely.

She nodded, then whispered, 'They won't let me out yet, though. Will I – be put in prison?'

'I doubt it. You were ill, not in full command of your senses.'

She let out a sigh of relief and looked at Georges. 'Who are you?'

'I'm a friend of Mary Ann's.'

Her face tightened into a sour mask again. 'That woman!'

'At the moment she's caring for Beatrice and wants her daughter with her permanently.'

'Well, she can't have her. I *need* Beatrice. She owes a lot to my husband and myself, and it's only right that she pay us back now.' She forced a laugh. 'I shan't be beating her like that again. I was overwrought.'

'May I ask why you need her?'

'To look after me. That's what daughters do, isn't it? Look after their elderly parents.'

'Ah.' After a moment's thought, he asked, 'If you had someone else to look after you, would you prefer that?'

'Of course I would! The girl's sullen. She's been a great disappointment to me almost from the start, though my husband was fond of her.'

'But you can't afford to pay someone else?' Georges guessed. 'Because you haven't much money left.'

'How do you know that?'

'We had to pay off your cook and I found the bills in your desk,' Sergeant Carswell put in.

She sat bolt upright, spots of red flaring in her cheeks. 'You haven't told anyone! No one will ever speak to me again if they know how badly off Alfred left me!' Her voice was rising towards hysteria again. '*Say you haven't told anyone!*'

Georges moved to sit on the edge of the bed. 'Of course we haven't told anyone, *madame*.' He patted her hand, surprised to find that he felt sorry for the poor creature. 'It must be very difficult for a lady like yourself.'

She nodded and gulped back tears. 'What am I going to do?'

'If you will let me help you, I can make sure you're looked after for life.'

She looked at him warily. 'Why should you do that? You're a complete stranger to me.'

'I'm Mary Ann's stepfather,' he improvised. 'If you were to let her have her daughter back, it would make her happy and I would be prepared to show my gratitude to you in a practical way.'

A nurse came to peer into the room, looking at the visitors suspiciously. 'Don't go upsetting her, now.'

Ethel flapped one hand at her. 'Go away! They're here to help me.' She looked back at Georges and let out a long sigh that was almost a groan. 'You'd really do that?'

'*Oui, madame*. We could find you a small appartment in a spa town, perhaps Buxton? Hire a maid. Give you an allowance which will enable you to live in modest comfort. How does that sound?'

She closed her eyes, relief showing in every line of her body, then opened them again and said, 'I accept.'

'She doesn't deserve it,' the sergeant grumbled as they left.

'If we only got what we deserved, many of us would be in a sad state,' Georges said mildly. 'And this way Mary Ann will be happy.' He held out his hand to the other man. 'I thank you for your help, sergeant. I must go and see the lawyer now. I shall do nothing on Mrs Bawton's word alone, believe me.'

When he got back he went to look for Mary Ann and Beatrice, finding them in the conservatory which seemed to be their favourite place. Gabriel was sitting with them, smiling broadly at something Beatrice was telling him.

Georges went to join them. '*Bien*. I'm glad you're here, Gabriel. I can tell all of you the good news at once.' He explained what he had arranged and Mary Ann stared at him in shock.

'But that'll cost a fortune, Georges! I can't let you do it.'

'The best use for money is to make people happy,' he said in his usual mild tone. 'And I have perhaps more money than is good for me.'

'Oh Georges!' She got up to hug him, then Gabriel shook his hand and, after a moment's hesitation, Beatrice gave him a quick, shy hug.

Mary Ann watched this with pleasure. Her daughter wasn't used to demonstrations of affection, as she herself hadn't been till she became one of Lady Bingram's Aides. Which reminded her that she must write to Daphne and tell her the good news.

She moved across to Gabriel who put his arm round her and smiled.

Georges and Beatrice exchanged glances and he winked at her.

The following Sunday the Kershaws turned out en masse, meeting at The Sycamores which Angela had offered since the Deardens' living quarters above the shop weren't big enough to hold them all in comfort.

Lizzie arrived first, walking from the Dearden's van hand in hand with her husband, her two small children following, attended by the lass who looked after them for her, because Lizzie didn't see why anyone should be left out of a celebration. As soon as she got inside she took charge, her exuberance quickly infecting the others.

Richard Mercer drove his wife Polly over from the Fylde Coast with her son Billy, well enough recovered from his accident now to limp along beside her. Richard's daughter Connie clung shyly to her father's hand, still not quite used to these large gatherings of Kershaws.

Eva drove down from Heyshaw with her husband and Aaron's two daughters.

Percy Kershaw came with his wife Blanche, her sister Emma, and their two children.

Johnny came by himself. He always insisted there were enough Kershaws around and he didn't intend to marry and produce any more – though his sisters simply smiled at one another whenever he said that.

As instructed, Gabriel brought along not only his daughters, but his mother and Carrie.

A bemused Angela Garbutt found herself being treated like everyone's favourite grandmother. Since Georges stayed by her side, she coped remarkably well with the influx of cheerful people who all seemed to be talking at once.

'I think we've been adopted into the family,' he whispered, 'and I, for one, don't intend to waste the opportunity. Who can feel lonely with such lively people around?'

She was near to tears as she admitted, 'I can't believe my luck.'

Margaret and her husband were less reluctant to join in and Dick was soon arguing cheerfully with Aaron about the future of radio while Margaret moved from one sister to the other, getting to know them, ending up sitting beside Mary Ann again.

'Your daughter seems to fit in well,' she commented.

Mary Ann turned a glowing face towards her. 'Doesn't she? The poor darling's been starved of affection. Well, she won't be lonely any more. She and Gabriel's daughters get on like a house on fire already.'

'I like your Gabriel.'

Lizzie came up in time to overhear this. 'So do I. When are you two going to get married?'

A shadow crossed Mary Ann's face. She looked round quickly but no one was close enough to overhear if she kept her voice low. 'We can't. His wife is still alive in Australia. Georges is going to try to help him get a divorce, but in the meantime I intend to live with him and pretend we're married, though we won't tell the girls the truth.' She looked at her half-sister challengingly as she said that. It was the final test, the thing which had been worrying her all week. Should she tell them or not? She'd spoken impulsively, now she waited for the verdict.

Lizzie grinned and linked her arm in Mary Ann's. 'Just what I'd do, too. You'll have to go away for a weekend and come back pretending you've got wed.' She hesitated. 'We could tell Polly and Eva, but our Percy's a bit strait-laced and the rest of 'em are too young to keep a secret.'

Mary Ann looked down at her diminutive sister, who seemed nonetheless to be the pivot around which the whole family turned. She could feel tears of joy filling her eyes at this instant acceptance of what she was doing, but she blinked firmly and they didn't spill over. She had wept enough.

Lizzie looked round and waved to Georges, who disappeared. Five minutes later he reappeared, accompanied by Mrs Garbutt's two maids carrying trays of glasses filled with a golden liquid which fizzed and sparkled.

He clapped his hands together and when everyone had been shushed into silence, he said, 'I have taken it upon myself, since Mary Ann has been kind enough to adopt me as a father, to provide some champagne and make a speech because I think this is a moment to celebrate.'

As Lizzie led the round of applause and laughter, glasses were passed round then Georges stepped forward. He looked at Mary Ann, his love for her shining in his eyes. 'You do not know this dear young woman well as yet, but she is, I promise you, a loving and generous-hearted creature and will be an asset to your family.' With a smile, he added, 'So I'll ask you to raise your glasses. And I have been in Lancashire for long enough now to know how the toast should be phrased: "Our Mary Ann".' He raised his glass to his lips and drank to her.

The room echoed with the toast and after Mary Ann had saluted them with her own glass she went round the whole group, hugging her new family and those they had taken into their ranks.

'I prefer to think of you as *my* Mary Ann,' Gabriel said softly when she eventually returned to his side.

Her smile was dazzling.

Beatrice watched them with a fond smile of her own. She had never realised until now how wonderful life could be. Frances came to put an arm round her on one side and Christina on the other. 'She's going to be our Mary Ann too,' Frances said. 'Isn't it just wonderful how much they love one another?'

Gabriel and Mary Ann were drinking a private toast and had eyes for no one but each other.

The three girls sighed happily and exchanged misty-eyed glances.

'Our Mary Ann,' they echoed softly.

Anna Jacobs is always delighted to hear from readers and can be contacted:

BY MAIL:

PO Box 628
Mandurah
Western Australia 6210

If you'd like a reply, please enclose a self-addressed, business-size envelope, stamped (from inside Australia) or an international reply coupon (from outside Australia).

VIA THE INTERNET:

Anna has her own web domain, with details of her books and excerpts, and invites you to visit it at http://www.annajacobs.com

Anna can be contacted by email at anna@annajacobs.com

If you'd like to receive email news about Anna and her books every month or two, you are cordially invited to join her newsletter list. Just email her and ask to be added to the list, or follow the link from her web page.